ROTTEN HEART

Kat Dunn grew up in London and has lived in Japan, Australia and France. She has a BA in Japanese from SOAS and an MA in English from Warwick. She's written about mental health for Mind and the *Guardian*, and worked as a translator for Japanese television. Her YA has been published by Head of Zeus and Andersen Press and has been nominated for the Carnegie Medal for Writing and shortlisted for the Nero Book Award and the 2024 Polari Children's and YA prize.

ROTTEN HEART

Kat Dunn

MANILLA
PRESS

First published in the UK in 2026 by
MANILLA PRESS
An imprint of Bonnier Books UK
5th Floor, HYLO, 105 Bunhill Row,
London, EC1Y 8LZ

A CIP catalogue record for this book is available from the British Library.

Hardback ISBN: 978-1-78658-397-0
Trade paperback ISBN: 978-1-78658-396-3

Also available as an ebook and an audiobook

1 3 5 7 9 10 8 6 4 2

Typeset by IDSUK (Data Connection) Ltd
Printed and bound by CPI (UK) Ltd, Croydon CR0 4YY

The authorised representative in the EEA is
Bonnier Books UK (Ireland) Limited.
Registered office address:
Block B, The Crescent Building
Northwood, Santry
Dublin 9, D09 C6X8
Ireland
compliance@bonnierbooks.ie
www.bonnierbooks.co.uk

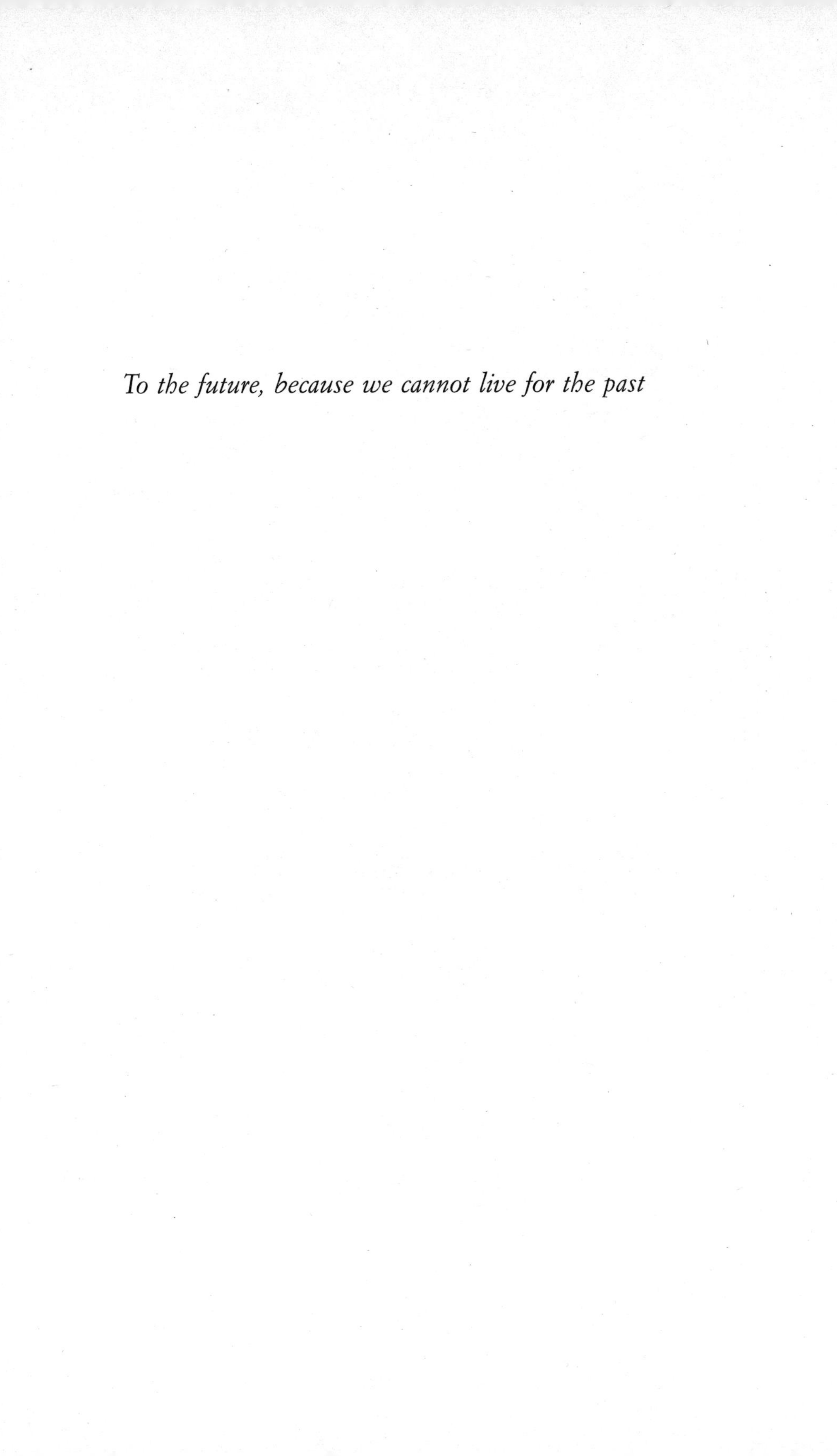

To the future, because we cannot live for the past

Frailty, thy name is woman.

Hamlet, William Shakespeare

I have gone mad. I love you: let me die.

Idylls of the King, Alfred, Lord Tennyson

Summer 1898, Herne House, Suffolk

IT IS THE TIME OF night when only the dead are abroad.

Three o'clock strikes on the plain Georgian long-case clock in the entrance hall, slender and solemn, and on the sleek French mantel clock above the cold grate in the drawing room, hemmed in by dried flowers and mezzotints of Burne-Jones and Rossetti. By Odette's bed, the pocket watch that hangs from a nail in the wall makes no sound as the minute and hour hands join together in brief union. She stirs lightly, brow puckering as her head shifts upon the pillow.

The shadows are heavy in the depth of the small hours, cool and slow-moving as a glacier, spreading out to consume the hallways and corners, retreating at the glow of an oil lamp upon a bedside table, drawing back to expose a slipper knocked upside down in carelessness, a crumpled shift, a torn sheet of writing paper.

There is a noise in the house.

A soft *tap-tap-tapping.*

Odette does not wake; nor does Cecilia, curled beside her, nor her father in his room along the corridor. The boot boy lying by the kitchen door senses nothing, and the maids in their attic bedrooms sleep deeply.

In a slice of moonlight that cuts across the dining room, there is a flash of movement, then a *tap-tap-tapping* like bare feet scurrying across the floor.

There are stories about Herne House. It is that sort of place.

Along a creek that splits around the timber-framed building to form a moat lie three storeys of argument between wood and stone and ivy, water seeping up from the marshland, reeds spreading close enough to brush the mortar. It is an old place. The moat once ringed a Norman manor. The curving staircase was built from an Armada wreck. There are bones beneath the flags of the hall – perhaps once a chapel; perhaps not.

The footsteps echo through the hall, through the dust and the spiderwebs.

In the corner of a mirror or in a pane of glass, there is the shape of movement.

Odette rolls over in her bed, pressing her face into Cecilia's shoulder. Cecilia is so still in her sleep that she is like an effigy carved on the tomb of some medieval lady in the church along the lane. If she wants, Odette knows she can stretch out an arm and hook it around her waist, and Cecilia will not stir.

A cold breeze rises from somewhere unknown – though that is not so strange in this old and crooked place. It is only that these August nights are not so warm, not here in Suffolk, where the wind blows fast and crisp from the North Sea over the flat salt marshes and fenland to the north and east. Nothing more.

The noise is on the landing.

Odette shifts again. It is colder.

Tap-tap-tap.

The noise is outside her door.

Odette, in her light sleep, frowns.

Wakes.

The flame in the oil lamp gutters as the door swings slowly open – just far enough for a pale hand to curl around the frame.

Cecilia is awake at once and slithers soundlessly from the bed. Odette cannot breathe. She watches the half-shape of Cecilia disappear.

There is a hiss of white skirts over floorboards and the *tap-tap-tap* as the footsteps glide towards the bed.

There is someone behind her.

The covers slip from Odette's shoulders, exposing the line of her neck.

Cold fingers slide across her skin, one by one, pressing against the fluttering point of her pulse. There is a breath to match, so close it is as though she is being embraced.

A fragile weight presses against her back.

'Mother,' says Odette. 'Go to bed.'

Lydia Fairfax-Waugh snakes her arm around her daughter's waist and curls into her. 'In a little while, angel.'

The back of Odette's nightdress grows damp, and she understands that her mother is crying.

'Please. I want to sleep.'

'Then sleep, darling, I won't stop you.'

The weight of her arm is like an iron beam pinning Odette in place. How can she turn her mother away when she cries so? How can she, and not be a monster?

'It is too much to bear,' says her mother after a moment. 'They put all these papers before me and expect me to make decisions. It is impossible. It is cruel.'

Odette pieces together what her mother has fixated on now. 'It cannot be so bad, for people make wills every day. Far stupider people than you manage it.'

It is the wrong thing to say. Her mother's arm tightens around her, and she weeps. 'I feel like a small child sent to work in some monstrous factory. No one has any care for me.'

Odette stares ahead blankly. It is quite dark, but the oil lamp sends a flickering shadow over her clothespress, illuminating the elaborate curls of the brass handle. She has learnt a trick where, if she focuses totally on one small point in her vision to the exclusion of all others, it is as though she disappears entirely. The world expands until it is all brass and the play of light on metal and the swoop and curl of an acanthus leaf. Her own body does not exist. She is not a girl with a mother. She is nothing.

'I would have no reason to live without you,' says her mother. 'Don't argue, because I am telling you, it is true. I know you will never leave me. You're such a good daughter.'

The screws in the handle need tightening. The left sags lower than the right, like a drooping mouth. It casts a long shadow down the walnut door panel, a wandering dark line, as though her mother has gone at the wood with her paints and dashed lamp black across the grain. There is a stray lock of Cecilia's hair on the carpet, spilling out from where she has hidden beneath the bed. They are too practised at this. They are too used to vacating their own lives.

'Will you?' asks her mother. 'Leave me?'

Their breathing evens out, matching speed and depth until they are one breath, one heartbeat.

It disgusts her.

'No,' says Odette. 'I won't leave you.'

There is no other answer to give.

Act One

Late September 1898, Hampstead, London

But now farewell. I am going a long way
With these thou seest—if indeed I go

Idylls of the King, Alfred, Lord Tennyson

1

Odette

THEY LAY HER OUT, feet bound and jaw tied closed.

Odette's mother has died in the London house, and there is much discussion as to where to put her.

Mrs Binx, the housekeeper, is a keen advocate of tradition and presses for the bed. Odette's father, George, agrees. He has long since vacated the marital room, and it is now less a bedroom than a domestic hospital ward. It is no worse to have a dead body there than a sick one.

The nurse says it must be a table, preferably in the kitchens, for it will be easier to move around the body, to wash it, to wrap it in its winding sheet.

'*Her*,' says Mrs Binx, overcome unexpectedly. '*Her* body.'

Aunt Claudine clasps her hands over the front of her dress and says it must be the dining room, for there will be visitors. They may put down a sheet of plain linen, to protect the cherry wood, and a board, so that it will be no trouble to move *her sister*.

Odette is not called upon to give an opinion.

The windows are thrown open and maids cover the mirrors with black muslin, which Odette recognises as an old petticoat of hers cut up into squares. They have been preparing.

At the front door, another maid wraps a black cloth around the knocker to muffle it. Outside, the leaves have begun their autumn turn on the waving boughs of the ancient heathland forest, and they cast a shimmer of crimson and gold light like stained glass across the floors.

It is busy – people everywhere – and, somehow, there are more servants than she has ever noticed before at every turn of the staircase; in the drawing room, the doctor still lingers, talking to her father, and hurrying through the front door is Aunt Penelope, her mother's oldest friend. The house is too tall, too big, her mother's exuberant decoration overflowing in each room in a mess of rugs and mirrors, lamps draped with scarves, sketches framed on the walls, the reaching leaves of aspidistra and parlour palms, lacquered screens and lattice work. It is intolerable.

Odette slips up to her room so quietly that she goes without notice. Her trunks are packed and waiting at the foot of her bed, ready to be taken up to Cambridge. That will have to wait now. She must write a letter to Newnham explaining her delay. Black-bordered paper must be bought.

She will have to write the words: her mother is dead.

Odette presses her hands to her stomach, against the hard bones of her corset, walks around in a circle, takes a pillow from her bed and holds it to her face, smothering herself. She imagines being numb, like the earth stretching across the hillside, like the steady trunks of the beeches and oaks, and the still, silent water of the ponds.

When her hands stop shaking, she puts down the pillow and goes to her dresser. Its usual chaos has been tamed: her pomade and scent and creams all packed, her letters tidied, ink bottles stowed and jewellery stored carefully in the lacquered box her mother gave her for her eighteenth birthday. From a coin purse, she retrieves two silver half-crowns, so small and ordinary, like beach pebbles or sea glass. They are so completely inadequate. They are all she has.

Grief, like a wave taller than her head, taller than the house, rises up, building, waiting to break.

Her mother is dead. Her corpse is downstairs.

Coins in hand, Odette slips past the servants and past Aunt Claudine, who is patting Aunt Penelope on the shoulder as she presses her face into a handkerchief and trembles, past the shut door of her father's study, past the nurse being paid by Mrs Binx – past it all, to the dining room.

She has left her mother's body for only a minute or two, and yet she is already trepidatious to step across the threshold. It is fortunate that it is a cold, preserving day; the fires have been extinguished and all the windows left wide open for the fresh autumn breeze to air out the stink of illness and death. And to let the spirit out – so her mother once told her, when she was still small enough that she had to stand on her toes to see out of the nursery window. There had been a death in the house opposite – white sheets tacked over the windows, the people coming in and out with black bands around their sleeves and their arms full of flowers.

Her mother lifted her under the armpits so that she could see the coffin as it left for the churchyard.

'The dead must not see their own reflection, or they will become confused and will not find their way to Heaven,' her mother said. 'You must let the spirit out, and close the eyes of the dead, or they will spy out who they will take with them into the afterlife. Hold the eyelids down with pennies.'

From the doorway, Odette can see bare feet tied with a length of muslin and the flare of the curtain as the wind blows through.

Blowing her mother's spirit away.

At once, it is too awful a thought, and she dashes across the room to slam the sashes down. Her mother must stay. She is not ready for her to go.

Slowly, stiffly, Odette turns.

There her mother is.

Lydia Fairfax-Waugh has died just shy of forty and is as beautiful in death as in life. Her chestnut hair is full and shining and lies around her like a cloak; she is small and slender, like an angel, hands neat and precise, with flecks of paint still caught beneath her nails and her fine-boned fingers curled as though ready to clasp a brush.

The servants who carried her in crossed her arms over her chest before the stiffness set in, so that she will fix in place. Odette has read there will be a smell, but none has come yet; there is only the tang of carbolic soap and the soft lavender water she scattered on her mother's pillow each night to ease her sleep.

Her mother's eyes are closed. Thank God.

She will place the coins atop the lids, but not yet. Not yet.

Instead, she reaches out one trembling hand to the pale skin of her mother's neck and spreads her fingers across her throat in the echo of a too-familiar gesture.

There is no pulse, of course.

'He has out soar'd the shadow of our night.'

Odette snatches her hand back and turns to find Cecilia in the doorway. Cecilia has no obligation to wear mourning, but she has come in a sombre grey and mauve day dress, her jewellery plain jet, with a ring of her late father's on her index finger, as a testament to the closeness of their two families for so many years. She looks only prettier in the soft colours, the flax of her hair and milky pink of her cheeks made delicate.

'*Envy and calumny and hate and pain can touch him not.*'

Shelley. Odette remembers Cecilia spreading the book of poetry open on her knees as they sat side by side on the roof of Herne House, the weight of a summer storm thick in the air.

Odette means to speak, to offer some answer to Cecilia's own line, but she can find nothing. She is no poet. The truth of it all is beyond words.

Cecilia pushes the door closed and comes to take Odette in her arms, to press their foreheads together like they are still schoolgirls whispering their love in the quiet dark.

'I am so, so sorry,' says Cecilia, and it is enough.

Odette curls into her warm body, lets the tears come, and shakes and shakes with the force of it.

'Please never leave me,' she speaks into Cecilia's shoulder.

'Never.'

They draw apart and turn to face the table.

'For the eyes,' says Odette, showing the coins on her palm.

Cecilia grips Odette's arm as she readies herself.

Before she can begin, the door opens again and the women of the house flood into the dining room. Odette quickly slips the coins into her pocket and presses her back to the wall. Maids carry in basins of warm water and cloths and a large pair of scissors to snip away the nightgown Odette's mother died in, should they prove unable to remove it themselves.

'You don't have to be here for this,' says Odette to Cecilia under her breath.

'Do you want me to stay?' It is not a simple thing to ask.

'It will be . . . taxing for you.'

'I'm not afraid.'

Odette chews the meat of her lip. There is no way of knowing what will be a comfort. The washing of the body, its preparation, involves no decision on her part. A ritual tells her: this is how it is; you are part of something bigger than you, and it has its rules. You are safe. Held.

It seems churlish to want a person as well. Demanding. Odette is too demanding; she knows this is her terrible flaw.

And yet, she *wants*.

She touches her fingers to Cecilia's, begins to speak, but Aunt Penelope interrupts.

'We can be of more use elsewhere. Come.'

Cecilia is ushered away by her mother, who has donned sombre black for her dead friend.

They are now five in the room: Mrs Binx, the nurse and one housemaid, who is sniffing pathetically – and Aunt Claudine.

She stands at the head of the table, eyes fixed on her sister. She is the taller, lither woman, with hair that runs to brown instead of chestnut, and her hard years of spinsterhood and teaching in Germany show in the lines around her mouth and eyes.

It is no easier to understand her now. She watches her dead sister's face with an intensity that could drive a hole through the wood, grey eyes flashing and dark.

Odette does not go to her.

'What can I do?' she asks Mrs Binx instead.

'Nothing, my love.' Mrs Binx pats her hand. 'Let the women do the work. We are here to see that it is tenderly done.'

First, the nightdress is carefully lifted up; the maid cradles Lydia's head as the gown is removed, and she lies naked before them all as she has never done in life. Her illness has made her fragile. Each bone of her ribs is clear, and her hips jut through skin that is sunless pale.

Water, soap and cloths are brought, and her body is washed. Each arm, each leg, across her stomach and chest. She is rolled over so her back can be washed, too, and then each leg and foot is gently attended to.

The maid lifts her mother's thigh, opening it out to the side, exposing her.

'What on earth are you doing?' asks Odette.

'We must stop up the orifices, Miss Fairfax-Waugh,' says the nurse, who is moving wads of cotton to between Lydia's legs. 'I would explain why, but I don't think you'd like to hear it.'

'Oh. I see.'

Claudine waves them on. 'Do not be prim, Odette.'

'I am sorry.'

Odette retreats to the wall again, catching her hands behind her to press them against the dado rail until they go numb.

They put cotton inside her mother's vagina and anus and nostrils and ears and into her mouth. She never thought a human body had so many broken places.

Odette has seen dead bodies before: carcasses in the kitchen, dead sheep bloated and rotting in the fields around

Herne House – even, a very long time ago, her grandmother laid out on her bed, ready for Odette to kiss her waxy cheek. She has seen unmoving bundles in rags on the streets around Shadwell, when she and Cecilia take the train east to sit in the dark corners of beer-soaked music halls where no one will recognise them and they can press as close together as they like. She has seen graveyards dug up to make space for more bodies, and a boat crammed with screaming people sink in the Thames.

Death is everywhere in this city. It is not so strange that it should be in her family, too.

When her mother's hair has been washed and spread out to dry, they dress her in her grave clothes. Claudine bought them from the finest funeral emporium on Oxford Street, and they are beautiful and pointless. The buttons do not fasten; there is no overstitching across the decorative embroidery, so they can never be washed, and they are fixed only with ties at the side.

Then Mrs Binx brings the shroud.

Odette made this herself. Cecilia sat beside her, stitching the hem as Odette sewed the pattern of ferns and lilies and chrysanthemums, while they kept vigil through Lydia's long dying.

'No. Wait.' Odette springs forwards. 'We must photograph her first.'

Claudine stops. 'Really?'

'Yes. Why not? People do it.'

Odette feels the weight of Claudine's gaze and every strained breath, every twitch of her mouth in exasperation – or perhaps distaste. That is what it is. However nicely she plays, Odette is not stupid.

'If you must,' says Claudine at last, and takes the shroud away.

The maid gathers up the rags and the scraps of cotton; the nurse takes the bowls of dirty water, and Mrs Binx brushes out Lydia's hair again.

It is mundane. It is monstrous.

Odette is powerless to change a thing.

2

Odette

ODETTE HAS LOOKED THROUGH the mourning clothes and picked out a plain day dress in bombazine with deep crêpe hems – but it feels wrong to have something shop-bought, so fragile and temporary.

Odette's family has never been large, but she feels its smallness now; so few of them will show their grief outwardly for long. Oh God, who will come to the funeral? Will they be alone in the church? It is too awful to think about.

Cecilia has come to help button and pin her into her new outfit, into her new life: a daughter in mourning.

'I should keep busy. That will help, won't it?' says Odette. 'Do you think it will take long for a photographer to reply?' They have dashed off notes to every photography studio they could find in the directory across Hampstead and Highgate and Kilburn. 'Did we write to enough? Or was it too many? Oh God, what if five all turn up together and it is a photographic circus?'

'Then they can all take pictures of each other, and it will set a new fashion,' says Cecilia.

It is not funny, but Odette rewards her with a tight smile.

Her hands shake too badly to fix the hook and eye at the throat of her dress, so she turns for Cecilia to do it. The brush of Cecilia's fingers against the soft hair at the nape of her neck is familiar – disconcertingly so. How can it be that this still feels the same? That her body will still respond to Cecilia's touch? That she is some ordinary, base animal made of muscle and skin and appetite?

'Do I really have to do this?' she asks.

'Not if you don't want to.'

But Odette does not mean the photograph. She means all of it. To grieve. To mourn. To remember. To grow into someone new who lives in a world with no mother, a world her mother will never know.

'Girls!' Mrs Binx's voice rises up the stairs. 'The photographer is here.'

Want does not come into *this* part. There is compulsion. Obligation.

This is something she knows she *must* do.

'I'll be right there,' says Cecilia, squeezing her hand. 'If you need something else to think about, think about me. The little flat in Bloomsbury.'

Odette smiles weakly. Their fantasy of a future seems so laughable now. 'The little flat in Bloomsbury. I don't suppose we'll ever have the money for it, after all.'

Cecilia falters. 'Do you not know what your mother wrote in her will?'

'No. We didn't . . . At the end, it wasn't really the sort of thing we could speak about.'

At the end, her mother could hardly speak at all.

Cecilia turns to her, surveys her new appearance. 'There. All done.'

'I suppose one simply has to go on,' says Odette, half a question.

'Yes,' agrees Cecilia. 'Though you could always turn to drink. Rend your garments and roam the Heath, gnashing your teeth at small children. I believe, traditionally, there has always been the option of going mad.'

Odette laughs, despite herself. This is what she loves in Cecilia: the unexpected cleverness to her, the sharp, canny imagination. Without thinking, she pulls Cecilia close and kisses her, languid and familiar.

A noise sends them scrambling apart; Odette smooths her skirt and resists wiping her mouth with her hand, as though Claudine will see the press of Cecilia's lips marked on hers. Claudine holds herself stiffly in the doorway, hand on the knob. There is always something of the schoolmistress about her, as though she is ever at the head of an unruly class of children plotting revolt.

'It is bad manners to keep tradesmen waiting. They are your tradesmen, after all.'

'Yes, Aunt Claudine.'

The photographer has set up in the dining room. Claudine has changed into mourning wear as well, and the servants wear crêpe armbands.

The footmen stand around Lydia's body, considering how to manoeuvre her into the chair that has been placed in the centre of the room. Finally, they take hold of her under the knees and armpits, and fold her awkwardly into place. She is already growing stiff, but they must fix her head upright as best they can.

How will they position themselves around her? Odette has considered placing another chair beside her mother, so they can be as close in death as they were in life. Then perhaps maybe her father behind them?

And Claudine?

Before the photographer has finished his preparations, Odette hears the front door open, and she steps out into the hall to witness the arrival of a tall man in his mid-twenties. His cheeks are pink from the exertion of climbing the hill to the house, and his honey-blond hair escapes its pomade when he removes his top hat.

'Leo!' Cecilia dashes to her brother to draw him in.

'Cessy.' He kisses her cheek, unwinds the scarf from around his neck. He has found a crêpe armband somewhere on his way, and now he unpins it from his topcoat to refix upon his smart frockcoat. 'I'm sorry I couldn't be here sooner.'

Leonard comes forwards, embraces his mother, then clasps Claudine's hand. 'I am so terribly sorry. I cannot quite believe she is gone.'

Claudine removes herself from his grip smoothly. 'She is with God now. Her suffering is over.'

They have clustered in the hall, half blocking the view into the dining room, but Leo is taller than them all, and he looks over their heads at Lydia propped in the chair. His mouth goes slack and trembles.

He kisses Odette's cheek next. 'She was the best of all of us,' he says faintly, though Odette knows none of them can think that true.

'Thank you. I know you loved her,' she says, as though she must lay out the people on her side, the people she can call upon to remember that her mother mattered. And surely she did matter to Leo? Surely he grieves, too? He holds her gaze and, for a moment, they are children again, growing up together in Herne House, the three of them sitting for her mother's paintings, hiding in the hay meadows, catching tadpoles and climbing trees.

Cecilia takes her arm, and Leo's expression shifts, closing down. He does not understand the true nature of the relationship between Cecilia and Odette, but he feels it all the same, a change that marked the end of them as a trio.

'Mrs Binx, tea for Mr Moore. In the drawing room,' instructs Claudine. She turns to Odette. 'Well, get your father.'

Aunt Penelope ushers Cecilia and Leonard into the drawing room, and Odette goes to her father's study.

It is a small room, tucked away at the back of the house, where the windows open onto the wild rose bushes in the garden, and is filled high with books and scattered issues of psychological journals. When the house was newly bought, most of the rooms were papered with William Morris designs; here, broad acanthus leaves twine across the walls in pale blue and ivory. Her father's red dispatch box sits atop the desk beside a ceramic model of a human head, marked with the sections and meanings of a phrenologist.

George Fairfax-Waugh sits behind the desk, face as grey and pallid as the hair scattered through his beard and at his temples, and he startles when Odette speaks.

'Father? We wish to take a photograph. With Mother.'

'A photograph?' There is a moment of horror, a flash of eye-whites and a mouth drawn into the beginnings of a grimace.

'Please,' says Odette quickly. 'The photographer is here, and it will only take a moment.'

His features settle into a more assured expression, the momentary glimpse of vulnerability gone. It hurts Odette more than she would have expected. She did not realise how badly she has wanted her father to join her in her grief, but he keeps himself apart from it, just as he has kept himself apart from the rest of them, shut into his private space since Lydia died.

Maybe there is no one who understands her now.

'Yes,' he says. 'A good idea. It is important for the human mind to progress through the stages of grieving in order to meaningfully separate the memory of a living person from the mortal remnants.'

He waits, wisdom proffered.

Odette does not know how to respond. Does her father think this is comfort?

'We are in the dining room,' she says instead.

The photographer and his assistant are waiting, the camera on its tripod and a space cleared around Lydia. Odette's father stays at a cautious distance from the body. He will not look at her. Instead, he inspects the rug, the silver on the sideboard, the tassels on the curtain ties, everything but his wife.

'George, don't linger.' Claudine ushers the photographer to begin his work.

The man dances round, positioning George behind the chair, his hand on Lydia's shoulder, and Odette alongside her mother. Then he hesitates, looking at Claudine in her mourning blacks. 'The whole family?' he asks.

There is a terrible moment when no one can meet the other's eye, looking instead to the photographer in the hope he will solve this unsightly problem for them.

Eventually George says, 'One like this. Then the rest.'

Claudine flinches almost imperceptibly and steps back.

Odette shifts closer to George. He is *her* father. This is *her* family. There is a fragile, final, fleeting moment when the three of them will all be together again. She must savour this.

One like this.

Apparently, only *one.*

The photographer readies the plate, and Odette braces herself. She must touch her mother. This is important; she feels it deeply in her bones. They must have a record of how much they meant to each other.

She holds her breath and places her hand on the cold fabric of her mother's shoulder. It is all she can do to suppress a shudder.

'Mr Fairfax-Waugh, you could place your other hand on your daughter's shoulder?' suggests the photographer.

The solid weight of her father's hand is enough that Odette can rally.

There is a bustle of activity at the camera, then a great flash, and now they must hold as still as they can.

It is uncanny, like this. Looking at her mother's shining hair and the set of her shoulder, it is as though she is alive again.

Odette is struck for a moment by the hideous sensation that if she were to lean around and look at her mother's face, she *would* be alive. Her quick, bright eyes and sensitive mouth would quirk, and Odette would feel her own heart flutter in response, because her mother would be here, she would not have left her, and it is so terrible and so wonderful she cannot bear it. If she looks, it will be true or not; she will know – if she never looks, it can always be true that, in this moment, that her mother was here. Her mother didn't leave her.

Oh God, she is going to cry.

'Very good!' says the photographer.

George steps back, snatching his hands away from the dead woman and the living.

'And now the whole group.'

The photographer brings in Aunt Penelope and Cecilia and Leo, along with Claudine, to group around Lydia's body.

Odette cannot move. She is staring at a fixed point on the wallpaper, her hand on her mother's shoulder. She must not cry. Not here – not yet.

The rest of the photographs are done quickly, then Mrs Binx announces tea. Aunt Penelope again ushers Cecilia away, taking Leo with her. Amidst the reorganisation, Claudine tries to touch George's arm with a tenderness Odette has never seen from her before, but he slithers away and, with a mutter about a vote in Parliament, flees the house. Claudine, cheeks pink with humiliation, snaps orders at the staff about printing funeral invitations and summoning undertakers.

The footmen come to move Lydia back to the dining table, and at last Odette must relinquish her mother. She shuts her eyes and steps away, holding the vision in her mind.

If she never looks, her mother is still alive.

3

Cecilia

THE AIR IS TOO COLD for Cecilia's bedroom window to be open as far as it is but, though it causes her to shiver in her nightdress and silk dressing gown, she cannot bring herself to push the sash down fully. From here, she can see all the way across the road and past the tree branches, to the neat square of light that is Odette's window in the Fairfax-Waugh house. On this clean, calm night, she can even make out the smudge that is the sketch above Odette's bed: Cecilia and Odette at thirteen, in the pond at Herne House, posing as water nymphs for a larger piece Lydia planned but never completed.

Cecilia holds herself at the window now, a hand pressed to each side so it frames her. Is Odette there? She cannot quite see; there is no movement, but that does not mean Odette is not just beyond her sight.

This is how she first saw Odette, seven years ago, when Cecilia and Leonard and their mother first moved into the private square in Hampstead. Penelope and Lydia's friendship stretches back long enough that, on the mantelpiece downstairs, there are photographs of the two of them together, before either Odette or Cecilia were born. But Cecilia only met the Fairfax-Waughs when Lydia summoned

Penelope back to London from their tidy, unobtrusive house in Richmond and installed them in Gate House set just across the road from the Fairfax-Waugh villa.

In the four grey walls of her bedroom, in this new, alien place, twelve-year-old Cecilia set out her needle and thread and her embroidery and pulled the dustsheet from the mirror on her dressing table put there by the movers and—

There.

In the reflection.

Like Lancelot to the Lady of Shalott, Odette appeared in a scene of colour and beauty. Cecilia could not at first put together what she saw: a curious girl wrapped in a swathe of velvet, a silver crown on her waves and a sword slung across her shoulder. It was strange and brilliant and confusing.

Cecilia spun around and pressed herself to the window, hauling up the sash so that she could hang out across the sill and drink in this apparition.

Odette held a fixed pose, face raised in some sweet victory, her hair flowing around her shoulders. Only when Lydia stepped into view in a stained painting smock, brush brandished at Odette, did Cecilia understand what it all was.

Penelope brought them to Lydia's house the next day, and there Odette was. Real. Tall and observant, leaning languorously across the arm of the settee, her hair flowing in burnished waves about her shoulders, her sharp, hawkish eyes following Cecilia about. It was like being stung, a shock rippling through her body at this sense of recognition, of some missing part to herself made flesh. She grew hot at once, flustered with yearning.

Odette took her up to her room, through the glittering maze of mirrors and paintings, shawls draped across lamps and Turkish lanterns dangling from the ceiling, silk wall hangings glowing in the gaslight. She pressed a volume of Keats into her hands, asked to be read to.

It was a bolt of sunlight into a gaol cell. Cecilia had been raised small and quiet, confined to a life reflected, the insipid shadow of something real and true and burning, but here Odette was, and she felt drunk on it. She knew then that she would walk after Odette wherever she went.

Only now, it does not seem so easy to follow.

The light in the window across the way flickers – it is Odette's form passing before the lamp. She settles now at her writing slope, lithe form curved over her work. Cecilia has watched her like this so many times, watched her dress and brush her hair and read sprawled across a chair and, sometimes, Odette watches her back.

Now, Odette looks up and meets her eye. She picks up a pen and stands it upright in the inkwell.

The signal for Cecilia to come over.

It still makes her heart stutter, even now. Odette wants her. Odette *needs* her.

She slips on her shoes, hooks her skirts into the belt of her dressing gown, and climbs from her window, onto the roof of the bay below, then down a trellis to the ground. There is no one abroad at this time of night, and she passes unseen across the road and into the grounds of the Fairfax-Waugh house. It is not so easy a climb this side, the house standing taller, but ivy winds wild up the brickwork, clematis and wisteria vying for space and proffering hand and foot holds.

Cecilia slips at last through the open window into Odette's room.

Odette waits, hands twisted together, a little distance away, as though she has forgotten how they can be together.

Cecilia will remind her.

She takes Odette in her arms and kisses her firmly, her mouth, her jaw, pulls their bodies flush and sets Odette steady. Here, she tries to say, this has not changed. This will never change.

'Do you think the photograph will turn out well?' is the first thing Odette says when Cecilia draws back.

Photograph? It takes her a moment to place Odette's thoughts. 'Of course it will,' she says.

'There are so few of her, and what if one day I forget what she looks like?'

'You won't.'

'I will. I can barely remember my grandparents.'

'She's your mother. You'll remember.'

'Do you remember your father?'

It is an abrupt and cruel question, and Cecilia smiles reflexively to hide the hurt.

No, she does not remember what her father looks like. How can she when he died before she was born? Odette knows this. She means nothing by it. There are a handful of photographs that her mother jealously guards in an album, and Cecilia has committed each of them to memory; she has quizzed Leo on what little he can tell her and turned each image – gentle hands, fierce temper, bright eyes – into something like a whole man. But she does not remember *him*.

Odette picks at her cuticles. It is painful to watch.

Cecilia takes her hands. 'It has only been a few hours. It is still such a shock—'

'Oh, do not try to be kind to me – I cannot stand it.' Odette snatches away her fingers, paces like a cat. 'If I cry, I don't know if I will ever stop. I can feel it all there, waiting for me, something so big it's like an ocean that will drown me if I ever stop kicking, so please, Cecilia, do not ask me to stop kicking.'

She presses her hands to her temples, pulling at the fine curls that are escaping their pins.

Cecilia comes to her again, kisses her cheek, then her forehead. 'I ask no such thing. Whatever it is you need from me, I will do it. Tell me.'

Odette's mouth twists, her full, Cupid's-bow lips and her fine dark brows drawn together. 'Distract me.'

This is a request Cecilia knows well. It is a game, their game.

She brings her to a sofa and sits in the corner so that Odette can rest her head in her lap. Cecilia strokes her hair, her eyes drifting around the room, to Lydia's sketches, the half-finished work Odette has been allowed to keep – *La Belle Dame Sans Merci*, *Isabella, or the Pot of Basil*, *Lamia.*

'One day,' she begins, 'we will take a train. We will go all the way to the coast.'

'To Brittany?' asks Odette, noting which picture Cecilia is looking at. *Tristan and Iseult.*

'To Brittany. Cornwall. Ireland. All of it.'

'No. I don't like that one. It all ends in death.'

She is not wrong. The stories that Lydia has painted them into court suffering and lovesickness, heartbreak and grief. Now, it seems a folly, inviting in something for which they were not ready.

'Then what about our flat in Bloomsbury?' Cecilia asks.

Odette curls her fingers into the fabric of Cecilia's skirt. 'Yes, I like that one.'

'So do I. I have been thinking, we'll have a little cat maybe, called Babette, and she will howl and howl every morning until we get up and feed her.'

'Where will our flat be?'

'Oh, in a narrow building full of poets and suffragists. It will be on the second floor but still quite spacious. The windows will look out onto a fine square, and if you stand just right and squint, you will see the British Museum or St George's.'

'There must be a little baker's down the street to buy fresh bread every morning,' says Odette, 'and I will always bring you back a strawberry tart when they are in season.'

'And in winter, it will be terribly cold, but we will stoke the fire high and I will knit you a scarf and the lights of the city will look so beautiful in the frost.'

The smile that had been forming vanishes from Odette's face. 'We will find the money for it, won't we? Could Aunt Penelope help us? It is not all lost, is it?'

Cecilia does not know how to answer. Instead, she taps her fingers against the hard shell of Odette's bodice, the bones of her corset.

'Perhaps I will get a job as a typist for a radical newspaper,' says Cecilia uncertainly. 'And you can be a clerk at the telegraph office and learn all sorts of secrets.'

But it is spoilt now. Odette's expression is far away.

Cecilia bites her lip. 'Are you still with me?'

'I am sorry. I am not good company.'

'I don't need you to be.'

'I do not know when I will be myself again. I think I died, and now I am in a new world and I recognise none of it.'

Cecilia presses a palm to Odette's cheek and turns her face to look at her. 'Then recognise me. I am still here. *Love is not love which alters when it alteration finds.*'

Odette covers Cecilia's hand with her own. 'What am I to do with myself?'

'I don't know,' says Cecilia, and it is the truth. 'But I do not think there is a wrong thing to do.'

Odette brings their foreheads together, and they stay for a while, united.

'My mother kept all the memorials her family wrote,' says Odette eventually. 'All these stories of the deaths of people she had never met. She said they were a comfort. Do you think it would be a comfort?'

Cecilia understands that she is not being asked her opinion. Odette needs someone to make a shape of the world now it has come undone, to lay down the edges afresh and say, here, this is where you are.

'I think it is beautiful to write it all down. To remember.'

Odette nods. 'To remember.'

Cecilia kisses her cheek. 'Will you sleep?'

'No. I think I will write.'

'You must sleep a little.'

'Later.'

They embrace once more before Cecilia makes her journey in return, working her way down one house and up into the other.

By the time she makes it back to her room, the light has been extinguished in Odette's.

But there is movement in another window now.

Two along: Uncle George's room. It is not one she has had any cause to look at before, for she has had no special reason to think much of Odette's enigmatic father. But there he is, plain before the open curtain, well-lit by gaslight.

And there, too, is Claudine.

It is this that gives Cecilia pause.

Claudine is dressed for bed in a silk robe draped over a nightgown, her hair let down from its pins. Why she is in Uncle George's room in such a state evades Cecilia for longer than it should, and it is not until Uncle George steps into view and lets Claudine touch his face that the truth is blunt and inescapable. There is no need for the confirmation of the kiss that follows, but it comes all the same.

Her stomach knots.

'Cecilia.' It is her mother's voice. Plain and flat, in a way that scares her. Her mother is in the doorway to her room, watching Cecilia watch Uncle George and Claudine. 'Come downstairs.'

'But—'

'Downstairs – now.'

Cecilia obeys.

4

Odette

AT THE DESK IN her mother's studio, Odette sits with her pen pinched between her fingers, nib hovering just above the page. A solitary candle burns low.

She has come up to the studio in some obvious gesture of closeness to Lydia, though it has been months since her mother painted here. The top floor of the London house was built for an artist, with large north-facing windows that arch up into the roof so that a steady light pours into the open space throughout the day. George bought the house because of the window – for Lydia – or so goes the story that Odette has always been told.

It is cold up here, but she loves it: the paints, the canvases, the rags and palettes, the pots of paintbrushes and knives, the tang of turpentine. She remembers playing here as a child, pressing her face against the fragile glass and looking down the long drop to the paving stones below.

There is a sheet of paper before her and a stack to one side, ready for her words. To the left are the open pages of the memorials from her mother's stash, taken from a box below her desk. They are a strange genre, a clash of different voices, all unfamiliar, marking down grief, shock, fear, carefully constructed bons mots about God and the Spirit and a Good Death, tirades against bad doctors and careless relatives. Odette has not read many memorials. She never could fathom what there might be in the death stories of so many, the grinding inevitability of decay and rot, of the end of human life.

She understands it a little better, now. It is like the photograph. This time is sacred: the final moments in which her mother still lives vividly in her mind. She must capture it all, while she still can.

Odette writes. About her mother's illness, about the days, weeks, spent with her as she died, the horror and the beauty, the work of witnessing, what it has cost her, what she has lost. It is laborious work. The words fight her; each must be dug from the ground like ore, smelted into something with meaning and laid in slow foundations. As she writes she cries, silently, seemingly without end. Is this what it is to mourn? Is this why each of those strangers from the past was compelled to write down their memories of the last moments they had together, as though committing them to paper would anchor the dead to the world of the living, so the writer would not be left so alone?

The clock on the mantel strikes a tiny chime only once – it is deep into the night, and her candle has burnt to the stub. She stretches, arms pulled high above her head, back aching. The shop-bought weeds do not fit her well; they pinch beneath her armpits, and the skirt is too loose around the waist.

Tap-tap-tap.

Odette stops.

Tap-tap-tap.

That sound. Where does it come from?

It is just a noise. She should not be so suddenly fearful.

But oh, it tugs at something in her mind, some familiar, awful recognition rooted deep down.

Tap-tap-tap.

She must know.

Odette rises quickly, quietly, puts on her slippers and lights a fresh candle.

Below, the house is silent, save for the interruption of that solitary tapping. Her father and Claudine are both in their respective rooms; her mother's bedroom door stands open, the room stripped and prepared for cleaning.

Odette checks it all the same, but it is a shell now, devoid of the warmth and softness and breath that makes a place alive.

Her mother is not here. Her mother is downstairs.

It is a comfort – and a horror.

Odette descends the stairs, only the hiss of her skirts on the carpet following her. Through the transom over the front door comes the soft orange glow of the street lamp, and somewhere very distant, she can hear the clop of horseshoes on cobblestones.

Tap-tap-tap.

The noise comes from within the dining room, she is certain.

Tap-tap-tap.

What if her mother knocks at the door?

No, it is mad; it is foolish – but Odette is struck so forcefully by a vision of her mother clawing at the door, feet and mouth bound, like those revenants who wake to find themselves already in their grave and score their coffin lids with nail marks.

It is too awful.

She must save her – she must let her out.

Odette rushes to the door, knocking her candle over in her hurry, extinguishing the flame, and she struggles in the dark to turn the latch and tumble into—

Nothing.

The room is still. Cold.

Her mother's body is flat on the table, grey in the moonlight through the open curtains, and beginning to smell ever so faintly of rot.

Odette covers her mouth and swallows a sob.

The tapping comes again, but now she sees what it is.

Only a bird: a crow, hopping from side to side on the windowsill, rapping its beak against the glass as though to get her attention. It cocks its head to one side, eyeing first her, then where her mother lies.

Then it raps again. One, two, three times.

Once for yes, twice for no. What do three knocks mean?

Odette is filled with a repulsion and horror so strong that she slaps her palm against the glass hard enough that the bird rises in a startle of wings and cawing.

The tapping is gone.

Her mother is still dead.

5

Cecilia

IN THE PARLOUR OF the Gate House, Leo sits in a chair by the mantelpiece, nerves betrayed by the manner in which he taps the end of his cigarette against the case, rapid fire. Penelope has brought the sherry decanter over with three glasses, something Cecilia has never seen her do without company present. She pours out three measures and hands one to Cecilia, who clutches it like an anchor.

She cannot think. Her mind will not let her. She cannot have seen what she has seen. It is impossible, and yet it has happened, and she bears witness to it in her own weak body. So it is a fracture, a split, a madness come into the world.

Penelope raises her sherry to her lips, then puts it down again, as though she is unable to look at either of her children. 'I must speak to you both. I am not sure you are fully aware of the situation we now find ourselves in.'

'Not when you continue to be so cryptic,' says Leo. 'Out with it, Mother. What terrible secrets have you been keeping?'

'Why must you be so dramatic? It is very callous of you. The fact of the matter is that it simply did not concern you before now.'

'But Lydia's death has changed things,' says Cecilia, less a question than an offering to her mother: her children are not stupid. She can trust them with the truth.

'Yes,' says Penelope. 'You both know how dearly I loved her, but the truth is: we as a family have relied on Lydia's kind nature more than I have ever made plain.'

Leo lifts the cigarette to his lips to light it, then drops it again, the fragile shape of it bent between his fingers. 'For God's sake, spit it out. What is it? Are we in debt? Did we borrow money from Aunt Lydia?'

Penelope looks to her sherry again. 'No. Lydia never expected any money repaid.'

'But we took money from her,' pushes Leo.

'We have taken everything from her, darlings. This house belongs to Lydia, not to us. When your father died, she promised she would give us her support to whatever end. She found us the house in Richmond first, then when she had the means she bought the Gate House and moved us here. We have never been charged rent, nor are we charged for the gas or the coal or the servants. It has allowed our small resources to suffice for our daily needs. It has allowed you, dear Leo, to work as an articled clerk until you qualify as a solicitor and you, Cessy, to indulge your desire to dally at university. You have both been raised in the manner I wished for you, and it is all down to Lydia.'

Penelope waits for her pronouncement to be absorbed.

There has been too much shock today. This, Cecilia cannot take in.

'You mean Father left us nothing?' asks Leo. 'That cannot be right.'

Their mother draws her shawl close around her. 'You know I don't like to speak of your father. I am sure he didn't mean it all to work out as it did, but there's no changing it.'

She knew it would not be easy for her and Odette to find the money to leave home, to afford their flat in Bloomsbury. Her mother would hardly have been willing to help them but – but this is . . . What does it mean? She cannot grasp its enormity.

'We have nothing?' she asks softly. 'We are out on the street?'

'That depends,' says Penelope. A different look has come across her face, one Cecilia cannot quite read.

She thinks of Uncle George and Claudine pressed together and is struck with the sense that Lydia's death is more than the passing of one life.

Leo frowns, fishing a fresh cigarette from his case and fitting it to his lips. 'Depends on what?'

Penelope grimaces. 'I have told you how I hate that habit.'

'Well, we shall all be in the workhouse soon, according to you, so I don't think I'll worry too much about my habits. So, this is Lydia's house – what of it?'

'It is no longer Lydia's,' says Cecilia softly.

'No,' confirms Penelope. 'It will be George's now; as her husband it will all revert to him.'

'Then what is the problem? Uncle George won't throw us out.' Leo laughs, looking at his mother and sister, as though he hopes that they will join in, the problem being slain.

'Don't be naive,' says Penelope. 'George is not a bad man, but he is easily swayed, and if we are no longer wanted here, we will have to go.'

Leo frowns. 'But I don't understand – who would not want us here?'

Cecilia glances at her mother, who returns her gaze with a look so forceful Cecilia feels light-headed.

'It is not important. The fact of the matter is that we are no longer under Lydia's protection.'

Leo stubs out his cigarette and tosses the end into the fire. 'So, what is it you think we must do now? I have my salary. It is not much, but I hope it will grow as I build my practice.'

It is easier to let Leo speak, to concede to his simpler understanding of their world. It is how the three of them have always been. Her mother speaks in stage dialogue, striking her poses, Leo steps in to act the gallant, golden son, the only level head amongst skittish women, and Cecilia – Cecilia relinquishes ground to them both, Cecilia is the audience.

'Thank you, my darling,' says Penelope, patting his hand. 'There is nothing to be decided tonight, but I could not sleep without telling you both the truth.'

'I doubt sleep is something any of us will be getting much of. I believe you're making a storm out of a drizzle. Nothing need change simply because Aunt Lydia has gone.' Leo seems to catch himself at the offhand way he speaks of her death. 'Well. You know what I mean to say.'

'Could you tell Masie to bring my tonic to my room?' says Penelope. 'You are quite right; I won't sleep a wink now, and it is the only thing that brings me any respite.'

Leo's face crumples with distaste. 'I am not the boot boy – tell her yourself.'

Penelope squeezes his hand. 'Darling boy, don't argue.'

When Leo is gone and the door has shut behind him, Penelope turns to Cecilia, eyes fiery, pinning her in place.

'Do not breathe a word of what you saw.'

Cecilia wishes she could look away from her mother but she feels as though at the mercy of some mesmerist. 'I cannot hide this from Odette,' she forces herself to say.

'You can, and you will.'

How does Leo laugh their mother off so easily? He has always done so and it has made her a jealous sister since they were children.

'Leo is right.' She throws his name in like some blocking move of a fencing sword. 'Uncle George will not throw us out.'

'Good God, girl – you act like you were raised to be stupid. A new wife will want a clean house. She will want her own allies, not to sleep in the sheets of a dead woman.'

'Wife?' says Cecilia, barely above a whisper.

'Don't look so shocked. All of good opinion know that it is only a matter of time before the Deceased Wife's Sister Bill passes. Until then, there are ways and means. George and Lydia had not been husband and wife to each other for a long time; surely you understood that. I loved Lydia, but George was a saint to put up with her ways. Of course he was desperate to find a sensible woman.'

'Is that what Claudine is? Sensible?'

Penelope darts up and pins Cecilia's jaw in her hand. 'Stop that. Do not make it complicated. It is quite simple: our future now lies with Claudine. Not with Lydia, and not with Odette.'

'But—'

'If Claudine takes against us, there is no university for you, and as you do not seem inclined to marry, you will be on your uppers, my girl, and I don't think you have the first idea what that means.'

Cecilia summons her courage. 'I don't want to lie to Odette. She trusts me.'

'This is not some childish game, Cecilia. Honour and virtue no longer come into it. If it comes to it, do you think Odette will put you first without thought to her own interest? Lord love her, she is a clever girl, but she is troubled – of course she would be, with a mother like that. She has eyes only for her own problems. Do not hitch your star to the wrong wagon.'

Cecilia thinks of the sharpness of Claudine's gaze, the way she seems to always be taking stock of the world before her and finding it wanting.

'I don't think Claudine likes me,' says Cecilia.

'Then you must change your tack.'

There is a noise at the door, and Penelope darts away, leaving Cecilia with an ache in her jaw where her mother pinched it so tightly.

Masie, Penelope's lady's maid, has come with her tonic, and it is as though the conversation has been spirited away. Once more, they are a normal, loving family exchanging pleasantries before bed, shutting up the house, dousing candles and coming together in comfort after a day of grief.

Lydia has died, and she has taken the world with her.

6

Cecilia

THE SECRET BEATS LIKE a second heart beneath Cecilia's chest.

A day or two passes, the mellow light of autumn slowing time and drawing the nights closer. There is so much to do. Death is a messy business.

She sits with a stack of black-bordered note-cards and writes to the world of Lydia's passing. Someone must do it, and the task has fallen to her. A clergyman, with a punched nose and widow's peak, all in black like a crow, comes to discuss the order of service. The undertaker arrives with a bag of samples. She is struck by the mundanity of their tasks, the separate world they have been pushed into. The chores. The detail.

And everywhere, lies.

Each time she looks at Claudine and Uncle George, she cannot bear the pressure that builds within her. She must tell Odette. It is unconscionable that she is keeping this from her.

But then, as she stands at the French windows that open onto the meadow-garden, rich with late-blooming flowers and the vines that climb the stone boundary wall, and again, as she replaces a book of Coleridge onto the shelves that teem with fine leather and gilt and endless, endless dreams – it strikes Cecilia that she might die if she were ever forced to leave this place.

There are two deaths waiting for her: the loss of Odette, and the loss of her safety. For so long, they have been one and the same, but now they have been split apart, and she does not know which road to follow. If her mother is right, then without Claudine's approval, without the continuation of the financial support that Lydia gave, no safe future is possible.

But without Odette, she can see no future at all.

Money and Odette. There must be a way to make these two things be one and the same.

Cecilia and her mother are sorting through a pile of condolence letters when Odette comes out the drawing room to fetch her. Her face is drawn and pinched, her sleep-bruised eyes sunk deep below her brows.

'There you are,' she says to Cecilia. 'They're starting.'

Penelope lays a hand on Cecilia's knee beneath the table to fix her in place.

Odette extends her hand.

For now, at least, Odette has authority here.

Cecilia wriggles out of her mother's grasp and lets Odette lead her through to where the undertaker has laid out examples of wood and handles and name plates. Claudine stands by the fireplace, stiff-backed and watching. Uncle George joins them, and the truth is so clear in the way Claudine's eyes track him around the room, assessing, possessive. His studied disregard is a little too overdone, even for him. It is almost unfathomable to Cecilia that this is the same man she has known half her life, that the man she always believed to be benevolent and wise could seemingly so lightly do something so grotesque. And yet now she knows, she can see it in his every gesture. Odette seems oblivious to it all, but surely she cannot be. She lives in this house; this is her father, her aunt. She *must* be able to see what is now so obvious to Cecilia.

'I want whatever is best. What do you think?' Odette asks the undertaker.

He coughs delicately and indicates a shining plaque in bronze with an elaborate engraving of lilies around the border. 'We find this design suits a more refined, sensitive taste.'

'Then we must have that one. And four coaches, at least, with ostrich feathers for all.'

Claudine makes a noise that she smothers quickly.

'Do you have a comment?' snaps Odette.

'An elaborate funeral is old-fashioned. Your mother would have wanted something small, for true friends only.'

Odette laughs, short and harsh. 'She would not have wanted anything of the sort.'

The truth, Cecilia thinks, is that Lydia would not have been able to make any decision at all about what she wanted. None of this is about Lydia, but then no funeral is ever about the dead.

They all turn to George, King Solomon sat in judgement.

He shifts in his seat. 'Ah. Well. Ritual has an important role to play.'

Cecilia always wonders how he manages to say so very little of meaning. It always seemed a little eccentric before, charming in some sort of inaccessible, academic way, but now it feels flat, so clearly inadequate. For the first time, Cecilia finds herself angry at him. Odette deserves more. *Lydia* deserves more.

Claudine is clearly displeased, but she can say nothing more than, 'Very well. But we must do it quickly. It is no good to linger over these things.'

Indeed, they do not linger at all. The funeral arrangements are decided in a rush of activity over the next day and a half; food is ordered for the wake, the coffin measured and bought, velvet lining and brass handles chosen, a service planned, and a plot paid for.

The coffin arrives the morning of the viewing, and they all gather around to watch as Lydia is lifted from the dining table and placed gently inside the silk and velvet lining like a ring into a jeweller's box. Odette clutches onto Cecilia so tightly it leaves finger marks. She wonders how much Odette is sleeping – if she sleeps at all – for she jumps at the tapping of the maid knocking the stub of a candle from its holder.

There is a distinct smell starting to rise from the body. The staff breathe through their mouths as they come near Lydia, and even Leo coughs into his handkerchief before excusing himself.

'Flowers,' declares Cecilia. 'Should there not be flowers?'

Odette rouses herself. 'Yes. Flowers. There were always flowers.'

They leave the rest of the household to prepare for the visitors who have been invited to view the body, and go into the garden, with a large basket and a pair of secateurs.

The sky is broad and beautiful, with the glory of a late-September sky when the air is fresh and strong but still made rich from the last of the light. The dahlia beds are a prism of colour, delicate asters and late-blooming clematis spilling down across the trellis. They place the basket on the lawn and begin their work.

Cecilia kneels beside Odette, reaching out to each stem and snipping it cleanly. On the wooden fence before her, a deathwatch beetle crawls from its hole and along the grain. A bee alights upon a hedge stake.

'I'm leaving for Oxford on Saturday,' she says. She wants to bring the future into the present, bring Odette onto this road she has chosen. 'When is your train to Cambridge now?'

Odette holds the stem of a pale mauve autumn crocus in her lap. 'I am not sure.'

'Have you the ticket already? I can go to the ticket office if you need.'

'I mean, I'm not sure that I am going at all.'

Cecilia sits back. 'Of course you are going. What are you talking about?'

'I don't rightly know, but how can I? I don't sleep, I cannot read, I can barely dress myself without crying. How can I do something so momentous when I am like this?'

'But, by your own logic, would it not be rash to throw away everything you planned, simply because you are "like this"? When it passes, won't you want to still have a life to go back to?'

Odette cuts the stem before her with viciousness. 'Passes? I am not sure this will ever pass.'

'Then why not go anyway? Lydia would have wanted you to.'

Cecilia casts around for something she can say that will pin Odette, keep her within the bounds of the girl she has always known. They have had their plan neatly set out for so long: university, then, somehow, an escape to a life of their own. What would she do without it?

All is in disarray, and Cecilia does not know how to position herself amongst the debris.

'You do not know what she would have wanted.' Odette throws down the flower and rises, brushing the grass from her skirt. 'She was drowning in life and would have taken me with her, if it would have kept us together longer.'

Cecilia scrambles up after her, nicking her hand on the secateurs so that she must pause and suck the small wound before she spills blood upon her clothes.

A white rabbit sits in the centre of the lawn, its side-eye trained on them, its nose twitching. In a flash, it is gone, into the vegetable beds, and Odette is walking stiffly inside, holding the basket of flowers close to her chest.

In the dining room, the coffin has been placed back onto the table with Lydia in it. The room is empty, and Cecilia closes the door behind them while Odette sets the basket down and idly takes up the round head of a hydrangea.

'Please,' says Cecilia, 'don't make any rash decisions about Cambridge. I don't think it would do you good to stay here with – Claudine.'

This at least seems to reach Odette. She knuckles her eyes. There are dark-blue smudges on the fragile skin beneath. None of them have been sleeping, but Odette seems to have been half pulled into the underworld.

'Perhaps not. Though I think she is trying, in her own way.'

Cecilia purses her lips. 'Do you?'

'Father says I must try harder to understand how difficult this has all been for her. She has been abroad for so long;

she has come back to quite a group of strangers. It must be hard to feel part of the family, as an outsider.'

Now, here is the moment. She must say it.

Cecilia's mouth is dry. Words abandon her.

'We must find a way to rub along now, I suppose,' says Odette.

Cecilia is a coward. A complete and utter coward.

She does not want to hurt Odette, she tells herself. She is protecting her. She will find out soon enough. Why take these last moments of ignorance from her?

So instead, she kisses her, less in passion than succour.

Cecilia will find the money for her and Odette to escape, and then whatever it is their parents do or do not do will not matter.

'Here,' says Cecilia, when they draw back. Fishing in a pocket, she pulls out two coins.

Odette smiles, small and tentative, but the first one Cecilia has seen in days.

Gently, Odette places the coins on her mother's eyes, then together they dress the body and the coffin in the flowers and greenery, until it is teeming with colour and verdant with life. The scent of sap covers the rot that has spread throughout the room.

'It is like something she would have painted,' says Odette, and then, without warning, the tears come flooding out.

Cecilia holds her tightly, as though they can weather the storm together and will survive by the strength of their grip.

Their moment is broken only by the sound of the doorbell, and a sudden flurry of movement in the hallway.

Visiting time has come.

Odette turns at once to the wall, scrubbing her eyes, and Cecilia takes a few paces away just as Claudine comes in. Behind her in the hallway, there is a mass of hats and scarves and coats being removed from heads and shoulders, the jabbering sound of conversation and even muted laughter, and George there in the middle of it, alive in the clasp of his circle.

Claudine surveys the flowers with distaste, which snaps to anger when she sees the coins on Lydia's eyes. 'What is this? Get rid of those at once before people see.'

Odette stands very still. 'She is my mother. Why should I not do as I please?'

'And she was my sister. Don't act as though I have no feeling in this. Remove them. At once.'

For a moment, Cecilia thinks she may challenge Claudine – and oh God, has the time come already for Cecilia to declare whose side she is on? – but then Odette goes slowly to her mother's face and plucks away the coins.

The Fairfax-Waughs' circle – Liberal politicians, art critics, poets and professors – crowd into the dining room and make unbearable conversation, rehearsing the same stale dialogue over glasses of brandy and sherry. George appears relieved to disappear into the safety of friendships that demand no real intimacy. It all reminds Cecilia of her mother's threats a few days before. Odette is surrounded by people offering their condolences and wringing her hand and telling her in detail who her mother was, as though Odette does not know best of all. They admire Lydia's paintings and sketches, which cover the walls. Odette's face is in more than half, the model forever at hand for whatever Lydia was struck to try.

Cecilia's face is there, too, but it is as though she is invisible. They cannot see her beside Odette in a sketch of Lancelot coming to Guinevere – Odette as Guinevere and Cecilia the maid who tends to her – or in the painting that hangs above the sideboard, of Cecilia's Cassandra, put to death by Odette's Clytemnestra on the return of Agamemnon, modelled by Leo.

She is drawn again to that painting, thinking of the cold spring day when Lydia dressed them in sheets and muslin, put a tin sword in Leo's hand and knocked Cecilia to the floor to bring her to a position of supplication and despair.

She is alive there, at least, in the moment captured in ink and oil. In the memory.

A gasp of horror snaps through the room, and Cecilia comes back to the present at once.

All stare at Lydia's face.

Her eyes are open.

There are mutterings of shock. A woman slumps into a chair, and there is a general drawing back from the body. Odette trembles, one hand holding onto the coffin, but a neighbour, a doctor, closes Lydia's eyelids, explaining how the muscles of the face contract after death and it has been known for a corpse to wink.

But Cecilia is watching none of them.

Claudine is at the door, one hand searching behind her for the handle, the other clutched to her chest in fear. She is ashen – the shock, of course, but it is more than that. She looks as though it is Judgement Day and the dead have risen to give their final testimony.

Odette is so caught up in herself that she does not see it. Cecilia glances between Claudine and Lydia, at the rictus of some unnamed emotion that fixes Claudine's expression.

Guilt at taking her dead sister's husband, perhaps.

Cecilia cannot rightly place it.

All she knows is that she must act with caution.

She only wishes Odette would do the same.

7

Odette

THE COFFIN SITS IN the hall now, open and covered in a black velvet pall with a white velvet border. Odette has chosen the old-fashioned shape that resembles a person, rather than the new oblong style that reduces a body into four straight lines. They are burying her mother; there is no need to hide it.

The dining room has been turned over now to the funeral breakfast, the mourners gathered together in their black, passing out scarves and hatbands and eating from the great piles of funeral biscuits that Mrs Binx has produced.

There is a buzzing in Odette's head as she comes to the open coffin.

Her mother's eyes are closed.

Of course they are.

Her cheeks have sunken in now, and her skin has become pinched and grey. She is dead.

She is dead she is dead she is dead.

And the thought strikes Odette, brief and giddy.

Odette is *free*.

Her father appears on the stairs, followed by Claudine, both in black, George holding his top hat, around which a crêpe band has already been tied. He is as hard to read as ever, but she notes that he appears dishevelled; his tie is set a little crooked and his waistcoat is misbuttoned. Perhaps his grief does work its way through.

The undertaker comes from the dining room with two of his staff, ready to fix the lid in place, and Penelope, Cecilia and Leo follow.

Penelope passes around a pair of scissors, and they take turns to cut off a lock of hair. Odette's fingers tremble so badly that her cut is jagged and a fine spray of hair falls across the shroud. She tucks the remaining strands in a handkerchief.

'You must go to the jeweller who handled my own dear Harry's hair with such care.' Penelope indicates the brooch pinned to her breast, which has a plaited lock of hair beneath glass.

The undertaker's men place the lid and set to nailing it down.

Odette is struck by a burst of hysterics rising within her, the urge to scream and beat her fists against these horrible men who have shut her mother into a box.

Cecilia holds her back, a rigid presence at her side.

It is done.

Penelope looks at her pityingly. 'Come sit with Cecilia and me; we can watch the procession leave from the drawing room.'

'I am going with them.'

Penelope looks between Odette and her father in surprise. 'No one wants a crying woman disrupting the service. You are of course deeply affected by it all, which makes you act so, but if you cannot control yourself—'

'"Act so"? What have I done that is so unreasonable?' demands Odette, cheeks hot. Who is Penelope to talk to her of grief? Who are any of them?

Penelope laughs uncertainly. 'I only meant—'

'What, that I should stay *here* and cry? That I should carry on this pretence that we do not suffer as badly as if we, too, had died? No, I suppose none of you do suffer like that. It is no pretence.'

'Oh, let her go,' says Leo. 'It's Lydia. She wouldn't have cared a jot for convention.'

'That's enough,' says Claudine.

Odette sets her jaw. 'I am going.'

They all look to George, who seems to shrink within his clothes. 'Very well. We will all go.' If this is all Odette gets, she will take it.

The front door is opened, and as the pallbearers arrange themselves to lift the coffin, the whole party take their places.

Leo squeezes Odette's arm as he passes. 'Buck up, old thing,' he whispers. 'Don't make a show.'

Odette keeps Cecilia close, as though she is the only tether preventing her from drifting away.

'I am not unreasonable, am I?' whispers Odette.

Cecilia does not reply, looking instead at the floor, at the flowers, anywhere but Odette's face. Odette means to ask something more, but the procession begins to move out, and she is silenced.

On either side of the front door stand two mutes, with their old-fashioned wrapped hats and sticks and streamers, like something her mother would have painted. They lead the group, followed by the featherman, then the hearse with the coffin placed carefully within.

Coaches are lined up, four horses a piece. George, Odette and Claudine take the first, and Odette snatches up Cecilia's hand to drag her in as well, leaving Penelope and Leo to take the next. There are several empty coaches behind, sent by those who could not attend in person.

It is a short, uncomfortable ride to Highgate Cemetery, where they dismount and file into the chapel for the service. After psalms and lessons are read, they move to the graveside, where fresh-turned earth lets out a loamy, damp smell of rotting leaves and rain.

Lydia's coffin is committed into the earth, and the clergyman continues to speak, but Odette hears none of it. That buzzing has come back into her ears, with a sense that she is far away from her unreal body. Is she crying again? She cannot make sense of anything she is feeling. Do her shoes pinch? Is she dying? They have taken her mother and put her in a box, and now they will put that box into the ground and she will be left there forever. It is mad. It is all mad. How can they do this to her? How can they be so done with a person, so certain her time with them is over?

She has been thrust through a door that she did not know was there and has found herself alone, cold and frightened and unsure how she will survive.

There is no poetry here. No art, no music. There is only this bleak, sharp reality, ugly and ill-formed and discordant, all laid bare by this one truth:

What is she to do without her mother?

8

Odette

ODETTE CANNOT SLEEP.

She has washed and changed into her nightclothes and slid beneath the covers, but she feels as far from sleep as if she were atop a mountain.

The London house makes everything impossible. She wants Cecilia in her bed, but there are too many servants here. It was a risk for her to come here the night of her mother's death and it would be too much to tempt the gods again. It is better out in Suffolk, at Herne House, where everything is wild and they can be to each other everything they feel. Cecilia waited for her at her own window tonight, holding her copy of Tennyson. Usually, they would indicate a page number and read together across the distance, but tonight, Odette left her book on its shelf, shook her head and sent Cecilia away. If she cannot have what she wants, she cannot pretend any substitute will do.

Now she lies staring at the stucco ceiling rose, the day repeating in her mind. Did she do everything right? Did it come off well? Would her mother be pleased?

Questions that have no answer.

She rolls over and presses her face into the pillow, willing herself to sleep.

Sleep and forget all of this.

Tap-tap-tap.

She freezes.

Tap-tap-tap.

No. Not again. It cannot be.

The noise comes from beyond her door, but it sounds far closer than when she heard it before, when she discovered the bird. Has the bird got inside the house? Should she check?

Tap-tap-tap.

She cannot bring herself to do it – to pull back the covers and swing her bare feet out into the open air.

When the noise comes again, she strains to hear it – and it is different. Not the tapping of a beak on glass but the light slap of bare feet on floorboards.

Dread floods through her at the familiarity of that sound.

It must be one of the servants, sneaking around at night. It cannot be anything else.

Can it?

Odette burrows into the bed. She will not hear it. This is not happening. She is asleep already, and this is a monstrous dream.

Still, the tapping comes.

Odette's heart races so fast she fears it will stutter and fail.

The door opens.

A gust of wind passes into the room, shivering through the curtains, and extinguishes the candle on her bedside table.

Odette does not move, does not breathe.

She has felt unreal all day, but now she feels so bitterly, acutely alive that she burns at every nerve ending, each inch of skin alert in the agony of anticipation.

A grave-cold hand slides about her throat.

She would scream, but the noise cannot escape her tight and twisted body.

'*Odette. Darling.*'

Her mother's rasping voice.

Odette thinks she will go mad – has gone mad. It is too much. Her mind has betrayed her, brought her horror at an unimaginable scale and yet – relief.

It is her mother.

She turns to look.

And there she is.

Lydia is as gaunt and pale as when they nailed her inside her coffin mere hours ago, dressed in the shroud that Odette spent hours embroidering. Even – there – the shorn lock of hair at her mother's temple, where her hands shook holding the scissors.

Her mother is here, but she is not. She is indistinct around the edges, ill-defined, like faded ink on old paper. If it were daylight, she might vanish entirely.

'*I need you, darling, my girl.*'

Odette will cry, will break in madness and hope. 'Mama?'

Cold fingers stroke her throat. '*Angel. You are such a good girl.*'

Oh, she is crying now. There is no stopping the way her heart splits open. 'Mama, why did you leave me?'

'*I did not leave you. I was taken.*'

Lydia shifts above her, unreal and weightless in her translucent body, but heavy as six feet of earth, the force of her spirit like a rock that will crush Odette.

'*Claudine.*' The words are harsh and indistinct, as though they are dragged from a depth with great effort, like larynx and vocal cords are no longer the meat and muscle of her body.

A shiver of fear spikes through Odette. 'What of Claudine?'

The cold fingers close around her throat again, and though it is not possible, it feels as though her mother squeezes.

Odette flinches away, but her view is filled by her mother's corpse-face, twisted in an inhuman snarl.

'*Revenge me. For I am murdered.*'

The Summer

July 1898, Herne House, Suffolk

Death, like a friend's voice from a distant field
Approaching through the darkness, called

Idylls of the King, Alfred, Lord Tennyson

1

Cecilia

'Do you believe in ghosts?'

Cecilia rolls over in the long grass, passing the cigarette to Odette, who is lying on her back, skirts pulled up to bare her legs to the summer sun.

'Ghosts?' asks Odette.

'Yes, ghosts.'

The sky is a deep, cornflower blue, dense with summer heat, and the wildflowers grow tall here, hiding them in the depths of the meadow. In this paradise, it seems impossible to believe that any sinister or hateful thing could ever happen, in an England that also contains cricket and chaffinches and the boat race and afternoon tea, sea salt and the crash of waves on pebbles, the sweet smell of newly mown hay, tennis and Tennyson, Marlowe and Shakespeare.

'Yes,' says Odette, knocking off ash with a tap from her forefinger. 'Oh, very much so.'

'Really?' Cecilia has plucked a long piece of grass and is tickling Odette's temple with its feathery seed pods. 'As in, the clock chimes midnight and the grey lady wails in the abbey?'

Odette bats the grass away, takes a long draw on the cheap smoke. 'Yes. It is all possible. Don't you think so?'

This is why Cecilia has asked. She knew Odette would say something delicious and unexpected. It is one of Cecilia's favourite things about her; she can study her every day like a botanist plucking petals from a hothouse bloom, and then a new season will turn and Odette will bear some strange, unexpected fruit.

Because it *is* all possible. The England of soft sun and meadows can only be so sweet because it is also the England of sacked monasteries, moons bright like sickles, black dogs, plague pits and sallow churches, ruined castles, battlefields beneath wheat and rye, graveyards thick with ivy, *batter my heart, three-person'd God*, and night-screaming from every wrecked house and manor.

Cecilia braces herself with her hands on either side of Odette's head, blocking out the sun. '*When by thy scorn, O murd'ress, I am dead and that thou think'st thee free from all solicitation from me, then shall my ghost come to thy bed, and thee, feign'd vestal, in worse arms shall see.*'

'Quite. Donne is appropriately dramatic.' Odette lets loose a stream of smoke into her face. 'Well, go on then. Kiss me.'

Cecilia grins and obliges.

With the heat of the sun on her back, she wriggles down through the grass to push Odette's skirts up to her hips. The first time she kissed Odette here, it was with the nervous confusion of a dare, a fumbling towards something that they had only heard about in whispers from the other girls at school, or in the bawdy jokes Leo would tell when Mother was out of the room. It had not seemed obscene to Cecilia, though Odette had wrinkled her nose in confusion – *what, your mouth? Your tongue?* It had felt more like an enticement, like putting a toe into ice water or testing the point of a knife on a finger. What *if*.

Odette obliged her curiosity, and though it took a little practice, they both found it was not so outlandish an idea after all. What an art she can make of coaxing noises from Odette, of moving her tongue just so, of causing Odette's hips to jump beneath Cecilia's firm hands and making the muscles of her thighs tense. Sometimes, Cecilia wonders if there would have been someone else, had she not met Odette, but it seems impossible. They are made for each other, and without each other, they will come undone.

When they are finished, Cecilia stretches like a cat, pointing her toes and reaching her arms over her head.

Odette slides a pair of small smoked glasses onto her nose to protect her eyes from the sun. It takes her a moment to steady her breath, and there is still a catch to it that makes Cecilia smile in satisfaction.

'I suppose we must go back.'

Cecilia slumps. 'Must we?'

'Don't tempt me,' says Odette.

'Tricky. I like tempting you very much.'

'And as soon as all Father's crowd arrive tomorrow, temptation will be entirely forbidden. It's better when it's just your lot and my lot, don't you think? You hardly count as other people.'

'It's like in *The Book of Common Prayer* and that big table of kinship laws. Once a couple are married, they become one family.'

Odette gives a small smile. 'Is that a proposal? It's terribly sudden; I shall have to disappoint all my gentleman callers.'

Cecilia swats her thigh. 'I think if a gentleman tried to call on you, you'd have his eye out with a hat pin.'

Odette sighs happily. 'More's the pity I can't use the hat pin on that dreadful lot arriving. God, they're such bores. I've never met people who thought so much of themselves simply because they've written one poor poem.'

'Poor poetry can be quite amusing.'

'Now, you mustn't start that again – I nearly laughed in poor Mr Wrexham's face, because all I could think of was you pulling his last piece apart.'

'*Fairy chimes trill in the dell, effulgently my heart it doth swell.*'

'Stop it.'

Cecilia pounces, straddling Odette's hips to pin her in place. '*By my troth, O my dear maid, all my life my love shan't fade, this I swear on pain of death, I pledge to you my knightly heft.*'

Odette covers her face with her hands. 'Heft! Christ.'

'All right, all right.' Cecilia rolls off. 'I suppose we ought to go.'

Odette does not get up. 'Do *you* believe in ghosts?'

Cecilia closes her eyes and holds out a hand to the aether. 'I sense avoidance. I sense procrastination.'

'Very funny. *Do* you, though?'

'Not a jot. I think we die and then that's it,' says Cecilia.

'Apart from Heaven.'

'Yes, apart from Heaven, of course.'

'Unless the papists had it right all this time, and there's purgatory and endless levels of Hell awaiting us sinners.'

Cecilia examines a grass stain on her skirts that is unlikely to wash out. 'I suppose there *was* a reason the village prostitute would wear green.'

'Darling, you make us sound sordid.'

'Very sordid. Simply obscene.' Cecilia smiles with the promise to make it so again and again and again. 'Perhaps the atheists have it right, and there's nothing at all after death. Just the cold soil and the worms.'

A thick band of cloud has blown in to cover the yellow disk of sun – an English summer.

Gooseflesh rises along Odette's arms. She hastens up, shoving their picnic into the wicker basket.

'I promise when I die to come back and haunt you, if I can,' says Odette. 'Teach you a lesson.'

'That sounds jolly.' Cecilia shoulders the bag with their books and paints, and Odette carries the basket as they walk back towards the house, hips swaying and lips sticky. 'I'll haunt you and you'll haunt me, and then we'll know for sure.'

At the kissing gate to the lane, Cecilia spits in her palm and holds her hand out.

Odette smiles. Palm wet with her own spit, she takes Cecilia's hand. 'Deal.'

In this summer idyll, they play like children, running barefoot through fallow fields and high corn, skirts tucked into their waistbands and unpinned hair streaming like a pennant behind a knight. Fields roll gently out across the land, golden with cut corn and dense with thickets of trees and hedgerow. A kestrel glides high, watching for the snuffling field mice gorging on dropped kernels, while butterflies and cabbage moths throng the blackthorn and hawthorn.

Odette is wild and daring, plucking insects from beneath stones, scrambling up trees and wading across moss-slick rocks, but it is Cecilia whose imagination is the dry wood to their blaze, turning mounds into mountains, conjuring castles from stumps of rock and dragon fire from clouds.

They are dying days.

With each moment, Cecilia feels as though she clasps her hand around dust motes in a sunbeam, around moonlight on water. Their days at school together are over. Each summer spent at Herne House, both families living together as one, elaborate picnics spread across the meadows, long evenings of party games and Leo at the piano, Cecilia singing, Lydia sketching – it will not be as it has been. It cannot be. Leo has separated already, too preoccupied with work. George spends more and more time visiting the Continent. Odette has bid them both to go away to university.

It is all slipping away from her.

Odette is slipping away from her.

It is only subtle – the smallest of closed expressions or the angle of her shoulder – but Cecilia can feel her tug against the bounds of their life at Herne House, and in turn, it is as though Odette tugs against her bond with Cecilia. If only she runs fast enough, then perhaps Cecilia can close the gap, keep the cord slack and easy, with no threat that it may break.

2

Odette

THERE IS A STINK like bilge water throughout the house. As soon as Odette crosses the threshold, the thickness of it meets her nose, and bile rises in her throat. The front and back doors are thrown open against its fetid presence, casting a stark dividing line between the blinding brightness of the sun-blanched courtyard and the cool flagstones of the hall within. The interior is all but impossible to make out – only an inky border to the open door at the back, through which she can see several men with bargepoles and billhooks bent over the moat where it meets the wall of the house and flows beneath the kitchens.

Herne House sits in a cupped valley between low Suffolk hills, surrounded on three sides by a squared-off creek that is known as the moat. A stone-built core remains from the medieval manor house it once was, rising in timber-framed storeys and expanded over time with mismatched wings. Inside, doors hang in the middle of walls; flights of three or four steps go nowhere; windows do not match up to any room, all made of uneven corners and slantwise ceilings.

Odette crosses the wide, oak-panelled hall – the last hold-out of the medieval house – and puts her head outside the back door. There is a strangely swollen mass of white and black and red wedged half under the stonework arch through which the moat runs. A sheep has fallen into the water and died, or died and fallen in; it does not matter much which, only that it has been pulled downstream by the power of the current, and now the bloated corpse has plugged up the channel, and the brackish, sour water has flooded out across the lawns. One man attempts to hook a limb and draw it out, but the flesh is too weak, and he succeeds only in pulling a leg from the mutton.

Cecilia comes up behind Odette and places a hand hot on her waist. The press of her palm through the thin material of Odette's shirt is a brand against her skin; she discarded her corset today in protest at the heat that shimmers over the grass, turning it brittle and brown in patches. Water and drought together – the world is dying of too much and too little.

'Wretched creature,' says Cecilia. 'Why is it sheep die so easily? I see them everywhere, caught in hedges or broken in ditches. It is like they have so faint a connection to life it cannot bear weight when leant upon.'

'That is a very poetic way to say they are stupid.'

Cecilia laughs and draws her back inside. 'I have an idea I want to tell you.' She stretches her arms above her head and toes off her shoes. Odette thinks Cecilia should have been a dancer, like her mother; she is so elegant it is distracting.

'A play?'

A cat-like smile spreads across Cecilia's face. 'Oh yes. A very good one this time.'

Their *plays* are a private game – something like a performance, a play-act, a co-creation of a world that lives between them, as if in one shared mind.

'Later,' says Odette, before Cecilia can speak. 'Mother said she wanted us for her new piece.' Odette sweeps into the morning room, untying the ribbons of her hat. 'Mother?'

Her mother is sitting in an upright chair facing the window onto the garden, where, at a slant, it is possible to see the jabbing of the poles.

And then she moves, and it is not Odette's mother at all.

Odette stops dead. For a moment, she thinks she has lost her senses. This woman looks like Lydia – the same mouth, the same set to her eyes and shape of her jaw – but it is as if one has been drawn in charcoal and the other in watercolour. This woman is her mother stretched out, blunter-featured, angular where her mother is soft, broad-framed where her mother is round and delicate, all pale lawn skirts and neat lace at her throat, unblemished by sweat or heat or any sort of human affect.

It is an astonishingly uncanny experience, like she imagines seeing a ghost must be – an echo of someone so familiar, distorted and wrong.

'I'm sorry,' says Odette, reflexively polite. 'I didn't know we were expecting company today.'

Cecilia stops behind her, like a shadow.

The woman lifts a perfume-scented handkerchief to her nose as a shield against the smell that reaches through the open door. Odette finds herself defensive of her home. *It is only the country*, she wants to say. The city has its own foul odour.

'You must be Odette.'

'How do you do?' says Odette, with a confused smile, not allowing herself to falter at her Christian name being used so bluntly.

'I am Claudine Hutton. Your aunt.'

Odette's father arrives, with a maid carrying tea.

'Getting to know each other?' he says warmly, as though none of this is a disorientating surprise. 'Sit down, sit down.' He seems to notice Cecilia for the first time. 'Of course you're welcome to join us.'

A flush crosses her cheeks. 'Thank you, but I had better see if my mother needs me.'

Cecilia slips away and Odette joins her father and Claudine. There is a silence while tea is poured.

Odette tries not to look at Claudine. It is too uncanny.

She searches her mind for anything she knows about her mother's sister but comes up with little. Older than Lydia. Teaching at a school in Dresden. It is not that her parents have spoken badly of Claudine; it is that they have never spoken of her at all.

'Claudine will be staying for a while,' says George.

Odette looks at her aunt and speaks before she can think. 'But I thought you and Mother were estranged?'

Claudine's face becomes tight. 'Is that what Lydia says?'

'We thought it was about time things were patched up. Time heals all wounds,' offers George, as though this is a profound comment.

Claudine does not look as though she agrees with the sentiment, and Odette feels a confusing sense of kinship in their reaction to her father's words.

What does he want from her? It is the question she must always answer with her father. To close up the gaps, to smooth things over – that, she knows – but this is too baffling. What is he thinking, bringing home her mother's estranged sister? She feels her own stupidity keenly. Surely she should be able to understand her own father. It is her failing that she always flounders just out of her depth; no one has ever said it to her in these terms, but she has come to understand it so. Her father expects more of her. She must be quick, she must be sharp, she must be one of the grown-ups. Odette and her father are the sane, rational ones lined up against her mother's irrationality. That is her job, that is what she can do for him.

But this – she cannot fit it together in her mind. She must keep up, but where has he gone?

'Where is Mother?' asks Odette. 'Does she—' *know Claudine is here?* It seems somehow too awkward to say it so plainly.

George's expression is fixed. 'She's resting.'

So that *we* did not include her mother.

Odette reaches around for something to say. 'I hope you will enjoy your stay in Suffolk.'

Make it smooth, make it easy. If her father has done something, then there will be some reason for it, and she must do her best to tidy up the loose edges.

Claudine sips her tea.

There is a little strained conversation, until Claudine announces that she would like to attend to her toilet after a long journey, and they break apart in unspoken relief.

A rearrangement of bodies: Hester, Lydia's lady's maid, is instructed to settle Claudine in her room, and George goes to attend to some matter, while Odette slips away to the painting studio.

The house is the same – stink and sun, old wood, stone, faded curtains and glass – and yet it is all wrong. The world has tilted over, as though it turns on some axis that Odette has, until now, been entirely unaware of.

Why has Claudine come? Why was this plan concealed? She must find her mother.

3

Cecilia

WHEN CECILIA WAS FOUR, maybe five – the memory is unrooted in that way of early life – Leo would laugh at how she said her own name. Too many sibilants, the vowels all tight and high and whistle-like. A little mouse, he called her, squeaking and snuffling. Cecilia cried over it, because she was not sure he was wrong.

In the vast, ancient emptiness of Herne House, she scurries along the corridors unnoticed, padding silently up the sweeping staircase, the noise of her own breathing flat against her ears. The house is so old it is as though it swallows her up in the expanse of its own past, as though she could cease to exist entirely. Here is Camelot, Cecilia thought, when Odette first drew her across the moat to the ivy-clad walls, through drawing room and solar. Here is Avalon, Arcadia.

Dismissed by Uncle George, she is untethered. With Odette, everything has purpose; severed, she is cast adrift.

What will Oxford be? comes the traitorous thought. *An entire undoing?* They will be parted for so long, with Cecilia at Oxford and Odette at Cambridge. Summer will stretch for weeks yet, but she has been bracing herself for the autumn, arranging it in her mind so that she can make some sense of it. Odette wants to go to university on her own, so Cecilia will want it, too; they will split for a time and it will only prove their love more constant, a test, or that is how she makes herself understand it. Cecilia can wait for Odette to be ready for their life together.

But it wasn't supposed to change yet.

Cecilia has heard nothing of an Aunt Claudine. She does not know what to make of this new actor upon the stage.

Her mother is in her room, sat before her dressing table, a pot of rouge open but discarded. She holds an oblong of paper in her hands, unfolded to be read.

'Is it true Aunt Lydia's sister will be staying?' asks Cecilia, tucking herself against the doorframe so that Penelope will not see her grass-stained skirts. 'We found her downstairs and now they are all talking in private.'

Penelope glances at her, distracted. 'Then leave them to it.'

'I didn't know Aunt Lydia had a sister. Did you know she was coming?'

Penelope shoves the paper into a drawer, shooing Cecilia from the room. 'So many questions! Anyone would think you'd been brought up in the gutter. It is rude to pry.'

'But—'

'Go along with you and keep out of the way.'

The door shuts firmly in Cecilia's face.

She scowls, as there is no one about to see. If Odette were here, she would do such a perfect impression of Penelope's tone, the twist of her mouth, that Cecilia's frustration would dissolve at once.

Fine. She will *keep out of the way*.

Halfway along the twisting corridor that runs the spine of the Jacobean wing is a section of panelling that does not lie flush to the wall. If Cecilia hooks her nails into the edge of the grain just so, she can prise out the panel that swings on concealed hinges. She steps through and finds herself in blessed darkness. For a moment, all she does is breathe. She is truly invisible now, a mouse behind the skirting boards.

The old servants' passages were closed up not long after Cecilia was born. When Uncle George inherited Herne House from his uncle, he declared them unfit for purpose, too narrow and dirty and poorly maintained. He considered himself a great radical; allowing his servants to see daylight was an act of magnanimity on his part. Now, they are all but derelict, the home of spiders and crawling things, broken furniture, leaks and smells and, in the bottom of the house, seeping, stagnant water.

The first summer she spent at Herne House, Cecilia discovered a way into the passages through the old priest hole beneath the stairs, in which Odette would lock her when they played at Reformation. She tried to share the passages with her, but Odette disliked the dark, recoiling, frightened, so Cecilia banished it from their play – and kept it for herself.

She is much larger now than she was then, and it is far more difficult to pass through the narrow space noiselessly, but she still remembers which steps to jump over, where the floor is broken or the ceiling lower.

At a shaft of light, Cecilia stops. Crouching, she can see into her mother's room. Penelope is at her dressing table again, the piece of paper back in her hand. Whatever it says, it is apparently more important than her daughter.

Along the passage, she comes to the next spyhole, a break between the hidden door and the panelling, looking into

Leo's room. It is in its usual state: strewn with clothes, books, papers, collars hanging off the door handle, shaving kit spread about, socks hanging out of the drawers. Once the books would have been poetry, now they are solid tomes on torts and contracts. She does not understand how her brother has managed to reinvent himself so completely, cutting out all feeling and sentiment as though with a razor, and recasting himself as a rational legal mind. She wants to watch him, to understand who her brother has become.

He is not there.

Boring.

There are any number of freshly aired guest rooms waiting for the arrivals tomorrow, all as dull as dirt, then at the end of the passage a narrow flight of stairs with several steps missing. At the bottom, she can spy on the morning room – but Odette, Uncle George and Claudine are gone.

Is she alone in the world?

Sometimes, she wonders if any of this is real. Perhaps they are all only marionettes in the paper theatre of some invisible giant, heads lolling and arms jerking about as they are tugged this way and that. Or perhaps it is all some great dream of a sleeping god? She has never been sure if she is the same sort of human as everyone else. Even Odette seems alien to her at times, a creature of action and want and purpose. Cecilia thinks of herself like the blank space around the object. Aunt Lydia has told her about the principles of art, as she herself was taught them as a young woman at the Slade. The artist was called to look at the empty space as much as the thing itself – the shape of absence, without which, presence would be lost entirely.

Cecilia liked that.

Upstairs again, she looks for Odette in her room and finds nothing but a cold grate and silence.

Then, unexpectedly, voices.

A snatch of conversation draws her along the passage – Uncle George and an unfamiliar woman, who must be Claudine.

'. . . you have me here – now what? What are you going to do?'

Cecilia frowns and presses her eye to the narrow gap around the concealed door. She can see a snatch of colour, a travelling gown, then black – legs – Uncle George.

He laughs in his placatory way. 'Unpack, rest. All that can come later.'

All *what*?

'You mean to keep me here like some entertainment. It is childish of her not to see me. I thought you said—'

'Lydia will come around. You'll see. She'll have her little tantrum today, and then tomorrow it will have all blown over.'

'Blown over?' Claudine's voice is rich with scorn.

'Unpack. Settle in.'

Uncle George has come into this woman's bedroom, alone. They are a bohemian household, yes, but this is – this is—

Now there is some softer exchange that Cecilia cannot make out, then the sound of feet receding. George leaves.

A sigh. Bedsprings creaking. Claudine remains.

Cecilia is torn. Should she follow George? Find Odette? Or stay to learn what she can of this stranger?

A new voice stills her before she can decide.

'Claudine.'

She recognises this one at once.

'Penelope,' says Claudine.

'What do you mean by sending me this?' Penelope stands in the doorway, clutching the note, pale as milk.

Claudine's lip curls, cat-like. 'You found it, then.'

Cecilia presses her eye closer to the gap, shifting to see more of the room.

'Whatever you think you have discovered, I can assure you, you are wrong.'

'Oh, I really don't think I am.'

'Nonsense.' Penelope hesitates for a moment, then rips the paper up into smaller and smaller pieces. She moves to toss the paper into the grate, but the fire is unlit, so instead she throws them at Claudine's feet. 'It is a fabrication.'

Claudine rises. Before, in the morning room, she seemed stiff; now she comes into focus, brought into sharp relief by purpose. There is a radiating sense of danger that Cecilia can hardly place. It is not that Claudine speaks threateningly, nor moves with violence, but it is as though some barely contained anger swells within her and fills the room with its scent.

'Lydia told me everything, you know,' says Claudine. 'You called yourself my friend first, but you dropped me so quickly I could never quite understand it, until she told me exactly what she knew about you—'

'Stop. Must you drag all this up again?' Penelope backs up against the fireplace, one hand thrust out in protest. Cecilia has always understood her mother as the dancer she once was – a performer, a creature of shape and artifice – and even now, when her disquiet seems too real, Penelope finds a way to strike a pose.

'I will not let you have your fun at my expense again,' says Claudine. 'This time, you will help *me*, or I will tell everyone. You will be finished.'

Penelope wavers, a narrow opening that can be grasped, pried apart. 'Help you with what?'

Claudine hooks their arms together. 'Walk with me. There is much I would discuss.'

Penelope resists for only a moment before allowing herself to be led out.

Cecilia waits, breath held, palm flat against the door, for any sound of their return. Her heart beats in her chest like a hammer against the anvil of her ribs.

Noiselessly, she pushes the door open and scurries across the rug to pick up a fallen scrap. The creamy paper makes her think of the formal documents sent to her from Oxford.

There is only one piece of writing, in a looping hand: *Penel.*

Before she can reach for another piece, there are footsteps and voices, and in a flash, the secret door is closed. Cecilia races away along her mousehole, as though even this small discovery could be stolen from her.

4

Odette

HER MOTHER'S STUDIO IS HOT, despite the doors propped ajar and the windows wound open to their fullest. Though built as a conservatory, it does the job Lydia needs: every inch is bathed in natural light. Canvases are propped against the walls in varying stages of completion, broken easels stacked to be repaired or become firewood – whichever strikes Lydia as fitting – and oil paints scattered in the drawers of an index card cabinet. In the corners are piles of dresses, lengths of velvet and silk, swags of cloth flowers and leaves, vases, crowns, swords, jewels, arrows, coins, goblets, and a large standing mirror, like the prop room of some London theatre.

Odette's mother is, as she suspected, on the chaise-longue tucked into a corner, alongside a short bookshelf and a card table. Lydia is still in her nightdress, a shawl tucked around her shoulders, her chestnut hair lank from lack of washing. Dotted on the table and shelves are apple cores dried to leather; a near-empty bottle of red wine is half hidden behind one table leg, and a fur of mould grows in the teacups littered about.

George always says that Lydia is too fragile to suffer the maids in her studio, though he likes to point out the mess, as though noticing is just as noble an act as doing anything to help.

'Angel?'

Odette perches at her feet. 'Mother. Are you well?'

Lydia closes her eyes in a grimace. 'My headaches are like the Devil himself has fixed a belt around my temples and is squeezing me until I break. Nothing touches them.' Lydia always has a headache, or a stomach ache, or her eyes are sensitive to the light, or she is too tired to come to dinner, or do whatever it is she has promised to do. 'You always seem so bright and easy when you have a headache. I do not know how you do it.' Odette plucks the fabric of her skirt. *It is not a competition,* she thinks, but she knows there is no use saying anything like that to her mother. It *is* a competition, and Lydia will always make sure she is losing.

'I found your sister in the morning room,' says Odette, for want of a better way of broaching the matter.

She waits to see if her mother will respond, but Lydia only sinks further into the chaise-longue, as though she cannot bear to carry the burden of her own body.

Odette tries again. 'I didn't think you were speaking to each other.'

'*I* have always been willing to speak to her,' says Lydia, then stops herself. 'It isn't important. She is here now, and I don't want to get in the way of you having your own relationship with her.'

This is such a baffling statement Odette does not at first know how to reply. What relationship? Her loyalty is to her mother, not this stranger.

'Will she be staying that long?' she asks.

Lydia doesn't look at her. 'Ask your father.'

Odette wonders if Lydia thinks she is effectively concealing whatever this secret is. There is so plainly *something* that neither of her parents wishes to acknowledge directly, but for all their careful obfuscation, the shape of the creature behind shows through. It is maddening to see it plainly and yet be told there is nothing there at all.

Lydia opens her arms in a too-familiar gesture, and Odette submits to be drawn to her grasp.

This is how it is. This is the only way it can be, with her mother.

Lydia is lost at sea, and Odette is the life raft.

'Never too old to be held by your mother,' she says. 'When you were little, it was the only way to calm you down.'

Odette makes a non-committal sound. The suggestion that she is not *calm* when she has done nothing but ask simple questions. There is some rising noise inside her, like the drone of cattle, too many voices lifting at once until it is unbearable, loud enough to fill her chest.

So Odette speaks. Not about her real life, or anything she feels or thinks, or her complicated, agonising love for Cecilia, or how she fears leaving for university on her own, or how tense she is with so many people always in the house, servants and guests coming and going, how she doesn't know how to behave in front of them, cannot work out what they want from her, how she cowers and tenses like a hunted animal and only finds solace in a closed door.

She tells her, instead, of the information Newnham have sent to her, of the lectures she will attend on Latin and Greek, of the papers she is expected to write, of the accommodation prepared for her and the rules set down about how she must live. She talks about what she might pack in her trunk, what books she will take, what she is reading now for pleasure.

A carefully penned portrait of a life.

It is a curious split she finds in herself: one part urgent in the need for some aspect of herself that her mother does not know, another in anguish to lose a moment of her attention. Her mother's eye is always wandering towards her own pain, and it would be all too easy to lose her entirely.

The question is: which can she bear? The loss of self or the loss of her mother?

'There is something I have been meaning to tell you,' says Lydia.

Odette stiffens. 'About Aunt Claudine?'

'No. Put her from your mind. I would like to find a way to give you some money. If a woman is to be free, she must have her own means.'

Odette is almost too stunned to speak. It is a rush of frantic thought and feeling all at once. Is this real? Is it one of her mother's fantasies? Will she remember this tomorrow? Can she be stupid enough to believe her?

After a moment's deliberation, she asks, 'What do you mean?'

'I have come up with something of a plan. You know how long Eddie has been pressing me to do a show, and he says his friend, Mr King at the Jermyn Street Gallery, will gladly find space. There are so many pieces cluttering up the place here; I could sell them all for you.'

Odette's heart pinches with a pain that silences her at first. It is a gift and a burden. 'That is – that is too much. Are you sure you could part with them? And a show . . .'

Lydia smiles, holds out a hand. Odette takes it, feeling the cool, smooth skin of her mother's fingers as she squeezes hers so faintly.

'You're such a lovely girl. You don't know what it means to me that you have found something you are passionate about in going to Cambridge. You are so independent and sharp; I am so useless.'

If Lydia struggles, is lacking, suffers, it is only ever because Odette is golden, good, strong. It makes Odette wonder who her mother was before her. If it is Odette's presence that casts her mother so deeply into shadow, then, without her, did she stand in the light?

It is as though they can exist only as two sides of one coin, and Lydia has decided that she must always be in the dark.

'I can't accept that much,' says Odette.

'It is my decision.'

There is nothing Odette can say to that. *Thank you* is too transactional. 'If you are sure.'

'You can always come to me. There will always be a room for you here, whatever happens. You are my girl.'

Lydia squeezes her tighter, and Odette feels suddenly repulsed. It is too confusing, these feelings of love and revulsion co-mingled within her.

How is it possible to love and to hate the same person so completely?

5

Odette

IT IS A HEAVY, moon-rich night, cloudless and still as mown hay. Odette is well-practised at climbing from her bedroom window up onto the roof slates. There is an area where the slope is gentle enough that two bodies can stretch out beneath the stars. Cecilia has reached their refuge first, still in her chemise, which she has pulled up to her thighs to air her bare legs. Odette lets her gaze roam over the stretch of bare skin and imagines touching Cecilia there, fingertips, tongue, teeth. Perhaps she will leave a bite mark there, that only the two of them will know about.

Odette sinks down beside her, sweating already from exertion. The air is thick and humid, promising a storm.

Her mind cannot settle.

After speaking with her mother, she scrubbed at her arms with her washcloth, yanked the pins from her hair hard enough that she took strands with them. The precision and care required by the climb has taken the last of the patience from her, and so, when Cecilia knocks loose a slate and cannot seem to slip it back in place, despite how obvious a task it seems, Odette snatches it from her hand and rams it back so hard it cracks.

'Fuck!' She throws the broken pieces from the roof with all the strength she can muster. It is uninspiring, their arc low and flat, and they drop into the gravel of the drive all but noiselessly.

Cecilia looks at her, a little cowed, a little nervous. 'I'm sorry. I shouldn't have knocked it out.'

Odette presses her face into her hands, her fingertips into the hollows of her eyes. Takes a breath. 'No. I am sorry. It is too hot, and I cannot bring my thoughts together. I am out of sorts.'

'It is nothing.'

'But it is not *nothing*,' says Odette, and she feels it keenly. It is Cecilia, her own Cecilia, without whom she would be trapped alone with her thoughts, and to do anything to push her away is to invite her own misery. 'I don't want to use you as some punching bag for my own unhappiness. It is only that sometimes I feel so frustrated and confused, and I cannot articulate what is wrong or work out what I could do to change it, so it feels as though I am being prickled by brambles on all sides, like there are ants crawling all over my skin, and I would rather rip it all off and throw myself from the roof than swallow it all back down.'

She peels her palms from her face and looks sidelong at Cecilia, unsure.

Cecilia fiddles with the frill of her chemise, tugging at a ribbon that runs through the eyelets in the lace. 'You don't have to pretend to be happy about your aunt showing up. Not with me.'

'Not only that. It is all very—'

'Unexpected?'

'Disruptive.'

'Was Lydia that bad?'

Odette should tell Cecilia about the money, but she can hardly think on it for fear of breaking the spell. Right now, it is a beautiful idea, a sketch unrealised. It *could* be possible. Her mother really *might* follow through this time.

If she says the words out loud, it will pin it down like a butterfly to paper.

Lydia is not possible to pin down.

Odette knows it too well.

But if she does not tell Cecilia, then she is no better than her parents and their dissembling.

She rearranges the drape of her nightdress, wafting the too-hot air against her skin in a futile gesture.

'My mother said something to me earlier.' Odette does not know how to convey the doubt and uncertainty her mother's words bring. 'She is thinking of selling some pieces. All the pieces she still has, in fact.'

'What do you mean, all of them? Absolutely everything?'

'She thinks she could do a show through a friend of Eddie's, Mr King, and sell the lot.'

'But whatever for?'

'To give the money to me.'

Cecilia's eyes widen. 'But that's – my God. You'd have—'

'I have no idea what it could be, but she seems to think it would be enough that I could set myself up and not worry about – anything really.'

Cecilia clutches her hand again and squeezes it hard, an unruly grin curving her mouth. Her joy is contagious. 'A little flat in Bloomsbury.'

'A little flat in Bloomsbury,' echoes Odette. 'It could be real.'

'*Could?* Will! Can you believe it? Finally. *Finally!*' Cecilia rains kisses on her cheeks, then falters. 'What's wrong?'

Odette closes her eyes. 'You know you can't believe my mother.'

'But Eddie Rutherford *is* coming. They're all arriving tomorrow.'

'That doesn't mean anything.'

'Don't be so pessimistic.'

'I'm not being pessimistic; I'm being realistic. What my mother says doesn't mean much.'

'But she wants you to have the money. It may take her a little time to work it all out, but she intends you to have it. Doesn't that mean *something*?'

'I don't know. Does it ever mean anything?'

When Odette was eleven or twelve, her mother took her to Dulwich and the Picture Gallery in the bright, posied spring. Lydia led her from Rembrandt to Gainsborough to Canaletto to van Dyck, talking through each style, each artist's use of colour and composition, the quality of oil and water paints, the play of light and dark, and brushstroke and blending. A small crowd gathered with them as they moved from room to room, mistaking Lydia for a learned guide, and Odette shone with pride. That was *her* mother.

These memories are like gold amongst the silt, a narrow vein she mines carefully, mindful of collapses.

Because Lydia is only ever one false move from collapse. The unfinished canvases abandoned in her studio, the promised drawing lessons that never materialised – each new vision of her future that Lydia conjures so vividly for Odette never takes form. It is all always too much.

And fool that she is, Odette swallows each hook and feels the pain of it ripping out each time.

She does not want to be gullible.

But she cannot help hope.

'Then we must make sure it happens,' says Cecilia. 'We will not let your mysterious aunt become a distraction.'

Claudine. There it is. The fault that runs through Lydia's new fantasy.

Odette leans back on her elbows, digging her nails into the moss that clings to the slates. She looks at the expanse of stars above them, the fog of the Milky Way indistinct against the bright wash of moonlight. A day ago, a moment like this would have brought her peace.

'She wouldn't say a word about her. It was all very peculiar. No one in my family ever wants to talk about anything.'

It is probably the worst thing she could do in her father's eyes: ask him to talk *honestly*.

Cecilia's expression becomes fixed. 'We shouldn't think about Claudine. What does it matter? We will be away at university soon enough.'

'I thought everything was set up for me to leave, but it can never be simple. There will always be something that comes along to drag me back to my mother's side.'

Cecilia finds her hand and squeezes it.

At once, it is too much. Odette cannot bear it. The hope, the anxiety, the risk of disappointment, the fear that it will all undo her.

She sits up abruptly, pulls her hand free. 'I don't want to think about my mother anymore. What a waste of being here with you. Earlier, you said you had an idea.'

'Oh!' Cecilia looks at Odette from a sly side-eye. 'Lady Godiva.'

Odette tips her head back and laughs. 'If you wish to see me naked, you need only ask.'

Cecilia's gaze flickers down to Odette's body, half visible through the thin material of her nightgown. 'Seeing you naked is why I know you will make the perfect Godiva.'

'And you want to be the dirty peeping Tom?'

Odette means it as a joke, but it lands flat between them, this suggestion that there is something sordid or perverse in what they do, that Cecilia is somehow as crude as the men who cluster on the Haymarket in the West End.

Cecilia's mouth is tight, waiting for the next blow.

'No.' Odette smooths over her mistake. 'I see you'll wish to be the horse. You would never tolerate me riding anyone else.'

At this, Cecilia goes pink and swats Odette on the knee – the tension is broken. 'Stop it. Do you not want to do it?'

Odette considers. 'You're right. It could be a lot of fun.'

'If you're sure.'

'Of course I am. We should do it as soon as we can.'

'Tomorrow, then,' agrees Cecilia. 'After all, we hardly need prepare.'

Odette laughs again.

How much easier it is to hide inside this fantasy.

That is what her mother's money will buy her: a way to make the fantasy real.

A flat with Cecilia. The means to live as she chooses.

If only her mother does not ruin it.

If only Claudine's arrival means nothing.

Then, perhaps.

Perhaps.

6

Cecilia

THE MORNING SUN COMES early and golden through the open curtains of Odette's window, picking out flashes of Lydia's chestnut in her hair. Cecilia lies beside her, watching the rise and fall of her chest as she sleeps, like a worshipper at the adoration of the cross.

Not for the first time, she wishes she had any of Lydia's skill. If she knew how, she would capture Odette on paper or canvas, freeze her in place to keep her forever. It is so hard to love a living being. There is always change. Always the unknown. The harder Cecilia grasps, the more Odette seems to shift and retreat.

There – a soft tap at the door, and the maid comes in, waking Odette. She makes no remark on Cecilia's presence. It is not so unusual to share a bed for warmth or company, and Cecilia is glad of how obtuse everyone seems. If she takes Odette's arm, kisses her cheek, sleeps in her bed, they will only ever be *good friends*.

As they wash and dress, they talk through the day ahead. Odette is doubtful of Lydia's resolve, but Cecilia sees no other way but to hold her hand steady and make this promise come true. There is, at least to her mind, a practical way to do this. Keep Lydia painting. Keep her focused. And when Eddie Rutherford and the other guests arrive, encourage the show.

There are complications, of course.

She has not told Odette about what she overheard between her mother and Claudine yesterday, and she feels a worm for concealing it.

'What will you do about Claudine?' she asks Odette as she plaits the length of her hair and wraps it around her crown.

'Endure, I suppose. I can ask Father how long she intends to stay. Surely it will not be so long.'

Cecilia passes the brush over her own hair. Claudine is a mystery that bothers her more than she would like. She cannot shake the look of panic on her mother's face. That scrap of paper – *Penel.* For Penelope, surely. Of course this secret had to do with her mother, that much was clear. But what sort of secret? What could be so awful that it frightened a woman like her mother?

She cannot allow this matter to disrupt their escape. Let her go back into her own mousehole and see what she can find. If Claudine wants to wield secrets like power, then maybe Cecilia can pull them out into the light and strip them of it.

There is no need to worry Odette about something they will soon leave behind.

But she must *make* sure.

Everyone is at breakfast when they arrive in the small room off the main hall; it is one of the oldest parts of the house and here crooked wood panelling turns even the summer day dark and the flags beneath temper the heat.

Uncle George is hidden behind *The Times*, Aunt Lydia beside him, cutting up fruit with a penknife. Cecilia's mother sits opposite, scraping butter thinly across her toast, and Claudine guards a cup of hot water and lemon. It is only Leo who has a plate full of everything from the sideboard: kedgeree next to cold lamb chops from last night's dinner, a boiled egg and three slices of toast and a pot of jam set directly before him.

Odette slides in beside Cecilia with her own plate of toast and marmalade, a few slices of cold ham, and a cup of coffee.

'How terrible,' says Penelope, scanning the local paper. 'A little girl over in Bures has drowned in the Stour.'

'You know, I read in some case documents the other week that a child can drown in total silence,' says Leo. 'Obvious, really, when you think about it – if you're struggling to breathe, you hardly have the opportunity to cry out.'

'Leonard, really, what a thing to say at the breakfast table,' clucks Penelope.

'This place all belongs to water,' says Lydia. 'The moat could really have been one. The angles are so regular and the sides so straight.'

'Or a drainage ditch,' says Leo, neatly puncturing the fantasy.

Lydia does not notice, only nods earnestly. 'Yes, absolutely. People have been draining the land for centuries, but it is not a battle we will win. The coast is eroding by several feet a year. We're only one large storm away from losing another village.'

'Aren't you going to berate Aunt Lydia for being sinister?' Leo says to Penelope. 'Or is it only me who has to keep chipper?'

Penelope tuts but does not intervene.

'Will you paint today, Aunt Lydia?' asks Cecilia. 'The light seems perfect for it.' She glances at Odette to catch her eye, but Odette has her head down, looking at her toast.

Lydia seems taken aback to be asked directly. 'Yes. Perhaps.'

'You've spoken so often about starting *Elaine* – why not today?' Cecilia sticks her elbow into Odette's side.

Finally, Odette joins in. 'I'd like to sit for it today. It would be nice to spend the time together.'

Of course, Odette knows the right thing to say, and Lydia comes alive with a mix of hope and guilt and relief.

'In that case, we must.' She pushes her plate away and stands. 'I'll see you girls in the studio.'

Cecilia is flushed with relief. Odette worries too much. Lydia *will* paint. She *will* hold a show. All they need do is keep her mind on her promise and smooth the path before her. If Cecilia must hold out hope for the both of them, then so be it.

George puts down his paper, and it signals the end of the meal. Leo joins him on a ride, despite the heat, and Cecilia's mother disappears immediately, saying she has correspondence to deal with. Claudine has said nothing throughout breakfast, but Cecilia is all too aware of the quiet way she has paid attention to each exchange. She worries for a moment that Claudine will try to speak to her and Odette, but instead she corners the housekeeper and talks of the preparations for the guests arriving today.

In the studio, Lydia is bent over a pile of costumes, sorting through dresses until she comes to one it seems she likes.

'Elaine is a much overdone subject,' she says. Her hair is looped up on top of her head in a chaotic Gibson knot, and she wears a loose emerald-green aesthetic dress with a stained painter's smock thrown over the top. 'I do not want some wistful scene in a tower with a loom or some maundering girl in a boat. The pathos is at the end of the story, the moment of reunion with Lancelot. For all his good intentions, it is too late. Elaine is lost. For all Elaine's hope, she is nothing but one part of his much larger story – and yet it is the ruination of hers.'

Lydia straightens and holds up a pale blue dress. '*Now fair knight and courteous knight, have mercy upon me, and suffer me not to die for thy love*. But she will die. He will bear that sorrow for the rest of his life. She gets no life at all.'

Cecilia's stomach dips as Lydia thrusts the dress at her. 'You will be Elaine of Astolat.' Next, Lydia takes a sword and a helmet and gives them to Odette. 'And you must be Lancelot. I would rather it be Leo, but he won't sit for me anymore. I suppose you'll do.' She digs in another box to hand Odette a length of cloth. 'Bind your chest and put on the mail. You know where it is.'

Odette's jaw tightens, but she does not protest. She does not like playing the male parts – Cecilia knows this – but she likes it less when Leo usurps her place in the tableaux.

The stage has been set: on a dais painted grey to look like stone or cobbles or flags – whatever it is that the scene calls for – is a bathtub that will stand as a boat. Around it lie heaping flowers, some dried, some dyed silk, and swags of golden cloth and jewels.

Cecilia slips on the dress, tying it snugly around her waist with a chain belt. Odette returns in the mail and helmet, her breasts bound as flat as they can be. She moves stiffly, whether from the weight of the mail or the constriction around her chest, Cecilia does not know.

'Right,' says Lydia, hands on her hips and a collection of brushes stuffed into the pocket of her smock. 'Lancelot is here. Guilty, heartbroken. You did this. It is your fault.' She chivvies Odette into position on the dais, kneeling over the bath-boat. 'And Elaine, here.' She indicates the bath.

It is, unexpectedly, half filled with water.

'I'm afraid it is cold, but there is nothing to be done about that.'

Odette frowns beneath her raised visor. 'But Elaine's boat does not sink. She is sailed down to Camelot; Malory mentions the man steering.'

Lydia's face grows soft with hurt. 'I am no great artist, but I thought the scene should look well. Elaine is sunk by her love, the boat unable to bear her great sorrow.'

'It will be so touching,' says Cecilia quickly. She does not want the spell broken. Without another word from either, she climbs into the bath and bites her tongue to stop herself from exclaiming at the shock.

Odette protests no more and takes up the position given to her. Lydia seems pleased, twittering about the studio, arranging the flowers, considering the golden light that pours in.

At last, she comes to Cecilia with a folded and sealed piece of paper. '*And while my body is hot let this letter be put in my right hand, and my hand bound fast with the letter until that I be cold.*'

Cecilia takes it and lies back, lets her hair float loose. If she stays still, it is tolerable. The temperature of the water becomes familiar, almost pleasant, as though it has warmed to her body – or her body cooled down to match it. She cannot see Lydia at the easel, but she can hear the sounds of brushstrokes and small metal tubes of paint being opened and squeezed.

A little numb now, dreamy and soft, she cannot feel her feet or the hand that drifts beside her. Cecilia is loosened, opened, stepping out of herself and into something more beautiful, more certain, more simple. It is a gift, this other life, this world inside her mind. Odette is the only one who will step through with her. They move and think in harmony, one shared mind, and never need trouble themselves with the cruel, cold world of others.

A faltering, then. A speck of rain falling from a blue sky. The turn of rot at the centre of the fruit.

This might end.

Claudine has come and changed everything, so subtly – a single flat note played in a great, swelling chord.

Odette's hand slipping from hers, her own cold, bare palm grasping nothing but night sky.

One day, this could all be only a memory.

And then, what will she do?

7

Odette

GREAT CLOUDS OF INSECTS rise off the stagnant moat, here and there flecked with the iridescent blue of dragonflies feasting. The roses and hydrangeas in the garden tumble and riot across the flowerbeds, and in the fields, the sheep bleat against the relentless sun. The whole household retreats inside, shutters closed.

'Where's my father?' Odette asks Leo, when she finds him trotting downstairs in a fresh change of clothes after his ride.

'Gone to his study, I think.'

Odette turns to go, but Leo stops her.

'You're off to Cambridge then.'

'Yes.'

'You think you'll be all right there, on your own?'

Odette wrinkles her nose. 'I think I can manage.'

Leo coughs, shifts his weight. 'I'm sure you can. You've always been better at the practical stuff than Cessy. What I mean to say is—' He coughs again. 'Look, the fact is I would feel as though I hadn't done my proper duty if I didn't tell you that you can always write to me, if you get into any sort of trouble.'

Odette flushes. 'Leo—'

'Let me finish. I know we haven't been all that close recently, and I'm not your brother, but in another way I am, you see, so I thought I'd best make that clear.'

He looks at her with such an awful earnestness that Odette feels a flush of guilt. It has not occurred to her that perhaps the closeness that has grown between her and Cecilia has had the effect of shutting Leo out from a sense of belonging he once had.

She squeezes his hand. 'I do know that. We'll both be fine. I promise.'

He nods, pleased to be dismissed.

Odette tracks her father to the island of his desk.

'Mother did well today,' she says lightly. 'I think this new piece will be a triumph.'

George continues to read the letter in his hand but acknowledges her with a brief glance.

Odette considers sitting, but it feels too formal, so instead she browses the shelves of books, the bound issues of *The Westminster Review* and *The Athenæum*, volumes of Catullus and Seneca that she has copied out too many times to recall, sat in the corner of his office like another object to display. Her father would always place her on her own chair at her own writing desk, tell her how good it was to see her, then bend his head to his own tasks. He is so busy, of course, she should be grateful for the scant time he gives her, and it is something special to be his companion, his helpmeet. She knows she was a good daughter, quiet and studious and never childish or demanding. She is proud to have managed what so few children do, smug, even, that she so quickly cast off her naivety.

He makes less and less space for her in his world as she has grown older, and she wonders what it is she could do now to please him. Not become burdensome like her mother, that she knows. She thought Cambridge would gain his approval, it is independent and intellectual, and that is the world they can comfortably inhabit together, but he takes little interest in it. She has meant, more than once, to ask him if he would go up with her to visit her new college – but she wants him to offer, not for her to *have* to ask, and so she has left it unsaid.

'She has me as Lancelot,' Odette continues. 'But I imagine she'll paint Leo's face in over mine, unless she's trying to be particularly scandalous.'

'Art is always scandalous,' says George, folding the letter and tucking it away. 'Otherwise, there is no point to it.'

Odette preens at saying something right. 'I quite agree. One can hardly call the heaps of cherubs on a Valentine card *art*.'

George laughs. 'Ice cream and a day trip for the masses, everyone is comfortable and nothing changes.'

Odette warms to her topic. 'I suppose I could make a fortune if I went into writing sentimental poetry or some sort of ladies' advice manual on how to make your underthings smell like roses at *any* time of the month.' His expression shifts – she has lost him there – too much women's business. Quickly, she continues. 'I hope Aunt Claudine's visit won't get in the way of Mother's work. You know she can be so sensitive.'

'I don't see why it should.'

She stops at a bust of Seneca. '*How* long do you think she'll be staying?'

'I don't know; it's quite up to her. As a member of the family, she is entitled to stay here.'

Odette cuts a sidelong glance at her father. 'That hardly seems to have been the case before now. Neither you nor Mother ever speak of her.'

'Of course we do.'

No. They do not.

'But why did you not tell any of us?' says Odette. 'I worry it has upset Mother.'

Her father laughs lightly. 'A badly boiled egg at breakfast upsets your mother. This is a lovely surprise for everyone. It's about time bygones were bygones.'

An invitation to smooth things over, to cast her mother as hysterical, unruly, and congratulate themselves on having mastered their animal passions.

Odette finds that she does not want to accept it.

There is some shifting in the ground beneath her she cannot quite identify.

'Aunt Claudine thinks so, too?'

Her father ignores her. 'I think it would be nice for you to have an older woman around. Your mother is not someone you can look to for any guidance. You live a very lonely life.'

Her cheeks flush. 'I'm not lonely.' She cannot work up the courage to contradict him about Lydia, and indeed she cannot honestly do so – but she will not admit he is right.

'George.' Claudine comes through the door, looking down at a notebook in her hands. 'The brougham has gone to collect someone called Rutherford and someone called King from the station already, but there is absolutely no writing paper in any of the rooms yet, and the housekeeper tells me there were no orders for any in the first place. If you want me to take over running this party, then you have to let me manage the servants how I want. Oh—'

She stops abruptly when she sees Odette but makes no apology for the interruption. Odette feels somehow that it is she who has made the faux pas and intruded where she is not welcome.

'What a fortuitous opportunity,' says George. 'Why don't you take Odette in the Victoria and pick up some paper in town? Odette can show you where everything is, and I'm sure the two of you would enjoy some time to get to know each other.'

Odette's expression hardens, and she is distantly amused to find a mirror in Claudine's face.

'I should stay to welcome the guests,' says Claudine.

George smiles in a flattening way. 'Lydia and I can do that.'

'I am not the staff.' Her voice is stiff with a warning that Odette's father does not seem to detect.

'Don't worry about that; no one stands on ceremony here. If you're worried about the paper, it won't take you a minute to find.'

There is some silent battle in Claudine, and Odette waits, breath held, to see which side will win. Eventually, Claudine nods to her. 'I will meet you in the hall when you are dressed properly.'

Odette blushes again. She had thought she was dressed nicely, in a plain but clean day dress. 'As you wish.'

All the way to Sudbury, Claudine leans forwards at regular intervals to order the driver to increase the pace, then settles back under the leather hood for a short while before tapping the driver on the shoulder again in impatience. It is sweltering under cover; the hood keeps off the blazing sun but traps the hot air, and Odette is sweating copiously between her breasts, along the length of her spine and the backs of her knees. Occasionally, a bead will roll down her forehead and catch on her eyebrow. Surely Claudine must be subject to the same forces of nature, but, if anything, she looks pale and drawn.

'I have been away from England so long I had forgotten these dowdy little houses,' says Claudine, assessing the low line of cottages that cling to the side of the road. 'No wonder English people are all so parochial, closed up in sodden little boxes.'

She speaks with a light yet pointed tone, as though delivering a great witticism, then looks to Odette for a response.

'I think the stone is pretty. It is like the houses are part of the landscape itself.' Usually, when she is with either parent, she is meant to smooth matters, to keep alive the light when the world is painted dark.

Claudine laughs archly. 'I suppose a peasant living in a hovel is as old as the landscape.'

'I have been visiting with baskets at Christmas, and they do keep their places very clean, even if they are poor.'

Claudine's jaw tightens, and she does not speak again.

Odette looks at her knees, heart fast with anxiety. A misstep – a stupid one. She does not know how to read Claudine or what it is her aunt wants from her. Agreement with her judgement, perhaps, but even then, she has the sense that Claudine's problem is with Odette herself.

The carriage slows as they reach the edge of town; a crowd has gathered in the street with some commotion, some in black, and more wear black armbands. A woman stands at the front of a cottage, hands covering her face. The door opens, and a coffin is carried out to be placed on a wheeled bier that stands waiting. It is a cheap thing, with only an old shawl for a pall cloth.

It is a small coffin, and Odette thinks, unbidden, of the girl that Leo mentioned who drowned in the Stour.

Then, of Cecilia submerged in the bath. Lydia changing the myth to drown Elaine, sunk by her love.

God, please let her mother finish the piece. Please let her be true to her word.

The bier is wheeled into the middle of the road, and a line of mourners forms behind it. It passes one side of their carriage, close enough that she could reach out to touch the ash, and then it is gone, and the procession streams past.

The driver gees the horses into movement.

'There is a stationer's on Market Hill,' Odette explains. 'They'll have letter paper, though it's only plain.'

'Yes, I do know.'

'You know Sudbury?'

'What a question. Of course I know Sudbury. I grew up in Herne House.'

Odette blushes. How stupid of her.

She has a thin grasp on her mother's lineage; she knows that Lydia – and, she supposes, Claudine – were orphaned at a young age and raised as wards of an unmarried family friend, whose nephew George was. Neither of her parents speak much of their pasts and she had not pictured them all together at Herne House. But of course they must have been, and it is only her childish myopia that has blinded her to this obvious truth.

'I didn't realise.'

'If you ask no questions of others, you will learn little.'

She is saved from further conversation by their arrival at the stationer's. Claudine waits for the driver to offer his hand while Odette drops down to the street without thinking. The heat is oppressive, with little breeze finding its way through the streets; the smell of standing water rises from the meadows nearby, and the manure, dried quickly in the sun, is enough to make Odette's eyes sting.

The stationer's interior is dark: displays of cards and envelopes, pens, nibs, ink, wax, twine, are arranged behind and in front of a counter placed across the shop. At it sits a woman a little older than Claudine, who fans herself with a sense of futility.

Before either of them can speak, the woman's expression abruptly changes, and her face opens up in wonder. 'Miss Hutton? As I live and breathe, it's like seeing a ghost – pardon my frankness.'

Claudine does not smile. 'I'm afraid I cannot return the compliment. I do not remember having met you before.'

'You wouldn't, but we all knew you up at the house. It has to be – oh, the best part of twenty years since you all but disappeared. Someone said you'd gone into a convent, but my Fred says you were away to the Continent.'

'Yes. I have been in Germany. It suited me better to be somewhere more cultured.'

It is a close to the conversation; Odette can tell, but the shopkeeper cannot.

'There – I'll tell my Fred he had the right of it. Only, we were all so shocked, waiting for the banns to be read at church any day, and then you were up and vanished.'

Claudine's expression is cold. 'We require letter paper. And a supply of ink, if you have anything decent.' Her voice is sharp enough this time that the shopkeeper understands the message and busies herself with bringing out samples.

The banns? A wedding expected? Odette files away this piece of information as she studies Claudine out of the corner of her eye.

Each type of paper in turn is dismissed as plain, low quality, inferior.

'What a trial it is to do anything out of the city,' says Claudine, removing her gloves to touch a sample. 'This is for guests, not the clerk at the workhouse.'

The shopkeeper has gone pink, and she bends over to rummage in a low drawer.

'This is the best we have, brought all the way from London.' She lays out thick cream paper, so fine it is like silk to the touch.

'I like it,' offers Odette. 'It's so smooth, I am sure it will write well.'

The shopkeeper wraps their purchase, and Odette carries it back to the carriage.

Once they have passed the last of the houses and are back amongst the open fields, corn swaying high and golden, Claudine speaks. 'I don't appreciate being condescended to.'

It is like a stone has dropped through Odette's stomach. 'I'm sorry. I didn't realise I had been condescending.'

'You undermined me in front of the shopkeeper. I will not allow myself to be humiliated publicly, especially not by an ill-mannered child.'

Odette is unpleasantly aware of how close she sits to Claudine, that only a few layers of cotton provide a barrier between herself and someone she abruptly realises does not like her. 'I really am sorry,' she says quietly.

They sit in icy silence until the gables of Herne House finally crest over the hedgerows. Odette stares at her knees as she has done before and, as she does with her mother, finds herself letting her mind detach from her body and float up through the leather hood and into the hazy sky.

8

Cecilia

FROM HER VANTAGE POINT, high under the eaves of Herne House, Cecilia watches the carriage depart, the driver mopping sweat from beneath his hat, the horses' tails twitching against the encroachment of flies.

Odette has left with Claudine.

Cecilia shoves her bitten fingers into the folds of her skirt and descends from the attic. Lydia made good work painting today, and Cecilia is sure it will make a fine centrepiece for a show. Odette's mood is difficult to predict, but Cecilia is pleased with her own careful reading of it, the right word said at the right time, silence left when silence is needed.

There is only the bother of Claudine.

Cecilia worries at the scraps of her cuticles. Why have they gone off together? What if Odette likes Claudine after all? What if Odette changes her mind about everything and Cecilia is left all alone?

Nonsense. It is nonsense. Odette will never leave her.

At the panel to Claudine's room, Cecilia waits, listening to the space beyond. Yes, it is empty. She knows the difference between the silence of a held breath and the noiselessness of a dead place.

The room has, of course, been cleaned since yesterday, and there are no tantalisingly obvious pieces of paper scattered to catch her eye. It is a tidy room, redecorated in a sparse style a century before, and it is almost clinical with its pale yellow walls and polished boards. It seems impossible for a place like this to harbour secrets. But Cecilia knows how to be a quiet, small, sneaking thing. She will wriggle beneath the bed, behind the chests of drawers and the bedside tables, ferreting out anything that has been lost or hidden.

There is more dust, the dried bodies of fallen insects, withered petals from long-rotten flowers, nothing, nothing, nothing – then there, a pale buff colour beneath the dressing table.

Cecilia wriggles her arm beneath it to pull it out. Her elbow catches, and she knocks the table badly enough that a few scattered objects fall to the floor. She turns her prize over eagerly in her hand. The same paper with its soft, torn edges, and the same looping hand. Here, there is written only: *art*.

Penel. Penelope. Her mother.

Yes, yes, she *knows* that.

Art – some other name? Christian name or surname? Or a segment of a word – start? Part?

Frustration is sour in her mouth as she gathers up the things she has knocked over. Amongst the cheap scent and combs and hairpins, there is one fine, glittering object: a silver bracelet with intricate workmanship, far more valuable than anything else. And yet, there are harsh scratch marks along a flat inside piece that once bore an inscription.

To CH, forever yours – and here the second set of initials has been so badly scratched out that it has torn jagged edges into the metal.

Cecilia turns it over in her hand, uneasy.

An official document that has frightened her mother. A love token vandalised in anger.

She likes none of this. Clues placed before her that she would rather have never seen.

Nonsense again. What is it a clue to? Claudine has a past that Cecilia is not interested in, and this bracelet is nothing more than a sad memento kept by a woman who is not welcome in her sister's home.

Cecilia tidies the table up, replaces everything as best she can remember seeing it and slips back into the walls.

Claudine needs to leave.

She will cause disruption – Cecilia can feel it – and disruption is something they can ill afford.

Lydia is in hand, at least for now.

All there is left for her to do is speak to her own mother.

She finds Penelope in her bedroom, standing in front of the full-length mirror, turning one way then the other, considering the dress she has chosen. It is a jacquard-woven white silk, patterned with a shock of brightly painted oranges, which would be garish on many women, and it seems that Cecilia's mother is deciding whether this includes her.

It would look well on Odette, Cecilia thinks.

On Penelope? She knows better than to offer an honest opinion.

'The oranges are too large. Don't you think?' Penelope twists again, tugging the material of the skirt into one place and then another. 'If they had made them a little smaller, it would look more tasteful.'

Cecilia sits on the end of her bed, twirling a length of ribbon between her fingers. The first guests are arriving with the busy sound of shoes on flagstones, the barking of dogs, cases being carried by servants, raised voices and laughter. It has all come too soon. Cecilia is not ready to share Herne House with the wider world, to share Odette.

'Do you have time to change?'

'Don't cause me such worry – why would you do that? Terrible child.' Her mother looks back at the mirror again, mouth turned down. 'You think I am embarrassing myself. Well. It is hurtful to hear it from your own flesh and blood.'

'I think you look lovely, Mother.'

It is partly the truth. Penelope has a fine bone structure that has aged well, though it is a sharp, self-conscious kind of prettiness that is better called *handsome* than beautiful. Leo has it as well, but the squareness suits him better. Cecilia touches her own cheeks sometimes, wondering if she has the same looks, but when she tries to see, her face blurs and twists in the mirror until she is a stranger, only a mass of skin and eyes and hair. Is she pretty? She would like to be pretty.

'You're trying to make me feel better,' says Penelope. 'It won't work. I feel quite distressed now.'

Cecilia goes to her mother's side, carefully positioned so she will not be in the reflection. 'It is very flattering. Bold and daring. You will put everyone else to shame.'

'They all call themselves artists, but few of them have ever really *lived* art.'

'Did they all know you, when you were on the stage?' asks Cecilia lightly. She learnt long ago never to come at a subject head on with her mother. She must turn sideways, move unobserved.

Penelope pinches colour into her cheeks. 'Some of them. George, of course, and Lydia; Eddie, too. Not that young creature Mr King, whom Eddie makes such a pet of – he is something of a late arrival.'

'And Claudine?'

Her hands still only briefly. 'Oh, yes, for a time. The rest are very interesting people – I would hardly take any notice of them if they were not – but they do have a tendency to complain, when they have never done a day of work in their lives.'

'But you married Father when you were nineteen,' said Cecilia. 'You've not been on stage since then.' How much does her mother know about work?

'And I was the most beautiful girl in all the London theatres. Everyone said so, even if they thought me a fool for believing I would make something of myself. But I worked hard and was discovered by a brilliant man, as I knew I simply must be. Perhaps I will write a novel about my life; it would do very well, I think.'

She pauses for Cecilia to comment.

'I should think so. It's so romantic – and tragic.'

'More romantic, I think. Yes, the oranges are a little large, but I think I can carry it off.'

Cecilia leans against the armoire, hands caught behind her back. 'What were Aunt Lydia and Uncle George like back then?' She bites the tip of her tongue. 'And Claudine?'

Penelope looks at her sidelong, eyes narrowed. 'Why are you asking about Claudine?'

Cecilia shrugs. 'Why not?'

'Curiosity is not an attractive quality in a girl. And don't lean like that – stand up properly. I taught you good posture, so don't pretend you don't know how.'

Cecilia straightens. 'When did Claudine go to Germany? It must have been some time ago.'

'That is not a subject that concerns you.'

'But—'

Penelope points a hairpin at her. 'Leave it alone. It is not your business. Lydia may tolerate you bothering her with your nonsense, but I will not, and nor will Claudine, so know your place and behave yourself or I cannot be responsible for—' Penelope cuts herself off and goes back to arranging the carefully dressed curls of her hair.

It is strange; Cecilia cannot imagine anyone intimidating her mother.

And yet, Claudine has done it.

'Responsible for what?'

'What do you mean, *for what*? Responsible for you, silly girl. That is your problem: too much imagination, not enough sense. Go on now. Get ready. You look a state.'

'Yes, Mother.'

Penelope shoos her away. 'Odette can afford to waste her youth on flights of fancy, but you cannot. Do you understand?'

'Yes, Mother.'

'Don't wear white,' says Penelope, as Cecilia goes out the door. 'Or yellow, or orange. Those are my colours today.'

9

Cecilia

'EDDIE!' UNCLE GEORGE'S VOICE rises up the staircase towards Cecilia. 'Looking sprightly, old boy. Always good to give into your tailor and allow him to take out your waistbands.'

'Very funny, Fairfax. So funny your hairline seems to be running away in mirth.'

Cecilia grips the newel post and denies herself the moment to peer over the banisters like a child. She does not want to be seen or heard or thought of, just for a short while. The voices carry easily in this echoing space, with its stone flags and too-high ceilings.

'Allow me to introduce Mr King,' says Eddie. 'Curator of the Jermyn Street Gallery.'

'How do you do?' says Mr King. 'I think we met briefly at the opening of the summer show at the Slade – was it last year?'

Cecilia is alive at once. Mr King – the Jermyn Street Gallery. This is it: Eddie, his friends, the show.

'Yes, of course. You will remember my wife.'

'I have admired your work for a long time, Mrs Fairfax-Waugh.'

'Oh – well – thank you,' says Lydia.

'Truly superlative.'

No, that is not the way to do it at all. Cecilia wants to run down the stairs and shake this Mr King and tell him that Lydia is not one for direct praise. She is not Penelope; she wilts in the light, unless it is angled just so.

The voices recede as they move from the entrance hall.

It is all she can think of now. She must find Mr King and align him to their cause.

In her room, a dress has already been selected for her, laid out on the bed like the shadow of a body. She strips her stained shirtwaist, changes into the new frock, a red dotted Swiss fabric with small leg-of-mutton sleeves and a ribbon-belted waist, then neatens her hair and applies a little scent.

Her confidence falters at the prospect of approaching Mr King alone. That is not the role she plays. She is the shadow, not the light. The echo, not the noise itself. What will she say to him? What will he think of her? Will Odette be disappointed if she makes a misstep? She needs Odette. She needs an anchor, some ballast to steady her in the storm.

Odette is not yet back.

Lightly, she slips into the dining room, a grand place with red silk wall hangings and paintings of battles from the ancient world, where an array of bottles has been laid out on the sideboard; music comes from the drawing room, the clink of glasses, laughter from some unheard joke. Cecilia pours herself a cup of lemonade to have something to hold.

Light hands on her waist shift her to one side. 'Excuse me, my dear.'

Mr King's voice shocks her into silence. He stands a little too close as he examines the selection of alcoholic drinks.

A man closer to thirty than Leo, middle height, handsome and with the tense athleticism of some kind of prowling animal, he is quite the different type to the usual sort in their parents' crowd. Cecilia thinks, abruptly, that this is not a man who has been comfortable. He does not move with the unthinking entitlement of Uncle George and his friends, but with a far keener awareness, alert and assessing. His shirt sleeves are rolled up, his dark hair is tousled loose from its pomade; when he knocks over a bottle, Cecilia realises he is already drunk.

It cannot be so easy.

Together, they right the bottles that have fallen like ten-pins.

'I'm sorry,' she says, for want of anything better. 'Am I in your way?'

'Not at all.' He seems to stop, taking Cecilia in properly for the first time. 'Melusine,' he says. 'It *is* you. My God – your face. I have seen it a thousand times.'

Melusine. A water spirit. It was the first painting for which Lydia used her as a model, sitting her inside a water butt in the grounds of Herne House, Odette nearby as Pressine, Melusine's mother, banishing her daughter from Avalon.

There, she should speak now – tell him who Lydia *really* is, how he can get what he wants, what they both want – but the words stick in her throat.

Mr King takes her in with his hungry gaze. 'Quite remarkable. You are even more arresting in person.'

He steps forwards, and she steps back without thinking, catching her heel on the foot of the sideboard. Before she can fall, Mr King's hands are on her waist again, steadying her. He does not remove them. They are close enough that she can see the red veins at the corners of his eyes and the speckle of stubble caught in the fold of skin below his nose.

'I've met many artists' models, and few are as beautiful when painted only by God's simple hand.' His breath smells of port, sweet and decaying, and she looks anywhere but at him: the floor, his shoulder, a point on the ceiling. 'Your look is so fresh and pure. I can see why artists desire to possess it.' His hand creeps up her bodice to her breast. 'Tell me, does she have you in your shift in the water, or are you naked?'

Cecilia freezes.

She is at once very far away from herself, very quiet and small and hidden.

Any thought in her head is gone like dandelion seed.

Before he can press his hand further, Eddie comes through the door. 'Charles! Where are you hiding? Come on – old Fairfax-Waugh says she'll show us the goods.'

Mr King does not remove himself. Cecilia fears he will feel her shaking from the effort of holding herself still.

Eddie stops dead. 'What are you doing?'

For a moment, Cecilia's heart rises.

'Hiding by the wine – you're far too predictable,' Eddie continues, and Cecilia's foolishness is laid bare. No one is coming to save her. 'Let go of Miss Moore. She's a family friend, you know, not a regular model.'

Mr King at last steps back, releasing Cecilia to sag against the sideboard.

'My mistake.' His eyes do not leave her face.

'Lord, Charles – can't leave you alone for a moment.' Eddie slings his arm around Mr King's shoulder and steers him back to the party.

There is the bang of the front door flying open again, more voices – and this time, Cecilia hears Odette. Thank God – she is back.

Cecilia has failed her here. Miscalculated. Or – well, misunderstood.

She is out of her depth.

She will not fail Odette again.

At the last moment, Mr King looks back at her, like she is Melusine, naked in the water, painted and pinned up on the wall.

10

Odette

'I HATE HER, I hate her, I hate her.'

Odette paces Cecilia's room, flexing her hands against the hot spark of loathing that runs through her. Cecilia is oddly quiet, and Odette thinks perhaps she is allowing space for Odette's anger to bloom. When she tried to touch her, Cecilia tensed uncharacteristically. Odette thinks, distantly, she should ask Cecilia why – but in this moment, her mind is filled only with thoughts of Claudine and how small and shameful she made Odette feel.

'I know I said I must try to have sympathy for her, but she is such an unpleasant *bitch*. I'm trying – I really am – to find some redeeming feature in her, but there is none. No one is a complete monster, but, my God, she runs it a close thing.'

Finally, they have escaped upstairs, as the late summer twilight turns the sky translucent. The heat has built ferociously, and the whole party became querulous over dinner, wine sloshing onto the tablecloth, the laughter of Odette's father and his friends unpleasantly alien. It is a careful dance Odette does at such dinners, to be her father's pet who can be shown off, clever and articulate, while knowing her place: she is not one of them, she can gain admittance only through a narrow door. If she gives a line of poetry, or makes some witty remark, she must not expect their approbation to mean anything real. She knows this, and that knowing should make the pleasure sour – and yet. Here she is, compelled.

Her mother shrank from it all and excused herself early, Odette expanding to fill the space, disguise the flaws of their family, while Claudine sat beside George, surveying the mess of bohemian artists and intellectuals with barely concealed disdain. The worst of it is that Odette doesn't *disagree* with all of Claudine's snobbishness, and that makes her hate her more. Penelope sat at one end, positioned carefully with a few chinless, fawning men, fanning herself and delicately accepting compliments. Leo gravitates to the men, keen to show himself an adult amongst equals.

Now the party has moved to the smoking room, where Odette knows they will stay up drinking and playing billiards until the early dawn drives them to their beds.

'Do you think she might feel scared, being here?' says Cecilia from where she sits cross-legged on the bed. 'That she will lose her place as quickly as George has given it to her?'

'Do not take her side, Ces. I cannot bear it.'

'I take her side in nothing, of course not. I only meant to try and understand her. England must be a difficult place for her, you told me yourself she had an engagement broken off.'

'I am tired of understanding. I owe her nothing.' Abruptly, Odette turns on her heel to Cecilia. 'Godiva. Let us do it now.'

'Now?'

'Yes. I do not want to be myself.' She half kneels on the bed beside Cecilia, takes her hands into her own. 'Make me someone else, Ces.'

Finally, some colour returns to Cecilia's face, and Odette sees that she has offered her a lifeline out of an unknown sea.

'Yes. All right. We can take Diana down to the lane by the water meadow.' Diana is the docile mare that both Odette and Cecilia learnt to ride on. 'I'll be Leofric and issue you the challenge.'

Odette pulls Cecilia to her and kisses her deeply, overcome by her love and excitement. There is no one but Cecilia who can understand what she needs, and in this moment, she wants to possess her entirely, to have something – someone – of her own. Their kissing grows passionate, but Cecilia captures Odette's wrist before she can push Cecilia's nightdress from her shoulder.

Odette draws back, mouth hot and wet, fearing for a moment that she will be chastised for her wanting.

Cecilia's eyes are dark. 'I would have you outside. Under the stars.'

Hand in hand, they slip from the house, as silent as spirits. There is a riot of noise still from the smoking room, of music and laughter, and they are careful to skirt through the unpeopled places. It is somehow even hotter outside, a dank, desultory heat that sticks Odette's hair to her neck and makes slick the rub of her thighs. A mass of stars wheels overhead, the turrets and gables of Herne House a dark outline marked out against them. They lead Diana across the yard, pressed together tight and giggling at their own brilliance. The sound of horseshoes is lost beneath the revelry, and above them, a gibbous moon swells in the sky.

At the meadow gate, they stop, and Cecilia draws herself into the character of Leofric.

'O Lady mine,' she says softly, voice low, 'I weary at your troublesome requests. I will lift the taxes from the people of Coventry when you strip naked and ride through the streets for all to see. That is to say: never.'

A rush of peace passes over Odette. Here, it is better. Here, she does not have to worry about Lydia or money or Claudine or the future.

'You are mistaken, husband,' she says, and reaches for the hem of her nightgown. 'There is no shame in doing what is right and good.'

In one movement, she lifts the dress up and over her head, baring herself to the night air and Cecilia's gaze. Her heart is racing, skin hot. It is quite something to be desired so greatly even after so many nights together. She wants Cecilia to look, to want, to hunger.

For a moment, all is forgotten, and she comes close enough to place Cecilia's hand on her bare breast.

'Husband,' she breathes, an invocation of something that will always remain out of reach.

'Wife,' responds Cecilia. She brushes her thumb softly over Odette's nipple, a claim and a promise at once.

'Who is out there?' a sharp voice calls across the yard.

Odette leaps away, scrabbles for her nightdress.

A light swings in the dark, and Claudine comes into view, striding towards them. They are far enough across the cobbles that the gaslight from the windows does not reach them, and this had given Odette a sense of secrecy – but now she realises how exposed they are, hidden only by the night and their own brazenness.

'Girls? What on earth are you doing?' She stares in incomprehension and dawning disgust.

Odette yanks on the gown, but it is too late: Claudine has seen her nakedness. For a moment, Odette is struck dumb by the terror that Claudine has seen them together, seen who they are to each other – but then Claudine's attention goes to Diana.

'Why have you taken a horse from the stable at this time of night? What is this?'

'A game,' stammers Cecilia. 'We wanted to do Lady Godiva.'

Claudine stares at her. 'Do you mock me?'

'No. I swear it,' says Odette.

'A game.' Claudine looks at the two of them in incredulity. 'A game to strip naked and cavort in the dark? Is this how my sister raised you? I cannot believe you would think this is anything other than wickedness. Inside, at once. There are guests in this house, and you choose to do something so utterly inexcusable. You will answer to your father.'

Cowed, they follow Claudine to George's study, where she leaves them to wait.

Odette's heart races. She does not get in trouble. That is not the kind of daughter she is. Will her father be angry? Will he shout at her? He has never done that before. She has seen him shout, yes, at leaking pen nibs and spilt coffee, his fury vented at the inanimate world – but at her? At her mother? Never. It would be far too much like honesty.

'I'm sorry,' Cecilia whispers, but Odette shakes her head. She wants to say they have nothing to be sorry for, but the shame has set in already.

She is stupid. Of course they shouldn't have taken such a risk. She has judged it all wrong, and she is ashamed of her foolishness. Claudine returns with her father sooner than she would have liked, a blare of chatter following them from the smoking room down the hall as the study door opens and closes.

'Girls. Claudine has told me everything.' George adopts a serious expression that ill fits his face, like an actor practising for an unwanted part. Odette wonders if he has read something in his journals of psychology about the best way to deal with conflict, with troublesome daughters.

'Don't be angry,' says Odette quickly. 'It was a silly game. Honestly. We got carried away and didn't think about it.'

She can solve this for him, at least. Give him a route out and through. She can still be useful to him.

'That's certainly true. Poor Diana doesn't need to be roped into whatever silly idea you had.'

'You're right. We should have left Diana alone.'

'I'm glad you agree. Well then. To bed, both of you.'

Odette is flushed with relief. There. Smoothed over. Is that not better? They both know that this should never have happened, and far better to avoid any unpleasantness when it is unnecessary.

Claudine looks at George incredulously. 'Is that all you have to say?'

George is distinctly uncomfortable. 'Misunderstandings happen. No harm done.'

It seems as though Claudine is going to speak again, but instead, she snaps her jaw shut tight, turns on her heel and stalks from the study.

With that, George slopes back to the smoking room, and Odette and Cecilia are left to return to their separate rooms.

At the top of the stairs, Cecilia brushes her fingers against Odette's in a silent question – do they risk staying together tonight? Odette shakes her head and withdraws. She has extricated them for now, but things are not as they once were. Claudine's arrival has changed the rules, and Odette does not yet know how to navigate them.

She is frightened. She wants to flee.

God, let her mother be true to her word. Let Lydia set her free.

11

Odette

ODETTE PUTS ON A CORSET the next day.

The heat has finally broken in a great, thrashing storm that batters against the windows and whistles down the chimney.

Clothes are not something she ever thinks about too deeply. It is the joy of Herne House and summer with Cecilia to pay no mind to manners or mores, to dress how she pleases, in shifts and loose tea-gowns, shirtwaists and skirts tucked up.

The night before comes back into her mind over and over: the scramble for her nightdress, the bobbing light approaching, Claudine's look of disgust.

It had not occurred to her before that anyone other than Cecilia could see her body and have thoughts about it – as though they lived in a world apart.

Foolish.

She dresses quickly, angrily. Corset. Plain dress. Conventional.

The breakfast room is already noisy with the morning crowd, and without thinking, Odette steers away from it and towards the studio.

Her mother sits before the half-finished painting of Elaine and Lancelot. The shape of Cecilia and Odette is sketched out in the centre of the canvas with a solemnity and carefulness that comes through even in the simple work. Around it, the scenery is blocked out in swathes of colour and shape. They will have to pose again, more than once, for Lydia to capture the detail of the scene, and Odette finds herself suddenly longing for it.

'Mother?'

Lydia looks round. There are dark circles under her eyes and no colour in her cheeks, but she seems alert, present. 'Darling.'

Odette sits on the floor beside her and rests her head against her mother's thigh. A hand comes to settle on Odette's loose hair, stroking the strands behind her ear.

'It's wonderful,' she says of the painting, and means it entirely. Her mother's brilliance is undeniable, and Odette cannot begrudge her it.

'I will finish it before the summer is out.'

Not so far away, a boom of thunder rolls in, and a cheer rises from the breakfast room.

Odette lets herself be soothed by the running of fingers across her hair, by the warmth of her mother's body, a childish instinct that has never deserted her.

'Did you always know you loved Father?' she asks. 'Did you always know you wanted to be together, no matter what?'

Her mother does not answer at once. 'Oh yes. Always. Long before he ever looked at me. Far *more* than he ever loved me.'

'But he loves you now.'

Lydia tuts. 'Why all these questions?'

Odette does not rightly know. Instead she asks, 'Will you be all right when I go away to university?'

Lydia thinks awhile before speaking. 'Of course. I am so very proud of you for going. I have let so much keep me scared. You are much braver than me.'

'I'm not brave,' she says reflexively.

'You are. And whenever you want to come back, you know you will always have a place with me.'

'I know.' Odette turns her face to press it into the stuff of her mother's skirt.

There is no one who knows her better. No one who loves her so unconditionally, so boundlessly that her love becomes shapeless, indistinct.

Cecilia may love her, but she knows it comes with conditions, that Cecilia needs things from her she fears she may not be fit to give, and that gap between them will only grow and fester.

Her mother has no world but Odette.

If she ever lost her mother – she thinks that unobserved by her, she might cease to exist.

Lydia says nothing, but she keeps smoothing her hair over her crown. Rain clatters against the glass, loud enough to drown out her own breathing. A flash of lightning is followed by thunder so closely that the storm must be right overhead.

Odette cannot explain herself. She is crying. There is a sense of some foreboding that has taken root in her heart, and it makes her sick – as though there is something she must do, if only she can think of what it is.

Her mother's cool fingers find her neck, soothing against her hot skin.

'You should eat something,' Lydia says when Odette is done crying and has mopped her face with a handkerchief.

'Will you come with me?' Odette looks up at her, open-faced.

Lydia baulks, then seems to catch herself, and forces a smile. 'All right.'

Odette rises, brushes down her skirts, wipes her eyes again.

But when Lydia stands, she stumbles. Steadies herself against the easel.

Then doubles over, retching up red blood.

Letters

October to November 1898

4th October 1898

My darling Odette,

I cannot believe I sit here at Somerville, writing my very first letter to you as a university student. I miss you terribly, though it has only been a matter of days, but I am unaccustomed to living even one hour without you near. It is quite taxing. I shall give you a description of my rooms so that you can picture me; please do the same for Newnham, as I dearly wish to hold an image of you there in my head, so that at any moment I can conjure you, like a ghost at a séance. I am proud of you for going, despite it all. I know this will do us both good.

I am in a building called West, for that is where it lies in the grounds of the college, and we have a great rivalry with the other building, called House. West is quite charming, and very newly built, so I am only the second or third girl to use my room. We each have our own bedroom, which is simply but elegantly furnished, and we share sitting rooms and dining rooms, so it is nothing at all like school but far more like being at home. We also have a paddock and an orchard and a vegetable garden, and some of the girls have already invited me to go punting, and there's a group who hole up in one of the sitting rooms and give dramatic readings, and I feel quite intimidated of course, but I thought I could read that section of Endymion you always complimented me on – I will try it and report back.

It is very strange to do all this without you. I could never picture it before, being all on my own, but I find it quite exciting. I have my books arranged on a shelf and much writing paper and ink in stock, and I have brought the sketch of you and me as dryads and hung it up above my desk. At dinner the other night, someone mentioned Lydia's Psyche and Venus, and I was dying to tell her that I modelled Psyche, but I kept quiet because no one likes a brag, and anyway they'd hardly believe me.

It is strange, I find myself missing my mother – I even miss Leo! I can hear you laughing at me. Of course I miss them, it is natural. It is only that I thought, being apart from her, I might finally come into some new sense of myself. But instead I feel as though a stark light has come on in a once dark room, and there I am, exposed, some spineless, wriggling insect. It is odd to think at least with Mother I always know where I am.

I am sorry. I shouldn't have written all that. It was thoughtless of me.

I miss Lydia too, very much. I think she would have obtained so much joy from seeing you at Cambridge, I really do. She would have some clever little story about all the brilliant people who have walked where you now walk, and some little fact about a college building being used for something during the civil war or a Roman general who once bathed in the Cam – that sort of thing, don't you think?

I must say sorry again, for I write far too much on matters you cannot want my opinion on.

My darling, I think of you all the time. I am pressing my kisses to your forehead (and elsewhere). Please write me a long letter. I want to know every last thing about how you are and what you are doing.

Your ever loving,

Cecilia

*

10th October 1898

Dearest Cecilia,

It brought me such comfort to receive your letter. I confess I have found it hard to be in a new place that feels so cold and alien. We are west of the Cam here, while all the major colleges are on the east; there is no one out here with us save Selwyn across the road, but that is full of missionaries and clergy, and people avoid them even more than they avoid me. I am in my blacks, of course, and send everyone letters on black-edged paper, and half the girls have offered their condolences, which I cannot but find hateful. I want to snap at them in their simpering faux kindness. They do not know me; they did not know my mother. They live their happy, untouched little lives and think themselves so generous for tolerating my ghoulish presence. It means something to me, that you remember her.

I think, sometimes, that I wish to go home, but then I remember with a sensation like a blow that home is gone. Purely a place of memory. I can never return there. Is it possible to be homesick for a person? A time?

Is this grief?

I think, often, of that awful weekend when Claudine arrived. Mother fell ill so abruptly. She had always been delicate, but at that moment, it was something quite different. I should have found some way to help her. It was all I was good for, helping her. She needed me. Oh God, she needed me like no one else, and in the end, I let her down, didn't I? She told me often that I was her reason to live, and now, she is dead. So I must have done a very bad job.

There is something I must come to. It will seem like a strange turn of conversation, but you must have faith that I write in all seriousness and earnestly wish to hear your sincere response. Do you remember when you asked in the summer if I believed in ghosts? I have been thinking on it quite often, and it strikes me that you were so very certain that you did not, and I must know: why are you so sure? What is it that sets things out so clearly in your mind?

Do not ask me why I have come to this matter – it is not important – but I would know your answer.

Yours always,
Odette

*

11th October 1898

Darling Odette,

A letter from you, at last! I will tell you that when the porter gave me this missive and I saw your hand, I took it straight to my room and did a dance between the bed and desk, in what little space I have. It is a tonic to hear your voice in my head as I read your words, to think that I hold this piece of paper that once, not so long ago, was in your hands.

I wish I could visit, but they are so strict about what we do and where we go. I cannot believe there are still weeks and weeks until I see you again. I have enclosed a list of my lectures and tutorials and notes about what we discuss in each, so that you may consult it at any time and know where I am and what it is I am doing. Will you send the same by return? My studies are engaging, but I have not found a girl of any fellow-feeling here. They are pleasant but all quite serious and many study the sciences, and I feel quite stupid when they speak at dinner.

I think you would like it here. Oxford is a lively place; there is always someone about at any time of day, and the Ashmolean is so close it makes me think of our own little flat in Bloomsbury that is waiting for us one day. I would be happier, I think, if you were here. It is a little lonely.

I have prevaricated because I wish to linger in the goodness of having news from you for a little while, but I must say also that your letter has made me so unhappy. You must not think like this, Odette. Your mother was ill; there was nothing any of us could have done about it, and it is certainly not remotely reasonable to think that you could have done any more to help her than a doctor. She loved you and she needed you, and she would want you to be happy, to live your life fully and not lose yourself to grief. Of this I feel quite certain.

I must, then, come on to your question as to the matter of ghosts. I will not call it strange, for I do take it with the gravity you give it – but I suppose I do not know what to say. It is not something I have given much thought to, but perhaps it is simply that I cannot see any way in which they are real. They seem like such an old-fashioned notion to me, something from a world before the Reformation, the idea of souls in limbo for whom we must still fight. But I think I understand why you have asked me this. Lydia has been gone such a short time; she is still so alive in so many ways. I have read stories of widows seeing their husbands or hearing their voices from another room. I cannot imagine what it is to lose a mother, but I know what it is to lose a father, and they stay alive in your heart for so long.

But it does not mean they are a ghost.

I do not think you haunted, Odette. Only grieving.

Darling, please will you send a list of your engagements so I can see if there is any way I can manage a visit?

Love, which in spite of darkness brought us hither,
Should in despite of light keep us together.

Your Cecilia

*

20th October 1898

Dearest Cecilia,

Cambridge is a cursed place; I feel it deep in my bones. When I rise in the morning, there is a damp mist everywhere, turning us all into demons from some level of Signore Dante's Inferno. The men are everywhere in their black flapping robes, clicking and fluttering, and I feel as though I have come amongst a colony of bats, in some hell-fire cave of damnation.

I am not sleeping.

Sleep seems so impossible.

I feel as though my mind is not my own, as though I cannot bring reason to bear on my own thoughts. I think that I am well and capable, and then I find myself at the back of a lecture with tears streaming down my face in the most humiliating manner, with nothing at all to have set me off, and I have to excuse myself before I become a topic of conversation.

I am troubled. I wish I could tell you all that is in my mind, but I fear you would think I have lost my senses, and I fear that I may have.

[The following is crossed out with deep incisions of the pen nib.]
I think I see things. Her. Oh God, she has not left.

You are wrong about my mother. I do not think she would release me so unbegrudgingly.

Do not visit. I do not want you to see me in the state I am in now. I think I have become quite selfish and utterly unable to tolerate the company of others. I stay up late into the night reading, for I do not wish to be myself. I hate joy in any form I see. I hate laughter or singing or any softness that I cannot have. People are more than strangers; they are some other species. Unmarked. Naive. They think death will not touch them. They walk as we all walk, on a narrow ledge above a great drop, but they do not see it – they do not know it is something to be feared. But I see now. I know.

There is horror in this world, and I do not understand how I can continue to live in it.

O

*

21st October 1898

My darling Odette,

I am so relieved to hear from you. I must confess, the delay in receiving a letter from you put me ill at ease. I cannot bear to think of you without a dear friend in such a difficult time. You must know that I am thinking of you always, and when you are awake late at night, I am awake also, reading our dear Idylls, though I find it means less without you here.

I am not sure I know what to do with myself without you.

What a silly thing to say! You don't need to hear my nonsense now.

Yesterday, I went to Blackwell's and bought a very fine volume of Keats, and I enclose it here. I have underlined passages where I felt particularly moved, and if we cannot be together, I can still share this with you. No, no, go not to Lethe, my dear Odette.

I do not know what else to write. It seems banal to tell you about my days. The work is difficult, and I find little pleasure in it. My rooms are always cold, and I have chilblains on my hands, which Mother would surely comment on most cruelly.

This university business is not what I thought it would be. I feel very stupid for being so naive about it. Mother and Leo did try to warn me, but I thought I was better than their idea of me. I fear I am not.

Would it be mad for us to run away?

I have been thinking of it. I have seen advertisements for typing courses, which we could both take, and then we could work as secretaries or clerks, and we could be together, which would surely be so much better than this horrible separation. What do you think? Am I being too wild?

Write to me soon.

Your Cecilia

*

31st October 1898

[There is no addressee, and the paper seems to have been scrunched up as though to be thrown away, then smoothed out again before being sent.]

Remember, remember. Do you ever think about all those Catholics burning up, being chopped into pieces?

Are they right? Do we all suffer after death?

Or is it just Hell and the Devil torturing us while we live?

The children push Guys down the street, bellowing for pennies with their frightful burdens, a human figure all twisted and cruel and unnatural. I am sick with the horror of it.

O

*

1st November 1898

My darling Odette,

I am worried about you. Are you still attending lectures? Leo says you have not written to anyone in Hampstead since you arrived, which is your right,

I suppose, only it does make me worry more. Our minds can become traitors when we do not sleep, and all manner of things can seem – real.

Is there someone in your college to whom you can speak? The vice-principal or some other mistress?

Please tell me when I may visit; only give me the word, and I will pack my things and take a train at once. I am always at your disposal. I think of you hourly. I cannot believe I have left you when you must need me so.

Oh, Odette, please tell me and I will be there at once.

Your loving,

Cecilia

*

9th November 1898

My darling Odette,

I have had no reply, and really, I worry very much about you. Please, when you have a moment, can you send me one message?

Yours always,

Cecilia

*

14th November 1898

Oh God, Odette, Mother has just written to me with the news. Are you all right? It must be an unbearable shock. She says Uncle George has written to you first, and surely the letter has reached you by now? I did not even know they had left the country – did he tell you?

I did not think it could be possible – the Marriage to a Deceased Wife's Sister Bill has failed enough times that we should certainly know if it had passed, but Mother has enclosed something from Leo who says it is legal because Claudine is still resident in Germany, and since she and Uncle George could marry there, then it must be accepted here.

I do not know what to say.

Odette, please reply to me.

I love you.

Cecilia

*

19th November 1898

[There is no signature, the ink is blotchy and the lettering spidery and unsure.]

I don't understand. I don't understand this.

What have they done?

I think I must go mad

Act Two

December 1898, Hampstead, London

Was it a vision, or a waking dream?
Fled is that music:—Do I wake or sleep?

'Ode to a Nightingale', John Keats

1

Cecilia

CECILIA STOPS AT THE unsettled earth below the wooden marker. A host of stone angels watch her from beneath the branches.

In the months since Lydia's death, she has learnt that gravestones are long, like teeth, stubby and blunt, with a tapering root going down to the nerve. One must wait for the earth to settle before they can be planted.

The winter day is low and pale. London spreads out to the south in a mass of smoking chimneys, coal smog settling across the houses below. It is not so cold, and already she sweats under her heavy woollen coat.

In her pocket is the letter from Odette that set out a time and location to meet. Cecilia has read and reread it, looking for some hint as to Odette's state. Is she angry at her? Hurt? It has been two weeks since her previous letter – longer since anything meaningful from her, and Cecilia has spent the intervening time fretting, conjuring up horrible accidents or terrible illnesses that have taken Odette away from her.

Highgate Cemetery is a half-hour walk across the Heath, and she is glad of the exercise to keep her worry at bay.

She checks her watch – she is a little early, and there is no Odette.

Then the church bells toll the hour from St Michael's at the top of the hill, and Odette steps out from behind a tree.

It is a piece of theatrics Lydia would have appreciated, like an attitude from one of her tableaux vivants. Cecilia can see it in her mind's eye: Antigone at Polynices' graveside, doomed for her forbidden mourning.

'Odette.' Instinctively, Cecilia goes to her, reaching out a hand in expectation that she will meet her halfway.

Odette does not move.

Cecilia falters, stops. Drops her hand.

I missed you, she almost says.

Instead, 'It is good to see you.'

Odette wears small smoked glasses against the low winter sun; she is still in her mourning blacks, darkest bombazine with deep crêpe hems in the old-fashioned style of mourning reserved for widows. She is used to Odette in flannel skirts and shirtwaists, rational dress or tea-gowns – it is strange to see her so neatly done, her corsets tightly laced and her dress so precisely fitted that it is like armour. She is beautiful in her grief, her cheekbones cutting a sharp line, features brought into precise relief like clear air after rain. It feels wrong to desire her when she is so acutely wrapped up in grief, and yet Cecilia does. There is no end to her wanting when it comes to Odette.

'You came,' says Odette simply.

'Of course I did.'

It is as though they are meeting for the first time, all the ease and familiarity with each other stripped away, and, God, if that is not enough to send a spike of fear through her.

Odette comes to her mother's grave, toeing the edge of the sinking dirt as if looking for something.

'Is there anything wrong?'

'No,' says Odette sharply. 'What would be wrong?'

Cecilia considers asking about her clothes, the smell of cigarette smoke about her, the way she is measuring the length of Lydia's grave with her footsteps.

'You stopped writing.' When Odette doesn't reply, Cecilia continues. 'Uncle George says they have heard nothing from you at all. You didn't tell anyone when you meant to come home, only in that last message to me, and even then you come first here – what I mean to say is: we worried about you.'

'*We* worried?' queries Odette, with an arched brow. 'I did not know you were so close with my father and aunt – forgive me, I suppose I must say *stepmother* now.'

'*I* worried.' Cecilia comes closer. 'I cannot imagine what you must be feeling about it all. Truly, it has shocked me beyond all sense, but—'

'I don't wish to speak of it.'

'But what will you do when you go home? You must say something to them. I do not know how you can bear it—'

'Of course I cannot bear it!' snaps Odette. 'My mother is barely cold in her grave and yet my father has found time to take a new wife and looked no further than my mother's sister. It is *sick*.'

'I do not disagree.'

'Then why do you ask so many questions?'

'Because you won't tell me what I can do to help.'

'If you cannot change history and bring my mother back then you can do *nothing* to help me.'

There is something unnerving about the perfectly formed carapace of Odette's appearance and the lurching, untempered emotion of her words, taking her from control to chaos in a single moment. She holds herself as though she is primed to run – from what, Cecilia does not know, but Odette twitches at the small sounds of birds and mice in the undergrowth, darting furtive looks over Cecilia's shoulder and to their sides.

'What happened in Cambridge?' asks Cecilia. 'Your letters were . . . They made me frightened.'

Odette laughs, forced and brittle. 'Nothing happened.'

'I cannot imagine how hard the idea of going back home must be now that—' She cuts herself off. 'Would it be easier if we went together?'

She is so simple that she hates herself sometimes. Would it not be easier to lie down in the dirt at her feet and beg Odette not to leave her?

'I cannot ever call that place *home* again,' says Odette. 'They have sown salt into the earth.'

'You have to go home sometime. You can't make it not real by never seeing them again.'

Odette stops pacing, so completely has she been struck. 'That's not what I'm doing.'

'Isn't it? I would not blame you if it were.'

'Fine. I will go back – only—'

'Only what?'

Odette hesitates, suddenly a girl again, young and unsure and lost. 'Nothing.'

'If it is nothing, then you might as well come back with me.'

They walk across the Heath together, stride matched for stride, but for the first time with Odette, Cecilia feels herself entirely alone.

*

'Well? What did she say?'

Cecilia's mother waits in the hallway of the Gate House.

When the letter arrived from Odette this morning, Penelope plucked it from Cecilia's hand the moment she was finished with it, then demanded the others, everything sent from Cambridge. Her eyes moved greedily over the words, eyebrows rising at Odette's scrawling hand and her strange sentences. It felt to Cecilia like being stripped and laid bare on the breakfast table. And the fear: will her mother see what they are to each other? Why had she given into her mother so easily? Why could she not say no?

'Well, you must meet her,' said Penelope.

'I thought you said I should keep my distance?' replied Cecilia, as much of a challenge as she could brave.

Penelope tutted. 'Don't be so literal.'

Cecilia did not know what to say to that, so she fell silent.

Now, she is faced with her mother again, and she is still mute.

She hides her face in the unbuttoning of her coat and unpinning of her hat. She has spent the walk home turning over the conversation with Odette in her mind. Whichever way she looks at it, she cannot make sense of Odette, other than that she is thrown around by the wild currents of her grief. There is nothing she can repeat to her mother that will not feel like a betrayal.

'You were gone for quite some time – surely she must have said something worth sharing,' says Penelope.

'I – don't know,' says Cecilia, slipping past her mother and into the parlour.

'Good afternoon, Cecilia.' Claudine is sitting on the settee, in a shocking pale-lilac dress and gold jewellery. It is not wrong for a sister to enter half-mourning so soon, but Cecilia finds it jarring all the same. Her mother has come in behind her, cutting off her exit so that she has no choice but to take a seat. Penelope shuts the door.

Why is Claudine here? Is this an ambush? What do they want from her?

'I believe you have seen Odette? A rare gift she does not bestow on the rest of us.'

'I have.'

'What of her? How did she seem?'

'I am sure you can see for yourself now she is back in London.'

'Enough of your cheek,' chides Penelope. 'It is a simple question.'

Cecilia stills her hands and focuses on a point on the wall behind Claudine's head.

'She is not . . . well,' she says carefully. 'I cannot imagine how she could be.'

Claudine is tapping her fingernail against the varnished surface of the end table, the only sign of her disquiet. 'The girl wallows,' she says to Penelope. 'I told you at the time – we should not have humoured her about the photography and the funeral. She has formed an unhealthy obsession.'

Penelope nods, quick to agree. 'It is natural to grieve a parent – none of us would deny it – but I must say that I for one think she takes this whole performance too far.'

'I do not believe it to be a performance,' counters Cecilia, but her mother ignores her. *You do not know her*, Cecilia wants to say, but the room is full of other people's words, other people's thoughts, and she struggles to regiment her own.

Claudine continues to speak to Penelope as though Cecilia were not there. 'If she spoils dinner tonight with her sulking, I will insist George gives her a talking-to. He is her daughter; he must straighten her out.'

'Quite right. She must learn to behave herself.'

Abruptly, Claudine looks at Cecilia, eyes sharp. 'You two seem very close.'

Cecilia does not react. 'We are old friends.'

'She trusts you.'

'Yes.'

'She will tell you the truth, I imagine.'

Cecilia moistens her lips. 'I am not quite sure I understand what you are suggesting. Tell me the truth about what?'

'About whatever it is she is hiding.'

Ah. There it is. This is why Claudine has come.

'I don't believe she is hiding anything,' says Cecilia automatically, but the lie sits dead on the floor between the three of them. Odette *is* hiding something – from her, as well as from the others – and it rankles like a pebble in her shoe. 'Or whatever it is, it cannot matter all that much,' she says weakly.

'That is for you to find out,' says Claudine. She leans forwards, and her manner changes, like a theatre backcloth being raised and replaced by another. 'You would be doing me the most terribly kind favour if you would speak to her a little, try to understand what lies beneath all this . . . extravagance.'

Penelope is staring at Cecilia with a too-familiar intensity, and Cecilia diminishes under the combined attention.

'If Odette wants to keep secrets, she is not easily swayed. She is quite stubborn. Even if I tried to make her tell me, it would only make her withdraw further.'

'Then try harder,' says Claudine, mouth in a tight smile.

Cecilia stares at her feet, a rushing sound in her ears. This is all wrong. She shouldn't be here, with them, drawn into her mother's scheming. It is a horrible betrayal of Odette, and she despises herself for it.

But she is ruled by fear. Of Claudine, of her mother's anger, driven by whatever secret it is Claudine holds over her. Fears the precarious future that balances before her.

She is a worm. She knows that much. She is pathetic and stupid and gutless.

The Gate House feels too small; Hampstead a prison yard, ringed round by watching guards. She is struck suddenly, intensely, by the notion that she and Odette *cannot* stay here any longer or she will end up in a grave herself.

A return to university is only a stay of execution. They need a way *out*.

There is only one narrow chance of escape: the money Lydia promised from the sale of her paintings. Odette has dismissed it as a lost cause, another broken promise from Lydia, but Cecilia cannot let it go so easily. Could Lydia not have put something in her will? What has happened to all the paintings that have been taken?

She must keep the peace until she can give Odette a way out. She cannot lose her.

If she must play along for now, then so be it.

'I will talk to her.'

'Perhaps I can ease the way for you a little,' says Claudine. 'Should you happen to speak to Odette as intimate friends, and should I happen to be in a position to hear what was said, then there can be no charge of a betrayal of confidence on your part.'

Cecilia's stomach turns in revulsion. 'I think I understand the idea.'

'Then all is settled.' Claudine rises from the settee. 'I am so grateful to you and your mother for making me so welcome. Mine is not an easy position, and I find myself in need of a friend.'

For a moment, the truth of the words bleeds through, and Cecilia does not like the new wave of guilt that comes with them. It cannot be easy for Claudine. She is no monster, only a woman.

She presses Cecilia's hands between her own. 'Your mother tells me you are a sensitive girl, and I can see it in your face. This must be quite distressing for you. I am sure it can all be straightened out neatly enough.'

Sensitive. She means *weak*.

Cecilia smiles, lets her hands be squeezed as though a pact has been made between them.

Claudine is not wrong.

She does not bend with the wind. She fears it breaks her.

2

Odette

THE LONDON HOUSE IS a sinking ship.

Odette crosses the threshold and feels the floorboards lurch beneath her feet. This is wrong. This is not home anymore.

She lingered as long as she could, stretching out the minutes between the Heath and the house until night fell and she had no choice but to return. To face whatever is waiting for her.

The hallway is the same, of course, and the front door, and the same maid takes her coat and hat, and there is the same smell of lemon and vinegar from where someone has been scrubbing the tiles – but it is all overlaid with another set of images, like two photographs exposed on the same plate. Here is where her mother's coffin rested; here is where the funeral party formed.

To her left is the door to the drawing room, closed tight, and Odette watches it for a moment – straining, she realises, for the tapping.

There is nothing.

Of course, there is nothing. It is just a house, and she is mad.

She has spent two months in Cambridge hiding from a ghost, twitching at shadows and sleeping in bursts. She has not seen the apparition again since the night of the funeral, and at times, she has convinced herself she has lost her mind. Nothing is following her. Her mother is dead and cold beneath the soil.

But here, in the house in which Lydia lived, touched the banisters, left hairs on the armchair, spilt wine on the rug – the house in which she died, in which they washed her cooling body and lifted her coffin.

Ghost or no, her mother is still here.

Her father comes down the stairs, a look of pleasant surprise on his face, as though this is normal – a daughter walking in as though she has only been into town, not gone for two months without a word since the death of her mother.

She notes the wedding ring on his left hand, and she wonders whether he took one off and procured another, or simply sent the old one for cleaning and then used it again at the church in Germany.

'Odette, we have missed you.'

Have they? Really? She misses the father who would not cast her mother off so easily, but perhaps this is who he always was, and what she misses is a construction of her own imagination.

She allows her cheek to be kissed. A few months away, and she sees it now for the affectation that it is. They are not bohemian and continental; they are awkward and English, and her mother was the only one of them with any true talent.

'You have time to change before dinner,' he adds, when Odette does not speak. 'Your things arrived from the station and have been taken to your room.'

Yes. The dinner. The celebration of her father and her aunt's wedding.

'Must I attend?'

Her father's smile becomes fixed. 'Claudine has made a great effort for tonight's meal, so I am sure you will do everything you can to make her feel at home.'

At home – the words send a bristle of anger through her. She wants to throw herself on the ground and beat her fists, reduced to a child in a way she finds hateful, embarrassing.

'She has made herself at home quite thoroughly, I should say,' she says instead.

For a moment, it looks as though her father will caution her, and she feels a thrill at it – that she might elicit a spark of honest emotion from him. She thinks of all the time she has sat with him in his study, or listened to him speak on his reading, his work, listened to him explain the world for her, set it out in rules and wisdom. Nailing it down so thoroughly until all the meat of life is twitching and limp, unable to fight back. He has always wanted her to help him in this effort, to agree with him that, yes, this is how things are, yes, his understanding of the world is right – because her mother's must be wrong, so fragile is it – therefore, his choices are the correct ones, his wants are reasonable.

What was once so certain is cast into absurdity. How can she go on as she had with him? How could she support him in this?

But he does nothing. As always, he sinks back into a vague smile, and continues as though he has not heard her.

He pats her shoulder. 'You're looking well.' With that he goes to his study.

Odette breathes hard through her nose. It is unthinkable to go upstairs, to change for dinner. Smile at their guests. Eat, drink. Make conversation. It is mad – this whole world is mad. What does it matter, then, if she sees a ghost? She is too alive with feeling; her hands are clammy, her breath short. How can she endure this? How can she be here?

It is all she can do to make herself turn mechanically into the drawing room, where Penelope, Leo and Cecilia have already gathered to wait for the dinner gong. Drinks have been poured, and above the mantelpiece the large painting of Cecilia cowering and scared as Mary at the annunciation has been removed. The London house is airy and modern where Herne House is ancient and brooding, and the effect is strengthened by the gaslights being turned up brighter than her mother would ever have set them. But they cannot dispel the winter dark, and the shadows seem to fall more heavily in spite of them.

Claudine stands a little apart in a purple velvet evening dress with beaded appliqué and regards Odette coldly.

'Are you not joining us for dinner?'

It is like the abrupt slap of a cold ocean wave to see her again. Odette cannot look at her – cannot look away.

Her aunt. Stepmother.

Her mother's murderer?

'I am,' says Odette.

'You are not dressed.'

Odette looks down at herself. 'I do not believe I am naked.'

Leo chokes back a laugh and earns a discreet smack on the arm from Penelope. Cecilia does not meet her eye.

Claudine draws her lips into a bloodless line, though she does not speak.

Oh. She should not have said that. What does she mean by it? Why does she draw Claudine's ire?

Revenge. Murder.

She can hear the ghost's words now as plainly as the night they were spoken.

Odette takes a glass of sherry and holds it tightly for support.

Can she really believe Claudine had a hand in her own sister's death?

She thinks again of her mother folding in on herself, the blood pouring from her mouth.

The sickness that started only after Claudine's arrival.

Claudine, who now sits prettily as a new wife, mistress of the London residence and Herne House, instructing her dead sister's servants and sleeping between her dead sister's sheets.

For a moment, Odette's eye is caught by the shape of a figure in the shadows behind Cecilia, in the lee of the chimney breast, and she thinks another of their party must have arrived – but when she looks again, it is gone.

Finally, George arrives amidst the safety of the dinner guests; Eddie Rutherford leads the way with Mr Wrexham, in hot debate over the merits of Hardy's *Wessex Poems* and Wilde's *The Ballad of Reading Gaol*, which have both been published this year. Mousy Mrs Wrexham follows, and a few of the usual crowd, though Odette notes that the more beautiful, artistic women have been replaced by stolid society wives whom Odette has heard her father call terrible bores.

'Are we all here?' says Eddie. 'I saw Mullen heading towards the gong.'

'Could Mr King not join us?' asks Cecilia.

'Unfortunately not,' says George. 'Do I sense a *special* interest in Mr King?'

Cecilia goes pink and stares at her feet. 'Not at all.'

'A most unsuitable match,' declares Penelope. 'I'll thank you not to encourage it.'

'I didn't mean it like that,' says Cecilia again, but only Odette seems to hear her.

The gong sounds. Odette is flushed into the dining room by Penelope and Leo behind her, and she sits down at the table where they laid out her mother's body.

There is an anger in her that feels like a sickness. Her skin fits wrongly; each breath is a task around this great boulder of sorrow and rage and injustice that has swelled and swelled, a great boil that is close to setting her howling.

She does not know how to say what is wrong. It is so obvious what is wrong that it makes her feel mad to have to say it.

But then, what is never said is how wrong it has been for so long.

She remembers, suddenly, her mother drawing her down beneath the blankets on the couch in her studio in Herne House, the smell of wine on her breath.

God. No. Stop it.

Silence is her best option, and she exercises it liberally, looking only at the pattern on the series of plates placed before her, mock-turtle soup, stewed eels, grouse, lobster, sweetbreads, lifting her glass in toast when required, and letting the conversation wash blankly over her. A woman passes the doorway, white skirts flashing in the corner of Odette's eye, and she looks around to see which of the guests has risen from their place – but they are all present.

The skin prickles along the back of her neck.

This is her mother's house.

Her mother would not leave it so easily.

No. A maid, the flash of her starched apron.

Only—

Odette drinks deeply from her wine glass and listens to Claudine, who is holding court.

'I must apologise for the potatoes – quite plebeian in their simplicity, but it takes time to train up a new cook.'

Odette has the distinct impression that Claudine thinks she has said something wry and witty, rather than simply rude. There is appreciative laughter and much discussion of the plebeian potatoes, and Odette realises how absolutely dull her father's set is. Leo laughs along, a little too obviously keen to be counted amongst them; he has grown a small moustache in the months Odette has been away and she sees now that it is a poor copy of Mr Wrexham's.

No wonder Lydia became a little strange when she had been trapped amongst these tiresome people for twenty years.

As if in response, there is a cold gust against her neck. The candles do not flicker.

Odette holds the stem of her glass tighter.

Here is the thought that has stolen her sleep, her appetite, stalked her through the fens of Cambridge:

What if the apparition was real?

She hides her face in her cup for a moment, suddenly hot, her heart racing, as though the people sat around her can hear her thoughts.

What if she is not mad at all?

Dinner progresses through the courses until dessert is placed on the table, with fresh fruit, bon-bons, dried and candied fruit intermingled with lemon-water ices and sweet wine.

Claudine sits amongst it, candlelight flashing off the jewels at her throat and the crystal of the glass in her hand, smiling, triumphant.

What if Odette has sat down to dinner with a killer?

*

There are worms in her mother's eyes and weaving through the slack flesh of her cheeks. The rasp of breath over the desiccated lips, fetid and damp air against Odette's cheek. Living-dead. Dead-living.

Her mother in her bed. Her mother dead. Her mother murdered.

From one breath to the next, Odette wakes.

For a moment, the dream exists alongside consciousness – a doubling, inner and outer world muddled.

She lies still, tensed like an animal scenting the hunter, listening to the subtle shifting of the room, the hush of the wind against the window frame, the soft hiss of the banked fire, the wood settling, groaning.

There is someone outside her door.

She is sure of it.

The door is flat and large and closed flush. She cannot see anything, cannot hear anyone, but she knows it in the same way that she knows the moment before rain begins to fall or—

Someone is waiting for her.

She did not know before what it meant to be frozen with fear. She thought it a turn of phrase, but now she understands that it is all too literal. Her body is rigid and beyond her control.

Seconds draw out like hours. The rush of her blood in her ears. The frantic thump of her heart.

The church bell strikes three beyond the window, and the moment breaks. The dream subsides, and the hush of the night-world grows human: the rattle of distant carriages, the maid turning over in her bed, the squeak of springs, a mouse in the walls.

Odette curls into herself, wrapping her arms around her knees. She cannot take her eyes from the door.

It is unbearable to be here in this house. To not know if what she saw was real. If what her mother's ghost told her is true. She must know or surely lose her wits.

More than anything, she wishes she were not alone in this.

It is her own fault for pushing Cecilia away, but it seems impossible to do anything else. How can she tell her the truth? She could not survive it if Cecilia's expression changed in distrust, disbelief.

She has no proof of anything.

How can a ghost be proved real?

Wait.

Odette moves at last, slithering from her bedclothes and crouching beside her travelling bag, compact and hunched as though she can conceal herself from watchful eyes. She pulls out an illustrated magazine she read on the train and turns to the pages she skipped over in fear before.

Communing with the Ethers.

Mediums. Séances. Automatic writing.

Perhaps there *is* something she can do to find out.

3

Cecilia

THERE ARE FLOWERS ON Penelope's dress. It is a fine print, delicate lavender and pinks, with a foaming spill of blossom along the sleeve and across the hip. Cecilia follows the curl of a vine over slender stripes, tracking lily and narcissus and peony.

'Cecilia?'

Blossom like Blodeuwedd, a girl made from flowers. It sounds peaceful, she thinks, to be a creature of broom and oak and meadowsweet. Of soft petal and perfume.

'*Cecilia*, are you listening to me?' Penelope pinches the inside of her arm.

'Yes, Mother.'

Claudine and Penelope look at her expectantly. The three of them stand in Penelope's dressing room, a sharp December wind cutting in through the loose window frame.

Claudine has been as good as her word: Cecilia will not have to report on Odette directly. It has all been arranged. She is to persuade Odette to visit the Jermyn Street Gallery, with the idea that such a familiar sort of environment may prompt some weakness in Odette that causes her to speak more freely. Penelope and Claudine will take up a position where they may wait unobserved; Cecilia is to draw Odette to this location and induce her to talk.

It is all so simple when they say it. Betrayal. Deception. Manipulation.

'You have the tickets?' asks Claudine.

'Yes.'

'And you know where we will be?' Claudine's gaze pins Cecilia like a specimen in a display case. There is nowhere for her to run.

'Behind the screens in the third gallery,' repeats Cecilia. She has had it explained enough times that she can close her eyes and picture the exact spot, the clack of heels on the parquet, the winter daylight through the high windows, the hum of voices.

'Make sure you are there before you speak of anything serious,' instructs Penelope. 'If she spills her heart to you on the way or after, you must tell us, but it is most important to encourage her to talk when we can hear. Bring up her mother, her grief.'

'I understand.'

'Good.' Penelope pats her shoulder. 'Don't dally. You must catch her quickly.'

They usher her out, and as she crosses the road to Odette's house, she can feel them watching. Briefly, Cecilia hopes Odette has already gone out, slipped from the servants' entrance where neither Penelope nor Claudine would have observed her. It would be better that way, with her failure at the task entirely natural.

But no. Odette is there in the hallway, again in her neat, closely fitted black, dark smudges beneath her eyes.

She is tugging on a pair of gloves when Cecilia enters. At first, Odette says nothing, only watches her, warily.

They have not properly spoken since their uneasy reunion at the cemetery a few days ago; it felt like a rupture, a discordant noise interrupting the melody of their love, and she is unsure where it leaves them both.

'Good morning,' she says to break the silence. 'Did you sleep well?'

'No.'

'Neither did I.'

Oh God, how is she supposed to do this? Her mother and Claudine assume everything is so simple between them, that it is no harder than fitting a key to a lock for Cecilia to extract the truth from Odette. Once, before, she thought they had no secrets. Now, she knows herself to be as guilty as Odette. She cannot truly betray her, she *will* not – but there is no escaping her mother. She will have to go through with this and endeavour to fail.

'I am sorry that we have not spoken properly since you came back. I think I went about things all wrong when we met at the cemetery, and I want to find a way to make it right.'

Odette busies herself with her gloves, yanking each finger in place with a rough motion. 'There's nothing to make right.'

'There is a new exhibition at Mr King's gallery. I thought you might like to go with me?'

'No, thank you. I've had enough of all that.'

She cannot let it sting. Odette is in pain, she does not mean to hurt Cecilia. It is not a rejection of her, but of – of—

Cecilia reaches for and fails to find a satisfactory end.

'Are you going somewhere else?'

She cannot give up so easily. Any failure must seem natural, it must seem as though she really did try.

Odette stares at her gloved hands. 'I had not . . .' She seems almost fragile, as though the tension within her has been wound so tight that one sharp movement will send her shattering to pieces. 'I cannot rest here.'

'Then come with me.' Cecilia hooks their arms together. 'We can laugh at all the women with blank faces and overly pert breasts. You enjoy that. And all the portraits of little dogs with ribbons.'

Odette cannot help but smile. 'There are always so many of them. I suppose it could be diverting.'

'Then that is settled – we will go at once.'

Cecilia guides them out into the street. For a moment, it is as though a ghost of their past has arisen, some scene that Lydia has conjured to paint: Odette and Cecilia, young and in love, dashing around the city as though it is all theirs. It can be still, Cecilia reminds herself. She will make sure Odette gets the money she is owed, and then they will both be free of their families.

Cecilia goes slowly, putting them first on the wrong omnibus, then on the right one but mistaking the stop. She lingers to fix her hat, pausing to look in the window of a Lyons' Corner House, commenting on the fashions, complaining that a street is too crowded so they must take another route – if she takes long enough, perhaps Claudine will give up?

They come at last to the gallery on Jermyn Street; it is one of the smaller galleries, but lively with the new showing. In the press at the entrance, their arms slip apart, and Cecilia finds herself walking alone, hoping Odette will follow. The rooms are hung high and teem with works, every new and interesting thing all pressed together; there are particular crowds around a new painting of Waterloo, and some piece on loan from a collection in Paris.

In a main room, filled with drifting crowds and poorly lit by the damp winter sun, they come across a painting that stops them both in their tracks.

It is a large, rectangular canvas hung at eye height, framed in gold, rich and dense with colour and light, as all Lydia's paintings are. There is Lancelot, kneeling on the stone quay of Camelot, face beautiful with grief, and Elaine of Astolat, the Lady of Shalott, dead in the water, Lydia depicting her boat half sunk and strewn about with flowers. Only the oval of her face rises above the river, and one hand, still clutching the letter for Lancelot.

Odette and Cecilia, recast by Lydia's brush: Lancelot a handsome, boyish youth with Odette's long, straight nose and high cheekbones, and Elaine a faded, washed-out mirror of Cecilia, a corpse of a living woman.

Unthinkingly, Cecilia grasps Odette's arm. She has not seen this work since its painting. It is unfinished – there are patches of bare canvas around the edges, where Camelot fades into indefinite blurs of colour or pencil sketch – but it is brilliant. Beautiful and maddening, some sense of things not quite as they should be. Perhaps it is in the blank, sightless eyes, or the unworldly, weightless way Lancelot and Elaine seem to hang within their surroundings. Cecilia has grown up with her world reflected back through Lydia's eye, and she has always taken it for truth, for wisdom, but now, with the link severed and Lydia in her grave, it strikes her as odd, a little disturbing. Was her work always like this, but Cecilia sees it only now? Or was the twist of Lydia's illness already altering her sight?

Odette has covered her mouth with one hand, frozen in place. 'Did you know this was here?' she asks, voice coarse with emotion.

'No. I swear it.' Cecilia hopes the shock of it is clear in her voice. 'Come away,' she says.

But Odette is not listening. She whips round, pulling away from Cecilia's arm, searching the gallery with wild eyes.

'What is it?' asks Cecilia. 'What's wrong?'

Odette searches a moment more, so tense that the lines on her neck stand out – and then, like her strings have been cut, she goes slack, closes her eyes. 'Nothing.'

There. Another lie. They both know it. It hurts Cecilia like thorns on a rose bush; she tries to grasp Odette, the bloom of what she must still believe moves between them, and yet each time it draws blood.

Cecilia steers Odette with a hand in the crook of her elbow. 'Come.'

It is not so many steps to the place in the gallery where a screen shields one part of the room from another. There is a shuffle of footsteps behind it, the rustle of fabric.

A bench is set before it.

'Rest a moment.'

They sit in silence, Odette pale and unfocused, Cecilia working up the courage to speak.

'You were not yourself at the dinner,' she says.

'Oh? Who was I then?' Odette speaks lightly, but there is an edge to it – an edge to everything about her.

'You hardly seemed in the room at all. And your letters—'

Odette stiffens. 'What about them?'

'I – I hardly know what to say. It is as though my Odette has disappeared somewhere and a stranger has come home.'

Odette gives her a look shot through with hurt and confusion. 'You would have me smile and pretend, as my father would?'

'No – of course not. I am trying to tell you I am worried about you.'

'Worry more about my aunt who has become my stepmother. Worry about your mother, who has forgotten her dearest friend so fast. Worry about my father who brings incest into his marriage bed. Worry about my poor dead mother who had to die for everyone to finally be happy. Were they simply waiting for it all this time? Has no one ever truly wanted her here?'

Cecilia has lost her footing. There is some dark, open void within Odette she has never seen before, and it frightens Cecilia to find her so changed. She had hoped to engineer a failure of Claudine's scheme, but Odette seems all too raw to contain herself.

'You don't mean that.'

'How do you know? Maybe I mean all of it, and it is only that I don't see why I shouldn't say it now.'

'You are grieving. I understand what that is like. I lost Lydia, too.'

'You haven't lost a mother. It's different.'

Now it is Cecilia who retreats, hurt. 'Is it so impossible to think I could feel some measure of what you do?'

It is as though Odette has stepped over the cliff edge, and now that she is falling, she cannot find a way to halt her momentum. Cecilia sees it in her eyes before she speaks, the inability to stop herself.

'No one has lost what I have lost. You cannot understand.'

'No,' says Cecilia quietly. 'I cannot if you will not tell me the truth of what is the matter with you.'

The pause stretches out long enough to become awkward, then heavy.

Eventually, Cecilia speaks. 'You grieve so strongly that I am afraid for you. There is something else troubling you – and do not say your father's marriage, because of course there is that, but, Odette, you look like a creature from the underworld. You send me strange letters from Cambridge; you jump at shadows. Yet you will not tell me a thing. It is like you have gone mad.'

There is a look in Odette's eye, and she thinks, for a moment, that she has touched some part of her, some old familiar place where they still know each other, where there is solid ground beneath her feet.

Odette's mouth twists down, and she looks away.

Cecilia has got it wrong.

'Mad. Yes. Call me mad. It is mad to live amongst all you lunatics. You bob about telling lies to each other, smiling and pretending anything makes sense, and you blame me for spoiling the party, for being *troubled*. Tell me, why am I supposed to be kind to Claudine? Why am I supposed to forget my mother so quickly? Like my father has? Was the earth even settled on her grave when he took another woman to his bed? I am sure Claudine could not believe her luck when my mother died so conveniently. Why must I shut up my feelings to make things easier for you all? Am I supposed to grieve quietly? Privately? Should I be on my knees in some chapel with a book of improving lines? Should I go and feed the needy or the sick? A dead mother is nothing so unusual, so the fault must lie in me. Is that not what you all think?'

'No,' says Cecilia, but she wilts under the force of Odette's words.

This is a mistake. It is all a mistake. She is stupid, clumsy.

It was Claudine who called Odette mad, but is that fair? What is madness? What does it look like? She heard Lydia called mad, and she was strange, yes, erratic, melancholy, with great highs and lows like a tide, and loving her must have been like building a house on sand. Cecilia has seen men raving on the street, talking to the air, seen girls throw themselves into the river. But what made it madness? Their misery? The trouble they caused others? What is it to be mad? Is it anything?

Is Odette mad in her grief? Has she become lost to them all?

'I don't think—' Cecilia stumbles over her words, and it is like bait.

'Go on. Tell me what you think.'

'I think – I think maybe you want to hurt us so we feel the pain you feel.'

'Oh. Clever. Very neat.'

'I'm not trying to be neat – I am trying to make you hear me.' Cecilia is losing her patience, and she can hear the childish, demanding note in her voice. It is embarrassing to do this here; exposing. People are already looking at them and her cheeks burn in shame. She modulates her voice. 'I know you are keeping something from me. I do not understand it. What have we ever kept from each other? Why will you not let me help you?'

She is seized by a sudden, urgent need to take Odette's hand and pull her away, run to the first train, keep going until their money runs out.

She wills Odette to soften, to come back to her.

But something catches Odette's eye, and she follows its movements.

She stands, backing away. 'I – I have to go.' She spares Cecilia one final glance. 'I am sorry. I truly am.'

She turns abruptly, knocking into a mother with her young son in a sailor suit, before bounding back the other way, pushing through the crowds with an increasingly frantic desperation –

And then she is gone.

4

Odette

THE PUBLIC CONVENIENCES IN the gallery are winter-cold, porcelain and tiles with frigid air pouring in through narrow, frosted windows. There is no one else inside, and with great relief, Odette shuts herself in a stall and locks the door before the great tide of her panic hits her.

She is seeing things. In every flash of white skirts, every face looking at her, there is her mother.

Her panic, and her shame.

Behind her closed eyes, she sees Cecilia's face crumple. The soft curve of the mouth she has kissed so often, pulled down in misery. Odette did that. Odette hurt her.

She worries that Cecilia is right: she is taking her pain and turning it into a punishment for all around her.

Cecilia is not wrong: Odette *is* concealing something from her. Cecilia, the one person she should trust above all others. The thought flashes briefly across her mind, like the warning glow of a lighthouse through fog: if she loses Cecilia, she will have no one left at all.

If only there was a way to *show* it to her, to have Cecilia understand for herself.

The idea is there, in the magazine. She *can* try to prove the ghost real. She must stop prevaricating and *act*. Her cowardice frustrates her, shames her. She has been weighed and found wanting.

The door to the room must have opened – though Odette did not hear it – because there comes, abruptly, the rustle of fabric.

She stills, sniffing back her tears. She does not want some well-meaning busybody enquiring if she is all right.

The rustle comes again, and then – soft footsteps.

A rush of cold sweeps through her.

Bare feet.

Unmistakably. It is the slap of bare soles against tile.

Odette draws back, pushing herself into the gap between the toilet bowl and the wall of the cubicle. The sound of her breathing is too loud and harsh and quick. It is as though all the noise of the world beyond has died away: the horseshoes on cobbles, the chatter of the crowds, the tolling church bells, all just beyond the windows – gone, and it is only her breath and the footsteps.

They come to a halt before her door. Beneath it she can see a dirty white hem and two ice-white feet.

It cannot be – it cannot be – her hands are shaking, and she is breathing so fast it makes her light-headed.

She thought—

Earlier – she thought she saw someone.

Saw *her*.

Just for a moment.

When she and Cecilia stood before Lydia's painting, there was the faintest sense of cold fingertips at her throat, and she whipped round at once, searched for that white shroud, the chestnut hair, in vain.

Perhaps the truth is this: she hides from the ghost because she is frightened by how badly she longs for it to be real.

In her sick, broken heart, it is her only wish.

She remembers that monstrous, unnatural voice against her ear. The horror of her own madness.

She aches to hear it again.

'Mama?' She fumbles quickly, desperately, with the lock on the door, jerking it open. 'I am here – it is me.'

There is no one there.

'Mama?' Her voice is plaintive. 'Mama, come back. Don't leave me.'

Silence.

*

On her return home, she meets Leo going out as she comes in.

'Are you quite all right?' he asks, searching her face.

She tries to sidestep him, but he blocks her. 'Yes – no – it doesn't matter.'

She fled the gallery, too ashamed to look for Cecilia. She has another task now: one she cannot put off. Not after what she has seen.

'Look, I know—' he fumbles for the right words '—all this is quite a lot to get one's head around, but don't you think you could lay off the dramatics a bit? It would be easier on everyone, and on you too, I think.'

'I don't want any more lectures, thanks.' She pushes past him.

'Odette,' he calls after her, 'stop being an ass. I'm trying to look out for you.'

Ignoring him, she heads up past her room, all the way to the top of the house.

She cannot be around them, any of them. They do not understand.

The slow rumble of approaching thunder greets Odette as she opens the door to her mother's studio. The rain has not yet come, but the sky is already dark, and with only an oil lamp to light her way, the room is a mass of shifting shadows and the bobbing reflection of her own hand carrying the lamp. No one has thought to come and cover the furniture with sheets, so there is a thickening layer of dust across each surface, and the windows are rimed with dirt.

Odette waits by the door for a moment until she is sure she has not been followed, then closes it and pulls a chair beneath the handle to fix it in place.

The last time she was with her mother in this studio, Lydia was bright and lively, dashing between her paint stores and the canvas as she made great, swooping brushstrokes across a scene of Ariadne arriving in Naxos.

The last time Odette saw her mother anything resembling her usual self was before Claudine came to England.

Revenge me. For I am murdered.

The spray of red blood across the front of Lydia's dress as she collapsed against Odette.

At the writing desk, she sits and considers for a moment.

Her mother's memorial still lies where she left it, the loose pages written in a messy, erratic hand. She reads through it, looking for some new understanding. If only she had written about her mother's illness from the start. It is too convenient that it began so soon after Claudine's arrival – does Claudine think her naive? Stupid? She had a hand in it, Odette knows this.

She reads the memorial twice, but can find nothing that paints any obvious guilt. It will be there, she knows it must; like some trick of the light, it will become clear when she least expects.

She folds the pages and slips them into her pocket, to take down to her own room.

For now, she must try another route.

How to do this? It is not the kind of task that comes with instructions in an issue of *Cassell's Magazine*.

A pen and paper – that is obvious. Or should it be a pencil? Yes, a pencil, so the nib will not need recharging with ink.

Odette finds both and sets them before her, then, after a moment's debate, holds the pencil loosely in her fingers and rests the tip against the paper.

What should she say? Should she speak to her mother?

Even alone, she is too embarrassed to do it.

Instead, she closes her eyes, lets her mind drift, loosen. Rain hammers at the glass, wind rushing down the chimney in gasps.

There is a flash of lightning as bright as daylight. Her eyes snap open, and in the arching glass window, Odette sees a figure in white behind her.

Her heart races, but she does not turn.

'Mama?' she whispers. 'Tell me what to do?'

What a foolish want. Her mother could never have done as she asked in life – what hope is there of it now?

Is she so sure she wants her mother back?

She shuts her eyes again and focuses on her hand where it rests on the paper; on the press of the graphite, waiting.

There. A sense of weight. Pressure. So faint it is almost nothing, but she feels her hand urged to move. Down first, then a loop, then down again – she cannot follow it. Her hand is cold, as though there is something laid atop it, guiding her.

It lasts only briefly, and then her hand is a dead thing, flaccid and inert.

She must look at what she has produced; there is no hiding.

A mess: that is what she has made. There are great loops and scrawls, lines bisecting lines, flourishes and curls. It is nonsense.

She picks up the paper to scrap it, but the changed angle causes something to catch her eye. It is a wobbling, misshapen word, like a trick-eye puzzle. At first nothing and then – *remember*.

Her eyes flick to her reflection in the window, to the figure she had seen behind her. Nothing. She is alone.

Remember.

Remember what? Her mother? The ghost's command?

It is not proof. Not proof she can share, not something she can show Cecilia. She must do something else. Something *more*.

5

Cecilia

'WHAT ON EARTH IS that girl playing at?' Claudine would be pacing if she could; Cecilia can tell from the tense play of her fingers around the strap of her umbrella, how the cords of her neck stand out above her high collar.

The three of them – Claudine, Penelope and Cecilia – are pressed into the carriage as it rattles north up Regent Street. Neither Penelope nor Claudine seem to notice her misery, and it is a blessing to be forgotten by them. Odette left her there in the gallery, watched by so many curious, judging eyes. Cecilia waited, hot-faced with shame and sorrow, for her to return, then went looking for her. But there was no trace.

'I will speak to George about her behaviour. She is putting on a show intentionally. She cannot abide not to be the centre of attention for even a moment.'

For the first time, the traitorous thought comes: perhaps Claudine is right – at least in part. Odette's misery has made her selfish, and they will all bear the cost of it.

And yet, she would go to her at once if she called.

God, she is crying.

Claudine focuses on Cecilia, takes her hand. 'You did not deserve to be the target of such hurtful words. I am grateful that you entertained my little scheme, and I am sorry that it came at such a cost to you.'

Cecilia's skin crawls where Claudine's hand rests on hers, and it is only because they are both wearing gloves that she does not snatch hers back at once.

'I am sorry I didn't find out her secret for you,' says Cecilia, taking the opportunity, as they jolt round a corner, to remove her hand and clasp one of the leather straps hanging from the ceiling. 'I am not sure I can be of any help to you.'

'I've always said she was a spoilt girl,' adds Penelope. 'Self-involved. Hardly surprising given her mother's own weaknesses, but it is quite intolerable.'

This speech is clearly aimed at Claudine, but she pays little attention, instead leaning in to speak conspiratorially to Cecilia. 'You know her better than either of us. You *do* believe she is keeping some secret?'

The tone in Claudine's voice catches Cecilia in the midst of her thoughts. There is almost a sense of nervousness, an attentiveness that is unwarranted. Cecilia knows why she herself fears Odette keeping something from her – but why should Claudine fear it?

What a thought: Claudine is *afraid.*

Cecilia considers her words. 'I cannot rightly say. Is there some specific matter you suspect she may be concealing?'

'No.' The reply comes too quickly.

'Let her have her secrets then.' Cecilia gives a hopeful smile. 'It does none of us any harm, does it?' She hopes she comes across naive, idealistic – unimportant.

For the first time, Claudine falters. 'I suppose that may be true.'

They turn into Regent's Park to take the Outer Circle north, then cross the canal by the Zoological Gardens. Penelope starts up some chatter, flattering Claudine's choice of dishes at dinner, the elegant way she has adapted to running a household. Cecilia cannot listen to it.

She spends the rest of the day in silence. Sewing in her room, watching Odette's window for her return. She is silent at dinner while Penelope and Leo chatter. Is it as easy for them both to cast off Lydia and Odette as it seems? How can they talk of the mutton and the new hat Leo thinks to buy, and the business of the journey to his office?

What of loyalty? What of love?

Perhaps Odette is right. No one grieves as she does. It is an inconvenience.

She sits silent, thinking.

The pieces lie before her, and she turns them about in her mind, considering how they might fit.

The weather has turned with a violence, a storm wind picking up and smacking the tree branches against her bedroom window. Cecilia sits on the end of her bed, shucking her shoes and stockings.

There are too many things she does not understand.

She does not understand Odette or what happened at the gallery. She does not understand why Claudine is so afraid of what Odette may be hiding.

Cecilia thinks of the bracelet she found with the initials scratched off. The scraps of paper with her mother's name, and that mysterious fragment – *art.* She should have some theory about it, she thinks, but she can come up with nothing. Her mother displays her past through a careful curation of scenes placed on show. It is immaculate and perfectly done, and there is so little to gain some scrabbling foothold on. If a secret is there, it will be no simple thing to find it.

And what of Odette's secret?

Claudine's own past is hazy. Cecilia has never given that fact much thought, but perhaps within it lies something Claudine does not want to come to light.

Is *that* what Odette is hiding?

No. Somehow, she does not think so. If it were, why would she not share that information with Cecilia?

She unbuttons her shirt and blouse, and hangs each item across the back of the chair by her nightstand. From her window, she can see Odette's room more clearly now that winter has stripped the leaves from the trees. There is no light, no movement.

In her dressing gown, Cecilia goes to hover in her mother's doorway. Penelope sits in front of her mirror, working cold cream into her skin.

'What happened to Odette's money?' Cecilia asks.

Penelope gives no reaction, smoothing the cream into the skin of her neck with precise upward motions. 'What money?'

'The money from the sale of Lydia's paintings.' Cecilia shifts, biting the inside of her cheek against her rising frustration. 'She was arranging an exhibition with Mr King. You must remember.'

'Oh, yes. That.'

'Did she not say anything about the money being for Odette? I thought it might come up in the will.'

Her mother pauses, in the act of removing an earring. 'Don't go snooping into that sort of thing. It is none of your business.'

'It is Odette's business.'

'Then let Odette ask.'

'I am only trying to help. She might not feel able to ask so freely now that—'

'Not this again.' Penelope shuts her jewellery box and rounds on her daughter. 'Leave poor Claudine alone. No one likes to think of how she has suffered in all this, but she nursed her sister through her last weeks and was the only one of us present at the death itself. Let her enjoy this time as a new wife.'

'But how does it affect Claudine for Odette to get the money she was promised?'

A cold wind snaps through Penelope, and in a flash, she grasps Cecilia by the ear, fingers pinching painfully tight.

'Are you deaf? Do you not listen to a single word I say? You will not help Odette cause trouble. Without Claudine, we are *ruined*.' She lets go of Cecilia's ear and wraps her arms around her, as though drawing her in for a maternal embrace. 'My sweet, silly, naive girl. I am doing all this for you, and you don't even know it.'

Cecilia's mouth and nose are muffled against Penelope's bosom, the tickly stuff of her nightdress irritating her nose.

'I forgive you for your childish blunders. If you will only listen to me and do as you're told, all will be well.'

'Yes, Mother.'

Cecilia slinks back to her bedroom. The air is heavy. She feels the beginnings of a pressure headache descend like a weighty hand on the top of her head. In the distance, a rumble of thunder rolls across the city.

When she goes to open the window, she spots Leo standing beneath it, tucked into the lee of the building, smoking. She goes downstairs, slips on a coat and joins him beneath the mulberry tree that hangs over the front path.

'Evening, Cessy,' he says. 'Come for some fresh air?'

The wind is strong enough that he has to hold his hand cupped around the cigarette to keep it lit.

'Couldn't stand to be indoors. It's all so . . .' She trails off.

'Mother ploughing around like a stately barge, sending backwash through every room?'

She smiles. 'Something like that.'

He smokes quietly, and she lets the companionable silence stretch out for a moment. Leo has always moved more easily under their mother's assessing gaze, but he is still an ally against her dramatics. Cecilia is not sure he knows how different it is for her with Penelope than it is for him – why should he, after all? It is not Leo who their mother will see herself in, not Leo who will face the world in a way their mother recognises. Cecilia understands that she draws her mother's ire because her mother fears for her in a way she does not fear for Leo. Her fate matters in a way Leo's does not.

But it is something, to have a brother. Something, not to be the only one. She has not considered before that it must be a different kind of difficulty to be Odette, and stand alone. There is no one who must suffer Lydia and George as she does – did.

Cecilia shoves her hands deep into her pockets.

'You really didn't know that we had no money?' she asks eventually.

She cannot imagine Leo being ignorant of something like that. He is her older brother, always quicker and smarter than her, always more of the world.

He grimaces. 'Mother was a fool for keeping it from me. If I had known I could have looked at the arrangement, spoken to Uncle George and Aunt Lydia about formalising it – but now it's a mess. I've looked at the numbers; Mother is right that we are in trouble. A good thing that she's so cosy with Claudine, I suppose. They were great friends back when they were young, so says Mother, but then Claudine went abroad the same year Father died, and that apparently was that.'

Cecilia is struck again with the thought of how little she really knows of her family's past. Lydia and George are old family friends, yes, and her father died before she was born, a riding accident, a mundane tragedy – these are the facts that add up to less than the sum of their parts.

What was it Leo just said?

Claudine went abroad the same year father died.

Odette told her, back in the summer, about the incident at the stationer's, the woman who had mentioned banns being read before Claudine abruptly left the country. It seems hard to read that as anything other than a broken engagement that meant Claudine felt she had no choice but to go. And now they know that it was around that time that their mother became financially dependent on Lydia, after their father died. Their mother, who had been Claudine's friend first, then switched allegiances because of a secret that Lydia knew, the same one that Claudine now used to bring Penelope back to her side, and turn on Odette.

There is something that catches in Cecilia's mind about the order of events. She cannot tell if there is a piece missing or if she is simply overlooking the obvious.

She wants badly to speak to Odette about it all, to share her burden. But she cannot.

She thinks again of Odette, standing before Lydia's painting of Lancelot and Elaine. The true, real grief on her face – and that strange, hunted look when she turned suddenly, as if searching the room for someone who had called her name. Cecilia was surprised to see the painting hung unfinished – such a thing had never been Lydia's way. She would guard her work closely, spending days – weeks – agonising over the final touches of the brush until she declared the canvas must be taken away or she would cut it to ribbons in frustration. Still, someone had got hold of it for display and—

Mr King.

There, anyone knows about the paintings it will be him.

She must return to the gallery as soon as possible. She must find Mr King and ask him directly.

The memory comes of his hands on her waist, his hot brandy breath on her face, but she pushes it away forcefully.

For once, she can play Lancelot. For once, she can save Odette. She will find the money and come to her with hope, with another path. Odette is lost, and she needs Cecilia to come into the dark to find her.

'You fret too much, Mousy.' Leo knocks her shoulder affectionately. 'Don't take everything to heart so.'

'Don't you feel uneasy about it all? Claudine and Uncle George?'

'Why should I?' He drops the cigarette butt and stubs it out with his toe.

Cecilia hesitates, warring with her frustration. Is it not obvious?

'Aunt Lydia was good to us, in her way,' she tries.

'Of course she was. We all love her still, but people move on.' Before Cecilia can protest he continues. 'You can't control what other people do, much as you may want to, or live forever on the hope that they will come round to thinking just as you do. You must look out for yourself, secure a path of your own, and leave other people to their own mistakes.'

'That seems a little heartless. Don't you think we all owe each other something?'

'Perhaps we do, but if the other party isn't interested in paying, what's the use in wasting your life rattling an empty tin at them? Uncle George and Claudine are looking out for themselves. So am I; so is Mother. It's simply how the world is.'

'I don't like it.'

'I know you don't, Mousy.'

He ruffles her hair in an exaggerated gesture of brotherly affection and she sticks out her tongue. For a moment, they are so young again, arguing about stolen toys and bruised knees. Family, she thinks, is loving people who cannot love you back in the way you need them to, and going on loving them all the same. She worries she is not very good at it.

A flash of lightning sends Cecilia and Leo skittering out from under the tree in shock and nervous laughter. Barely a breath later, thunder cracks through the air and the deluge comes.

6

Odette

ODETTE SLINKS DOWNSTAIRS AS softly as she can in rubber-soled boots. She does not want to be caught leaving. She might be asked where she is going – and that she cannot answer. But at the morning-room door, she pauses, looks inside.

'Who gave you that?' she asks Claudine with a frown.

Claudine wears a shawl of lavender silk embroidered with white lilies.

She lets the shawl hang casually from her arms. 'This? George thought I might like something of Lydia's as a keepsake.'

'It wasn't enough that you took her husband – you had to take her clothes, too?'

'I beg your pardon?'

Before Odette can reply, George steps into the hall and steers her away. 'Oh dear,' he says, smiling. 'You two really are chalk and cheese, aren't you?'

Odette stares at him, blank with shock. He cannot be serious, surely? 'Chalk and cheese?' As though they are simply two clashing personalities in a West End play.

'Give it time and the two of you will find some common ground,' he says, almost jovial in his tone. 'You are unused to a mother like Claudine, so naturally it will not be easy.'

Odette bristles. 'She is not my mother.'

'No, perhaps you are too old for that.'

She steps away from his grasp. 'I'm going out.'

'May a father ask where?'

'Only – out. With Cecilia.'

He smiles, glad of an easy way to please. 'Of course. I'm glad to see you two getting on again.'

Another maddening statement. When did he think they fell out? What does he know of any of it? And yet he will tell her how it is, define the world for her.

Was he always like this? Did she simply not notice before? Or has it come with Claudine, this evasiveness? He has more to hide now, she imagines, and Odette loses patience with it. She cannot play this game anymore, she cannot work to uphold his narrative.

She thinks, abruptly, that now her mother is gone, there is no irrational figure to range themselves against, stood side by side. Her father must have an abject counterpart, so he can stay the steady one, the sane one. Who stands on the other side now?

It is her, Odette realises. It is her.

*

She rings the bell of the Gate House and waits on the doorstep, making a concerted effort to keep her hands still.

The maid brings Cecilia to the door. It is not their hours to be at home to callers, so Cecilia wears a loose house dress.

'Odette!'

There is something closed and wary in Cecilia's face that she cannot interpret, and it makes Odette feel so utterly, terribly alone. They have never been this alien to one another. 'I have made an appointment,' she says.

'What sort of appointment?'

'Would you hate me if I called it a surprise?'

Odette's heart is racing, but she hopes her agitation is not too obvious. If she tells Cecilia what she has planned, she might say no, and that is unacceptable.

Cecilia hangs back, watching Odette a little warily. 'I'm not dressed.'

'There is time for you to do so.' Odette has not seen her since their visit to the gallery yesterday, and she has made no apology for her behaviour. Should she? Maybe – but later. Right now she cannot find the words, it is all she can do to hold her nerve.

Cecilia hesitates for only a moment before nodding and disappearing inside.

Odette paces the small, tree-filled garden, sweat gathering beneath her heavy bombazine.

At last, Cecilia emerges, and they set off.

London is perpetually busy, with omnibuses and trams rattling past dressmakers and bakeries, dray carts delivering milk and vegetables and meat, shop awnings jostling for space, women with prams, children dashing about in mittens, men posting advertisements for music halls, auctions, boarding houses and temperance preachers. They make it only a few streets before it begins to rain, so Odette hails a hansom cab. Is this a bad omen? Is she making a terrible error?

The clatter of the wheels and horseshoes makes conversation difficult; Odette is grateful for the reprieve. How odd that she does not know how to speak to Cecilia – Cecilia who is half her own mind, half her own heart. She wants to reach for her, in this brief private space, but it is as though these next few hours are a test through which they must pass before she can be at ease around her again. It is strange and unsettling, and Odette feels like she has missed a step on the stairs, is lurching out into the void.

'Where are we going?' asks Cecilia.

Odette evades the question. 'You are quite sure you don't believe in ghosts?'

'You asked the same question in your letter. Why does it matter?'

'Tell me. Please.'

'Odette, you are frightening me.'

Odette is agitated, her leg bouncing. This must go as she hopes, or she will simply not survive it. 'Don't be ridiculous. It is just a question.'

Cecilia swallows. 'Well, I suppose I cannot say for certain. I don't think anyone can say for certain.'

Odette rounds on her, eyes narrowing. 'But you were certain before.'

'Yes – I mean – as certain as I can be.'

'But you might change your mind?'

Cecilia shrugs helplessly. 'I suppose any of us may change our mind about anything.'

Odette can barely sit still; they crawl so slowly along the crowded streets it is as though she has been placed in fetters. She needs to *move*.

'We are attending a séance,' she says plainly. 'I suppose that will make it clear one way or another.' Before Cecilia can reply, Odette bounces up. 'For God's sake, we will be late if this damned driver cannot do something more clever about this traffic.'

She lets down the window and hangs out to have a quick and caustic argument with the driver that results in a handful of coins being exchanged – near thrown – and Odette marches off with Cecilia in tow.

They are soon in the residential streets of Camden. Odette turns into one of the newer developments, built in the style of thirty years ago, long rows of flat-fronted townhouses with wrought-iron balconies along the first floor and the servants' entrance down an alley to the side of each pair of houses. The plane trees planted at intervals along the pavement have shot up like weeds and will soon overshadow the fine buildings.

Cecilia catches up at last. 'You cannot simply tell me we are going to a séance and run off.'

'I didn't run off.'

'Why did you keep it a secret?'

Odette hesitates beside a tree, pressing a hand to the trunk to steady herself, and for the first time, she feels real, horrible doubt. What is she doing? Why bring Cecilia into this?

Still. They are here now. Cecilia is watching her.

She schools her nerves, straightens. 'I thought you might not come.'

Cecilia looks at her reproachfully. 'Don't you know I would follow you anywhere?'

If they were not in the open street, she would kiss her. She must not lose Cecilia. Who would she be without her?

But Odette has no words for any of it.

'We're late,' she says instead.

Cecilia must see for herself. If the ghost is real, then it must show itself at a séance, surely?

It would be a relief to know she is not mad. That she is not alone.

Odette checks the house number in her notebook and mounts the steps to a nondescript front door. There is no sign or plaque explaining what this place is; through the window, she can see only a very ordinary parlour with a fire burning in the grate. A maid shows them inside, and they wait a moment before there is the sound of footsteps descending the stairs.

Odette squeezes Cecilia's hand so tightly she knows it must be painful.

'Whatever you see, whatever you hear, you must promise to report it to me faithfully,' she says. 'However mad it may seem. I must hear your complete and truthful account of it. Do you understand?'

All Cecilia has time to do is nod before a plain, friendly-looking woman comes into the room.

'Miss Fairfax-Waugh.' She takes Odette's hand in an overly familiar way. 'I feel as if I already know you.' Then she turns to Cecilia. 'And Miss Moore. I am Mrs Emilia Weston. Thank you both for joining me in my home. I hope that today I may offer two grieving souls some small comfort. The spirits are always with us, my dears, and it is my greatest joy to reunite love lost too soon.'

'Thank you for seeing us,' says Odette mechanically.

Cecilia says nothing, only takes a step closer to Odette.

In the hallway is a slender girl whom Odette would have assumed to be one of the staff, if not for the smartness of her dress and the clean pink of her hands.

'This is Rosina, my assistant.' Mrs Weston waves her in. 'This will be our little party for today. Tea first? I find my clients often welcome a moment to remember their dear departed before we begin.'

'No,' says Odette abruptly. 'Let's get on with it.'

Mrs Weston falters but smooths it over quickly. 'Of course. Please come this way.' She indicates for the group to move from the parlour.

Odette and Cecilia are led past the main staircase to a door at the back of the house. It is murky with shadows, but Mrs Weston guides Odette's hand to a rope that hangs on the wall and ushers them in.

As they are closed into the darkness, Cecilia leans forwards to speak into Odette's ear. The light breath against her neck is all too familiar. 'I don't like this. Say the word and we can leave.'

'Please. I have to,' is all Odette can say.

Cecilia touches one hand to her back, in a gesture of comfort.

They stumble along the corridor, clutching the rope, the wall, and the immense sense of vulnerability feels too much. Odette stubs her toe on a step and gropes her way up a set of stairs that are narrow and steep.

This is not safe.

What is she doing? Oh God. Please let this be worth it.

The stairs level out, and the rope takes them through another doorway and to a table.

Odette fumbles into a chair, and there is the brief press of an arm against her shoulder as Cecilia takes the chair to her left.

'Odette?' whispers Cecilia, and Odette realises she is not beside her after all, but across the room. A flare of panic grips her.

'Let us join together,' says Mrs Weston, from somewhere in the darkness. 'Take the hands of those each side of you.'

Odette bites her lip. The hand to her left is unfamiliar, childlike and clammy – the assistant, Rosina's, she thinks, not Mrs Weston's. To her right, she hopes to feel Cecilia, but instead the hand is cold and smooth and bony. This must be Mrs Weston – though she was sure from the sound of her voice that she was somewhere more distant.

'I call today upon the dear spirit of Arabella, my guide, poor soul, poor unloved soul. Arabella, will you come to me again and open the way between the worlds?'

There is a pause, and then a gentle tremor across the table.

'Will you introduce yourself to the kind people who have joined us today?'

The table rocks in rhythm with the subtle motion of the assistant's foot – Odette can feel the movement to her left, and she is so disappointed. Mrs Weston is nothing but a fraud. Of course she is. Of course this was a stupid idea. It is like going fishing with a stick and a length of string and hoping to catch a shark.

The next time Mrs Weston speaks, her voice is high-pitched and childlike. 'Oh, Mrs Weston, it is cold today, so cold I can't rightly get warm no more.'

Odette hears a snort that can only come from Cecilia.

'Darling Arabella is my spirit guide,' says Mrs Weston, in her own voice. 'She has been with me many a year – haven't you, my darling?'

'So cold, madam, and so dark, down at the bottom of the water.'

'Drowned in the Serpentine,' Mrs Weston explains. 'Dear girl, we have come here today hoping that there might be someone waiting to speak to the young lady at this table. Is there any such spirit?'

Odette wants to sink down out of sight, though there is no hiding in the dark. She has done this foolish thing, and Cecilia is here to witness the depths to which she has fallen.

'It hurts,' says Arabella's voice. 'It presses all about me like needles.'

This is hateful.

'Try harder for us, little one – let the door open! Throw it wide!'

The air turns icy, as though a window has been flung open – and perhaps it has, but it is not so cold outside today; it is unnatural. Odette frowns. Is there a block of ice brought in, a fan to send frigid air across them?

'Yes – yes – she is here,' says Arabella. 'Oh, she is so angry. So *angry*.' The word twists with a sound that must pain Mrs Weston awfully to make, the high-pitched child's voice dropping into an animalistic snarl.

There is a sudden spattering of rain droplets across Odette's forehead, as though the roof were open to the sky.

Something is turning. She doesn't like it; in some unspeakable, confused way, it feels wrong. She can hear her own breath coming too fast, the pulse in her wrist pounding.

'We long to hear her,' says Mrs Weston. 'Go on, Arabella. Let her through.'

There is an unexpected note of ill-ease in Mrs Weston's voice, and in response, the table jerks violently, scraping along the bare boards before slamming back into place hard enough that it catches Odette across the stomach.

'She remembers!' The snarl tears its way out, Arabella's sweet voice now like gravel. 'She sees! She will not forgive!'

There is the touch against her ankles, something fleshy and warm, patting along her legs up to her knees – and then at once, it is gone. A pressure builds in Odette's head. Her ears are muffled. For a moment, she is underwater, an immense weight pushing down on her, her ears and nose filled up – and Mrs Weston's voice comes through distorted, anxious.

'Restless spirit, take pity on us – this is – too much,' she says, voice shot through with panic.

The hand to the right is gripping hers so hard she can feel the bones in her fingers grind together, and her breath is strangled in her throat.

'Stop it – this is a cruel joke,' cries Cecilia. 'Stop it at once.'

The hand to Odette's right yanks her sideways, ripping her other hand from Rosina's grasp and almost pulling her out of her chair. She grabs at the table with her free hand – and then, as suddenly as it moved, the bony grip is gone.

She breathes hard for a moment, white hot and unreal with fear.

Almost too quietly to be heard, she whispers, 'Mama?'

Cold fingers close around her throat.

Shock runs through her from her toes to the top of her head.

Odette thinks of the cold grave dirt under her hand at the cemetery. Undisturbed. Her mother is *dead.*

Then breath, rank with rot and loam, hissing in her ear. '*Odette, why do you run from me?*'

She says nothing, moves not an inch. She cannot breathe; she cannot even let herself think, for fear this apparition will comprehend it.

'*Why do you leave me alone, in the dark and the cold?*' The voice is soft and sibilant, like air whistling through bone. '*Why do you not save me?*'

She can almost feel desiccated lips against her skin. The voice is so close, as though it is coming from inside her own soul.

'*Odette, let me hold you.*'

Two rangy arms close around her in a vice-like embrace. She breaks. She cannot tell herself this is not real because it *is* – she can feel it, hear it. She can never *stop* seeing her mother's mouth howling *revenge*, *murder*, and she would rather leap from a bridge into the Thames than hear it a moment longer.

She flings herself from her chair with a howl, fighting to be free, and she is blind, desperate, struggling. She knocks the table, hears something fall, and there is shouting, the clamour of voices, Mrs Weston's and Cecilia's, and Odette stumbles until she hits a wall, hands grasping in the dark for the doorknob. She has to get out – she has to get out.

Behind her comes a flare of brightness as Mrs Weston lights an oil lamp, but Odette has found the door and is stumbling into the corridor, half falling down the stairs, cold fingers chasing at her throat.

The Summer

August 1898, Herne House, Suffolk

That I might drink, and leave the world unseen,
And with thee fade away into the forest dim:
Fade far away, dissolve, and quite forget
What thou among the leaves hast never known,
The weariness, the fever, and the fret

'Ode to a Nightingale', John Keats

1

Odette

ODETTE LETS HERSELF INTO the studio.

A long cane chair is positioned so that Lydia can look out across the grounds. It is piled with cushions and rugs, despite the sultry summer heat that lingers. Lydia is leaning back, book open in her hands, but she looks over the top of the pages to the *Elaine* canvas that still dominates the room. Odette and Cecilia have sat several more times, but the painting is not yet finished.

'Mama?' Odette comes slowly into the room, waiting for her mother to register her presence.

Lydia comes back to herself, vacant face slowly warming. 'Darling.'

Illness has stripped the flesh from her bones; her cheeks are hollowed, the lines of her collarbones clear where her house dress falls loose at the throat. Of all the changes, it is this one that has upset Odette the most: her mother's body, almost as familiar as her own, is suddenly that of a stranger.

Odette pours fresh water into the glass at Lydia's side, gathers the untouched lunch things onto the tray and leaves it by the door for the maid to collect.

Lydia has always been temperamental – the kind of thing called nerves or hysteria, *women's trouble*, easily dismissed. But now she is truly, dangerously ill.

She is so used to her mother being fragile, unreliable, she thought she was inured to it.

She finds she was wrong.

There is always something left to lose.

She comes to sit on the floor at Lydia's feet, her customary place once she became too big to sit on her lap, and she rests her back against Lydia's leg. Her dress smells of cedar from the mothballs in her clothespress, and the sharp note of turpentine.

It has been a month since her mother fell so gravely ill, a month since Claudine arrived. The summer has been given over to doctor's visits, the airing of sickrooms, tinctures and delicate broths, the sound of vomiting, the smell of blood. Cecilia and Penelope stay on at Herne House, though Leo comes back and forth when work can spare him.

Claudine has martialled it all. At some unseen point Odette cannot identify, Herne House became Claudine's domain. Directing Lydia's care, the running of the house – she has become necessary. It almost seems too neat, her place solidified with such readiness. It is as disorienting as the change in her mother. The year is rushing by too quickly, the turn of the seasons, the day of her departure to Cambridge drawing closer – though how can she even think of leaving for university with her mother so gravely ill? – and she cannot find a firm grasp on anything.

At times, Lydia rallies, at others, slumps again; across it all there is a slow, sloping descent towards – towards something that no one wants to name.

It is a constant push and pull. Every moment with Lydia is unbearable, as though Odette is being swallowed up, but each one apart feels like a betrayal. She cannot know how much more time she will have with her mother, whether this illness will pass like a storm or drown them all, and the fear of it drives her back to her mother's side time and time again.

Lydia runs her fingers through Odette's hair, which Odette has left loose intentionally, then begins to pull it into a French plait.

'Do you mind awfully having a mother who is ill?' she asks.

'Of course not. You do not want to be ill.'

Lydia does not reply for a while. There is only the soft carding of her fingers through Odette's hair.

'I have always been weaker than others, even at your age. No one ever made any allowance for it. They couldn't understand that I had a fragile constitution, and they forced me to keep up with them all, when it was quite beyond me. I suppose it is no surprise I would find myself enduring an even greater suffering.'

'Is the medicine helping?' asks Odette.

'A little.'

There has been a course of treatment prescribed; the doctor is due back in a few days to assess its efficacy.

'You will write to me about Cambridge, if you have time?' asks Lydia.

'I will. And you'll visit me,' says Odette.

She must paint the fantasy of it: the future when Lydia is well again.

Lydia smiles faintly but does not reply.

'I suppose I ought to begin packing before long, though I do not like to go.'

'You must go. It is such a balm to me to see you excited.'

They do not talk of the money and the exhibition anymore. Odette cannot bring herself to ask. She wants the money, but she wants her mother restored to health more, so she must leave it alone. Of course it was never going to happen.

Lydia is fading again, so Odette takes up the copy of *Emma* on the table and reads to her, as she has done all summer. Lydia plaits, and Odette reads, and like this, perhaps it is possible, pleasant even, to be together.

At the end of the chapter, Odette closes the book. 'We can cancel my birthday party tomorrow,' she says. 'I do not want to be with anyone but family.'

Lydia ties off the plait, lets it run down her back. Odette turns around so Lydia can admire her work.

'You must not let me ruin things,' says Lydia.

Before Odette can reply, there is a knock at the door.

When she opens it, she is surprised to see Mr King on the threshold.

'My apologies, I did not realise I was interrupting.' He smiles, and it seems entirely genuine and open. 'Miss Hutton invited me up for the party, and I thought I would pay my respects – but I see perhaps you were not told.'

Odette schools herself into pleasantries. 'It is our pleasure, Mr King.'

'I hoped I might be bold enough to ask for a private viewing of your work, Mrs Fairfax-Waugh, as an ardent admirer – but I can come back later.'

Lydia rises from the long cane chair, fingers worrying at the trailing edge of her shawl. 'Mr King. It is good to see you again.'

'Please, call me Charles.' His eyes alight on the *Elaine* canvas. He gives it his careful attention, with true admiration as much as dealer's eyes. 'Most magnificent. Eddie says you have not done a show for a number of years?'

'No, I have been working in private.'

'I am sure the public would be greatly interested to see what marvels you have been conjuring. Miss Hutton mentioned you had been considering it, before your recent illness.' Mr King pauses, looks around at the other works, assessing. 'I hear you are interested in selling as well as showing?'

Lydia's eyes dart towards Odette, a certain trembling of her top lip. In this precise moment, Odette feels attuned to her, like a delicately calibrated scientific instrument. Lydia is balanced like a spinning coin, poised just so on a fine edge: now it slows, lurching to each side; now it begins to fall.

It is selfish of her. Odette looks away.

'Yes, why not?' Lydia's tone is artificially breezy, and Odette wonders if Mr King can tell. 'There are so many canvases cluttering the place up that I would far rather they go to better homes.'

It is childish and simple, but all Odette can think is: her mother *does* love her.

'The Jermyn Street Gallery would be delighted to accommodate you – if I don't presume too much?'

There is no knock this time when the door opens; Claudine enters with the medication the doctor has prescribed to dose

Lydia. There is a downturn to her mouth, a brusqueness to her movements that reveals her irritation with her task. She wears an expensive lavender house dress and silk slippers, her hair pinned up with careless elegance. It is still strange to see her in the house, so much her sister's overexposed copy, too tall, too prepossessed, too *healthy*. Odette has always been taller, stronger than her mother, and she wonders, with a jolt, if she more resembles Claudine than Lydia.

'Oh, Mr King. I see you have found our patient.'

Odette tries to slide into the background. It is a delicate moment, and she does not wish to unbalance things – or to draw Claudine's attention. Odette finds herself cringing away each time her aunt rounds a corner, a spike of panic catching her in the throat. She is ashamed of herself – and confused. She must try harder to anticipate Claudine's moods. Odette has had enough practice moulding herself around her own mother; it should not be beyond her to distil whatever it is Claudine wants of her and provide it.

'Odette, have some tea sent in for our guest.'

She does as she is told, and Claudine follows her out.

'You are overtiring your mother,' she says. 'It is selfish of you to demand so much of her time.'

At once, Odette's cheeks flush. 'I'm not – that is to say, I only wanted to keep her company.'

'She is always tired after lunch – something you would know if you tried a little harder to be a member of this household.'

'I'm sorry,' she says, because she does not know what else to say. She does not know if what Claudine says is true. Is her mother more tired after lunch? Does Claudine know more about Lydia than she does?

'We would all appreciate it if you gave others a little more consideration. You may gad about with Cecilia, or you may take your mother's care seriously – you cannot expect to do both.'

Claudine goes back into the studio, leaving Odette hot with outrage. How has her aunt so swiftly touched upon something so utterly untrue? What does Claudine know of *duty* to Lydia? How dare she accuse her of abandoning her mother?

Odette cannot bear to stay trapped with Lydia – but if she goes, she does not know what will become of her.

2

Cecilia

'WHAT HO, MOTHER – YOU look like half of Kew Gardens,' says Leo as he saunters into Cecilia's room. The whole household has been in gloom since Lydia's abrupt illness, but Leo alone seems immune.

Penelope laughs and swats Leo on the arm, scoldingly.

'You honour us with your presence,' she says. 'Can the partners spare you for so long?' She has come to rifle through Cecilia's jewellery for something that suits the pale ivory evening dress she has chosen. A series of necklaces are laid out for her inspection.

'Oh, I should think so. Half of them have taken off to Mont Blanc to attempt a climb and the other half have gone to Monte Carlo to take the waters – or rather to have half their wallets taken from *them*, so I shan't be missed at all.'

Penelope fixes a bracelet around her wrist and looks Leo up and down. 'You are looking quite fine, I must say. They keep you sharp on the London fashions?'

Cecilia knows that Leo is restraining himself from rolling his eyes. Instead, he leans on the dresser and lights a cigarette. 'We've much more important things to be doing than worrying about *fashion*, Mother. That's yours and Cecilia's domain.'

'Hardly Cecilia's,' says Penelope, eyeing the stained hem of Cecilia's skirt. 'University girls don't go in for that sort of thing, apparently.'

Cecilia tucks away the soiled patch. 'I don't think there's any rule in the college handbook that says we can't take an interest in dressing well. I suppose it is simply that the women worry they will not be taken seriously if they come to lectures dressed as finely as they might wish to.'

Leo snorts. 'Tell me, are blue stockings evening wear or only for casual use?'

Cecilia scowls. 'I am not a bluestocking.'

'So, why *do* you want to go to Oxford? Isn't it a bit much? I thought there were correspondence courses and lectures for ladies in London.'

Leo went to Durham and feels the slight keenly. He told her once that it was far easier for her to study at Oxford than it would be for him, because of all the allowances they made for girls.

'Somerville suits me, and I believe I will be happy there. Besides, why shouldn't I go?'

'I suppose I just don't know what it's all *for*,' he says. 'You can't take a degree – you're hardly going to get a *job* after, so why bother?'

There are more reasons than she can count, but none that Leo or her mother would understand. In the midst of Lydia's illness, university has been the bright star on the horizon, the moment when the world will be set back on its proper track. Odette, who is hazy and distracted, Odette, who cannot leave her mother's side, will be given respite. They can take the first step into the life they have planned for themselves.

That is only for her to think about. She must have some private things, some places in her mind where her mother is never allowed – otherwise she will become so filled with hatred and anger she could take a letter opener and stab them all.

Cecilia smiles sweetly. 'Would you be happier if I went to a finishing school?'

'Lord no, what a waste of money – no school could finish you up to a decent standard.' Leo laughs, and Cecilia lobs a hairbrush at him.

'Stop it at once,' snaps Penelope. 'You are both adults; do not replicate the schoolroom for want of anything else to do. Leo, go downstairs and be good company. Cecilia, put something clean on – you embarrass yourself. Now, don't protest – you must come down and occupy Odette so that she doesn't sulk about like a dark cloud. And do not exchange those glances that you think the rest of us can't see. It is quite trying.'

'Yes, Mother.'

Penelope appropriates a necklace in gold and the bracelet still on her arm, and returns to her room.

Cecilia considers the clothes in her wardrobe churlishly: all picked by Penelope, all entirely fine and proper. She would rather go naked than wear them.

No, she will not go downstairs yet.

Whenever Odette is with Lydia or otherwise indisposed, and Cecilia finds herself untethered, she slips again into the walls and makes her mouse-like way between morning room and scullery, attic and bedroom, tracking each of the occupants of the house, picking up each discarded line of conversation and unguarded look.

It pleases her to have some small thing for herself, a secret to carry around like something to nurture.

Everyone in Herne House has their secrets.

Claudine most of all.

At school, they did not call Cecilia 'Mouse'. They called her 'Rat'. Always squirming and scurrying and putting her twitching nose into unwelcome places – so the girls would tell her as they held her down and scrubbed her delicate skin with a nail brush or poured ice water down the back of her neck. They would never dare do the same to Odette; they only called her cold and haughty behind her back and ignored her when she was present. Cecilia didn't care. She and Odette only ever needed each other.

For Odette's birthday, Cecilia has bought her a fine volume of John Donne's *Holy Sonnets*, bound in green leather and inscribed with a coded message of love. It does not feel like enough. She wants to give Odette something truly special, to take her to the top of a mountain and shout about her love or to swim an ocean for her. It never feels like enough.

Claudine must not ruin it.

Cecilia has seen no more strangeness in Herne House, beyond the strangeness that Lydia's illness and Claudine's rise brings – and perhaps that is strange enough. But of the blackmail, the secret her mother harbours – nothing.

It worries her, like a snake in the long grass. It does not move while she stays still, but if she were to act, she fears it would strike.

So, to her mousing.

In the kitchen, the cook is scolding a kitchen maid over blunt knives. In the study, George stretches his back at the desk. Several guest rooms are occupied, and in the morning room, a game of bridge is being fought over. Mr King pours the drinks, the dark curl of hair hanging across his forehead again. Cecilia does not want to look at him. Does not want to remember.

Lydia's studio has no easy spyhole. That will be where Odette is, with her mother.

The closest she can get is a view of the door.

At which she finds Penelope listening.

It is naive, perhaps, that her first instinct is to reveal herself.

'Mother, what are you doing?'

Penelope startles, blushes. 'What are you talking about? I'm not doing anything.'

The truth strikes Cecilia like a bolt: she is spying. What need would Penelope have to spy on her friend? Only if, for example, she had been instructed to by someone who was controlling her.

This is what Claudine has asked her mother to do, in exchange for the keeping of her secret.

Turn traitor, sell out her oldest friend.

And her mother has done it.

Penelope lets anger carry her through. 'Don't sneak up on people; it is dreadfully rude. And did I not tell you to get changed? Be off with you, at once.'

Cecilia lets herself be chivvied upstairs. There is no point arguing with her mother.

It is time she finds an ally of her own. She cannot burden Odette with this, not now, not with Lydia the way she is.

Leo is smoking in his room, looking down through the window at the Herne House crowd. The three of them spent far too long as children around Uncle George's friends to ever truly walk amongst them as adults, but Cecilia knows Leo will not admit that. The few years he has on Odette and Cecilia is his prize to lord over them.

She hovers at the door, reaching the limit of her bravery.

How is she to do this? She trusts Leo in one way – but not in others – and it is so difficult to know where she will stand with him on this matter.

But who else is there? She must take this risk.

Leo peers at her, frowning. 'You're looking quite peaky. You're not going to be ill like Lydia, are you?'

'No.'

'Good, there's only so many invalids one house can tolerate.'

Her hands are slick with sweat, and she rubs them on her skirt. She does not know if she is brave enough to do what she means to.

'Leo, can I tell you something? You must promise not to tell anyone else.'

His expression falls, a rare moment of seriousness. 'What's wrong? Has someone done something to you?' His fingers flex, as though preparing to reach for some throat.

She blushes with the expected pleasure of the attention. She is right to trust Leo. He is her brother, and that must count for something.

'It's not me, it's—' She stumbles over the words. 'It's Mother.'

At once his demeanour changes. 'I'm not weighing in on some disagreement. I know she's a frightful menace, but you will simply have to find a way to rub along together.'

'No, Leo, listen to me.' She comes inside and shuts the door behind her. 'It's about Claudine. I overheard something of a row between them when she first arrived.'

'Been spying again, Mousy?'

Cecilia wrinkles her nose in annoyance, then stops at the thought of the image it conjures.

'You're so nosy, Mousy. No one is going to like you at Oxford if you keep it up.' Leo stubs out his cigarette and begins to change his collar.

Always that name. It shouldn't upset her anymore, and yet it does, and of course that is why Leo uses it. She has never found a way to wound him so neatly in return. Would he like her better if she could?

'I know I shouldn't eavesdrop, but Claudine is *blackmailing* Mother, I am sure of it. There is some sort of secret, about Mother. Claudine had sent her something that looked like an official document, but Mother tore it up – I found a few scraps with Mother's name on, and a few letters – I didn't understand it at all, but I've never seen Mother look like that. It frightened me.'

Leo hesitates, turning the freshly starched collar in his hands. 'You're quite serious about this?'

'I am.'

'Surely it is some sort of misunderstanding. If you only hear half a conversation, you're sure to invent a dozen mysteries to make sense of it.'

'I heard it all, Leo. And just now I found Mother spying on Lydia and Odette – I think that must be what Claudine is using her for. I hoped it was all a fuss over nothing, like you said, but – but I don't think it is.'

'You haven't spoken to Mother about it?'

Cecilia does not dignify this with an answer.

'Yes, I suppose that would be impossible. Why are you telling me?'

'I thought you might help.'

'By doing what, precisely? Having it out with them?'

'No – don't say anything to anyone. But this document she sent Mother. There must be something in it.'

'What do you want me to do, go hunting through every official document in London – Lord, the whole country? It could be anything.'

'I know that. But you are far cleverer than me – surely you must have some idea where to begin. It is a secret about our family, about Mother in particular. In the row, Claudine said Lydia had told her about it so that must make it a secret from when she was still in the country. Doesn't that narrow it down?'

The flattery mollifies him. 'And then what?' he asks. 'What do you want to do with the information, if I find it?'

'I don't know if we need to do anything with it, but at least we won't be caught unawares.'

Cecilia is determined to know what it is Claudine holds over them. The truth is that she is frightened of her. Frightened of the way Claudine behaves towards Odette. Of the way she has taken over Herne House.

'I confess I cannot resist a tantalising mystery. Though it is quite hopeless a task – you know that?'

'So you'll help?' says Cecilia eagerly.

'Yes, all right. But I can't promise I'll find anything. It's less the proverbial haystack I'm looking in than half the fields in England.'

Cecilia throws her arms around her brother in honest relief. 'Thank you.'

'Steady on.' Leo removes her arms, but he is smiling. 'Don't get so girly about it all.'

She wonders if she is laying it on too thick, but Leo doesn't seem to notice, fixing his collar in place with its studs and whistling a tune off-key.

There. That is something. Whatever it is Claudine plans, Cecilia will have some insurance against it.

3

Odette

It is Odette's nineteenth birthday, and she spends it in much the same way as she has for more years than she can count.

Herne House is busy about its own work, as on any day. George entertains his circle, the servants go to their work, mayflies cloud above the standing water, and the wind moves through the willow trees and the peonies. Cecilia wakes her early with kisses pressed across her face and whispers in her ear of a surprise later. The perfect line of Cecilia's throat, the dip of her clavicle, tempts Odette to linger in bed, and she lets her finger drift over the curve of Cecilia's shoulder, the swell of her breast below thin linen and the crest of her nipple. There will be time for that, later.

Then she is summoned to her mother's studio.

Lydia is already up and busy when Odette comes in. She has a trailing shawl flung about her shoulders and before her is a mess of half-used tubes of paint, brushes, pencils, caked palettes, all spread about a fresh canvas. The *Elaine* painting is gone from centre stage, leant up against a wall with its back to the room. Lydia is ragged around the edges, the colour too flushed in her cheeks.

'Should you not be resting?'

'Good morning, my angel.' Lydia stops and surveys Odette. 'And what an angel you are. You look so much better with a bit of weight on you.'

Odette ignores the flush of shame. 'Does this mean you feel well today?'

'Well? Well? Who amongst us is well?' She pulls open another drawer in the index card cabinet where the paints are stored, to reveal a scatter of different peach tones. 'I feel as though someone is driving knives through my stomach and has let all the air out of my head, but you know, they give me very good medicine.' She lifts her skirt up to use as a basket to carry the paints over to her easel.

Odette picks through the mess spread about the floor.

There is a present waiting on the stool, wrapped beautifully in marbled paper and tied up with ribbons.

'Is this for me?'

Lydia diminishes a little. 'Oh. Yes. You may not like it, and you must say at once if you don't; it is only a trifle and really very unimportant. Happy birthday.'

Delicately, Odette unwraps the object that is unmistakably a book.

It is a copy of *Persuasion* – a first edition, she sees when she turns to the title page, in a brown leather binding with a maroon and black-banded spine. The pages are lightly speckled and the edges soft where they have been clipped and turned countless times.

Her mother watches her hopefully.

'It is wonderful,' says Odette.

And it is.

'You like it?'

'Very much.'

'I thought you might find Anne's story a comfort.'

Odette's smile is fixed. 'What do you mean by that?'

'It is her best work, I think,' says Lydia, as though Odette has not spoken. 'Her most mature.'

'Thank you.'

'Now. Come here.' She gestures for Odette to stand in front of the canvas, as though she is to sit for another painting. 'I have an idea. It's quite, quite brilliant. It will simply *make* the show. I cannot imagine making any work public without it.'

Odette's breath catches. 'Then it is settled? You will show at the Jermyn Street Gallery with Mr King and sell the paintings?'

Again, Lydia continues, disregarding her. 'Mr King said it is a busy market and we must find a way to draw attention – something that will get the press interested. Publicity, he called it. And I have just the thing.'

'What is it? Shall I fetch Cecilia and Leo?'

'Oh no, this one is quite special. I want only you.'

That warm flush of pleasure. What it is to be wanted. 'Of course, Mama. I'll sit for anything you want.'

Lydia takes up a pencil and begins to consider angles, shapes. 'Help me lift this.'

Her mother indicates a small square trellis that is interwoven with cloth flowers. Odette remembers it from a work of *Tristan and Iseult* that she and Cecilia sat for last year, and from *La Belle Dame sans Merci* that Cecilia and Leo modelled the year before. The sittings would go on so long, the three of them came up with games to play, The Minister's Cat or I Spy: silly, childish parlour games. One year, Leo had insisted that the minister's cat was a frabjous cat, and argued that as it had been published in a poem, that made it a real word. The resulting argument had derailed Lydia's work and they had been banned from any mention of Lewis Carroll for the rest of the summer.

It was a beautiful time. They had so many beautiful times.

It cannot be possible that this is the last summer they will spend like this.

Together, they position the trellis where Lydia wants it, and Odette waits in anticipation. It is so rare that Lydia asks her to model alone. She would sketch her often as a child, while Odette was reading or concentrating on her needlework, but her paintings are all grand pieces with multiple characters.

'Strip down,' Lydia orders.

'To my shift?'

'No, all of it.'

'You mean—'

'Yes, all of it off.'

Odette stands stock still, suddenly unsure what to do with any of her limbs. She feels burningly hot. 'Do I have to? Can't I just leave my shift on, and you make it up?'

'Make it up? Do you know how hard we had to fight as women artists to draw from life? This is about craft and skill and expression. How can we ever be taken seriously as artists if we do not do as all the greats do and study the human form?'

Odette wraps her arms around her chest. 'I suppose. Maybe we could do it another time?' It is all unreal. She cannot think. Her mind is a great empty white space, like some Arctic waste.

'Don't be prudish. It's not anything I haven't seen before; I looked after you as a baby, or have you forgotten I am your mother?'

Odette stares at her. There is a frantic light about Lydia's face that she had thought was excitement, pleasure – now, with the gaunt hollows of her cheeks so pronounced and the sheen of sweat across her ashen forehead, Odette is struck again by the horror of her mother's illness.

She is not well. She is badly ill.

Now may be all they have.

She cannot bear to disappoint her mother.

Odette unbuttons her shirtwaist and unfastens her skirt, folding them to place them on a chair. With her back to Lydia, she takes off her petticoat, loosens her corset, removes her stockings. And then her shift.

She is naked, and the air is colder than she thought. The studio is such a big place, high ceilinged and all glass and empty air.

Lydia gives her instructions on where and how to stand, and she does so, acutely aware of her breasts and her stomach and her hips. She is on display. Her body will be displayed in a painting. Perhaps there will be mezzotints or prints made. Perhaps the show will be a wild success and half of London will go. She thinks, wildly, of asking her mother to paint a different face. But speaking is impossible. She is only a collection of parts.

She is gone.

*

The birthday party brings all the usual crowd to the dining room that evening: Mr King, of course, and Eddie Rutherford, and the simpering Mr Wrexham, and a new libretto writer of whom her father considers himself patron, the earl of somewhere Odette can never remember, an old school friend of her father's, who is an amateur philosopher, and many countless others who come teeming in when the gong is struck. Lydia is swaying a little from a glass or two of wine too many, playing the hostess well.

The meal is not to Odette's taste at all: far too fussy and formal, complicated dishes that take a long time and taste of little. *Fricandeau de veau à la Jardinière* and *capon à la Financière.* It smacks of Claudine's orders to the kitchen, and Odette swallows down any disappointment that no one who knows her better took charge. Cecilia catches her eye and gives her a commiserating look. A few gifts are presented – a new pen, a silk square, a delicate bottle of scent – while beneath the table, Cecilia keeps her hand on Odette's thigh. Her father presents her with an academic diary for her first year at Cambridge and she strokes the soft leather of its cover with a bloom of hope. Her father *does* think of her.

Then, the real entertainment starts.

The weather is still fine, so the party moves to the garden, and a few scratch recitals are given as more wine is passed around. Penelope makes a show of fanning herself, insisting she could not possibly be called on to recite, having been retired for so many years, but sure enough, a moment later, she is working her way through a soliloquy from *As You Like It.* Leo joins his light tenor voice with another guest's for a duet of a music hall number about Maria Marten, murdered by her lover in the famous Red Barn. George eschews the limelight, watching his household, Odette thinks with pleasure, but she realises perhaps she does not understand him as well as she believed. What *does* he want with all these hangers-on? Is he content with his talented wife, or does he feel overshadowed? It is strange, she felt so sure he thought as she thought, but it seems she has got everything round the wrong way.

Odette stays as close to Cecilia as she can risk, legs pressed together where they sit on a blanket, hands carefully apart. Even Claudine seems to be making something of the evening, holding court with a rotating cast of admirers to whom she dispenses bon mots and witticisms, as though she is mistress of the house and not her sister.

Abruptly, Odette notices that Lydia is not here.

'Where's my mother?' she asks Cecilia, peering around. 'Have you seen her?'

Panic thrums in Odette's chest, and she is struck by the image of her mother collapsing, red blood splattering across her shoes.

But then Lydia arrives in a burst of colour, timed, somehow, to a flare in the music as she steps through the French windows.

'Darlings. How dare you have fun without me.'

She is sly, tipsy, posing against the doorframe as though she is Sarah Bernhardt in a photograph card. Behind her are several boxes of fabric and props that she has dragged from the studio.

'I think we can make a few good scenes together, don't you?'

There is something like a cheer, and wine is pressed into Lydia's hands, and she is ushered into the circle, the boxes pulled after her and outfits handed out.

Odette blanches at the memory of this morning. It strikes her now that anyone who steps into the studio will see it, see *her*. When Claudine goes with Lydia's next dose, there Odette will be. Exposed.

Tonight, Lydia is brilliant.

Quick, creative, light, charming.

Odette has seen this rarely – too rarely. Like a sun that barely breaks through thick cloud, it will not last. It is easier for Lydia to do this if Odette fades into the background, she has learnt – and sometimes, it makes Odette wonder if she was the cloud that blotted out the light from her mother. What was it like before Lydia was a mother? Perhaps it was better.

The first tableau vivant is a motley collection of scoundrels as the Pirates of Penzance, which quickly descends into an abysmal rendition of 'I Am the Very Model of a Modern Major-General'. Odette and Cecilia are dragged in to play the daughters, and then soon enough, the scene is changed again, and now they are Byron, Percy and Mary Shelley, Doctor Polidori, all gathered around the fireplace, telling stories in a Swiss thunderstorm.

Then, almost inevitably, comes the tableau of Shelley's pyre on that lonely Italian beach. Odette has a mezzotint of the Fournier painting above her writing desk.

'Someone be Trelawny and retrieve the heart,' cries Eddie. 'Here, Odette – you be Mary, and prepare to receive it.'

The new tableau is set, and Odette is handed a windfall apple in place of her lover's heart.

'Love surpasses death,' says Lydia. 'She kept his heart with her for the rest of her life.'

Claudine laughs. 'Are you sure it was a token of love? It might have been proof he was dead.'

There is general protest and amusement at her statement, and quickly, it is lost.

But Odette is watching her mother's face all the while.

And Lydia looks frightened.

The tableau changes, then changes again, and after a moment, Lydia regains herself.

Odette's father sits to one side on a folding chair, enigmatic and quiet, speaking with one or two people who drift to his side, resting his chin on his hand with an air of mystery. He watches her mother, and now and again, she directs her performance to him, but his eyes slide away each time she tries. Her mother is hard to love, Odette understands this. She must have been a different woman when he chose to marry her, the one who existed before Odette arrived and changed everything.

When Lydia does begin to flag, it is with a healthy colour in her cheeks, and Odette allows herself to feel hope. Lydia will get better. If she was truly sick, she would not exert herself like this, surely?

People are ill all the time, and they recover.

Odette cannot conceive of a world in which her mother will not get better.

The party winds down, and the guests make their way to bed. Odette waits where Cecilia has instructed her to, in another of her hiding places, and when the house is quiet, save for the sound of the servants, Cecilia appears.

'Are you ready for your surprise?'

She leads her up through the hidden passages until they reach the attic, dim and dusty and hot under the pitched roof. The place has been transformed. Once forgotten bookshelves have been righted and filled with an assortment of volumes. A cloth has been put across a table with a vase of flowers, chairs set out as though waiting for someone to sit down to tea. A bed has been made up from blankets and pillows, and Cecilia pulls her down into it at once.

'My gift to you is one night of actual, absolute privacy,' she says. 'One night alone together, just as we will be in our little flat in Bloomsbury.'

Odette's smile widens. 'You are quite mad.' She looks around and sees it: Cecilia's vision, the home they might one day share.

'I am not mad at all. Lydia has spoken to Mr King. Surely it is done.'

Odette squeezes her hand. 'Yes. I suppose so.'

Cecilia rummages in the blankets and pulls out two books. 'These are your actual presents.'

'This is too much.'

'Don't complain; just say thank you.'

'Thank you.'

Each is wrapped in cloth, and Odette removes it to reveal an edition of John Donne. She turns it over, unsure.

'Don't you like it?' asks Cecilia. 'I thought it was fitting.'

It is not that she dislikes the gifts, only that they are too close an echo of that morning.

'I'll take them back.'

'No.' Odette speaks reflexively. 'I want them. It was only – nothing. It doesn't matter.'

She leans over to kiss Cecilia softly. 'Thank you.'

Cecilia tries to draw her into another kiss, but Odette cannot, not now, not after—

'I'm sorry.'

'Don't apologise.' Instead, Cecilia brings her down to lie at her side, chaste and chivalrous. 'I love you like this, too.'

Odette closes her eyes. She will not cry. *Don't leave me*, she wants to say, but it feels unfair. No one can promise to stay forever. No one can promise to never change.

Dying is the only unbreakable promise.

The end is all there is.

4

Odette

ODETTE DREAMS ABOUT THE water rising up the sides of the house from the moat, stagnant and still and silent, swallowing it all up – worse than a tide she cannot stem; a slow, inexorable sinking.

Her mother is sinking first. Odette swims down, reaching out her hand, but her mother's fingers always slip through. Then she has swum down too deep, and all is dark and cold, and there is no way back to the surface.

She wakes crying, and Cecilia rests her head in her lap and strokes her hair.

What to do with all this pain?

Nineteen. Money that will be hers alone. A place at university. A great love.

There is nothing wrong with her life. She should not feel melancholy or disturbed. She is lucky. Wouldn't everyone say so? Why can she not *feel* her luck?

They are due to return to London in a handful of days, if the doctor agrees that Lydia is well enough to travel. It is a delicate decision, George has explained to Odette. The travel will be disruptive to Lydia's health, but staying in the waterlogged house as the weather cools will be no better. Aunt Claudine is to accompany them.

There are plans to be made for her move to Cambridge: clothes to be packed, books to be bought, other essential items that she is sure she should be able to think of, but her head is too muffled. The future feels like a terrible thing, one that she would hold at bay at all costs, if she could.

*

She is walking in the gardens with Cecilia the morning after her birthday when her father comes to find her.

The weather is turning early for August, the brutal heat dying away as if chasing in the harvest. Herne House hunkers low amongst the trees, the stone and wood turning dull in the cooling light. The fields are full from dawn until nightfall with the sound of the drays pulling the new reaping and binding machines or the swish of scythes and bent-backed labourers. The cloud draws in, a silent threat.

'Come and sit with me,' her father says with a soft smile.

She is glad of it. Glad to be remembered by him. She thought that something between them had begun to drift, that her understanding of her place with him was wrong – but he is still here. First the diary, now this. He is still an anchor point to which she can fix herself.

They walk a little further, under the fruiting trees of the orchard, to a stone bench set in seclusion from the house.

'I wanted to speak to you,' her father says, gesturing at the bench beside him.

Her gladness turns at once. She sits, a rock in her stomach. 'It's Mother, isn't it?'

He frowns. 'No, the doctor will not come until tomorrow.'

'Then what?'

Her father fidgets like a schoolboy, and Odette realises that he is attempting to organise his expression into something authoritative. Not as he did the night Claudine caught Odette and Cecilia playing at Godiva; this is something real.

Odette stills, in confusion, then in apprehension. She does not speak.

'The way you have behaved towards Claudine is not acceptable, and I have been derelict in my duties as a father for not disciplining you sooner.'

The birdsong is too loud. That is all Odette can think. Why is the birdsong so loud?

Maybe she can get up and start walking and walking and walking and travel far enough away that this isn't happening.

'I don't understand,' she says quietly.

'She went to a great deal of effort to arrange a special dinner for your birthday, and you gave her no thanks at all. In fact, she told me she saw you making childish faces at Cecilia, pretending you didn't like it.'

'I – I did say thank you. I'm sure I did.'

She is a good daughter because she is discreet. Pleasant. She needs nothing, no guidance, no scolding, no help. Her mother demands so much, there is no space for Odette to demand too, and she knows what a comfort it is to her father that she asks so little from him.

Some lurching gap opens beneath her. She has not smoothed things over. She has not made things easy. She has failed.

Oh God, here's the fear: will he stop loving her if she stops being easy?

'Claudine has taken so much responsibility off your shoulders since she arrived, and you have not shown gratitude for any of it. She has been caring for your mother and running the house on your behalf so that you may go off to university, and you act as if you thought yourself entitled to all of it.'

Odette thinks she might be sick. It would be odd to be sick here, in the garden, on her nice shoes. She barely ate breakfast – would there even be anything to throw up?

'But . . . but Mother is her sister. Why should she not look after her?'

George gives a short, mirthless smile. 'You have a sharp tongue, Odette, and you cut more people with it than you care to know.'

She is hot with shame. This is all wrong, but she cannot put her finger on what or where or how. Her tongue is fat and stupid in her mouth; she cannot work out how to say what it is she thinks, what it is that seems right, to defend herself. No, she does not like Claudine, and perhaps that is obvious, but if Claudine is to string her up for her offences, then should Odette not get her chance to list Claudine's own failings?

But she cannot find the right words.

'I am sorry.' Those words again. Is she? No, she is not, but she does not know how to fight, only how to roll over like a craven dog and bare her soft underbelly.

'There. You'll find a moment to say it to Claudine. I am sure she will understand.'

No, she won't. Odette knows that already.

She feels the ground shifting again, the lines redrawn – and she finds herself pushed out and out.

'Best behave yourself today; you know how women are.'

Her father pats her hand and leaves her in pieces.

5

Cecilia

CECILIA FINDS ODETTE DOWN in the meadows, watching the farmhands build bonfires.

She disappeared after speaking to her father, and Cecilia cannot shake the worry that has crept around her. Something is wrong, something she doesn't understand. Odette is slipping further and further into a world apart, and Cecilia would do anything she can to keep her.

Cecilia takes up position beside Odette, leaning on the fence that surrounds the field where the farmhands are stacking dry brush and hedge trimmings.

'Come. We have a few days more. I would see you happy.'

'Happy? I don't think that's what I'm made for.'

Cecilia tugs her elbow. '*Come*. Trust me.'

Odette relents and follows Cecilia into the open fields and towards the forest beyond.

This is the one thing Cecilia knows how to do: draw Odette out of herself, give her someone else to be, a private world of their own.

The sun is broad overhead, beating down in glory and gold. It is not a time for sad things – Cecilia will not have it so.

She sets off running through the meadow, past the bobbing heads of wildflowers and down, down, down, to the winding banks of the Stour. At a fairy ring amongst a stand of beech trees, Cecilia lays Odette down and heaps her with leaves, a slain King Arthur ready for Avalon. Cecilia gathers foxgloves and irises and sprays of meadowsweet to cover Odette where she lies, hands clasped at her breast over the hilt of a stick-as-sword. Kneeling at Odette's side, Cecilia speaks Sir Bedivere's words.

'*Whither shall I go? Where shall I hide my forehead and my eyes? For now I see the true old times are dead.*'

Odette sits up, brushing the petals from her face. 'No, don't say that. Nothing is dead. It is only changing.'

Cecilia leans back in the grass, her expression dropping. She does not want to talk about this. They will leave for university so soon, and the thought of it makes her quail.

'*The old order changeth, yielding place to new*,' she offers.

'Yes, more like that.'

They run again, right to the edge of the river, where the weight of the heat casts a shimmer across the water and dragonflies dart between the reeds. Odette stands on the bank, eyes caught on the glittering water.

'Here – I have an idea. Let me go into the water. I can be Shelley, and you can find my body washed up and rotting.'

Cecilia frowns. 'Let's not. Won't you sit down? I stashed some brandy around here somewhere.'

But Odette is wading into the water, up to her knees. 'It is not so fast-flowing. Here, I will lie face down in the shallows.'

Before Odette can suit action to word, Cecilia catches her elbow again and drags her away. '*And* I have strawberries. I don't want to get wet – it'll make my petticoats all itchy.'

They are silly protests, trifling things she fills the air with, smothering Odette's fire. It is as though Odette wants to push and push, to find the edge where someone will call her bluff, will see that she is not all right. But it is not Cecilia's attention she wants; this is not something she can give her. It is Lydia's she wants, George's, Claudine's even – for them all to come to their senses and see what they are doing to her.

Cecilia knows they will not. Their only path is to get out. Odette will never get what she wants from them, and if she cannot see that, Cecilia will make the path for them both.

Because without Odette, what life will there be for her? Her mother. Home. Four walls, a tea set, never saying what she thinks. Her own inadequacy. Her own failure.

There is a sense of a great, yawning empty space around her, ahead of her, her whole life blank and cold and hopeless. It is a life sentence, to be herself.

She finds the brandy and strawberries and sets Odette down with both.

'We'll write to each other all the time,' she says, as though dictating to the universe.

She pictures it now: a dowdy writing desk in a room at Somerville, pen in hand as she writes amidst the stacks of books and blotting paper and notes from lectures, looking out across emerald lawns, to tell stories of her adventures, and read Odette's in turn.

'And we'll be together every vac.'

Odette chews a strawberry, considering. 'Yes. I suppose so.'

Cecilia pulls a book from the basket and instructs Odette to lie down so she can read to her.

'*O what can ail thee, knight-at-arms, alone and palely loitering?*'

Odette throws a strawberry at her. 'You've done that one enough times. Something new.'

Cecilia throws the strawberry back, and it splatters on Odette's shirtwaist, so she unbuttons it and casts it off, red-stained and crumpled into the grass. Cecilia lets her eyes linger on the soft curve of Odette's breasts above her corset and the dip at the hollow of her throat.

She licks her lips and continues reading.

The first time she read to Odette, they had climbed out of the dorm windows onto the roof of their school, to smoke a handful of half-crushed cigarettes lifted from Leo's case and drink from a purloined bottle of port. Odette had complained before that Cecilia asked so many questions that she didn't get a chance to enjoy her smoke in peace, so this time Cecilia brought out a volume of Byron and gave Odette her favourite lines until she found herself reading the whole poem under the cold November stars, the two of them curled together for warmth in their winter coats and mufflers. What started as lips shyly coming together, sticky with stolen port, as though daring each other to be the first to blink, had become giddy, illicit, magic.

Cecilia puts down the book, draws Odette's hands from her face to kiss her, at first lightly, goading, until they move in more earnest passion. Cecilia is greedy for the feeling of Odette against her, for each touch of her fingers, each press of her hot, slick skin. It is always like this, her mouth between Odette's legs, trying to serve her. How can she serve her? What does she need? Cecilia feels like a solider with no captain to follow.

From somewhere over the water, the church bell tolls and Cecilia sits back, wiping her mouth clean. Odette lies flat and boneless, staring at the sky above as she regains a steady breath.

In this, at least, they still belong to each other.

6

Cecilia

CECILIA LOOKS AT HER TRUNK at the end of her bed and considers what it will look like in her room at Oxford. It is a mad thought. It is not much more than a month now until she will go, and it seems like a joke, a fabrication, as though she has made plans to visit the moon or breathe underwater.

The doctor is in with Aunt Lydia now, and Odette has spent the past half-hour pacing up and down Cecilia's room, snapping when Cecilia makes any comment on it. Lydia will be well; Cecilia knows it. It is not possible that something so awful could happen to Odette, not now. Lydia will recover like Hippolytus being restored by Asclepius.

There comes the sound of voices and footsteps from downstairs, and Odette is out of the room like a shot, hanging over the banisters to watch the doctor and George descend the stairs in close conversation. Odette is hesitant now to talk to her father – she has explained to Cecilia how she has been berated for her perceived slights against Claudine. It is unjust. Cecilia wishes there was something she could do to wish away Claudine from their lives, but she cannot.

'We had better speak downstairs,' George says to Odette.

Odette reaches one hand back for Cecilia.

'Yes, you too,' George adds, looking at Cecilia, then behind her. 'All of you. Claudine will stay with Lydia.'

Cecilia turns to see her mother peering from her doorway and Leo at the end of the hall.

George seems at first as though he will lead them to his study, but at the last moment he redirects them to the morning room. Odette and Cecilia sit together on a low couch, Penelope perches on a chair to the left with Leo stood behind her, smoking, and the doctor sits before them. George steps away, folding his hands behind his back and looking out at the meadows beyond the window.

Cecilia holds Odette's hand tightly.

This will be fine. It will be fine.

The doctor explains the situation as he understands it so far, the treatments he has offered and Lydia's response. He is a short, stocky man, with sandy hair thinning at the crown and large, blunt hands; but there is a softness around his eyes and mouth, and Cecilia can see why he must be well-respected in his field.

Then he comes to it.

'It is my professional opinion that Mrs Fairfax-Waugh is suffering from severe and extensive peptic ulcers throughout her digestive tract,' he says, as though speaking to them of the weather. 'They have not healed with rest, and now they are affecting her body's ability to take nourishment from her food. With her signs of fever, I fear they may have become infected. I can give no explicit prognosis, but I guard you all to make your peace and help Mrs Fairfax-Waugh face her passage from this life into the next with the grace and love of God.'

There is silence.

Penelope covers her mouth with her hand and lets out a small sob, genuine in its quietness. Leo puts his hand to her shoulder, though his own mouth trembles. Does he remember the news of their father's death, Cecilia wonders? George stays at the window.

Cecilia squeezes Odette's hand harder, looking at her out of the corner of her eye, but Odette seems hardly present.

Cecilia is aware of a great, deep howl lodged inside her that she cannot give voice to. It is not fair. Lydia is not her mother – her grief will be different – but, *God*, it is a wound ripped through the centre of her chest, and her very heart aches.

Eventually, George turns and dismisses the doctor with a handshake and a request for a full report to be sent to the physician in London.

George's shirt has come untucked and pokes out between his waistcoat and trousers; the dishevelled display disgusts Cecilia. Lydia is dying, and he cannot ensure his shirt is properly tucked in?

There is a catch in his voice. 'Lydia is sleeping now. I'll leave you to your business,' is all he manages before he turns and takes himself to his study.

To cry, Cecilia wonders – or not. She does not know if men cry or if it is a vulnerability they have wholly removed from themselves and allocated to women. How unfair on all involved. It would be inhuman to not let oneself cry, but she is not sure George allows himself to be human very often.

Penelope twists her fingers together. 'Well, we had best see about packing, girls. We shall take the train to London tomorrow, where the doctors will be far better. He was a very pleasant man – I will allow that – but surely a London doctor will know what to do. Don't think about it at all, Odette.' It is the first time Penelope has directed her words specifically at Odette. 'Don't give it any thought. We'll find a better doctor.'

Cecilia's mother hovers for a moment, as though coming near Odette will bring some of her misfortune upon herself, but then she seems to decide it is worth the risk and pats her arm before leaving.

Leo stops before Odette, eyes red.

'Rotten luck, old girl,' he says, helpless. Language fails him, and he turns away, leaving Odette and Cecilia on their own, hand in hand in the empty, lifeless shell of Herne House.

Odette still has not spoken.

Cecilia turns to her, to say something, God knows what – there is nothing she can possibly say – but Odette's face stops her short. It is the perfect picture of misery, Cecilia's own grief reflected back a thousandfold in her face: the world ending, the walls of the house crashing down, the earth rising up to bury them all.

Odette shakes her head. She cannot speak.

Cecilia trembles at the burden placed on her shoulders.

She cannot make this better.

She cannot make this right.

All she can do is bear witness and not look away.

They walk out of the house and across the meadows, over the wooden bridge that crosses the moat and past the sheep that like to die, past the orchard and down the track deep into the pastures with their boundaries of hazel and blackthorn, the leaning alder and ash trees. They sit together in the crook of an alder, and Cecilia holds Odette as the hurricane of her grief rips through her. There is nothing to be said. Cecilia only holds her, strokes her hair, offers a litany of soft noises, prayers, comforts.

When the evening turns frigid, she coaxes Odette back to the house, to suffer morsels from the cold tray of dinner that is brought up to her room. Cecilia reads to her until Odette falls asleep in her lap, and then she dozes upright, watching the thin summer night fall and lift too soon.

Odette wakes with the dawn, misery replaced by a sharpness behind her eyes. 'I have an idea for a play.'

Cecilia stifles a yawn. 'Are you sure? We could wait until later.' Until she is not ripe with grief, Cecilia means, but she knows this cannot be said.

'I want to do it now. Claudine prevented us from doing Godiva, but she will be occupied now. There is no one to spoil it.'

'You want to do Godiva again?'

'No, I have a better thought. Get up – come on.'

Cecilia follows her from the bed, drawing on her dressing gown and slippers, then down the hall and out of the house, along the path they took yesterday.

'Do you see the bonfires set in the bottom field?' asks Odette.

The dawn is fresh and new. A thin mist is cast over the ground that dissipates as they pass through. Flower heads droop under the weight of dew, and the birds announce the day to each other with urgency.

'Yes.'

'They will be perfect. They'll be tinder-dry after the summer we've had.'

'Perfect for what?'

Odette turns round, walking backwards. 'The tableau vivant from my birthday. I want to burn Shelley's pyre.'

When Cecilia hesitates, she continues.

'Please, Ces. I need to do something big.'

There is an intensity to her that Cecilia cannot cross. 'All right. I mean, I suppose it is going to burn anyway.'

'Good.' Odette squeezes her hand tighter and pulls her along.

In a divot in the landscape is the field where she found Odette yesterday; empty grazing land where a bonfire has been laid in a neat oblong, quite like a pyre. Cecilia did not look at it closely before, but now she can see why it took hold of Odette's imagination. The scene is no desolate Italian beach, beset by storms; they have no bloated, rotting body, but all the same, the picture creates itself.

'Damn,' says Odette. 'I should have brought a copy of *Lamia*. That was how Trelawny identified Shelley.'

'It will look well all the same.' There is a chill in the air, and Cecilia tucks her hands under her arms. 'How will we light it?'

Odette produces a book of matches from her pocket. 'Always come prepared.' She laughs, then moves round the bonfire, striking matches and tossing them in between the stacked branches.

Cecilia hurries after her. This is happening too fast. 'How will we play it?' she asks. 'Will you be Hunt or Byron? Or Trelawny?'

'I don't think you can trust anyone who would *choose* to be Byron,' says Odette, tossing in another match.

The fire has caught in the depths of the wood, smoke seeping out from within. Odette stops to assess her work.

Cecilia cannot read her face, and it is disconcerting. She did not ever think there would be a world in which Odette was a stranger to her.

'*Nothing of him that doth fade, but doth suffer a sea-change, into something rich and strange.*' Odette quotes the passage from *The Tempest* that is inscribed on Shelley's grave. She worries at the book of matches, ripping up the card and tossing it and the last of the matches into the rising flames. 'It is not complete.'

'We could strike poses?' suggests Cecilia. 'One of us could kneel like Mary Shelley in the painting?'

'No. It needs a body.'

Without warning, Odette flings herself towards the pyre and tries to climb the side, as though she intends to lie upon it and be immolated. With a shriek of horror, Cecilia throws herself after Odette, grabbing at her nightgown. The flames seem to have come to life at once, swallowing the base of the bonfire and gusting up through it in long licks of red and orange. The smoke burns Cecilia's eyes. The whole thing will go up in a moment – she knows it. This is madness, madness.

Knotting her hands in Odette's nightdress, she pulls her back, spins her round so that Cecilia stands between her and the flames. Heat rises up her back, startling and close.

Suddenly, Odette's horrified face is almost touching her own.

'Get down!' she cries, pushing her to the ground, rolling her over on the dew-wet grass – and then comes the slap of cold, as brackish water fills her nose. Odette has thrown her into the stream at the foot of the fields, quenching the flames that singed her own nightdress.

Coughing, they sit together in the shallow water.

'Don't ever do that again,' says Cecilia, when she can find the breath to speak.

If she were a different person she thinks she would slap Odette.

Instead, she clings to her. They wrap their arms around each other, press their bodies together and take some familiar animal reassurance from the feeling of hot skin and heartbeat.

'I'm sorry,' whispers Odette.

Cecilia shakes her head, beyond herself. 'Why would you do that?' She is crying, hot angry tears. 'I love you so much – why would you do that to the person I love?'

Here, Odette breaks. 'Because I don't know what else to *do*, Ces. What do I do? What do I do if she dies? What's the point of me? How do I live if she dies? I will be dead, too.'

She buries her face into Cecilia's shoulder and sobs again.

Odette's expression makes Cecilia more afraid than she knew she could be. There is some new, broken wildness in her. Odette has stepped through a door into a place where Cecilia does not know if she can reach her anymore.

As they walk back up to the house, shamefaced and shaking, the clouds darken and a squall of rain blows through. Behind them, the smoke from the bonfire slopes away, rain hissing as it meets the still burning fire.

It is the end of one world. The next one will meet them, whether they are ready or not.

Act Three

December 1898, Hampstead, London

I owe a longer allegiance to the dead than to the living

Antigone, Sophocles

1

Cecilia

'ODETTE, *ODETTE*.'

Cecilia scrambles down the pitch-dark steps, following the sound of Odette's feet, and bursts into the too-bright hallway of the medium's house. The front door is open, and Odette is just out of sight, skirts flashing down the winter London street.

She catches Odette halfway to Camden Road station and places a hand on her arm, half expecting to be shaken off.

'What happened?' asks Cecilia.

She is not sure herself what she thinks happened. The séance was a sick charade – she knew it would be. Penelope dallied in them once or twice when Cecilia was a child, and she can still remember the sickly smell of the medium's heavy violet perfume, the obvious trickery of the performance.

There was something uniquely sinister this time. It began with the same old tricks, but this medium seemed to have some particular skill at deception – perhaps a background in the theatre – and her sleights of hand frightened Cecilia. She is angry at herself for not stopping Odette from going through with it, and it has only ended in heartbreak and horror as she feared.

'I can't talk here,' says Odette. 'Not – in public.' Her hair is escaping its pins, and she is breathing too hard; they are drawing attention.

Cecilia nods, mouth tight, but loops their arms together, leads them into the station, buying two tickets so that they can go down to the platform and walk along to a quiet end. She sits on a bench, but Odette does not join her.

She does not pace, seemingly too fractured for even that much co-ordinated action. Instead, she flutters around, first holding onto a pole, then the back of the bench, then going right up to the edge of the platform and back again. As before, her gaze is always drawn back to someone Cecilia cannot see.

Cecilia does nothing, says nothing, hoping patience will go some measure towards reassurance.

Eventually, Odette stops before her. 'What did you experience?' she asks at last. 'You promised me your true and honest account.'

Cecilia's mouth twists – she has never been good at hiding her expression. A train rattles into the station, and she waits for the alighting passengers to thread their way to the exit before she speaks.

'I am not sure what to make of any of it. It was quite – strange.'

'Yes? What was strange?'

'All of it. You could have warned me.'

'If I warned you, would you have come?'

'No.' She pauses. 'I don't know.'

'You would have tried to persuade me not to go, at least, and I had to go because—'

Odette stares over Cecilia's shoulder, face distorted with grief. Cecilia reaches for her hand, but Odette does not react when she takes it. It is as though Odette has stepped through to another world and left Cecilia all alone.

'I understand,' Cecilia says quietly.

Finally, Odette looks at her, eyes shadowed and glinting. 'No. You do not.'

This again. Cecilia feels an unkind flare of frustration. Does Odette really think she is the only person to have experienced a grief so devastating? Perhaps she meant it when she told Odette she was taking out her pain on others. It is blunt, but perhaps it is true.

'They cannot—' She stops to choose her words. 'I do not believe they can reach your mother, if that is what you wanted to know.'

'That is not what I wanted.'

Cecilia's frustration boils over. 'Then what was it? Why did you leave like that? I am trying to help you, but you will never tell me what is going on. You leave me in the dark.'

'Answer me first,' urges Odette. 'What happened back there, for you? The truth – not what you think I want to hear.'

It is a low blow, a little too well observed, and Cecilia does her best not to crumple from it.

'Nothing. Nothing happened. We went to a dark room, they did a few tricks, then you gave such an awful cry and ran away, and I thought someone must have hurt you, and now you will not tell me what the matter is.' Cecilia pulls up short, a little breathless. 'There it is. My honest account.'

Odette does not speak.

For a long while, they stay in silence, trains rushing into the platform, disgorging passengers and swallowing them up again. The day is cold, and Cecilia shivers despite her gloves and coat.

'Then I have my answer,' says Odette. 'You cannot understand me. I am alone.'

Cecilia stands abruptly, unsure what to do with her anger. 'Only because you choose to be. I am right here, Odette. I am not dead. I love you. But that does not seem to matter to you anymore.'

Another train pulls in. Cecilia loses her nerve.

'I will see you at home.'

She turns quickly before Odette can speak, steps onto the train and closes herself into a compartment. A cloud of steam obscures the platform, and then they are moving, splitting, as far divided as they have ever been.

*

Penelope catches Cecilia as soon as she sets foot inside the Gate House. 'There you are. Come in here and help me with my wardrobe. There is so much that needs altering that I cannot possibly manage it myself. Of course there is no immediate question of leaving this house, but it is wise to be prepared. You would learn that if you were to become a wife. There are a few things that can be sold, just to be sensible of course . . .' Penelope trails off, chattering to herself, always smoothing, arranging, schooling the world to suit the story she must believe.

Cecilia is too jumbled up from the events of the morning to refuse, and she finds her arms full with a mound of dresses and skirts and blouses and jackets, all of which must be examined for wear, for style, for fashion, for what is unbecoming, what is passé. Penelope chatters through it, discussing

Leo's prestige at his firm, the shows she wants to see in town, the poem she thinks Mr Wrexham will write about her.

Once that is done, Cecilia is tasked with sorting through Penelope's writing desk, piles of correspondence, albums, diaries, pens, cards. Amongst them is a worn photograph album of red leather that Cecilia has not looked at in at least a year. It shows all their summers at Herne House. She opens the cover and leafs through the images that have become as familiar as Lydia's paintings: Odette and Cecilia in their school uniforms, lined up together at the front door; a sprawling party on the back lawn, George dressed up as Nelson and Leo a diminutive Wellington; George stood proudly by a shy Odette presenting a school prize book; Penelope and Lydia arm in arm in front of a wall overgrown with honeysuckle.

With a pang of regret, Cecilia wishes she had a photograph of Odette's nineteenth birthday to add to the collection. She should have documented those last moments before they were parted.

At the end of the album, the pictures become older, showing summers from her mother's youth, which have little interested her before. The only ones she has ever paid attention to are the ones of her father – the man who died before she was born. Her favourite is one of him leaning against the fireplace in the smoking room in Herne House, wearing a waistcoat that she can tell from the pattern must have been brightly coloured. It is only a little detail to hold onto, but it is to Cecilia as though she can conjure a whole man from one small trace.

'Did you never want to marry again?' she asks.

Penelope does not look up from the dressing table where she is sorting through her jewellery, but there is a sharpness to the set of her shoulders, a sadness in her voice. 'No. I loved once and lost it. When you know a love like that, you know there is no love after it.'

Cecilia thinks of Odette and knows that what her mother says is true. If she lost Odette, there would be nothing else left for her. It would be the end of her life.

On the opposite page is a picture of George and Lydia, looking extremely young. Lydia is sitting on George's lap, and George is kissing her cheek.

Cecilia looks again and stops.

No, it is not Lydia.

She would have thought it was before, when there was no reason to ever doubt it.

But now she has seen Claudine, she has observed the clear differences between the two women.

Claudine is sitting on George's lap.

Claudine is being kissed by George.

The previous engagement. The estrangement.

Claudine must have been engaged to George, until it was abruptly called off and she went abroad. After that, she was estranged from her sister.

Her sister Lydia, who married George.

Suddenly, Cecilia feels very cold and very frightened of Claudine.

Before Cecilia can lose her nerve, she speaks. 'Odette mentioned that a shopkeeper in town said Claudine used to be engaged. Years ago, before she went to Europe. Before she became estranged from Lydia.'

Her mother looks at her sharply. 'Yes. Well. It happens.'

Cecilia's heart is a painful pressure in her chest. 'She was engaged to George, wasn't she?'

Penelope changes in a breath, face distorting into a mask of fear and anger. 'Never say that again. You have no idea what you are talking about.'

'It's true, isn't it?'

'What happened in the past doesn't matter.'

'If it doesn't matter, why was it kept secret? What do you know about it?'

For a moment, Cecilia thinks her mother might throw the perfume vials across the room or smash the mirror on the table.

'Be quiet this instant,' she hisses. 'You overstep. You know nothing about what is going on, and believe me, my girl, you are better off that way. Do not trifle with Claudine – it will not serve you well, trust me. Ask fewer questions, and do what you're told.'

Cecilia's bravery is washed away in the face of her mother's fury. 'I'm sorry. I just wanted to know the truth.'

Penelope ignores her, pacing before the bed, then lighting upon a pin on the table. 'Your appearance is shabby, and I won't have it,' she declares. 'You run about like a child but play at being an adult, going off to university. You won't even pierce your ears. I am still your mother and what I decide is law. Silly modern notions.' She advances on Cecilia, who backs away.

'I'm sorry. I won't ask any more questions.'

'Keep still.'

'Mama – don't—'

Penelope has backed her against the bed.

'I don't want to change my body for fashion,' says Cecilia, choosing the words Odette used when they agreed they would be like the suffragettes and new women and spurn piercing.

Penelope laughs. 'You're a hypocrite, my girl. You wear a corset and shoes with a heel, curl your hair and pinch your cheeks red. You cannot opt out of living in the world, and the world will not let go of you so easily.'

'No – I don't want to,' says Cecilia, her eyes fixed on the pin in her mother's hand.

'Stay still. This will only hurt if you make a fuss about it.'

Penelope pushes her flat on the bed, puts a cork behind Cecilia's earlobe and pushes the pin through.

There is a pressure against her ear and then a tearing sensation, like paper ripping. Then the pain and shock hit her body. She is hot and cold at once, shaking and about to cry.

Penelope leans across her to the other side, repeats the action.

This time, Cecilia's body is braced for pain, and the needle is sharp enough that she feels as though her whole head is being stuck through with it.

Penelope pushes stud earrings through the holes and fixes them in place. 'There. Leave those in.'

She gets up and goes back to organising her jewellery, the anger seemingly expended from her body.

Cecilia lies flat on the bed, staring at the ceiling. She thinks she is crying. Her head throbs on both sides, like a pulsing noise too big to think around.

Penelope looks over at her and tuts. 'Stop crying – that was nothing. Sit up.'

Cecilia sits.

'Would it hurt you to look up from your books once or twice while you are at Oxford?' She takes in her daughter. 'There will be any number of young men around, and I am sure many of them will be in want of a wife.'

Cecilia says nothing.

'Of course, I do not encourage you to any indiscretion, but it is no crime to flutter your eyelashes at a boy or two. They are quite simple, really; they want to feel wanted. Smile, ask them questions and *listen* and don't talk about yourself too much, and you will find no trouble gathering suitors.'

'I suppose.'

'You think I don't understand that you have a different life planned to the one I lived, but you are wrong. Life is not the easy thing it seems at nineteen, and I would not see you drowned for want of learning how to swim. So put on a nice dress and, for God's sake, smile. Do you understand?'

Cecilia looks at the floor. 'Yes, Mother.'

2

Odette

ODETTE HAS NO MEMORY of how she has come to be on Waterloo Bridge. She is standing in the middle, carts and carriages rolling behind her. The reflected gas lamps shiver in the dark waves of the Thames, hiding the sewage and flotsam that lap against the embankment stones and grit-sand beaches.

Death has left on her only the beautiful.

Odette shudders at the image. Hood's suicide, *Owning her weakness, her evil behaviour.* Lydia never wanted to paint Hood's 'The Bridge of Sighs', no matter how much she was encouraged, calling the story of romantic suicide a cruelty forced on women by men. Odette first saw the Millais etching as a child, and the shrouded figure with her face so stricken with horror drove deep roots into her. The Watts painting, *Found Drowned*, seemed too peaceful when she came across it, too kind an end, as though those who had driven the woman to her death by malice or indifference could be acquitted of their guilt by imagining. Lydia hated it, so Odette did, too, listening earnestly as her mother explained that drowning was not so peaceful as people would tell you.

Only now does she wonder how Lydia might have known what drowning felt like.

Odette will not be brave enough to do it. She knows this. She can lean far over the stone balustrade and watch the rushing, muddy Thames pass beneath her and understands she is trapped.

Her mother stands a little way off on the other side of the bridge, obscured by passing vehicles, but Odette knows she is there, in the flash of white shroud and the glimpse of her pinched and yellowing face.

She will not come any closer, not yet. Odette knows this, too.

It is as though a veil has been ripped down between them and Lydia's mind is her mind. They never were two different people, only sound and echo.

It would be easier to be dead like her.

But instead, she is mad, and she has lost Cecilia.

She saw the look in Cecilia's eye when she asked her what she had experienced at the séance.

Nothing was her answer.

Lydia has come only to Odette, and so it is Odette's duty to avenge her, to keep her alive in the memory of all those so keen to forget her.

Her mother walks behind her all the way back up to Hampstead. It is a long walk, and Odette lets her mind turn over the problem of Claudine.

Revenge. Murder. Remember me.

This is what her mother asks of her.

The air is brisk and fresh as she walks up and out of the smog that hangs low across the city. The colour is high in her cheeks by the time she steps back inside the house. It is quiet, and she pauses in the entrance hall, listening instinctively for footsteps, for a tapping.

Of course there is nothing. Her mother is gone, for now. She is doing what her mother wants. She does not need reminding.

Odette strips her gloves and hat and fixes her hair in the hallway mirror, touching her fingers to the brooch at her throat, the one that contains a curl of her mother's chestnut hair. She pricked her skin pinning it in place this morning, and if she looks closely she can see a rusty speck on the black fabric where the blood has dried.

As she goes up to her room, she hears noise from the top of the house. Hammering, sawing. She follows it to her mother's studio, where workmen have erected ladders and worktables as they set about boarding up the great arching window.

Odette flushes hot with outrage. It is her mother's rage that runs through her, twined with her own, finding her voice before she knows it. 'What are you doing? Who told you to do this?'

She realises too late that Claudine stands to one side, supervising.

'These are long overdue repairs,' she says. 'I would remind you to moderate the way you speak.'

Odette is too angry to heed the danger Claudine poses. 'This is my mother's room – how dare you come in and destroy it?'

'You forget this is my house now. This room is draughty and lets in damp. The window is impractical and no longer needed.'

'Why not burn the whole place down? Then you never need think about her again,' snaps Odette. 'Surely that would suit you best.'

Claudine is about to respond, but suddenly her expression softens, and she transforms into an angel of the hearth. Odette turns to see her father in the doorway, filling his pipe.

'What's this?' George saunters into the room. 'Both my favourite girls together.'

For a moment, Odette and Claudine are united in horror.

'Really, George,' tuts Claudine.

'Have I interrupted something?' He smiles in confusion, and Odette cannot believe it is not feigned. Surely he can sense the tension simmering? She looks at him anew, considering this man who would so blind himself to the truth for the sake of an easy life.

Then he looks directly at Odette and beckons her. 'Join me for a moment. There are a few matters I would speak to you about.'

Claudine's mouth is a set line, but she seems pleased, as though some argument that Odette is not aware of has been won.

Odette allows herself to be ushered downstairs and into her father's study. It is warm, the fire banked high and the thick curtains half drawn against the cold that radiates from the windows. She has always liked this room, the jewel-box quality of it, the towering shelves of books and wood panelling and the great globe by one side of the fire. There are paintings on the wall of racehorses, prints of the Boxing Day hunt near Herne House, oddities her father picked up in his youth on his Grand Tour: a long, spiralling tusk, a curved sword, an embroidered hat. As a child, she loved to sit and listen to her father tell the histories of each item, like bedtime stories, the same words repeated over and over until she could tell the story herself, as though they were her own memories.

'Sit, darling, sit.'

George takes his seat behind the desk and Odette takes the one before it. She knows he likes to talk to her in this way, as though he is holding an audience with a member of his constituency, or some junior minister come to press his case for a certain policy.

'Are you well?' he asks, steepling his hands. 'Is it very different being at home after Cambridge?'

Odette pauses before she replies. She has not thought about how she wants to play her hand before her father. 'I find things quite changed,' she says. 'I wish you had told me of your plans sooner.'

'Yes, perhaps I should have.' He moves on without further thought. 'Do you intend to return to Cambridge in the New Year?'

'I – yes, I suppose so.'

'Good, good. We are always happier when we can strike out from our parents. Lydia could never really be a proper mother to you, and I see now that you suffered for it. After everything that has happened, I think it is very healthy for you to want a life of your own.'

Odette cannot follow his meaning, and she is left with only a creeping sense that maybe he does not *want* her at home.

'But it is only university,' she says slowly. 'I have not left home.'

'No, no. Of course not. Until you marry, you will live here.'

Until she marries.

'I have no plans to marry,' she says, though she hardly understands why she has to state it.

He wants something from her, there is some crack she is to smooth over, but she cannot work out what it is.

'At the moment, no. But you will want to.'

There is a bitter tang in the air, something a little like burning, the undercurrent of a danger she cannot yet place.

'Claudine and I have been speaking, and we agree it is time that you consider your future.' George smiles, leans forwards. 'This childish antagonism towards Claudine must stop. She and I do not see eye to eye on everything she has said to you, but it is simply that you are very different people.'

'That is hardly—'

'It would be better for everyone if the two of you were no longer under the same roof. Claudine is very understanding of how difficult this must be for you. But you are not a child, Odette. This is Claudine's home now, and she cannot welcome someone who treats her in the manner you have.'

She is back in the gardens of Herne House that summer, her father calling her sharp, entitled. Casting Claudine as the victim.

The crack splits wide and there is nothing she could do to cover it. It would eat her whole to do it. Send her mad.

Odette can barely speak. She feels Lydia's shaking fury in her bones. 'Are you throwing me out?'

George laughs. 'Don't be so silly – of course not. You have said yourself that you plan to return to Cambridge in the New Year, and you will be there for some years yet. I will make enquiries to find a suitable husband if there is no one who catches your eye. Then everyone will be happier. You are too attached to me, Odette. It is not healthy.'

Odette stares, unable to believe what he is saying. 'You are my father.'

'Yes, and Claudine is my wife.'

He is captured. It is Claudine who speaks, not her father.

She stands so abruptly she knocks over her chair. 'I need no reminder. It beggars belief that you expect me to sit here and accept all this without a single word. I am a *saint* not to have said more, in these circumstances. How can you expect me to swallow it? Mother was barely *cold*—'

'That's enough.'

Her father does not raise his voice. Not even now.

He only becomes cold as marble, every human thing in him closing off. He is a stranger, not the father who has loved her since she was born.

'Fine. I understand the message you have delivered. I am not welcome here.'

He does not look at her. Maybe this is how his true fury takes shape.

Is he really angry at her for how she has behaved towards Claudine? Or is it that she will no longer play his game?

'If that is how you choose to interpret it, I cannot stop you.'

A lightness takes her as she leaves. That is the end of that.

It is all so simple now.

If she is to lose, she will take Claudine down with her.

In her room, it is there, just as she left it. The oblong of folded pages, tucked carefully away on her desk. The memorial. Her last memory of her living mother.

It is like a dream. She can barely recall writing the words before her, though it is her slanting hand, her erroneous spelling. It has not been much more than two months, and yet those days after the death feel like a fiction she has built for herself.

She turns the pages like the delicate leaves of an old bible, tracing her finger along each line as she reads. The last time she saw her mother, she was frail, a little distant, muddled by the laudanum, but their eyes met; there was a sense of communication between them, of interest in her presence.

There must be evidence here of Claudine's actions, if only she could find it. Claudine was hurting her, Odette is convinced, and there must be some telltale clue within this record. But there is one unassailable fact before her: her mother is dead and buried. This is not a detective novel. There is no body to examine, no crime scene to assess. If she has her suspicions, then they are only taken from the situation as she knows it.

It dawns on her, slowly, heavily, like the weight of a tide drawing back to expose the soft and sinuous things on the seabed: if there is no proof, then the only path is to force a confession.

What a thought.

A confession? Could she really do it?

The rain comes now, drumming against the window loud enough to drown out any noise from upstairs.

How could she do it?

There is something so impotent about her position that it half makes her want to smash the window, break the furniture. How can she bring her will to bear on Claudine?

Does Claudine hope no one will ask about Lydia, think about her? That the memory of Lydia will dissipate from the world until no murder was committed at all?

There. That is it.

Odette cannot let her forget.

Odette must make her remember.

As her mother's ghost has come to her, she must bring her ghost to Claudine.

If Claudine is guilty, then it will burden her conscience, and any weight Odette brings to bear upon it will make it untenable.

If she is not, then any antics Odette performs in aid of her goal will be easily cast off as grief, madness.

Very well. She will take it on as a mantle, as armour. Let them believe her driven from her senses with grief, believe that she is blind and deaf to anything beyond her own misery.

Let them think her mad.

So this is it then – the task before her.

She locks the memorial into her desk drawer. She must keep it safe.

There, on the neat surface she has yet to unpack onto, is a single photograph: herself, her father, Claudine, and the corpse of her mother, head tilted sideways as though she is asleep. She thinks of the cold hand at her throat.

She has an idea.

She fetches her hat and coat and slinks out of the house.

She will make her move first.

She must see this through, whatever the end.

Whatever the cost.

3

Cecilia

IT IS NOT STRAIGHTFORWARD to find Mr King at the Jermyn Street Gallery. There is no neat sign pointing towards the private offices – of course there isn't – and Cecilia is not so naive as to think she can simply present herself to an attendant or one of the women selling tickets and expect to solicit an audience with the proprietor.

She hovers on the street opposite, watching the crowds drift in and out of the entrance, the matinee-goers turning off the Haymarket, the boys darting across the road to sweep the manure from the paths of the gentry, a newspaper seller pushing *The Illustrated London News* into the hands of anyone who makes the mistake of catching his eye. Her earlobes throb with her pulse. The feeling of the rip through paper, the blow of pain to the side of her head, is still vivid from earlier that day.

She thinks back to her encounter with Mr King in the summer.

He was all human. Flesh and stink and hair and mouth, and every base thought *The Illustrated London News* could possibly cry about.

Perhaps there is a way she can present herself to gain an audience.

Perhaps she simply needs to understand the tableau she wishes to create and the role she will play in it.

She checks her reflection in the window of a restaurant and pinches some colour into her cheeks, then darts between the traffic to the gallery. She pulls a card from her case and presents it to the man at the front of house.

'To see Mr King,' she says simply, presumptively.

The man assesses her card. 'Is he expecting you?'

'He knows me,' she says. 'I am one of Lydia Fairfax-Waugh's models. Mr King and I met at Herne House.'

The man's expression changes at the word *model*, and he moves his roving gaze from the card to Cecilia's face and body. Whether he recognises her from Lydia's paintings, she does not know and refuses to let herself consider.

'I'll tell him you've called for him. Wait.'

She is left standing awkwardly to one side as visitors come in and out, and she tucks her gloved hands into her sleeves against the cold. People are looking at her; she is sure of it. Did they hear her call herself a model? What will Mr King think of her solicitation?

Before she can talk herself out of such boldness, the man returns.

'He'll see you. Through the door on the left and up the stairs.'

Cecilia does not look at him again. She hurries inside and through the small door to the left that leads immediately to a narrow set of stairs. They are almost blocked with boxes of flyers, paperwork, stacks of rolled canvases, broken lengths of frame. All the glamour of the gallery disappears at once; it is like stepping into the wings of a theatre and seeing the lengths of rope and waiting props, the illusion of imagination transformed at once into junk and scrap.

There is a tight landing above. At one end, a door is open onto a storeroom, piled with chairs, broken plant pots, heaps of scrap fabric, discarded posters and paintings. At the other end is a closed door, from behind which the sound of a gramophone spills.

Cecilia hesitates before it. She is struck by a sudden longing for Odette. She could be braver if Odette were here. With Odette, she has climbed across rooftops, swam in rivers, drunk herself sick, taught herself the fumble of two bodies together. She has been ignorant and out of her depth, and the fear has turned instead to excitement. Curiosity. The desire to know. Odette makes her bold – perhaps it feels like the only way to keep her attention – but that boldness has fled her now, and she falters at the door, heart racing.

Mr King has heard her footsteps, though, and the door opens whether she wants it to or not.

He is as handsome as she remembers, dark brows over flashing hazel eyes and a wide mouth that curls with an edge of something that could be humour or could be predation.

'Miss Moore.'

'Mr King. I hope you will forgive me for this unexpected intrusion.'

'There is nothing to forgive. Come inside.'

He steps back, and Cecilia is left no choice but to cross the threshold, brushing uncomfortably close to his body in the limited space.

The office is as jumbled as the staircase: an overlarge desk takes up most of the centre of the room, stacked with newspapers, magazines, opened letters, bills, invoices, empty ink bottles and broken nibs, blotting paper and several dishes of cigarette ash. The bare floorboards are layered with overlapping Turkish rugs, at first dazzling but on closer inspection stained and moth-eaten. On the walls are countless posters of the gallery's exhibitions, and frames are stacked up in the corners, chairs piled with sketchbooks, portfolios, ledgers.

There is no chair for her to sit in, and Mr King only leans against his desk and lights another cigarette.

'To what do I owe the pleasure of your company?' he asks, shaking out the match. 'I am surprised a shy little thing like you would come knocking on my door.'

Cecilia knots her hands together to keep from fidgeting. 'I will not beat about the bush, Mr King. I come to you with a simple problem I hope you can assist me with.'

'If you are hoping I can put you in the path of another artist who recognises your *unique* talents but who, unlike our dear Lydia, might pay for them, then I might have a name or two in mind.'

Cecilia blushes furiously. 'No. You mistake me.'

'Ah. Forgive me.' Mr King takes a long drag on his cigarette, the glowing tip reflected in his eyes.

'My business does concern Mrs Fairfax-Waugh, but it is about her paintings. When we met at Herne House, you had come to discuss an exhibition of her work with a view to selling. Is that correct?'

'It is.'

'Of course Mrs Fairfax-Waugh sadly passed away before any exhibition came to pass. I want to know what has happened to those plans and whether any buyers had already been located—'

'My, my, so mercenary.'

Cecilia clenches her jaw. 'It is important to me to know what became of those paintings she wished to sell.'

'If there is a piece you would rather not see the light of day, I'm afraid I don't have as much power in the world of art as you might suppose.'

'That is not it at all, Mr King. I would appreciate it if you would answer me directly. What happened to the paintings she gave you for the exhibition?'

Mr King takes another pull on the cigarette and lets out a stream of blue-tinged smoke towards the ceiling. 'I can't rightly say. She intended to exhibit with us, yes, and use our services to find interested buyers, but her illness overtook her. I was deeply saddened by her death.'

Cecilia deflates. 'But her paintings are all gone, and you have an unfinished piece of hers on display—'

He waves this away. 'A loan.'

'Oh.'

Cecilia has fumbled all the cards in her hand. The paintings must be somewhere, and it is impossible to think Mr King does not have some role in the matter. Instinctively, he is not a man she trusts, but perhaps he does not understand the full situation, and if he knew what Lydia had intended with the sale of her work, he might be more inclined to help her.

It is worth trying.

'The money from the sale was promised to her daughter,' she says. 'I thought perhaps some of it had been secured before she passed.'

A limp throw, and it lands flat between them.

Cecilia is outclassed.

Mr King stubs out the cigarette and straightens from the desk. 'If you do think of modelling again, I hope you will call on me. I can think of a few men who would know what to do with someone like you.'

'Thank you,' says Cecilia mechanically. Humiliation burns her cheeks.

Mr King opens the door, and she slides out, pressing herself against the wall to avoid him.

On the landing, she squeezes her eyes shut. The shock of the séance that morning, the yawning gap growing between her and Odette – it is enough to overwhelm her.

The path of escape she had pictured for the two of them shrinks before her, dwindling into nothing.

As she starts down the stairs, she glances into the storeroom – for no reason really. Perhaps something in the light catches her eye, or perhaps it is a premonition, some buried sense calling to her – but she looks up.

From the storeroom, Odette looks back at her.

A stack of paintings leans up against the far wall and one, taller than the rest, peeks above a frame – the top of Odette's face, her watchful, attentive eyes and the curl of her brown hair along her brow.

Cecilia hurries into the room, pulls back the stacked canvases to reveal Odette – and freezes, a gasp caught in her throat.

The painting comes up to her shoulder, and it is a long, narrow thing, like a coffin. It shows a full-length figure amidst the vines and leaves of a Dionysian revelry, pomegranates and apples scattered throughout the foliage.

Odette is entirely naked.

She faces the viewer, head cocked shyly and hair loose about her shoulders. Her breasts are exposed – her whole body on display. If Cecilia didn't know Odette as she does, she would think her the model for the face alone, that Lydia found some other body to stand in for her daughter.

But she has not.

It is Odette, as Cecilia has known and loved her. It brings a blush to her cheek, but it is – disconcerting. She did not know this painting existed. Odette never spoke of modelling like this. It feels – wrong.

She puts back the canvases quickly and turns to leave, only to find Mr King blocking the doorway.

'Ah. You've found her.'

Cecilia struggles for words. 'You lied to me.'

He smirks and holds his hands up. 'You can't blame me for trying.'

'I think you'll find I can. Why did you not tell me you had the paintings?'

'Lydia's work is extraordinary, and I had the luck of my life to come into possession of some of it. I didn't lie to you. Lydia died before we got as far as dealing with the money, and I thought if I laid low, my great fortune might go unnoticed.'

'But I have noticed it. The money rightfully belongs to Odette.'

'On that front, I have no case to settle. I have paid up.'

Cecilia frowns. 'Paid who?'

'The late Mrs Fairfax-Waugh's estate.'

'I don't understand.'

'I suppose a chit like you has little reason to know how legal matters work, but it is customary that the executor of a will identifies and disposes of the deceased's assets.'

'Executor?' Cecilia fumbles to make sense of it. 'Who?'

Mr King ignores her. 'I expressed an interest in acquiring the paintings, and the estate agreed to the sale. You might think many things of me, Miss Moore, but I'm a mere reprobate, not a criminal. I settled the bill, so I have no case to answer to you.'

'But why did you not say?'

'As I said, I never lied. When a stranger comes to ask me the details of my business, I find myself under no obligation to give any details of my clients or their arrangements. Who knows what pieces of Lydia's the estate might discover and feel inclined to sell. I'd rather keep her confidence than yours. But I wouldn't expect a girl like you to understand the way business works.'

If Cecilia were Odette, she would give Mr King some lecture on *art* versus *business*. But Cecilia is not that sort of girl. She has exhausted her own supply of confidence, and she can feel herself shrinking under his gaze.

Of course, the matter is settled. She has been away for two months, and much has changed. Uncle George married Claudine. The money has been tidied up. Aunt Lydia is rotting in her coffin.

What use is Cecilia?

She cannot undo any of these things.

She lowers her eyes. 'I understand. I apologise for my intrusion. I will gladly take my leave.'

Mr King steps to one side, and this time, when she passes, he puts a hand on her waist as if to help her through, though it is only a step from the room to the landing and she needs nothing from him.

He has won. She has failed again.

4

Odette

ODETTE WAITS FOR NIGHTFALL before she begins.

The household is not up late; they are not entertaining tonight, and soon Mrs Binx is securing the shutters and the doors. Odette lies in Lydia's studio, where the workmen have made a mess of everything: a foot put through a canvas, brushes snapped and paints shoved haphazardly to one side. Here, she listens. There is the turn of the key and the scrape of the bolt. The steady footsteps patrolling the hallways to snuff out each gas lamp. The murmured goodnights.

Then – silence.

The Hampstead house is nothing like Herne House. It has no maze of forgotten passageways and priest holes, no easy way to step into the gaps between worlds – but that does not mean it is impossible. Cecilia has shown her one or two places where the veil grows thin: the airing cupboard into which a whole person can fit and conceal themselves behind the laundry, the turn in the stairs where, stood just so, a body can disappear.

And downstairs, there was once a connecting door between Lydia's room and the blue room, where George and Claudine now sleep. In the blue room, the door was nailed shut and papered over, but in Lydia's room, the deep alcove into which the door was set prevented this, and instead a wardrobe was pushed in front of it. Cecilia once discovered that, with a little care, it was possible to wriggle behind the wardrobe and into the alcove.

Odette listens to the church bells chime through the night, until she marks a quarter to three. She slithers downstairs and into her mother's bedroom, then worms her way into her hiding place.

It is too dark to see a thing, but she can feel the shape of the door, the hinges, the handle that has no counterpart. On the other side, her father and her aunt lie together. Behind her is her mother's deathbed.

With a slow and firm hand, she gives three loud knocks.

Silence reigns.

Perhaps only the scuffle of a mouse in the walls.

Carefully, three more loud knocks.

Now, a shifting. She imagines Claudine rising up on her elbow, blinking around the dark room, half in a dream.

Three knocks in sharp succession.

Did she imagine it? Was that a gasp?

Odette lets the tension draw out, fine as a knifepoint. Just when she imagines that Claudine might be lying down again, she knocks low, near the floor, a steady drumbeat, slow enough that she can hear movement in the room.

Footsteps on the other side of the door. Claudine is up.

Hissed words, then a low voice. She has roused George.

Odette stops.

Murmured voices. A rising frustration in Claudine's tone until she grows loud enough for the words to break through.

'—am not mad.'

Hmm. Yes. Now.

Odette gives a single knock.

The silence that follows is exquisite. She can picture them both, George sat up in bed, Claudine stood beside him in her nightgown, staring at the wall that separates them from Lydia's death room.

She gives three short raps.

'Hello?' says Claudine.

Three more raps.

George's voice is still low, but now he moves. Mattress springs – heavier footsteps.

He comes close enough that she can hear him clearly.

'It will be something come loose and knocking in the wind.'

Odette cannot resist giving another three knocks in response.

'There, it is steady – don't you see? There will be a simple solution.'

'It's coming from her room,' says Claudine, her voice strangled.

'Maybe so. It is not being tended to, so it would be easy to overlook an open window or broken shutter.'

The footsteps move away and into the corridor. Odette keeps up her knocking, a steady siren, until the door to Lydia's room opens and she stops at once.

They are here with her now.

She waits, imagines them pacing the room, inspecting chairs and tables for uneven legs knocking against the floor or checking for unsecured curtains at the window.

Will they hear her breathing? No, surely not, she is quiet as death.

She changes approach. With the heel of her foot, she stamps on the floorboards, a low and resonant sound that travels through the space, seeming to come from everywhere at once.

Claudine shrieks. 'That is no broken shutter.'

George does not reply. He cannot dismiss the noises so confidently now.

The footsteps move around again – searching, Odette assumes – and she lets them stew in it. They will find nothing.

'Houses settle,' says George eventually. 'The winter weather means the wood contracts—'

'Don't patronise me,' snaps Claudine. 'Someone is doing this.'

Odette freezes.

'A disgruntled servant still loyal to their old mistress. It is common trickery.'

God – a reprieve – but if Claudine were to sniff out her hiding place—

'Oh, well, now, I hardly think one of the staff would do something so unkind.'

'How wonderful for you.' Claudine's voice drips bile.

'It has stopped now. To bed, I think.'

Odette cannot make out what Claudine says in response, but both sets of footsteps recede.

The moment the door closes, she hammers as hard and as long as she can.

The door is flung open again, crashing against the wall, and footsteps march in.

'Whoever you are,' cries Claudine, 'I will find you out, and the punishment will be severe!'

Odette crouches and taps rapidly along the base of the wall, as though something is approaching the bed where one of Lydia's sketches hangs above the headboard.

'Stop it!' shrieks Claudine. 'I order you to stop it!'

'Darling, calm down,' says George.

'Do not touch me!'

'You're getting overwrought.'

'Of course I am overwrought, you fool – do you not hear this?'

'I will admit it is unusual.'

'If they mean to make me feel guilty, they will not succeed,' snaps Claudine. 'I have done nothing wrong!'

'No one has said you have,' says George soothingly.

'I did what I had to! I lost twenty years of my life because of her – I will not lose the next twenty!'

Odette stops the noise at once.

What does Claudine mean by that?

But it is guilt – some sort of guilt.

Claudine takes the silence as success. 'I will find out who you are, and you will be gone with no reference – I promise you that.'

George says something soft again, but Claudine interrupts.

'This room will be completely stripped back and remade. You will engage the tradesmen tomorrow,' she instructs.

'Yes, darling.'

One set of footsteps leaves, and finally Odette risks peeking out around the edge of the wardrobe to take in Claudine, stood in the middle of the room, hair falling out of her plait, colour high in her cheeks.

Behind her, in the shadows, is a face.

Lydia's gaunt and angular skull looms out as she emerges, one hand reaching for Claudine's throat.

Claudine stiffens and spins around.

Lydia is gone.

Claudine flees.

Once the house is asleep once more, Odette squeezes out from her hiding place and patters back up to the studio.

Amongst the detritus of her dead mother's half-life, she curls up and laughs and laughs and laughs.

5

Cecilia

CECILIA EMERGES LATE FROM her room in the morning. She has missed breakfast, claiming a headache kept her in bed. It has: her ears throb badly, though she has iced them, and she cannot bear to look at them in the mirror. Mired in thought since leaving the Jermyn Street Gallery yesterday, she feels strongly in need of a hot bath to scrape the last of Mr King from her. She can feel his eyes on her still, the touch of his hand at her waist.

Leo is in the parlour, stretched out on the settee, reading a document.

'Not at the office today?' she asks.

'I do get some time off, you know,' he says. 'But as it happens, I'd left some papers at home, so I have to crib them now before meeting some terribly clever fellows who are likely to eat me alive.'

'I see. Where's Mother?'

'Claudine called her round to discuss some crisis or another. The cook used lemon instead of lime in the ices, or the haberdasher's sent half a yard of Belgian lace instead of French, perhaps.'

Cecilia pictures the bath she could have drawn in a peacefully empty house, how long she could spend reading in hot water until it felt as though her whole body slipped off her like meat from the bone.

But Leo is here – they are in private – and she will use the opportunity that has presented itself.

'Were you there when Lydia's will was read?' she asks, leaning against the doorframe.

Leo twists to look at her. 'What a bizarre question. Why do you want to know?'

'I'm curious. Neither Odette nor I were here, so I wondered about it.'

'What's there to wonder about? It's a will. Entirely typical, run-of-the-mill stuff.'

'There wasn't—' Cecilia catches herself.

'Wasn't what?'

'I don't suppose Aunt Lydia made any unexpected gifts in her will?'

Leo snorts. 'Hoping to have snagged something? Sorry, Cessy – you weren't mentioned once. Everything goes to Uncle George as her husband.'

'Nothing to Odette?'

'Bits and pieces, but it's all held in trust until she reaches twenty-one.'

Cecilia considers. 'How does it work if, say, Lydia was in the process of selling some of her work when she died? What would happen to the money?'

Leo begins to pack away his papers. 'That would be a matter for the estate. Once you get a grant of probate from the courts, the will usually names an executor who will sort out the estate of whoever snuffed their glim, so to speak. That means totting up all debts and assets and settling the bill. Then they're in charge of distributing what's left as per the will. So I suppose in that case, the executor would finalise the sale and add the money to the estate's assets.'

'And if the money had been verbally promised?'

Leo fastens his briefcase and sits back. 'Then you're out of luck, Cessy. I don't know what Aunt Lydia promised you, but everything reverts to her estate, and that's that.'

'Oh.' Cecilia sits down in an armchair, staring at the spread of her skirts over her knees. 'She didn't promise me anything. It's Odette I'm asking for.'

Leo winds his scarf around his neck and fetches his walking stick and top hat. 'Then there's no problem, is there? Everything has gone to Uncle George, and he'll give her any money she needs, surely.'

Cecilia turns the problem over in her mind. It makes sense, and yet it doesn't. 'Is Uncle George the executor?'

'Oh, no, it had been their old family solicitor, but when Aunt Lydia fell ill she updated her will – standard stuff, but Claudine asked me to take a look, to help her sister with the more onerous odds and ends, that sort of thing. And, as part of that, Lydia named Claudine the new executor.'

'Claudine,' echoes Cecilia, numb.

'She's been very efficient about it all. Uncle George would hardly have had the time what with all the demands of Parliament.' Leo puts his hat and coat on and pats her on the shoulder. 'Stop fretting. Mother is doing what she does best and ingratiating herself with old Claudine. It's all in hand.'

Cecilia looks at the cotton of her skirt, the weave of the fabric and the places where the print has been poorly applied, smudging an acanthus leaf into a blur. There is an anxious tightness to her chest that she cannot place. Everything feels fragile, like the world is made of tissue-thin china and she is tied into hobnail boots. There is no way for her to move without breaking something.

It is so clever a ploy that she does not know what to think. As Lydia's executor, Claudine has control of everything – and yet it's a role that casts so little suspicion on herself. If Claudine had encouraged Lydia to change her will to benefit her, it would have been so obviously mercenary. And if she was already planning to marry George, the money would all go to him anyway. As executor, she can tidy up any loose ends and cut Odette out entirely.

She wins whatever happens.

How neatly Claudine has plotted it all.

Because Claudine always intended to marry George. Cecilia is certain of that now.

'And I haven't forgotten the so-called blackmail business, if that's what you're worked up about. Of course, I need to know what's going on, so I appreciate you telling me about that, but it's dealt with. Mother and I will manage the money situation, and Claudine, and you will work on behaving like a normal girl. How about that?'

'I hate you,' she says miserably and sinks into the chair.

'And I you, Mousy.' He pauses and pats her shoulder. 'It *will* be all right. I promise. Just hold your nerve.'

She accepts the comfort. He is infuriating, but he is her brother, and that means something.

'Mother managed to square things up when Father died – we can do it again now,' he says.

When Father died and they lost all their money. The same time that Claudine's engagement to George fell apart and she left for the Continent.

Wait.

It comes together so suddenly that Cecilia cannot believe she did not see it before.

Claudine went abroad the year Father died.

That is what Leo said before. That is the thought that caught in her mind.

Their father died while Penelope was pregnant with Cecilia – this is a fact she knows. Which means Claudine's engagement was broken off while Penelope was pregnant. But Cecilia is only a few months older than Odette – so Lydia must have been pregnant at the same time or very soon after.

Oh. *Oh.*

Claudine and George. Lydia and George.

How long has Claudine been planning her revenge?

The front door bangs in the hallway, and the parlour door opens to admit Penelope and Claudine, as if they have been summoned.

Penelope goes straight to her son. 'Ah, there you are, Leo. We'd like a word with you.'

Cecilia freezes in her chair, rotten through with fear. Claudine looks so ordinary where she stands: a human face, human mouth quirked in impatience, human hand upon the doorframe.

'Can it wait?' asks Leo. 'I'm overdue at the office.'

'It cannot,' says Claudine.

It is the first time Cecilia has seen Claudine look anything other than calm and controlled. She is pale with – anger? Fear? Cecilia is unsure – and moves in jerky, impatient movements.

'I suppose if it's urgent,' says Leo.

Penelope rounds on her next. 'Cecilia. Do you have some matters of your own to attend to?'

'My own matters?' Cecilia begins, but from her mother's expression, she understands the meaning below the words.

Get out.

Cecilia leaves, and Penelope shuts the door behind her.

All glass, everywhere – porcelain so thin the light shines through.

Cecilia sits at the top of the stairs, folded into shadows. The voices in the parlour are low and constant. Only a few words reach her.

Erratic behaviour. A rest cure. Odette.

She was mistaken before. She had thought the world fragile but intact, and that, if she moved ever so gently, she might find a way through it.

But it is too late. It is shattered, and she will cut herself whichever way she turns.

6

Odette

ODETTE DOES NOT SLEEP, but it feels better that way. To sleep is to be weak. If she loses the thread she is following, she may not find it again.

This morning, her mother is in the garden, standing sentinel beside the apple tree, staring up at her with blank, black eyes.

She is trying her best. She knows her mother understands.

She loses the morning somehow, and then it is lunchtime, and she brings herself to leave her room.

Claudine is alone in the entrance hall when Odette slips down the stairs. She is stood close to the wall, concentrating on the floor. At first, Odette cannot understand what she is doing, but then she sees she has cornered a mouse.

Odette stays quiet, tucked in the half-landing, waiting for Claudine to call for a maid.

But she does not.

She simply lifts her foot and brings it down on the mouse with force.

When she is done, she scrapes her shoe on the mat and goes into the dining room with a perfectly placid expression.

It is the most profoundly disturbing thing Odette has ever seen, and she thinks she might be sick.

If she had any doubt that Claudine was dangerous, she has none now.

She pelts upstairs again, only just making it back to her room and her chamber pot in time before she throws up.

By the time she comes downstairs again, the mouse corpse has been disappeared by an unseen servant.

George, Claudine and Odette sit at the table in silence. Odette can hardly breathe. The only thing keeping her steady is that she can feel the press of her mother's hand holding hers, just as it did at the séance, cold and bony and stronger than it ever was in life.

She is not alone. She will not let them destroy Lydia.

The silence is such that snatches of the maids' conversation drift in from the hall.

'What if it *was* a restless spirit? It would make a certain sense if Mrs Fairfax-Waugh didn't want to go so easily . . .'

Claudine puts down her glass with an audible clink. 'Edith, Agnes – you will present yourself to me in the morning room after lunch,' she calls, with a voice like cracking ice.

'Yes, ma'am.' There is the sound of footsteps as both girls disappear.

Odette feels sorry for them. She cannot protect anyone. She does not know if she can even save Cecilia.

She knows she cannot save herself.

'A delivery, sir.' The butler enters the room and hands her father a flat package wrapped in brown paper.

'Ah. The photographs.' George unties the string and removes the prints, then hesitates. 'Oh dear.'

'What is it?' Claudine leans over to see, but George holds the prints out of her grasp. 'Stop that.'

She snatches the pictures from him, and there is only a fraction of a second between her looking at them and the colour draining from her face.

'Don't look.'

She does not fight when George takes them back, putting them face down on the table.

Odette watches closely. Claudine has gone so grey she thinks she might faint – and a moment later, she does, slipping sideways from her chair onto the floor, pulling the tablecloth with her.

The crash brings servants flying into the room, and Odette skips back, away from the chaotic scene. It is almost something Lydia would have painted: the bright slash of colour in Claudine's limp form, the gathering of servants and husband like some great image from antiquity.

The photographs have fluttered to the floor, landing off to one side. Odette kneels on the moth-eaten Turkish rug that Lydia loved too much to throw out and picks them up.

They are of George and Claudine, newly wed and standing together in a photographer's studio, their hands clasped together, with an elaborate painted backcloth behind them showing a window overlooking a continental square, beyond the drape of a curtain. They look very fine, and it is expensive work.

Of course, it is perfectly marred by the ghost.

Odette runs her finger over the surface, tracing the outline of her mother's face.

She appears there, in between George and Lydia, eyes closed and face blank, just as she did in that final photograph they took together after her death. It is as though she has refused to leave the bounds of her marriage and now presents herself as the irrefutable third party to an unspeakable act.

Claudine has come to and is clutching a bottle of smelling salts as she is carefully manoeuvred upright. There is a tightness around her mouth that conveys a real fear, and her hands are white at the knuckle where she holds the bottle.

Interesting.

Claudine seems to sense Odette's eyes on her and she turns, face narrowing in anger. 'Spiteful, horrible child. You did this. I know it was you.'

'Now, that is a little much,' says George. 'It is a mistake at the photography studio, surely.'

'Oh, you dismiss me too easily, George,' says Claudine. 'You make all sorts of excuses for her when this so clearly oversteps the mark.'

'*If* Odette did this, then yes, it does, but for goodness' sake, everyone, you take it far too seriously.'

'Don't you dare defend her. This is beyond some servant's trick.' She rounds on Odette. 'I suppose that was you last night as well.'

Odette stares at her blankly. 'What do you have to fear from my mother's ghost?' she asks. 'If you have not wronged her, then she has no business with you.'

'How *dare* you—' Claudine surges up, but George restrains her with a hand on her shoulder.

'Easy now. You should rest.'

'If you are hiding something,' says Odette, 'then there is nowhere you can hide from the dead.'

For a moment, Odette thinks Claudine will push past George and corner her where she kneels by the photographs, but it seems that Claudine is mollified, at least for the moment, by the press of George's hand and the gesture of care.

'You are right. My nerves have been too greatly taxed these last days.' She gives George a dark look. 'I have had quite enough.'

She takes the smelling salts upstairs, and George repairs to his study.

Odette watches them go.

She witnessed real fear in Claudine's face. It was subtle, yes, but it was there.

Alone in the dining room, the cold of the floorboards seeping up through her stockings, Odette examines the picture again. The photographer did a fine job. It took most of the money she had in her purse when she slipped out to the studio yesterday to persuade him to create a double exposure with the plates from Lydia's death portrait, but his work has been far more effective than she could have imagined. The image is uncanny, the half-formed shape of her mother so like a spirit, like an angel.

Claudine saw something more in it. A pointed finger. An accusation.

There was fear – and guilt.

It is only a matter of time before she slips. One more push, and she will go over the edge.

Odette is sure, for a moment, that she can feel icy fingertips against her throat – then her cheek. A caress.

Her mother is with her. Her mother is pleased.

7

Cecilia

WHEN CECILIA HAS STEADIED HERSELF, hours later, and she has cried herself hoarse, she dresses to go out, taking care over the setting of her hair and the touch of red on her lips. Her earlobes are red and tender; she hasn't dared change the studs, and her skin is hot to the touch.

She must speak to Odette. It is past time.

Cecilia does not know if it is still possible for them to have any meaningful exchange, so far gone do things feel, but she must try. She will present Odette with the things she has learnt and make a final bid for their escape. Surely if she sees the true threat Claudine poses, she will be willing to listen, to leave.

As she pins her hat, she is struck by the certainty of it: if they do not leave now, this will be the end of them.

Penelope catches her before she can go. 'You look very well,' she says, with an approving smile. 'I am glad to see you taking more of an interest in your appearance. You are a pretty girl.'

'Thank you, Mother.'

'Where are you going?'

'Only on an errand or two.' Cecilia hopes the lie is not obvious. She hardly thinks her mother would be keen for her to speak to Odette.

Some sentimental mood has clearly taken Penelope, and she draws Cecilia into the parlour to sit with her, clasping her hands in her own.

'I am so sorry things have been so trying for you. You must believe that it has all been for the best.'

'I am not sure how I can,' says Cecilia, but she is unsettled to see real emotion on her mother's face.

Penelope tucks a stray strand of hair behind Cecilia's ear and cups her cheek. 'Things are never clear when we are in the middle of them. I love you so very much, my girl. I have spent much of my life frightened and trying to pave a road ahead of myself. I do not want to see you reduced to the same.'

Cecilia thinks she should make some smart remark, reject her mother's assessment of life, but she cannot. She is not that sort of daughter. Her mother *does* love her; she knows it. This would all be so much easier if she did not.

'There is nothing wrong with marrying a man who is boring but safe and living a small life.'

'Mother—'

'Adventure seems terribly exciting when you are young, but consequences will follow you into middle age, and it all seems much more foolish with hindsight.'

'I am not so keen on adventure as you might think.'

Penelope smiles. 'No? Odette is an adventure, is she not? My darling, I know how these passionate friendships can cut deeply, but you must not take it to heart. She can always be important to you, but you do not need to cleave your future to hers. I only want you to be safe and happy.'

Cecilia cannot help crying again. Penelope draws her in to rest her head on her bosom, and Cecilia curls into her gladly.

She thinks: this is what Odette has lost.

Perhaps it is so awful. Perhaps it is maddening.

Penelope strokes her hair, as Cecilia turns it all over in her mind.

Safe and happy.

Cecilia is not sure she can have both at once.

While she is within Claudine's world, safe is not possible.

But perhaps there is still a chance left for her to be happy.

*

The air is wrong inside the Fairfax-Waughs' house when Cecilia steps inside. It is like a subtle scent, some undertone of rot beneath the smart façade. It is tidier than usual, she realises. Some of the lamps and ornaments have been removed, rugs taken up from the floors, mirrors and artwork stripped from the walls.

She is let in by a distracted maid who pays her little mind. By the doors down to the kitchen, Cecilia spots one girl crying into her hands, another comforting her, before the door is rapidly closed to hide them. There are whispers she cannot catch, about noises in the night, about a photograph.

Raised voices come from the study, Claudine's and George's, so Cecilia slips past as quietly as she can and scurries upstairs to Odette's room. There is only so much courage she can scrape together within herself, and she will need all of it to unfurl to Odette the secrets she has been holding.

Odette sits on the end of her bed, looking sightlessly into the corner of her room.

No, not quite sightlessly. She is focused on some point in the middle of the air, gaze fervent.

'Odette?' says Cecilia softly as she closes the door behind her. 'It's me.'

It takes Odette a moment to register her voice and turn. Her expression falls, at first in anguish, then closes off, hard and blank. 'Why have you come?'

'What do you mean? Do I need a reason to want to see you?'

'You shouldn't be here. It's not – I don't know what's going to happen.'

The dark hollows beneath Odette's eyes are more pronounced than ever, and she cannot keep her hands still, picking at her cuticles and twitching at the buttons on her cuffs.

'Have you slept?' asks Cecilia, coming to sit on the bed with her.

'That's not important.'

Cecilia tries to take her hand, to still her worrying, but Odette yanks it back as though the touch burns, and she looks over her shoulder, through the window into the street beyond as though tracking something.

'I wanted to apologise for how I reacted to the séance yesterday,' says Cecilia, hoping to draw Odette back. She has thought about how to approach this, and there seems no obvious way to go back to how things used to be between them, but she can start with softness. 'You put your trust in me, taking me with you to that place, and I don't feel like I honoured it.'

Odette pulls at a hangnail hard enough that the skin grows red. 'You gave your truthful account. That's all I asked.'

'It frightened me. I wasn't kind. But it mattered to you, and I should have treated it more carefully.'

'It was stupid.'

'I don't think it was.'

'Don't lie to me,' Odette snaps. 'I don't need your pity.'

'You assume it is pity when it is not. Will you listen to me?'

Odette seems to war with herself for a moment, then drags her attention back to Cecilia and nods.

'There is something I have been meaning to speak to you about, but it has hardly felt like the right time for so long, and now it all weighs on me too heavily to wait any longer.'

Odette's expression grows wary. 'More secrets?'

There is no point denying it. 'Yes. Though I never meant to keep them.' Cecilia is out of her depth in a conversation like this; she can feel her feet reaching for the bottom that is not there. 'I have been trying to find out what happened to the money Lydia promised you.'

Odette considers her for a moment, with a searching, sharp look, and Cecilia is struck with the sense that this is not Odette. Not *her* Odette. The person she knew has gone, and she is left with this shadow, this imposter. She wants to clutch at Odette and shake her, will her back into her rightful shape.

'The sale never happened.'

'No, but the paintings were gone all the same,' says Cecilia. 'I tracked them down to Mr King's gallery. He claims he has bought them all from the estate.'

'I don't understand.'

'Neither did I, so I asked Leo.' Cecilia draws a breath to steady herself. 'Lydia changed her will before she died to make Claudine her executor. Leo said Claudine was "helping" her with it. Which means she has been in charge of your mother's estate, and she sold all the paintings to Mr King directly, and the money has all gone back to Uncle George and – and – Odette, I'm so sorry. I should have told you I was looking into it all but I didn't want to say anything before I had something meaningful to tell you.'

The silence is too long. Cecilia cannot let it lie.

'I'm so sorry. Can you forgive me?'

Odette still does not speak. She closes her eyes, draws a slow breath, and Cecilia thinks she might be crying.

'You should stay out of Claudine's business,' she says eventually.

'But, Odette, she—'

'I don't want to hear it. Don't speak of her. Don't look into any of this anymore. Forget it ever happened.'

'I don't understand. Are you listening to me? She has been planning all this from the start. I mean the real start: before you were born, she and—'

'*Cecilia.*' Odette's eyes snap open. 'Shut up. I don't care. Keep your mad theories to yourself. This isn't one of our plays. This is my real life.'

Cecilia draws back, wounded. 'I know that. I'm not making it up.' She has the terrible sense that if Odette speaks again, she will say something that will cut a jagged line between them that cannot be undone. She grabs at her hands again. 'Let us go. Anywhere, you name the place. Let's run away, like we planned. Bloomsbury, or – or Paris – or anywhere. There are ways to survive. We could manage it.'

Odette sneers. 'For God's sake, don't be naive. You still think we have any chance of that without money?'

'Why not? We have both tried our hands at living away at university – we are not so ignorant.'

'My mother is dead and gone, and every promise she ever made is gone with her. She traps me even now. I will never be free of her. There is no future for us.'

'There is, Odette – I know there is. There must be, or else – or else—'

'Or else what? You would have to think for yourself who you are?'

Cecilia stills as though she has been slapped. 'That's not – you don't mean—'

'I don't mean it? That is what you fail to understand, Cecilia – I mean *all* of it.' Odette's face grows cruel in anger, in disgust. There is some haunted, unnatural look behind her eyes that Cecilia does not recognise at all.

Odette has never hurt her before. Not intentionally.

She trusts Odette. She holds nothing in life more dear than the faith she has in her.

Perhaps it is that grief has cracked through to the truth of the matter.

Perhaps this is what Odette has been hiding from her.

She does not love her anymore.

Perhaps she never loved her.

Odette does not stop. 'You cling to me like a drowning man because you have only ever been a poor copy of me, only alive when my mother and I let our light fall on you. Well, now she is dead and gone, so what are you now, Cecilia? What of a shadow when the light is gone?'

The blows are delivered with no pleasure, but are precise and cold and devastating.

'Stop it. I won't hear this.' Cecilia speaks low and trembling. 'I won't let you ruin everything because you suffer. There will be a future after this – I know it, I promise you.

Do not tear down everything you have – you will want it when you come through.'

'Don't you understand, Cecilia? This doesn't matter. We do not matter. *Nothing* matters. Love is like a dew – it lies across the world so briefly, then the weight of the day burns it out without fail.' Odette is speaking wildly, hair falling loose from its pins and lips drawn back from bared teeth. 'She is dead. My mother is dead. *I* am dead – the Odette you knew. The things she wanted, that she cared about – how can I care about them now? They were desires in a world that is lost to me forever. It all means nothing. Do you hear me? You tell me I am changed, and you are right. Stop looking for me, because I am not here.'

Odette throws herself away from Cecilia, shaking like a dog, panting and beside herself.

Cecilia does not reach for her.

What will she do if Odette really does push her away for good?

The thought has not fully occurred to her before – but now it feels horribly possible.

Maybe they are not forever. Maybe they were only ever mayflies, for one bright, short summer's day.

She does not know how they can come back from this.

8

Odette

THE HEATH IS A SPLASH of oil and watercolour. Great murky cloudbanks fill the sky with ashy light; the bare ground rolls out, in turns ochre-muddy and the golden-green of fallen leaves on frost-brittle grass. The barren trees reach up together, tangled, more brown bark than vegetal. It is a nothing kind of weather, neither the full frost of winter nor yet the fresh budding of spring, not for many months. They are caught in some island damp, the humid, sodden mess of England, London, coal smoke and fox dung, fog and the half-light of early dusk.

Odette walks. The Heath spreads from Hampstead to Highgate, and she crosses it once, twice, doubling back on herself and drawing in tighter knots.

She is angry. If she stops, she feels it rise up from her stomach, in the heat in her throat and the shake of her hands.

It cost her everything to push Cecilia away. This is what Claudine has taken from her: not only her mother, her father, her home, but the very act of love itself. She has become cruel. She has given herself up to damnation.

Cecilia may never forgive her, and she should not.

But it is the only way Odette can think of to keep her safe.

Claudine murdered Lydia. Odette is sure of it. Oh, maybe she is trading on nothing but a look, a moment, but it was like a fire iron striking her chest, like a bell rung inside her head, echoing still. How is she to explain it? How is she to make that same epiphany bloom for any other? Claudine's guilt must be writ high; she must make everyone see it. Her aunt cannot be allowed to keep her secret; it must be split open like the spiked shell of a horse chestnut crushed beneath a boot, the soft heart yielded and turned to a pulpy mess.

Her mother's ghost trails her, somewhere behind her and to the left, a white shape moving between the trees, as skeletal as the leafless branches.

Odette will break Claudine open. She will expose the unjust heart of her.

She can see no other way. Claudine must be driven from her home like vermin. Ever since she arrived in their lives, there has been some invisible battle of wills unfolding. Claudine has declared that there can be only space for one, and thus first Lydia and now Odette must go. They are trapped in a place of want and scarcity; there is not enough to go around, and Claudine will ensure she gets her due.

Odette cannot share with her. There is nothing to be shared.

Odette must win.

And to win, she must destroy.

It is past dusk when Odette returns at last to the house. It is lit up bright as a furnace, each window blazing into the night, as though it is a castle, a fortification, into which she now delivers herself. A little of its old glory remains, in the tapestries of rich thread, the carpets, the Turkish lamps and the paintings hung on every wall. This is what Claudine wants to claim: this perfect nest, this comfortable bower. A husband, a place, a home, a position. She shores up the defences around herself – George, Penelope – and cuts off each piece of land beneath Odette's feet until she is standing with her back to a cliff edge. Odette has been so blinded by her misery that she has not seen the moves made against her from the start.

Poor Lydia would never have seen any of it coming.

The fury rises up in Odette again as she strips her hat and coat, changes her boots for her indoor shoes and climbs the stairs to her room.

Her mother was defenceless. She was always a weak, fumbling thing, like a kitten, like a doll – she needed protection. Odette was the only one who could ever truly offer it.

Those cold fingers slip along her jaw, the line of her throat, in comfort, in claiming.

Odette will see justice done.

She will not let Lydia be forgotten.

The door to her bedroom is open, and she halts in confusion. The locked drawer of her desk has been forced open, and Claudine stands before the glowing fire, where a handful of papers are turning into ash.

'What are you doing?' Her voice sounds alien to her, as though coming from an immeasurable distance.

She crosses to the drawer, yanks it out and searches its empty interior, but she already knows what it is Claudine has burnt.

'The memorial – what have you done?' There are tears choking her throat. She goes to the fire at once, but it is too late. The last memories of her mother curl and char, lost. 'How dare you? That was *mine*.'

'This is my house. Everything in it is mine. I do not need to explain my actions to you.' It is as though the mask has been removed, and Claudine no longer feels any need to disguise her hatred of Odette. 'Something you are too self-righteous to admit. This is *my* house, and you live in it by my good grace.'

It is almost shocking to hear it stated so openly.

'It was my home first – and my mother's,' counters Odette. 'You have only stolen into it like a cuckoo. I do not understand why you want it. Everything here is so intolerable to you. Everything is hateful. Does it ever occur to you that you are the sour and hateful one?'

The words pour out of her, and it is like falling, giddy and frightening and free.

Claudine's eyes blaze. 'You cannot help yourself, can you? I don't need to be preached to by some sanctimonious child. Everyone walks on eggshells around you, so afraid to upset poor dear Odette, but you are so caught up in your own self-pity you do not see it.'

'It is *grief*, and you are all so insistent to deny me it because it inconveniences you. But it is *human*, and I believe more and more that you are not.' Odette keeps looking back to the scraps of paper in the grate, the last moments of her mother's life, which she had taken painful care to record – gone. It strikes her like her loss all over again, a blow to the body so full and inescapable it all but knocks her to the floor. 'Why did you do it? To hurt me?' she asks. 'Or was there something in there you don't want anyone else to know?'

Claudine holds herself back, seems to shake with her anger, with the effort to hold onto the last shreds of control.

'These endless dramatics. It is always about *you*, isn't it? I am sick of it. I will not stand for it any longer. You have everything granted to you – your father indulges your frivolous demands to waste his money at university. You have us all bowed to your precious *grief*. Yet you do not spare a moment's thought for the feelings of others. You do not consider what *I* have been through. When I was not much older than you, I was orphaned and had to go abroad to earn my own wage. But you do not have a shred of empathy for anyone but yourself, and it is sickening. I will not tolerate it. I will see you put straight.'

Odette is crying; it is like a broken riverbank in a flood, and she is subsumed, the strength of her emotions taking her to pieces, working away at the mortar between the stones. She does not know how to defend herself against Claudine, against such a vicious attack; she is not built for it, and she fears that she has made a grievous error moving against her.

Those cold fingers press against her neck again, and she all but leans into them for some scant comfort. It is like feeling ground at last beneath her feet, a tree trunk to brace against as the flood waters wash over her.

She returns her focus to Claudine, eyes narrowing. 'Don't you mean see me gone, like my mother? Father told me I am on borrowed time. You will throw me out.'

'Once again, you insist on perceiving everything through your hysterics. It is about time your father took you in hand and had you married and settled.'

But Odette feels the force of her mission now; she holds right on her side. 'Did my mother know you had designs on her husband when you came back?' she asks. 'Convenient for you that she died. Almost like you had a hand in it.'

The slap stings sharp across her cheek.

Odette holds her face in shock. 'You hit me!'

'I am teaching you a lesson that your parents have been too cowardly to teach you.'

Claudine raises her hand, as if to strike again.

Before she can, there is a noise beyond the door, and she steps hastily away from Odette.

Their commotion has drawn attention. George appears on the landing, and behind him are Cecilia, Penelope and Leo, dressed for dinner. Odette did not know they were due to join them tonight. No matter. The more people who witness this, the better.

'Now, girls,' says George, coming into the room with his hands raised as though he is calming a skittish horse. 'This is not called for.'

'Do *not* patronise me, George. Your spinelessness has caused half this problem – you cannot bring your daughter in hand.'

He wilts at once, as though pushed back by the force of Claudine's anger.

Odette's cheek burns. She wants to go to her father, hold onto his sleeve like she is a child again and cry. Tears prickle her eyes, and she feels humiliated to be made so small, so scared.

'What's happened?' Leo frowns from the back of the group. 'Are you fighting?'

'Of course they're not fighting,' says Penelope. 'Odette is overwrought. Let us all go downstairs and leave her be.'

Cecilia has slid through the group and is edging towards Odette's side. Odette wants to reach for her, but she must not. Not now, not here.

Still, it is like a cut to the heart that Cecilia will come to her after everything.

The girl walks blindly into danger, for love.

How dare Claudine take so much from all of them.

Penelope touches her hand to Claudine's elbow, tries to draw her off. 'Come now. Leave her to her own dramatics.'

Claudine shakes her off. 'No. I will have this finished now. I will not allow a spoilt child to dictate the way we live. Odette owes us all an apology for making a misery out of what should be a joyous time.'

Odette is not looking at Claudine as she speaks. Over her shoulder is a flash of white, the outline of a figure moving from the darkness.

The room is dimly lit, only the glow of the fire and an oil lamp placed on the desk holding back the winter gloom. But it is enough to see the face drift into shape, the line of a nose, the too-familiar mouth, eyes all drained of colour.

Lydia's ghost steps forwards, the soft tap of bare feet against the floor.

No one else seems to notice.

Of course.

This is a gift just for her.

Like a shadow double, her mother stands behind Claudine, a pale echo, a restless spirit.

Her mother has not left her. Odette could cry.

Her mother is *here*.

Odette pinches her thighs through her skirts, clenches her toes inside her shoes, forcing herself back to life.

This is *her* house.

She must be brave.

Claudine will not win. Even if Odette destroys herself in the eyes of her family, her friends, she will take this woman down.

'You killed her, didn't you?'

The silence is thunderous.

'What did you say?' whispers Cecilia.

Leo's face twists in anger. 'For God's sake, will you stop this. You're not doing yourself any favours, Odette. Everyone is sick of you.'

Odette ignores him and looks straight at Claudine. 'You burnt the memorial because there was evidence in it you wished to hide. I think you were so tired of her. More tired of her than any of us could have realised. She was not an easy woman – I know that well – and she was your sister. You endured having her for a sister longer than any of us knew her. Of course you ran out of patience, fell to jealousy. Because it was jealousy, wasn't it? She was the talented one. She married well. She had the life in London you wanted for yourself. And now here you are – you have taken it from her.'

'How dare you – how *dare* you! George – stop her. Shut your mouth.'

Claudine lunges towards her, but Odette dances back, grabs Cecilia by the wrist and pulls her to the bed, pushing her down onto it. The rest of the group is frozen in confusion and horror.

'What an affront it must have been to be asked to nurse her. This terrible sister who had taken everything you felt rightly yours.'

'Lies – slander!'

'That last night, you were all alone with her.' Odette takes up a position beside Cecilia, who now lies prone, like Lydia once did. Odette cannot meet her eye. 'You saw her in the bed, and you saw your chance to be rid of her.'

Lydia's hungry spirit comes closer, milky eyes grown wider. '*Yes. Yes, my girl. Just like that.*'

Odette is shaking with fear, hysterics. She cannot stop herself now, even if she wanted to – she is too caught up in the truth that pours through like a conduit.

'Stop it – stop it, you mad, hateful girl. These are your own lunatic inventions!' cries Claudine.

'What did you do? Did you dose her morphine too high? Did you feed her poison from the start? Or were you so full of spite and jealousy that you smothered her when she was too weak to fight you? It would be easy, just like this.'

Odette snatches up a pillow and presses it down over Cecilia's face.

Penelope screams.

At once, Leo and George are at her elbow, trying to pull her away from Cecilia, but Odette knows she must make a full performance – they must see clearly what it is that Claudine has done. Claudine must be forced to witness her own cruel and base wickedness. Surely this will break her; surely this will force the confession from her lips.

Beneath her hands, Cecilia struggles, scratches at Odette's wrists in real panic. Odette does not know if she is strong enough to continue, but then she feels her mother's cold arms around her, pressing down alongside her.

A voice against her ear. '*You are mine. You will not leave me. You will not leave me alone in the cold and the dark.*'

And Odette will not. She will not fail her mother again.

'Get off her, you lunatic.' Leo hooks an arm around her waist and, like he is executing some rugby tackle at school, hauls her away so that they fall to the floor, panting. Cecilia lurches up, knocking the pillow from her red face, cheeks wet with tears; Penelope is at her side, close to hysterics. George watches in horror, frozen in place.

Hungrily, hopefully, Odette looks around for Claudine. What has she said? Why are they not all looking at her?

Claudine has backed right up to the doorway, framed in light from behind, but it is enough to see her expression, stricken.

Odette smiles at her, giddy and sick. 'Was it not just like that?' she asks.

'You will regret this,' is all Claudine says before she turns on her heel and flees.

Odette drifts away – the noise of too many voices, hands shaking her, all drowning out her thoughts. She is exhausted, euphoric, miserable, broken. Her face is wet; she is crying.

All she seems to do these days is cry.

Dimly, she is aware of Cecilia being helped away, of a heated exchange between Leo and George.

And then the door slams.

She is alone.

Except – she is not.

Lydia strokes her hair, hands cold as the winter ponds on the Heath.

'*You are doing so well, my girl.*'

Odette nuzzles into the touch.

'*Keep going.*'

9

Cecilia

IT IS SO QUIET. Perfectly, impossibly quiet. Cecilia cannot hear the noise of the servants downstairs or the chime of the clocks or the wheels of carriages outside. There is nothing.

They have left her in a spare room to rest, as though lying amongst more pillows is what she best needs. Her mother near-fainted away and was too weak to go back to the Gate House. She sleeps now in an armchair in the corner of the room, head tipped back.

Cecilia cannot believe what Odette has done. It feels unreal, impossible, like the product of a fever or one of their own plays gone so darkly wrong. She could not have meant it, surely. She would have stopped, whether or not she had been dragged off.

Wouldn't she?

And yet Cecilia can still feel the press of the cotton against her nose and mouth, the weight of dense down and the bar of Odette's arm behind her, stealing the breath from her lungs. It felt like she thinks drowning must, breathing but finding no air, lungs heaving against nothing.

At least in drowning, there would be the give of water, something to fill her.

This was an absence, a panic, a hard stop.

Odette did this to her.

She cannot sleep.

Cecilia wriggles away from the pillows, out from beneath the covers, and pads softly from the room without waking her mother.

She must speak to Odette. So much poison lies between them now. If she cannot draw it from the wound, then it will fester and kill them both.

Perhaps it already has.

Perhaps she is doing nothing but chasing a ghost.

When she comes to Odette's door, she can hear crying from the other side.

At least they are not so lost as all that. At least emotion touches them still.

So she goes inside.

Odette is slumped on the floor, leaning against the wall. The fire has died down low, and the cold has begun to creep in from the windows.

'You shouldn't be here,' is the first thing Odette says. 'It's too dangerous. You shouldn't be here.'

Cecilia does not sit near her. Instead, she drops down onto the rug before the bed and puts her back to the footboard. 'No. Probably not.'

She thinks, for a while, that Odette might apologise. There is such a torturous look of despair and shame on her face that Cecilia cannot imagine that any other thoughts occupy her mind.

Eventually, she speaks. 'It – went too far,' she says haltingly. 'I am sorry.'

Cecilia finds, abruptly, that she is furious. 'I never thought you would hurt me. I never thought I would be scared of you.'

Odette buries her face in her hands. 'You don't know how it pains me to hear you say that.'

'No, I don't. If you did truly feel pain over the way you've treated me, you would have stayed your hand long before now.'

'I couldn't! You don't understand. This isn't about you – it's—' She cuts herself off.

'What is it about, Odette? I have been begging you to tell me, begging you to let me help you, and instead you make wild accusations and turn your back on me, take a knife to everything we have held dear between us. Why? For God's sake, Odette – why?'

Odette grinds the heels of her hands into her eyes, taking several ragged breaths. 'All right. All right, I'll tell you.'

Cecilia's breath catches in her throat.

It is like some different creature lifts its head from Odette's hands, a ruined, ancient thing.

'I have seen my mother's ghost,' says Odette, voice low and flat.

Cecilia searches her face. 'You mean – you mean *really*?'

'Yes. I thought I was mad at first, but she has haunted me since the day of her funeral. It's real.'

'Is that why you took me to the séance?'

'Yes. I wanted you to see her for yourself.'

Cecilia does not speak for a while, turning it over in her mind.

'I see.'

'She told me Claudine murdered her and I must seek revenge. I have been frantic with it. It is true – don't you see? I have to get Claudine to confess. There – that is all of it. Do you believe me?'

There is a long, cold silence. The room is so quiet and so dark, and Cecilia feels herself sinking, sinking.

This cannot be.

'You mock me,' she says softly. For what else can it be? How can she trust Odette now?

'I do not mock you. Cecilia, please—'

'Do not,' she cuts her off, sharp and shaking. 'Do not ask me to make a fool of myself for you again. I have stood by you through all of this – this—'

'Madness?' says Odette.

'Yes! Perhaps.'

'So you side with them.'

'For God's sake Odette, you know I do not. I told you today that I have been trying to find the money your mother promised you so we can escape. What I do not understand above all is why you are being so *cruel*.'

What escape is left to them now? They cannot escape what they have said to each other. What Odette has done. Perhaps she should tell her now about George and Claudine's past engagement, but what would be the point? Odette needs no more fuel on the fire of her obsession.

Odette slumps back against the wall, and a hard mask falls across her face, mouth pulling into a tight line.

'You have said it yourself. I am mad. Mad for grieving my mother, mad for detesting my father for marrying my aunt, mad for railing against those who mistreat me.'

'Madness is not the same as being self-absorbed and cruel. You are not the only person in the world to have felt loss.'

'So you agree with Claudine.'

Cecilia all but throws her hands up in frustration. 'I have loved you and loved you, and you toy with me and mock me and *hurt* me. Perhaps you *are* mad if you want to destroy all that you have.'

Odette falls silent.

There is a horrible, dizzy, lurching feeling that makes Cecilia place both hands on the floor to steady herself.

'I am sorry I have disappointed you,' she says. 'I . . . I do not know how else to be other than how I am.'

'You do not believe me,' says Odette again.

'How *can* I?' says Cecilia, angry and distraught. 'This is – it is too much. I do not know how to help you anymore.'

Odette turns away. 'Then stop trying. I don't need your help.'

'Fine. As you like.'

Trembling, Cecilia goes.

Odette does not need her. There it is. That is the truth.

Beneath her, the world cracks open, a void dropping all the way down into the core of the earth, into Hell.

10

Odette

ODETTE WAKES EARLY.

There doesn't seem much point in sleeping anymore. She does not dream – or, she thinks she doesn't, but she wakes clammy and sick, twitching at sudden noises and with a need to scrub herself all over in the ice water left from yesterday on the washstand. She heard Penelope and Leo take Cecilia home very late last night. No maid has come to replace it with fresh, hot water, nor to stoke the fire. They have been forbidden to, she supposes – Claudine marking out her territory within the house and placing Odette outside of it. She may be present, but she is not welcome.

Or perhaps it is a punishment.

She deserves it, she thinks.

Her mother isn't here.

It is strange, how this apparition has gone from a horror to a comfort. Easier to bear, maybe, now she has accepted her fate. She will never escape her mother. Whether she is here or not, she carries her mother inside her, in her mind and her heart.

She dresses in black: black stockings, black petticoats, black bombazine skirt and black bodice, black jet at her throat and ears, and pins her hair up in a simple style, then sits at her writing desk. The drawer hangs loose from where it was wrenched open last night, pitifully empty. She has not unpacked most of her things from Cambridge: the desk is bare save an empty inkpot, a pad of blotting paper. Through the window, she can see past the leafless trees to Cecilia's room in the Gate House. Odette leans forwards, straining to see her. If she could just catch one glimpse of Cecilia, it would be like a light breaking through cloud, like a benediction.

It is empty. The light is out.

Cecilia has abandoned her.

It is only right, after what she did.

And it is safe. It is better this way.

There is no way out now, only *through*.

A knock on her door interrupts her thoughts.

It is her father.

He does not come inside, only stands on the threshold, dressed formally. 'Good. You're up. Come along.'

Odette rises from the desk. 'Where are we going?'

'Herne House. Don't pack a bag, we will have your things sent on. We must go at once. I don't think anyone here will want to see you.'

It is a worse blow than he seems to acknowledge, and Odette follows him meekly downstairs and out of the house. She feels sick. What will he say to her? He is so remote and serious that it makes him alien, forbidding.

He walks down the street in great strides that she must hurry to match, steering them towards the station. It is a flat, grey day, cold enough to pinch at her nose and fingertips.

Her father must be angry at her – but she feels a flare of injustice at the thought. Why should he be angry? Why does he not take her side? Surely he must see that Claudine's behaviour is extreme? Why can he not see the guilt writ so plain?

At the station, he waits for a train heading into the city, then finds a compartment in which they can be alone. The seats are upholstered in stiff fabric that has gone dark with dust and dirt, and the foot heaters give off a smell of burning metal. They sit in silence as the guard slams the door and the train slowly pulls out of the station.

It is an agony. Will he say something?

They roll along the tracks, between high-sided brick embankments, the dawn light flickering between buildings.

Odette feels alive with anticipation. She wants desperately for him to see her, to see what is happening, to defend her. Surely he will – surely he will remember that his duty is to his daughter and not his new wife.

'This is too much,' he says, after a great deal of thought. 'It must stop now.'

'I agree,' says Odette quickly. 'I am beside myself that Claudine destroyed my memorial of Mother – it is too cruel.'

He does not meet her gaze. 'Yes. Well. Claudine and I don't see eye to eye on that.'

'Don't see eye to eye? What is there to disagree on! If you don't believe me that she was destroying the evidence of what she did, then it could only have been from cruelty and how could you excuse that?'

'We can all do hurtful things in the heat of the moment. Claudine has suffered greatly in her life,' he says, 'and she has learnt to survive through attack.'

'And so I must stomach it?'

George shifts uncomfortably. 'You take it all so seriously. A little grace would go a long way.'

'And you will do anything for an easy life,' snaps Odette. 'I don't see what reason she would have to destroy it other than guilt. She had a hand in Mother's death, it is so clear. Why can none of you see it? Mother only became so sick after Claudine arrived. She knows I know the truth, so she comes for me too.'

Odette pushes. 'She's guilty. I saw it on her face. Father, listen to me.'

He pinches the bridge of his nose. 'Is that what this has all been about? A . . . delusion about your mother's death?'

'You saw Claudine last night – you saw it as clearly as I did. I know you must have. She knows she has done something wrong.'

George sighs. 'Yes, she might feel guilty that she failed her sister in the end. She nursed her through her last days, and that takes a toll on anyone. You assume too much and give little generosity towards others.'

Odette is hot with offence. 'Because you have all been so generous towards *me*? As though I did not also nurse my mother through the end of her life? You make me a problem to be tidied away.'

'That is not fair.'

'It is *true*. You have all decided me mad, but I think I am the only sane one here. You want me to bite my tongue, and I *will not*. Why must I swallow my pain to be more palatable for everyone else? You are all allowed your pain and your weaknesses, to nurture and coddle yourselves as victims. Why is *my* pain intolerable? Why am I expected to eat all the sin myself?'

George says nothing. He has become distant again, and of all things, is winding his pocket watch, as though her misery is an apt backdrop to his chores.

Does he mean to hurt her? Or is it that she overwhelms him, and he must vacate himself in whatever way he can?

His detachment frightens her, and stokes her fury.

'Are you quite done?' he asks, tucking the watch away.

'No. I have a question for you. How could you forget Mother so quickly?'

There it is: the plain truth of it, the wound she nurses in her heart.

At last, something cuts through. He recoils.

'I do not forget her.'

'Forgive me my mistake, your wedding nuptials were so distracting I did not notice your grief.'

Yes, she is cruel, maybe they are all correct and she is a monster. But she no longer cares. Let her be the Devil, let her be mad, she will suffer and die either way.

'Did you ever love Mother?'

George's mouth trembles. 'Of course I did. In my way.'

Ah. And what *way* was that?

'You judge so quickly, but you love different people for different reasons.'

'You did not love her as you love Claudine.'

He gives an almost helpless shrug. 'Claudine is a force of nature. Once she has fixed upon something it is pointless to try to stop her.'

'And she fixed upon you.'

'I know you do not believe me, but I truly hoped that one day you could be happy for my happiness. I have done my best to be a good father to you, but when you have your own children you will understand that it is not a straightforward thing.'

She is sour all through, sick with bitterness. 'Is it being a good father to throw your only child out to suit yourself?'

It is hurt for hurt's sake. She does not know what she wants him to do with this, only that she cannot bear it all being buried within her. She must get it out, and onto anyone who will take it.

'Odette,' he says, half a warning, but can find no further words.

Nor can Odette. She is worn through. What else can she say to make anyone listen?

The train rattles into a tunnel, and they are cocooned in the dark with only the gas lamp. The window becomes a mirror of their mirthless faces.

No one is going to listen.

Claudine could confess before them all, and still no one would listen to a word.

The train draws into the station, and the conductor proceeds along the platform, bellowing *all change*. Their compartment door is yanked open, and the chaotic noise blares in on them. George has not said where they are going, so she follows him, curled around her own pain like it's a fragile thing cradled in her arms.

The platform is narrow and overfull, passengers waiting for a delayed train on the line opposite, their own train disgorging more people than should be possible. They are buffeted and pushed by the tides, until they are trapped in a slow-moving crush for the stairs.

George seems to have drawn back into himself, gathering himself up, standing a little taller, straighter. Perhaps she has made it easy for him now, to do what dirty work is needed.

'We have agreed that it is better if you do not stay in London.'

'You mean to keep me at Herne House?'

'No. We have arranged for you to spend time at a spa town in Austria.'

'A spa town,' Odette repeats.

'For a rest cure. I am told it is an exceptional place and has brought many young women into better health. You will stay in Suffolk for a few days while we make the necessary arrangements, then you will be escorted to the Continent. Claudine has found a well-regarded ladies' companion to accompany you.'

In the distance, the chug of an oncoming train grows louder, the first billow of steam rolling beneath the station awning.

She is struck then by the understanding that, without her mother, there is nothing holding her family together anymore. She has no family, no home. Perhaps it was always an illusion, a staged scene they all took their places in, but now the canvas has been destroyed, the paints spilt. Her father knew this, and he has taken off his costume and walked away. There is only Odette left, in some cheap costume jewellery, stiff with pain from holding her position.

For nothing.

For *nothing.*

Out of the corner of her eye, she sees something move, a flash of lavender silk embroidered with white lilies.

Lydia's shawl, stolen by Claudine.

Claudine.

At once, Odette's sorrow turns to fury – how *dare* Claudine follow them? This is unbearable, for her to witness Odette's humiliation, her powerlessness.

She spins around amid the crowd, causing a ripple of movement around her.

But it is not Claudine.

It is Penelope, in the purple shawl. She stumbles back reflexively, recoiling from Odette, her face contorted with shock and guilt. Was she spying on them? Had Claudine sent her?

They are so close to the platform edge.

Odette did not realise how close.

Nor did Penelope.

The train bores into the station, thunderous and heavy on the tracks.

The crowd surges, but Penelope is unsteady on her feet, buffeted, with nowhere else to go.

It is the work of a moment. The slightest of missteps.

There is no ground beneath her feet.

Odette is frozen in horror.

Penelope goes over the platform edge just as the train hits her head-on.

Late Summer

September 1898, Hampstead, London

Darkling I listen; and, for many a time
I have been half in love with easeful Death,
Call'd him soft names in many a mused rhyme,
To take into the air my quiet breath;
Now more than ever seems it rich to die,
To cease upon the midnight with no pain

'Ode to a Nightingale', John Keats

1

Odette

A DARK AND BITTER AUTUMN comes early to greet Lydia's return to the London house, she the sick and stately queen, and the rest her muffled retinue. A squall of rain daily sheets across the Heath, scattering against the many windows like pebbles flung in anger. The place is battered, wind howling in the chimneys and water blown in beneath the doors; a phalanx of servants mop and dust and sweep, but there is no keeping nature out.

The world turns around Lydia's illness.

Confined to bed, she is pale and weak and gripped by stomach pains, and Odette spends much of the thin daylight by her side, reading to her from *Emma*. Sometimes she listens intently, sometimes Odette is waved away by one hand, curled into a claw, a drawn expression closing down her mother's face. Her mother is sliding away from her. Odette is swallowed by a panic that she cannot race fast enough to keep up.

Odette and Cecilia have spread out the sheet of stiff white cotton that will form Lydia's shroud. Of course, they could have bought a fine shroud from any number of tasteful outfitters in town, but Odette has chosen to sew one herself. She cannot bear the thought that there is nothing more she can do for her mother.

They work up in Lydia's studio, where the best light can be had from the soaring glass. Already, the close stitching hurts Odette's eyes, and her fingers tremble. The cloth is cut into a simple pattern, like a nightgown but open at the back, and together they begin the careful work of inserting the sleeves into the armholes. They have been cut large to make it easier to manhandle onto a lifeless body.

Around the cuffs and collar of the shroud, she thinks she will embroider baby's breath for everlasting love, red carnation for heartache and marigold for grief.

Claudine arrives in the doorway, stiff-backed and holding a tray of untouched food. 'I have business to attend to,' she says, then leaves without waiting for a response.

Odette knows this is her summons. She secures her needlework and replaces the thimble in the sewing box.

This is how it goes now: Claudine will not explain herself, and Odette will not ask. There has been no further conversation between them since her father took her into the orchard and explained her flaws to her. It could be cowardice, but Odette has shied away from any further discussion, saying very little to Claudine while also being mindful when she does to be unfailingly polite, quiet, to tidy herself away into corners and keep her eyes downturned. She does not know how to face the fight: better to be diminished, placatory. There is no need for Claudine to attack her if she takes herself out first.

'Do you want me to come with you?' asks Cecilia.

Odette hesitates. The truth is that she is afraid of her mother, as well. Afraid to be alone with her, to witness what is happening. 'For a little while, if you can spare the time.'

A polite fiction that Cecilia indulges her in. They both know Cecilia will spare her anything she asks.

Lydia's bedroom faces onto the garden; the fire is stoked high and the surfaces are cluttered with the detritus of the sickbed: medicine bottles and handkerchiefs, spouted cups to help her drink, ceramic bowls to catch her bloody vomit, sprigs of lavender against the ripe smell of a body.

Odette enters, braced – to be cheerful, to be patient, to swallow down her horror and shape herself into her mother's helpmeet. It is frightening to see her mother so reduced, to see her beautiful face twisted in pain, her bones standing out against her skin. These are memories she will never be able to scour, her idea of her mother forever indelibly changed, and she rails against it, the horror and the grief, and the desire to turn away and bury herself in beauty and noise and pleasure as though she can blot out what is happening if only she does not give it quarter.

But she has been enough of a coward. There is nothing she can do but offer witness to pain: that is the only gift she has left to give.

The curtains are closed tight against the day; Odette opens them, allowing only a gentle light in, just as her mother likes it.

Lydia lies in the bed, and briefly, Odette thinks she is sleeping, until she stirs, her chestnut hair shifting across the pillow and catching the light like the scales of a fish darting under water.

'Angel.' Lydia reaches out a hand to her. Odette sits in the chair drawn up to her bedside.

'Mama.'

Lydia doesn't speak again. Her face is pinched and drawn.

Cecilia draws up a chair on the other side of the bed, takes the prayer book from the bedside table and turns the pages to a few marked passages.

They have not told Lydia what the doctor has said. It has been the subject of much fraught debate. Aunt Penelope worries that in hiding the doctor's assessment, they are denying Lydia the chance for a good death, to reflect and make her peace with God and give a comforting example of the way a good Christian can face death. But Odette could not stomach it. The doctor has not said it is the end for sure, only that they must prepare for it. These are different things. While there is still a chance, surely they must ensure Lydia focuses on life?

In the end, Claudine forbade anyone from distressing her patient, and George offered no opinion, glad to see the matter settled.

But looking at her mother now, Odette wonders if she can possibly be in any doubt about her own failing body.

Around each of her eyes is a dark shadow, and when she speaks, her gums are pale and seem to be receding from teeth that are over-prominent. It is ghoulish, as though her living body gives way already to the grave.

It has occurred to Odette that her mother may starve to death, if she continues in this way for too long, unable to eat more than a little. Perhaps it is a mercy to be hoped for that the fever will take her first.

No, no. Nothing will be taken.

The rain softens against the window, and the wind slows its assault across the Heath. Odette holds her mother's hand, stroking her thumb across her fingers, and thinks about the nights her mother would climb into bed with her, press them close together as though Odette were a small child again, as though there was a way to make them again one entity in two bodies. It should not be possible for them to be severed by death in this way. Surely while Odette lives, her mother cannot leave her. 'I want to paint.' Lydia rouses suddenly, struggling up from the covers. There is a feverish urgency to her movements, a clumsiness.

'Mother?'

'Up, help me up!'

Odette and Cecilia obey, supporting Lydia on both sides to lift her up to sitting, pressing pillows behind her back and around her head to support her weak body.

'Paper – charcoal – I can sketch if nothing else.'

'I'll get it,' says Cecilia quickly, and she slips from the room.

Lydia is too animated, bright-eyed and pink-cheeked. The heat radiating from her is something fierce.

'I really think you should rest,' says Odette, but Lydia ignores her.

'Get Leo. I have a scene. Marat in the bathtub. It must be him.'

Odette tries to grasp Lydia's hand, but she rips it away, nails catching sharply on Odette's skin. It is a sharp slap of shock to be hurt by her mother in this way.

Lydia does not seem to notice.

Cecilia comes back with sketching paper and a tin of charcoals.

'I said get Leo. We will do the scene right here.'

'He's not at home, Mama.'

He avoids her, Odette thinks. She cannot blame him. They are all so helpless here, she understands that it is easier for him to go to work, where he can *do* something.

'Oh. Well, we must make do.' Lydia spreads the paper about her and makes a few initial sweeping lines with the charcoal. 'A knife – we need a knife. Cecilia, lie across the foot of the bed. It is a bath – you will have to think about that.'

Cecilia and Odette exchange looks, unsure. Hesitantly, Cecilia sits on the end of the bed and lies back so that she is spread across it.

'Odette, a knife, quickly.'

Perhaps it is better to humour her. Odette finds a letter opener on the writing desk and returns, hovering awkwardly by Cecilia. 'Just a brief sketch,' she says. 'But you must rest – the doctor said so.'

Lydia is working already, with jerky, uncontrolled movements. Her hair hangs lank around her face; it should be washed, but Odette does not know how to hold her mother in that way. She thinks, abruptly: who deals with her mother's bedpans? Is it Claudine? One of the maids? Should it be Odette?

She does not know what she owes her mother, and she is frightened that, to pay the debt racked up, she must give herself up entirely.

'Hold the knife to Cecilia's breast. Open your shirt a little, darling – yes, like that. Now – press down. It is important to see the skin depress under pressure. Harder.'

'Mother—'

'Break the skin. Only a little – break it – there must be blood—'

'*Mother.*'

The pain in Odette's voice seems to shake Lydia back into herself at last. Odette drops the knife to the coverlet, tears welling. Cecilia sits up, fixing her blouse, looking between Odette and Lydia.

Lydia covers her hand with her mouth. 'Oh. Oh, I've ruined it.'

Odette takes a shallow, shaking breath, before she can speak. 'Nothing is ruined, Mama.'

Lydia is going to cry. It is old familiar weather passing through, and Odette finds herself comforted in some unkind way to at least stand on known ground.

'Maybe we should ask Mrs Binx to sit with her for a while,' says Cecilia. 'Until the doctor can come again.'

There is the unspoken message beneath it: *you do not have to stay here. You do not have to do this.*

It is what Cecilia always says to her.

But Cecilia is wrong. She doesn't understand.

This is everything that Odette must do.

'No,' she says. 'You go. I'll stay.' She climbs onto the bed beside Lydia and holds her hand. 'She needs me.'

Cecilia looks as though she will insist again, and when she doesn't, Odette is strangely disappointed.

Instead, Cecilia gathers up the sketching materials and takes them with her.

Now, Odette is alone with her mother, as it always has been.

She rests her head on her mother's shoulder, feeling the warmth of her that is still here.

She cannot leave her. She knows what she owes.

She cannot leave.

2

Cecilia

THE ROAD BETWEEN THE Gate House and Odette's house is as wide and painful as a wound, an unnatural dividing line dug deep between Cecilia and Odette. The workings of illness have separated them as painfully as a severed limb, as a body rendered into parts. With each downward turn Lydia takes, Odette sinks further into the earth with her.

Cecilia does not know what she is supposed to do. Should she insist on crossing the threshold? On inserting herself into Odette's life? What does Odette need from her now?

What could Cecilia give her that could compensate for the loss of her mother?

Cecilia sits in her window, watching Odette's room, waiting for the light to brighten the glass. Sometimes, Odette will still come to look out across the dark to her, and they will find their old place together: Cecilia will hold up a book of Keats, Coleridge, Milton, Malory, and they will read across the void.

There is much still to prepare for their departure for university. They have packed trunks and toiletries and books and stationery. All continues as though Lydia will last long enough for Odette to go and return. The only time Cecilia dared ask Odette whether they should reconsider taking up their places, Odette gave Cecilia no space to explain herself, insisting that Cecilia *must* go.

Mostly, she sees nothing of Odette.

It frightens her.

Where has her friend gone? Her lover?

Who is she without Odette?

It is as though, somewhere in the last few weeks, the world has gone wrong, splintering and fracturing until she is consumed with panic, like she is only an animal body in fear. Sometimes, in her bath, she sinks under the water as long as she can, holding her breath, as though she can hide down there, as though total immersion can cleanse from her this intolerable sense of danger. Submerged, lungs aching, it is an experience so total that for a brief moment, it is enough. Death is like a rupture that breaks open new ground. This is not earth that she ever knew before was there to be trod. Now, it is irrevocable. She has learnt of some new, frightening portal through which all will walk, and the only comfort is to pray it does not come too often or too soon.

Sometimes she watches Penelope and Claudine speaking, heads bowed close, in the hallway of the Gate House or on the front step of the Hampstead house or walking along the street in tight conversation. Do they plan together? Do they speak of the blackmail?

And then there is the matter of the paintings, the exhibition that Lydia is too ill to even think of. Might she leave something to Odette in her will instead? There is no way Cecilia can ask about it now without being deeply insensitive, and again, it is all speculation that leaves her powerless.

It is no good. She must see Odette. If she sees her, maybe she will understand some way to help her.

She packs away the sewing box and puts on her hat and coat. There is a van waiting in the street, but she pays it little mind. She is unpinning her hat in the hallway when she hears voices. There are no walls for her to disappear into here, and panic rises up her throat. Will she be seen? Will she somehow be in trouble?

She holds her hat before her and stays as still as she can.

The voice, she thought, was Claudine's, but then two men appear, carrying a canvas wrapped in sackcloth. They nod at her but do not stop, making for the front door.

'Where are you taking that?' she asks as they pass. The paintings must surely be those that have been carefully transported down from Suffolk in hope of Lydia's exhibition.

The first man gives her a practised blank look. 'I don't know, miss. Instructions to take these, that's all.'

They pass and carry the painting away to the van.

Before she can think what else to say, she hears Claudine's voice again. It is coming from the drawing room.

As quietly as she can, she slips down the hallway until she can hear the words more clearly.

'. . . do you girls know *nothing* of nursing? It should not fall upon me to explain that bedsheets must be changed *regularly* if used by an invalid, no matter how much extra laundry that might entail. And do not turn your nose up at washing a bedpan, because I know you have done much worse in your sordid little lives—'

'Miss Moore.'

Cecilia turns to see Mr King coming down the stairs.

'Mr King,' she says, darting away from the door at which she has been listening.

'I take it you have also come to pay your respects to Mrs Fairfax-Waugh?'

He is much as she remembers him: dark, appraising eyes, mouth ever on the edge of a smirk. She is struck that again she finds herself alone with him, and she dislikes it.

'To support the family,' she says simply. He does not need to know the intimacies of her life.

A door opens, and Claudine emerges behind them. 'Mr King. How kind of you to call.'

He dips his head in acknowledgement.

'Please, do join me.' Claudine's gaze turns to Cecilia finally. 'Odette is upstairs.'

With that, Mr King brushes past her into the parlour, and the door shuts behind them. She is dismissed.

Cecilia takes the stairs slowly, her stomach clenching. What business does Mr King have with Claudine? He has come to take the paintings, surely, but is not Lydia too ill for the exhibition? And what business is it of Claudine's?

Is there no one who can be trusted?

No one but Odette.

3

Cecilia

THE SHROUD IS ALMOST DONE.

Cecilia sews alone in Lydia's abandoned studio, fixing a trailing line of flower blossoms, adding leaves and petals until the piece is a work of art.

Lydia should be buried with art. That feels important.

The doctor is here again. Each time he comes, Odette sinks further, retreating inside herself, away from Cecilia and into Lydia's dead world. Sometimes, she will sit beside Cecilia, sewing the shroud, and speak not a word for hours.

The shroud is beautiful. Cecilia is strangely proud of it.

When Odette is not here, she will slip her arms into the sleeves – to judge the span of embroidery and the decoration to the chest, of course – and imagine what her own shroud might be like. She has a photo card of Sarah Bernhardt sleeping in a coffin, posed for some part or another. It must induce a special kind of madness to put yourself inside a coffin, to close your eyes and greet death early.

Cecilia touches the delicate embroidery and wonders whether it will be Odette who has to choose the trappings of her end. She cannot imagine outliving her. A world without Odette is no world at all.

Odette bursts through the door in a flurry of skirts, loose hair streaming behind her. 'Ces! Ces, oh God, Ces.' She throws herself into Cecilia's arms and shakes, somewhere between a sob and laughter.

Cecilia holds her for a moment, then pulls them apart enough that she can look into Odette's face and read whether this portends disaster or hope. 'What is it?'

'The doctor – he said she's getting better.'

Cecilia cannot believe it. 'What do you mean? What did he say?'

'Too many things, which I did not understand the half of, but he said he was *happy* with her progress. Happy! Is that not the best thing you have ever heard?'

'I don't understand. What has changed?'

Odette is hardly listening. 'He said her pulse is strong and she has a good colour. He has not said anything so positive in weeks. He even thinks she may have put on a little weight, which surely means her body is healing!'

Cecilia does not want to press her, to unpick what the doctor may have said and what Odette has taken from it. It would be too cruel to wrench that hope from her, but there is a great tremor of fear beneath it. Such miraculous recoveries are not impossible, but they are rare, and she fears what may happen to Odette when – if – this fresh hope is shattered.

Odette bounces up, pulls Cecilia with her. 'Come on – my father has said we must all go to the drawing room and hear it for ourselves.'

Cecilia follows Odette downstairs, where Uncle George, Claudine, Penelope and Leo are already ensconced in armchairs or pressed together on the settee.

The London doctor is very different to his country counterpart. He is long and thin, with a sharp nose and quick, intelligent eyes. He has less of a bedside manner, but Cecilia finds this leads her to trust what he says more.

He is already speaking when Cecilia and Odette join them. '. . . all promising signs. If she pulls through, I am afraid she may be an invalid for the rest of her life and require diligent care, but I am pleased that she is keeping more food down, and there are good signs that the ulcers have begun to heal themselves. It is a tribute to your attentive nursing,' he says to Claudine. 'Mrs Fairfax-Waugh is lucky to have a sister so adept at the feminine arts. You will be a great aid to her recovery. It is the joy God gives to unmarried women to provide such careful ministrations.'

He smiles as he speaks, and Claudine inclines her head in acknowledgement. She sits stiffly upright on her chair, and Cecilia wonders if she is the only one who notices that Claudine is clasping her hands so tightly the knuckles show white through her skin.

There is some more light conversation. Odette is keen to have the doctor repeat his good opinion, at which she cries, to the discomfort of all, announcing the end of the gathering. Odette disappears back into Lydia's room for the remainder of the day, and Penelope ushers Leo and Cecilia home, insisting that their intrusion is no longer wanted.

They eat a simple meal braced against the cold that the unending rain has brought with it. The turn of the weather has come sooner than expected, and half the chimneys still need clearing out of birds' nests that have filled them through the summer, so there is only a fire in every other room. Cecilia's bedroom is like ice, the bedding so cold it feels wet to the touch, and her muscles ache with the tension of holding herself against the onslaught.

When, late that night, Odette beckons her through the open window of her room across the road, Cecilia needs no second invitation.

It is trickier for them to find private ways to be together in London, in their two separate houses. Lydia's illness has given Cecilia good reason to stay close to her *friend*, but also ammunition to her mother to insist that she does not disturb a household under stress. Her mother has a library of etiquette books to fortify her claims, and Cecilia struggles to counter them. But here, in the brief opportunity of night, when the house is locked up and the servants are busy with their final tasks, Cecilia knows how to climb out of her window, slip across the road and clamber up to Odette's own room.

Odette waits for her at the window, to haul her in – and, once Cecilia is inside, Odette is on her at once, with an intensity that takes her by surprise. Odette's hands pull at the collar of her shirt, at the hooks and eyes at her waist, as her mouth presses a hot line along Cecilia's throat.

It is impossible to speak; Cecilia cannot find the words. It is easier to guide Odette to the bed, to introduce some softness to her touch. But still, Odette is hungry, desperate, Cecilia's shift lifted up over her head while Odette remains fully dressed. It is never quite like this between them. Cecilia likes to lead, to serve, trying out each stroke of her fingers or lap of her tongue as though making an offering to her god, attentive to what is welcomed and what is spurned.

Now, it is as though Odette has become a vengeful, demanding spirit of old, capricious and instinctual. She pushes

Cecilia back onto the pillows, kissing her with sharp teeth, biting at her throat, her collarbone, before covering Cecilia's nipple with her mouth. Her other hand pushes Cecilia's legs apart and strokes a line up the inside of her thigh.

Cecilia gasps and arches back, overwhelmed by the twin sensations.

'Odette – slow – slow down.' She is not sure she means it, but there is something wild and frightening about this passion, as though they are riding full pelt into a rising tide. 'Talk to me.'

Odette gives her response with a scrape of an incisor across sensitive flesh, before moving her hand to dip between Cecilia's legs. All thought dissolves like mist against the bright sun of Odette's touch.

They have been with each other long enough that Odette knows too well exactly how to bring her pleasure, and Cecilia surrenders into it. If she tries to move, squirming against the building sensation or canting her hips into Odette's hand, the teeth against her breast press dangerously close to a bite. Odette wants her submission, and Cecilia will give it to her. Cecilia would give her anything.

At some point, Odette moves to straddle Cecilia's leg, grinds herself down against her thigh in rhythm with the movement of her hand, and they fall over the edge together, Odette's voice muffled against Cecilia's body and Cecilia with one hand across her own mouth to silence herself.

When they settle side by side on the bed, naked and clothed, Odette cannot look at her. She curls into Cecilia's side, hiding her face against her body.

'Are you – is everything all right?' Cecilia asks, and it is so worthless a question, so profoundly inadequate.

After a moment, Odette says, 'I do not know what I am.'

Cecilia strokes her hair.

'Life is—' Odette pauses. 'It is too much. How can anyone endure it?'

'I don't know.' And it is the truth. 'We will weather it together. Promise me we will always be together.'

Odette is silent for too long. 'No one can promise that.'

Cecilia swallows. It is a blast of icy Heath air across her skin.

No. She supposes no one *can* promise that.

But she wishes Odette would lie to her.

Cecilia slides free with a plea of needing to use the privy. She finds Odette's dressing gown and slips down the corridor, a well-practised ghost. The whole household should be asleep, or she would not risk it.

'This is not what I agreed to.'

Cecilia freezes, one foot resting lightly on the hall runner before her. Has she been caught? Did she make a noise?

No, the voice is coming from Uncle George's room.

Claudine's voice.

'No one is suggesting any firm arrangements now – let's not overreact.'

Hissing, now. 'Overreact? I will not let my life end being Lydia's nurse. She has taken enough from me already; she cannot demand this.'

Cecilia is endlessly overhearing things. It would be better, she thinks, if she could blind herself, stop up her own ears, make herself the unthinking, compliant girl her mother wants her to be. She is Eve, too tempted by the serpent, too weak for knowledge that can only bring her pain.

'You're tired. Let's all get some sleep, and things will look brighter in the morning.'

It is precisely the sort of bland platitude that Cecilia is all too used to from George.

'Has middle age made you a coward or was I too much of a fool to notice it when we were younger?'

She shouldn't be listening to this. She should go; she *must* go.

'Calm down. We've talked about this. The hired nurse is arriving in the morning. You'll have help.'

'*Help*,' Claudine sneers. 'I am telling you now, I will not give Lydia the years I have left. I will be no one's caretaker. Whatever it costs me, I will not bear it.'

Cecilia screws up her courage and flees.

4

Odette

LYDIA HAS A DELICACY to her, as though she were one of the paper dolls she made when Odette was a child. They used to sit together in Lydia's studio, sketching faces, Odette turning the pages of magazines, studying fashion plates to choose which dresses Lydia would paint, slowly building a wardrobe of outfits for her army of dolls. Lydia always gave her plenty and left Odette alone with the thin, unfeeling paper in place of a mother.

Now, her skin is as transparent as tissue, the map of veins and arteries beneath more like some drawing from an anatomical textbook than one of her paintings. Odette holds her hand, at once eager to be close and repulsed by the thickening of her curved nails, the sense that if she grips too firmly, the skin will tear apart.

Odette sits a long vigil. The hired nurse is here during the day now, but the household still take turns to stay by Lydia's side. Odette takes as many shifts as she can, guilt driving her to stay awake through the night, reading by lamplight until her head aches.

But there is hope now. The doctor says so. This has not all been for naught. Her mother will recover, and they will both know that, when things were at their worst, Odette did not turn away, that she stayed true. She will never leave Lydia, just as Lydia will now never leave her.

Lydia sleeps fitfully, drowsing between worlds, pushed under by the medication the doctor leaves and dragged back up by the pain that still scourges her.

'Angel.'

She is awake now. Odette sets down her book.

Her mother lifts her arm, a weak copy of a gesture Odette knows so well, and she obeys its summons, climbing onto the bed to tuck herself against her mother's small frame and feel her fingers rest against her neck.

'You're such a good girl,' says Lydia. 'My own angel.'

'I'm not that good, Mama.' Odette looks at a point on the wallpaper where it has not been hung quite right and the pattern judders out of shape.

'Oh, far, far, better than me.'

Their breathing falls into synchronisation; Odette feels the swell of her mother's ribs press into her own, the soft flesh of her slack breast as they move as one. Even when her mother has slipped away from her, into her own distress, her own despair, there has always been the solidity of her body to return to. Her mother may not have been present in her mind, but there has been a warm, breathing piece of bone and meat that Odette can hold and know is her mother. Some things are beyond words. There is a world in a touch, in an anchor. Her mother is alive. The world turns around this point; she knows where she stands.

'I have something for you,' says Lydia. She tries to sit up, but her strength fails her and she slumps back. 'I promised you I would give you a safe future, and I mean it.'

'It's all right, Mama, rest now. We have time. You know what the doctor said: you're recovering.'

For a moment, it seems as though Lydia might protest, but she is too pale, the pulse fluttering in her throat. 'It is important to me that I look after you. I have not – I have been neglectful. I know it. I told myself I was a good mother and hid my troubles from you well, but I don't think that is true.'

Odette blinks back her tears. She feels like a cup overfilled. There is too much within her, and she cannot begin to recognise one feeling from another. 'You did your best,' she says.

It is true. And it is not always enough.

They lie there awhile longer, mother and daughter curled together like an ammonite fossil in rock, like oak and ivy, and it occurs to Odette that she does not know which of them is which. The ivy helps the oak grow tall and strong, though the tree will stand without it – but without the oak, the ivy is nothing but a weak, strangling thing, struggling towards any support, no matter how ill-suited.

'I want to see the sky and the light,' says Lydia.

'Mother, it is late—'

'The sky and the light,' Lydia repeats, almost keening. 'Darling, please.'

Odette goes to the windows and opens the curtains onto the canopy of cloud that hangs above the Heath, blotting out any stars. No sky. No light.

But Lydia sighs, sinks back into her pillows. She is not seeing this world, Odette realises. She is somewhere else.

Odette strokes her forehead, as she remembers Lydia doing for her as a child. There. A body in space. Her mother is still here.

The door opens softly. Claudine stands in its frame, the light from the corridor casting her face in darkness. 'You can go now,' she says plainly.

Odette cannot stifle her yawn. It is painful to stay awake, but each time she leaves her mother, it feels like a betrayal.

Claudine steps aside, leaving the doorway free. The instruction is clear.

Odette hates the anxiety that cramps in her stomach when she is alone with her aunt, the shame of it, of not knowing how to behave to avoid bringing down her anger. Her mother's illness has filled the house so totally that Odette has been able to hide behind it, but she cannot help feeling her skin crawl, her hair prick, when Claudine looks at her.

'Thank you for sitting with her,' says Odette carefully.

'You forget she has been my sister far longer than she has been your mother. This is my duty.'

'Yes. Of course. I'm sorry.'

'Go on, then. I have enough to be getting on with.'

Head down, Odette scurries from the room.

Her own bed waits for her, a warming pan freshly removed from between the sheets to counteract the cold night. It is only September, but the year has turned hard, the leaves on the trees sagging under the weight of the rain, and the earth of the Heath becoming boggy and swollen. She sleeps fitfully, reaching for Cecilia, who is not there, and dreaming of a powerful tide of rain washing all the ground away to expose a skeletal network of tree roots and sewers.

Odette wakes to the grey dawn light, confused. What has woken her?

The maid has not yet been in to light her fire or deliver a jug of hot water, but there is the sound of footsteps moving up and down the stairs in haste, doors closing, the urgent murmur of voices.

She pulls herself from bed, wrapping her dressing gown about her, and goes into the corridor. Her father and Claudine stand at the top of the stairs, in quiet conversation. At the sound of her door opening, they both turn to her.

And Odette knows.

She falls back against a side table, grasping reflexively for something that will hold her weight, but nothing can support the weight of this. *She* cannot bear it. It will crush her down and press all the air from her lungs, and she will die, too.

Her father comes to her, stops an awkward distance away, as though he does not know how to cross the divide between them.

'Odette, I'm so sorry,' he says. 'Your mother is dead.'

Letters

December 1898

8th December 1898

My dearest Cecilia,

I do not know how to begin a letter such as this, but I feel I must write or I will lose the very last scraps of my mind that are still left to me.

I cannot begin to express how sorry I am for the death of your mother.

There, it is said.

It is intolerable to think that you have been dragged into the same misery that has consumed me. What is there I can say that will be of any comfort? There is nothing, and there can be nothing. We must simply reel from the blow and let the weight of our pain act as some bittersweet anchor.

Do you blame me? I think you should. It was my fault she was there. I lie awake each night and think of every different thing I should have done that would not have led to the three of us on that station platform. I wish I had been sharper, faster. I wish I had done something, but no matter how I think on it, I cannot see anything that could have been done.

You do not need to hear this from me. I am sure my father has told you it all.

I wish they would let me home to see you.

They have plans for me. I am still at Herne House, but there is talk of a lady's companion and a journey to the Continent. I think I am to be exiled for a time.

Please send me word. I wish I could be there with you but – well, I suppose it is better this way.

Your loving,

Odette

*

10th December 1898

My beloved Cecilia,

Of course you do not write to me. How can you write to me? You must be so angry.

I will sail from Harwich in a matter of days. It is better, I think, that I go. But please – if you want me with you, send me word – any word – and I will find a way to you.

I am possessed by thoughts that you need me, that you would rather I stay – and yet I know that cannot be true. I think about you every moment. You are all I can conceive of. What a fool I have been to let the world come between us. You have always been my true, dear, constant friend and the greatest love in my life, and I have used you most cruelly. I have – God, I cannot write the things I have done to you. See how my pen shakes? I am a monster.

Know that while you must rightly hate me, I love you, and you have all my heart.

I am yours, always,

Odette

*

11th December 1898

[The paper is scrunched, unblotted, smeared with ink and torn where the pen nib has punctured through. It has been thrown into the embers of the fire and already the words disappear into smoke.]

God, please, Cecilia, any word from you. I beg you.

I love you I love you I love you. Who can I ever be without you? Am I anything at all?

I told you the truth, but you would not hear it. That pained me so dreadfully I cannot begin to explain it – it was as though you took the worst fear in my heart and played it out perfectly before you.

I am sick to ask it, but I must know: does your mother come to you, too?

Lydia is with me all the time now. She will not let me know peace, exactly as she would not in life.

I am so frightened that truly I have gone mad.

I think, I know, I am terribly selfish.

I do not deserve you.

I think I have taken everything I truly valued and torn it up like a child in a tantrum, so filled with fury I must make all my internal pain external.

There is no excuse for it.

Is my mind lost? Will I be caught up in my own worst acts for ever? I do not understand why I am compelled to do the things I do. You do not deserve it. I do not know who does.

My father. Claudine.

My mother, even. She tried her best, but it hurt to be loved by her.

Or perhaps no one. Perhaps blame creates nothing but more anger.

But can I forgive? Should I? Why must I? Why are we told to forgive those who trespass against us? Should they not suffer? If we do not believe in blame and punishment, then why do we have lawyers, courts, prisons? Why has the gibbet long stood atop the hill? Why do we even now send people to their deaths for their actions?

Why is my pain not worthy of retribution?

If I am lost already, why should I not bring those who hurt me along with me into Hell?

What a fool you are, dear Cecilia. I have plunged you into Tartarus for no crime other than loving me.

For that, there can be no forgiveness.

I must accept my fate now. Perhaps this is all there is.

I have failed. I cannot see through the revenge tasked to me.

I have failed at it all.

[Here the letter is abandoned.]

*

[This, written hastily, with a shaking hand, undated and received on the twelfth of December.]

Peace, peace! he is not dead, he doth not sleep,
He hath awaken'd from the dream of life;
'Tis we, who lost in stormy visions, keep
With phantoms an unprofitable strife,
And in mad trance, strike with our spirit's knife
Invulnerable nothings. We *decay*

Like corpses in a charnel; fear and grief
Convulse us and consume us day by day,
And cold hopes swarm like worms within our living clay.

*

14th December 1898

Dear Odette,

I thank you for your condolences.

You write to me so loquaciously that I wonder where this woman has been these last few weeks. Where was she when I wrote and wrote from Oxford, and in London reached my hand to you only to be kicked like some craven dog.

I would let you kick me still, if it were not for this emptiness that has taken over me. It is all for nothing, don't you think? All those games, all that love, your mouth on mine, the poetry and the fantasy. That is all it ever was. Fantasy. I do not know what there is left to me in poetry. I let the words pour through me like sand, fine-grained and fleeting.

We are not children anymore. We must put away childish things.

You are not the only one who has lost a mother now. Perhaps that finally makes us equals.

[This, scratched out so violently it cannot be read.]
I don't think I want to be here anymore.

Yours,
Cecilia

Act Four

December 1898, Herne House, Suffolk, Hampstead, London, and Germany

She murmured, 'Vain, in vain: it cannot be.
He will not love me: how then? must I die?'
Then as a little helpless innocent bird,
That has but one plain passage of few notes,
Will sing the simple passage o'er and o'er
For all an April morning, till the ear
Wearies to hear it, so the simple maid
Went half the night repeating, 'Must I die?'
And now to right she turned, and now to left,
And found no ease in turning or in rest;
And 'Him or death,' she muttered, 'death or him,'
Again and like a burthen, 'Him or death.'

'Lancelot and Elaine', Alfred, Lord Tennyson

1

Odette

THE *TICK-TICK-TICK* of the clock fills the quiet drawing room. Odette sniffs, rubs at her eyes with her sleeve. The noise seems so loud that it fills her whole mind, as though she has been scourged and left empty but for the mechanical count of minutes and seconds.

Her mother stands in the corner of the room, silent, pale, accusing, shot through with light from the window like the half-shadow that she is.

She has stood there in life. Odette can remember it so clearly: her mother touching her fingertips to the china milkmaids on the mantelpiece or the oil-stained antimacassar on the back of the armchair, as though there were secrets hidden within the flotsam and jetsam of the world that she could discover if only she looked closely enough, some solution to the problem of her own existence.

Odette was delivered to Herne House a week ago in a flurry of whispers and averted eyes. No one has said a word of blame to her directly, but the accident hangs around her like a miasma, sickening all who come too close.

Odette has eaten little since that moment, and she feels faint, unreal. It is *not* her fault. She tries to make this thought whole, shape it into something that can exist outside of her. She did not push Penelope. She did not tell Penelope to be there. It was an unfortunate tragedy in a busy station, and Penelope will neither be the first nor the last poor soul to be crushed beneath the wheels of a train.

It is no comfort. It should not be.

The worst thing is that she can imagine the colours her mother would have chosen to paint the bloodstained scene.

There was chaos at the station when Penelope fell. Odette screamed – or those around her did – and the world became all noise, the whistle of steam and stamping of feet, slamming doors as passengers alighted, and Odette and George shouting for the guard, for anyone.

She will never forget what she saw when she knelt at the platform edge to reach down for Penelope. There was a hand reaching up to her, pale fingers wearing Penelope's rings, extended as though in supplication, and Odette strained to touch them.

When she did, the hand toppled sideways, the arm sliced off above the elbow and was tossed, somehow, to stand upright. A trail of blood and torn satin led to the rest of Aunt Penelope.

Odette knew she should not look. And yet.

There was not a person left anymore.

How awful, then, that she is now so profoundly grateful to have been gifted the body of her own mother to wash and dress and bury.

What is left to Cecilia but scrap meat in a box?

It must be right that she does not see Cecilia. They have shared one mind, one thought; how could Cecilia not look at her and at once see everything Odette had seen? Experience each horror as her own?

Cecilia's first and only letter has come with the morning post. It is kinder than Odette deserves and harsher than anything Cecilia has ever said to her before.

It is done, then. Odette has pushed and pushed, like a cat nudging a glass towards a table edge, curious to see the glitter of the shards as it shatters on the ground. If the splinters cut her, then it is only fair. It is her doing, after all.

The door opens to admit Claudine and a short, brown-haired young woman in her early twenties, wearing a travelling dress, with an unremarkable, watchful face.

'Ah, there you are,' says Claudine. 'Odette, this is Miss Rosebury – she will be your lady's companion and travel with you to Bad Gastein. Miss Rosebury, this is Miss Fairfax-Waugh.'

Odette rises mechanically and the two women exchange the obligatory pleasantries.

'Pleased to make your acquaintance,' says Miss Rosebury.

She has not taken off her hat and gloves, and from this, Odette understands that they are expected to depart at once. It is good that she did not unpack her trunk from Cambridge. It has simply been delivered to Herne House intact and will go with her now to the Continent.

Miss Rosebury is unreadable. She makes no reaction to Odette's hair that escapes its pins, the red rings around her eyes, the bitten quicks of her nails. Odette supposes she must have seen women in all sorts of states in her career. There is a trailing thread on the lace at Miss Rosebury's collar and the flash of a fine gold chain at her throat – a locket? A family? A sweetheart? Maybe she is kind. Odette hopes she is kind.

'Well, you will have time to become acquainted on the journey,' says Claudine, when Odette says nothing more.

'Miss Rosebury, the kitchen will have some refreshments for you, I'm sure.'

There is a slight flicker in Miss Rosebury's eye at being relegated to staff quarters. She will no doubt perceive it as a slight, occupying that strange in-between position that governesses and companions find themselves in, neither welcome below stairs nor with the family. Odette wonders for a moment if Claudine meant it intentionally. She has been a governess, too, and a teacher in Dresden. Perhaps it is a reflex, to hurt, to put people into the places she once found herself.

Miss Rosebury leaves, and Odette sinks back into her chair. She is too tired to think more hateful thoughts about Claudine. She has lost the battle. Surely she has. Aunt Penelope has died. It has gone too far now.

Lydia drifts across the room, the white train of her shroud dragging across the carpet. Her eyes are so dark now, sunken into her skull. It is as though her ghost rots along with her corpse in the ground, the softness of her mother in life sloughing away into something hard and cold and angry.

A bony hand comes to rest on her shoulder.

'May I – may I see Cecilia before I leave?' Odette asks. She knows what the answer will be, but she cannot go without asking once more. 'I thought I should attend the funeral with her, if she intends to go?'

Claudine's expression grows pinched. 'I don't think you should speak of her. She will do far better without you in her life.'

Odette is crying again, the tears a hot wet line along her raw cheek. 'I only want – if there's some way I can make it up to her.'

There is a moment's pause, then the rustle of skirts, and Claudine sits on the settee beside her.

'The best thing you can do is leave. You might not think it, but I am trying to help you.' It is a shock to hear a near-softness in her tone. When Odette looks up at Claudine, it is to see the flash of Lydia in her face, the shape of her eye and the line of her nose. 'You aren't happy here.'

'I don't want to leave,' says Odette.

Claudine taps a finger against her knee. 'We do not always want what is best for us. I am not—' She breaks off, as though something nearly got the better of her and now she has schooled it into obedience. 'I am not the monster you think me. Go. Distance will help us all.'

Her mother's cold hand digs into the meat of her shoulder.

If only distance were something possible.

Fine. Very well. Let her leave. Let her go far, far away from this failure she has made of her family, her home, her love for Cecilia, her duty to her mother. She is not wanted here by anyone, so it is immaterial whether she stays or lets herself be ferried to Austria by Miss Rosebury.

George puts his head around the door.

Odette stands rapidly. 'Is the carriage here?'

If it is to be done, better to do it now.

'Yes,' he says. 'The trunk is being loaded as we speak.'

'Then I will not keep Miss Rosebury any longer.'

Her father gives her that gentle, paternal look, as though they are an idealised parent and child in an illustration, as though he can cover over the rot beneath with layers of thick, oily paint. He has rejected her as completely as he has rejected Lydia, and yet even now he wants to pretend. She hates him.

And yet, she would still cling to him if only he opened his arms.

'I will write,' she says, because she cannot find any other words.

Her father smiles again. 'It is a few weeks' rest cure. You will feel the better for it. Your nerves have been too badly upset – we cannot blame you for your behaviour. But you must rest and recover.'

That is his explanation then. Ah, well. She cannot change him, as she cannot change herself.

'I understand.'

The carriage waits at the front of the house. There is no one to see her off, save her father. Claudine watches from the hallway, hands folded tightly before her.

Miss Rosebury takes a seat first, and Odette lingers, looking at the roofline of Herne House against the sullen grey sky, where she and Cecilia have climbed out at night to share poetry and kisses; at the ivy curling around the windowpanes, working its roots between the mortar, the edge of the studio to one side, where she has spent so many hours with her mother as she worked.

Lydia has gone now; the ghost has not followed her into the daylight. She thinks, for a moment, that she sees a flash of chestnut hair in the studio.

Her father does not kiss her cheek as he once did. Instead, he shakes her hand and steps back, leaving her alone between the carriage and the house.

She looks again, one last time, at this wreck of a life.

And turns away, sunken, defeated.

2

Cecilia

A DRIVING RAIN CHASES CECILIA into the Gate House, Leo dashing behind her, holding his coat over his head.

The funeral was washed out. The rain was strong enough that it eroded the sides of the fresh-cut grave, and Cecilia, stepping too close, felt the ground give way beneath her feet. It was only Leo's swift, strong hand on her arm, hauling her back, that saved her from entering the grave before her mother did.

Claudine did not think it proper for anyone but family to attend, sending instead a carriage on behalf of herself and Uncle George, and though they had sent out notices to many, there were only two mourners, Leo and Cecilia. Cecilia has read of funerals that were attended by no one. She should be grateful her mother was at least spared that.

In the hall they shake out their clothes, stamp the water from their boots. Cecilia does not feel the cold, nor the sodden wool against her skin. The colour has run from her hastily dyed dress, leaving a grey cast to her hands when she removes her gloves.

She can feel nothing.

How strange.

She did not know such numbness was possible. It is as though she has been cleanly severed from her body by the surgeon's knife, soul and meat cleaved in twain, and without a chest to ache, a stomach to knot, pain is nothing – it disappears.

My heart aches, and a drowsy numbness pains
My sense, as though of hemlock I had drunk

Keats. Oh, she needs Keats. How can she be alone with her own mind? She is so alone now. One by one, everyone leaves.

Cecilia thinks about opening all the windows and screaming until her mouth is bloody.

There is a neat little edition of Keats on her bookcase upstairs, bound in blue cloth, a nightingale upon a branch stamped into the front cover. Odette's favourites were always 'La Belle Dame sans Merci' or 'The Eve of St. Agnes', and Cecilia would read them to her gladly, her long hair spread out across her lap as they dozed in the shade of the great oak tree on the grounds of Herne House.

But privately, with herself, she always came back to the Odes.

Nightingale. Grecian urn. Psyche. Autumn. Indolence. Melancholy.

Grief, loneliness, betrayal, corpse, murder, death. She could write her own.

Love. Should there be one on love?

Her grey hands that once touched Odette. Her dead hands.

Do they all know yet that she is dead?

'Lord, the tea is cold. Mary? Mary!' Leo stands at the parlour door, yelling to the maid. 'Hot tea this time – we are all soaked through, and you feed us tepid water.'

'Yes, sir.'

The tea is taken away, and Leo returns to the fire, kicking the coals and holding out his hands to the flames. His anger seems outsized, overdrawn to fill the space where once were three but now live only two.

Cecilia laughs.

A ghost: that is what they need. Just as Odette claimed she saw. If the ghost of their mother were to join them now, then they would be three again, and Leo would not need to bluster and shout. Cecilia would not drift unmoored.

'What on earth could possibly be funny at this moment?' says Leo in irritation.

'Oh, nothing. Nothing. Only life.'

Leo is not placated. Top hat removed, there is a dry ring of hair around his crown, while the ends are wet, stuck to his forehead and temples and neck from the sideways rain.

What a silly thing. How made up of the sublime and the ridiculous and the cruel is such a thing as life. What if Leo had hair that was wet in the middle and all that ringed around was dry? What if her mother had stumbled left instead of right?

What if she had never met Odette at all?

Cecilia laughs again.

'What is wrong with you? Neither of us should be laughing. Life is a serious thing, and you will have to take it seriously now Mother is not here to shield you.'

Cecilia looks at him blankly. 'Shield me? From what?'

Leo kicks a log further into the fire with his boot. 'Mousy, Mousy, I am never quite sure if you are really this naive or if it is all put on. I love you but I often feel like I don't know you at all. Sometimes, you can be so sly, then at other times, it is like you were dropped here by the fairies.'

'Fairies are the cunning folk, so that would make me sly either way.'

He stares at her for a long minute. She does not know what grief looks like on him or how to read his misery. Surely, he is as broken as she is, but it has turned them into strangers.

'I looked into that secret you said Claudine was blackmailing Mother with,' he says.

A memory from the past, from the before her mother died, swims into view. Yes, the document. *Penel. art.* The blackmail. All these things she cared about, because she cared about Odette.

Odette who left her long before she was bodily gone.

Cecilia blinks. 'I suppose it doesn't matter now.'

'Unfortunately, it very much does.'

Leo goes to the writing desk and unlocks a drawer to remove two buff pieces of paper. He holds them out to her, and when she does not come to take them, he pushes them into her hand.

'Go on then. This is what you wanted to know.'

Cecilia looks down at the papers, both oblong in shape, printed with red ink and black where they have been filled out by pen.

Leonard Moore Hart. Born 1876.
Mother: Penelope Hart.
Father:

Cecilia Moore Hart. Born 1879.
Mother: Penelope Hart.
Father:

They are both blank. The spaces for a father.

She looks over them again.

'I don't understand. What is this? Where is Father?'

'Where indeed.'

'Is it some error?'

'They weren't married, you fool. That is the secret Mother was keeping. The secret Claudine was using to blackmail her. You know, I went digging in all sorts of places looking for some sort of nastiness in Mother's past and I found nothing, but when I was organising Mother's things after she died, there it was. In the simplest, most obvious place: our birth certificates.' Leo has returned to the fire, as though its heat gives him some anchor amidst his fear and anger. 'We are illegitimate.'

Cecilia stares at the certificates again.

Oh yes. She sees it now.

It is quite neat. Claudine must have sent Penelope a copy to show she knew about her secret.

'But Mother had a ring,' she says slowly. 'She told us all about their wedding.'

'Because no one ever lies, do they, Mousy? There's no marriage record I can find, so it was all, as they say, utter horseshit.'

No wonder her mother was terrified.

Cecilia wonders if she should be feeling anything yet.

Leo gives the fire another kick. 'The worst thing is, the more I think about it, the entry for "father" being blank must mean that Father wouldn't attend the registration. He could have gone with Mother and agreed to have his name on the paper. Hell, they could have even lied to the registrar and put themselves down as a married couple. But they're both dead now, so I suppose we can never ask them why they did the stupid things they did. We just have to live with the legacy of their actions.' Leo laughs. 'I suppose you had the right of it. Life's quite funny really. We were only financially ruined before – now we're socially ruined, too.'

'If we tell anyone.' There is something else welling up inside Cecilia, like the laughter, only wilder.

'Yes, Mousy, *if* we tell anyone. I'm sure everyone will be flocking to see a bastard lawyer. Well. The good thing is you've no marriage prospects, so we hardly have to deceive anyone there.'

Penelope tried so hard to protect them, and she has ended up dead for all her troubles. It is as though her mother's death has revealed a grand secret to Cecilia, far grander than this talk of illegitimacy and ruin. The special knowledge with which she is now privileged is that there is no sense to the world. Just and entirely that. Sense is a conspiracy that people walk around creating together, telling each other that the unjust are punished and hard work gains reward. That it is possible to make plans, to live in an ordered way, to exert one's will upon one's life. But it is all an illusion.

Chaos is all there is. Directionless, unexpected chaos.

Fresh tea is brought in, but Leo and Cecilia leave it unpoured. Leo sits in an armchair, on the edge of the cushion, elbows on his knees and hands clasped so that he can lean forwards in some mimicry of a serious pose he has seen men adopt at his office.

'I suppose we'd better talk about it now. Sit down.'

Cecilia sits down.

Perhaps tomorrow, she will wake up and it will be summer again. Perhaps the house will burn down in the night. Perhaps she will be the Queen of Sheba or a house cat, or the trees will start to speak.

She cannot play the game anymore. She cannot pretend.

'Do you think we can eat jam tarts for supper?' she asks Leo.

His expression doesn't change. 'Odette isn't here to humour your silliness. The both of you have been given far too much free rein and look where that got Odette. She should have been brought under control long before now. You must listen to me.'

'Only they are so colourful and everything is so grey. We could eat all the colour and then we'd carry it around inside us and we'd never have to feel grey again.'

Leo ploughs on as though she hasn't spoken. 'Mother was right when she said that after Aunt Lydia died, we were living on Claudine's good graces. Claudine has spoken to me, and while she was happy enough to let the three of us live here, things are different now. Mother is dead. I've been considering moving into digs with some friends for a while. It so happens that a place has come up, and I was rather meaning to move out. Which just leaves you.'

'Me,' she echoes. Last on the list.

'Yes. And it doesn't really seem a good use of the place to house only you, especially if you're off at university half the time. We can't afford to pay for you to have two places to live.'

Cecilia pours a cup of tea for something to do with her hands. The china is fine and delicately painted, and the heat burns against her cold fingers. The set was an unexpected gift from Lydia, found in Herne House and given with that confusing generosity Lydia had, which sometimes seemed more like self-flagellation.

'I don't want to go back to university,' she says. 'It isn't what I imagined. It is the greyest place.'

Leo laughs, harsh and unkind, and for the first time Cecilia wonders whether the love between them will be enough to withstand the hate they have been left with. She understands now that she is the only thing Leo has inherited. Another difficulty to overcome.

'That's your problem, Cessy – always imagining, never thinking. The tuition fees and your accommodation are already paid up for the year, so you'd better go back, as there won't be anywhere else for you to go.'

'But what about Mother's stipend?' she asks, hating herself for how plaintive she sounds. *What about Mother's stipend, what about Lydia's paintings, what about Odette.* There are no simple answers, yet she keeps searching.

'Will you listen? There is no stipend. Mother and Father never married – when he died, we were left with nothing. All we have inherited from Mother is debt. She said she had the finances sorted, but the truth is: she kept up appearances, running up bills anywhere that would credit her. It's all come due now. Claudine has said she and Uncle George will cover the debt, but they cannot fund us now we are grown. As I said, you're paid up at Oxford for another two terms, but after that, you can look for positions as a governess. Claudine said she might know a good family or two who'd have you.'

Cecilia curls back into the chair. 'Oh.'

'Now, don't look at me like that. It's not my fault you dallied around with Odette instead of finding yourself a secure match. And now – well. You're a bastard. No man will take you.' He speaks so plainly. It is fact.

'Spoilt goods,' she says. 'Bruised fruit from the market floor.'

'If you want to be dramatic about it. I don't think Mother did you a kindness by indulging you. She let you believe you and Odette were the same for too long. You will have to take a position as a governess, and now you have looked at reality head-on, if you don't like that idea, you can work out something else.'

Cecilia stares into the tea, pale with too much milk, just as she has always drunk it, since she was a child. 'I don't think I'll be any good as a governess.'

'Then work out how you can be.' Leo rises, takes his coat from where it has been drying by the fire. 'I am just as alone as you are. I will have to work for my bread. I know it is harder on you as a woman. I am sorry, but that is simply how it is.'

He shakes the last droplets from his coat as he puts it on and knots his scarf tight around his neck.

'I'm going to the office. Probably won't be back for dinner, so don't wait for me. I suppose Cook can have a tray brought to the parlour for you.' He pauses, one glove on, and regards her curiously. 'I suppose you are mistress of this house now, even if it will be only for a short while.'

Mistress of the house. Employment as a governess. Yes, yes. All these plans.

Claudine has so many plans. Why is it that she alone has brought her will to bear upon the world? What magic does she possess to be so in control of her life? Has she struck some strange bargain that grants her a freedom withheld from the rest of them?

The front door slams behind Leo, and Cecilia watches from the window as he dashes through the rain, umbrella overhead. He has somewhere to go.

All Cecilia has is herself.

3

Odette

THE CARRIAGE TRAVELS THROUGH the frost-rimed Suffolk countryside to Sudbury, where Miss Rosebury efficiently and emotionlessly has Odette's bags stowed on the train to Colchester, and Odette stowed in a compartment. Odette finds she has absolutely nothing to say. She finds she does not know herself. All seems lost, fractious, confusing. Who should she be now? Is she a conversationalist? Is she a wallflower? Does she like to sew, to read, to sing?

With her mother, her home, Cecilia, all stripped away, there seems barely anything left of her. Maybe there was never anything real to her, underneath her mother and her anger. Maybe there was never a whole girl.

She thinks of Cecilia as they travel. What does she do now? What does she wear? Does she eat, sleep? Could Odette smell the perfume of her soap if they were together? She longs for some token of Cecilia, a lock of her hair to curl around her wrist, but she has nothing.

The winter sun tracks low over the fallow fields; soon they are dropped into the darkness of midwinter, and there are only their own reflections to be seen in the window. Miss Rosebury reads a Henry James novella, the title of which

Odette does not recognise. There are travelling rugs to put across their knees, and when they change trains at Colchester for Harwich, Miss Rosebury produces, of all things, a seed cake, which, once seated in their new compartment, she slices, handing a piece to Odette. It is a strange kindness that she can hardly bear. How mundane, how simple, how alien to the sort of life she now finds herself caught within.

The ship departs Harwich at nine p.m. They dine simply in the port before they embark and pass the night in a shared cabin. Odette lies awake, looking at the snatch of stars through the porthole. Her mother has not shown herself, and she wonders whether the spirit can travel over water, so far from where her bones are laid to rest.

Rotterdam is a noisy industrial port, the water slick with oil and the flotsam of smashed crates, paper, cabbage leaves, bottles, dirty scrap cloth and other effluvia bobbing around the docks. A steamboat meets the Harwich ship and takes passengers through the canals directly to the city centre and then on to the station, where the train to Cologne awaits.

The train is modern and clean, with a corridor connecting the compartments, but it is busy enough that they share theirs with a family with two small girls. Odette gives up the window seat to the children, and the girls cluster, faces pressed against the glass as they roll through the flat, reclaimed land of Holland, then across the border into Germany. The sky is as broad and blank as in Suffolk, and Odette finds herself falling into a trance against the clatter of the tracks, the stop-start of the stations, the whistle and billows of steam, and the chatter in languages she barely speaks.

Here she is then. This is where all her *Sturm und Drang* has got her. It is a quiet kind of failure.

They reach Cologne in the late afternoon, when the winter sun has cast its fiery streaks across the clouds and a thick, clammy night has fallen. The gas lamps are lit everywhere, and there is the same noise of carriage wheels and horseshoes as in London, though the clothes strike her as a little different, the smells a note shifted. They will see nothing of the city. There is a little under an hour before their sleeper train to Munich, and Miss Rosebury leads them to a coffee room within the station.

Odette has a sense that Miss Rosebury has done this before, perhaps many times. A minder, a pack horse, delivering delicate, flighty young women to their destinations, women who are allowed a fragile, porcelain quality of femininity that Miss Rosebury is denied on account of her birth – or her circumstances; Odette does not know which have led her to be on one side of the equation and Odette on the other.

It was an accident of fate that sent Claudine to teach in Germany and Lydia to Herne House, though neither woman seemed to have been happy with their end of the bargain. It is not that Odette cannot sympathise with Claudine – she makes the horror of her life so plain – but still, Odette cannot understand why Claudine is compelled to take that pain and fear out on her. It is as though Odette is some rival, some threat who possesses a terrible power to throw Claudine out of this new life that she has snatched for herself – and, Odette thinks, perhaps that is true. If Claudine killed Lydia, and Odette is the only one who suspects, then of course Odette is a threat. But before Lydia's death? What harm had she done her then, other than to be a different person, living a different life, with different struggles? It is as though any other suffering threatens to usurp and diminish her aunt's, as though there can be none but her own, no one in pain but her.

She thinks, abruptly, of the last words she and Cecilia exchanged.

Cecilia accused her of the same thing. Of making her pain a punishment for others.

It is frightening to think that she and Claudine may not be so very different.

It is all not worth thinking on. Miss Rosebury orders them only a pot of coffee, as they will eat a meal on the train, and while they sit in silence, Odette stares at the plaster moulding that spiders out across the great ceiling of the room. Claudine should be happy now, at least. Odette is gone and Lydia eliminated; she has George to herself.

Lydia glides into view – at first only a shadow in the corner of her eye, then the slow movement of the white shroud. A sharp nail comes to rest against the side of Odette's throat, and she thinks of how she has read that the nails seem to still grow on a dead body but it is only the desiccated flesh shrinking back.

She is a bad daughter. She has failed her mother.

Miss Rosebury folds her napkin and excuses herself. Odette rests an elbow on the table and her chin in her hand as she watches her companion weave between the tables. Ever since her mother died, the world has been so perfectly ordinary and so completely unreal. People drink coffee, laugh, run for their trains, consult maps, stack sugar cubes, blow their noses, as though they exist, as though any of this means anything.

She will not cry in public.

What is the point? Crying means nothing. Pain, nothing. Madness—

Her mother drifts to stand beside the empty chair, where she raises one withered finger, pointing.

Odette turns her head away. There is a blare of emotion, a wave of anger and frustration that makes her cower. She understands; God, how she understands. She has failed. Her mother is angry.

'*Look.*' The words are dragged through stone, harsh and insistent.

Odette glances to where her mother indicates.

Miss Rosebury's bag sits on her chair, worn, oiled leather, her initials embossed on the flap. There – where the flap has not fallen closed, is the corner of a letter. Odette frowns.

'*Look*,' her mother insists.

Odette does not know the significance of this glimpse of cream paper, but she cannot disobey now.

She leans across the table and pulls the letter free. It is addressed to a Frau Sterne – but before she can look further, her mother's hand closes on her neck and she is back in her seat with a jerk, just in time to see Miss Rosebury returning from the conveniences.

She slips the letter into her pocket, her mother a cold, silent figure beside her.

4

Cecilia

THERE IS A WINDOW at the turn in the stairs of the Gate House that overlooks the Heath; in it is set a seat, and here Cecilia makes her home. Leo stays out at the office and comes home late. Cecilia takes a tray of soup or mutton chops in the parlour. The servants come to her with the small decisions that are to be made about the house, what preparations she would have them begin for Christmas, and she gives answers as best she can. There is no deference to her, and she commands no authority. It is all like a game, the cook and maid humouring her as though she is a girl playing with her teacups and dolls. Cecilia is happier to shrink away from the questions, to pad up to the window seat and sit, watching the wash of the wind through the treetops.

leave the world unseen

fade away into the forest dim

There are no new letters from Odette, so she takes the volumes of Keats and Coleridge, Malory and Tennyson, and runs her fingers over the soft pages, the words that have been their secret communication.

There have been no letters from anyone else either. She has no family other than Leo, no friends other than Odette. She has no hobbies, no skills. She doesn't even *write* poetry – she only reads it. She consumes, and makes nothing – she offers nothing. There is nowhere to go and nothing to do and so little in herself to fall back on. She has not quite understood it until now, how friendless she is. Perhaps her mother was right; she has built her life to orbit Odette's sun alone, but she cannot find it in herself to regret it.

She does not cry. It is all beyond that now. She would be crying every moment of the day if she were to start, and it is easier simply to run into her mind, leave her body, her life, the world to one side like worn clothes.

She misses bodies. Odette's warm and vital against hers. Her mother's frightening and comforting in turn. Bodies are real. Her thoughts – it all unravels.

to think is to be full of sorrow

She should not have written to Odette in the way she did. It was a moment of anger, confusion, when the world rushed in and pressed against her with clammy hands, steaming winter breath – Odette betrayed her, left her, and she cannot understand it still. How is it they have ended here? How is this where they find themselves?

She must write again.

That rouses her at last.

She must write to Odette and tell her to come back as soon as she can. That she forgives her. God, she has done nothing but tell Odette she loves her, and it hardly changed a thing, but maybe this time – this time, she will hear it.

She has no address for her. There is little she remembers about Odette's departure – something about the Continent, a rest cure.

Now, it seems imperative to know.

Claudine has won. There is nothing to fight anymore.

Odette will come home, and maybe – she doesn't know how – but maybe, they can find each other again.

If they cannot, then Cecilia will be utterly alone.

She will be as good as dead.

She walks across the road to Odette's house – *Claudine's* house – through the mizzling rain and to the doorway under the portico. The pull of the bell and the long wait.

She will only be here briefly. It can be lightly done. She does not need to show her soft underbelly.

A maid answers whom Cecilia does not recognise. How strange. She has known all the staff at the London residence and Herne House for years.

A memory of her mother's words comes to her: *a new wife will want a clean house.* She hated her mother for her disloyalty to Lydia and Odette, but now Cecilia can see that Penelope understood more of the truth of the world than Cecilia was willing to admit.

'Is – Mrs Fairfax-Waugh at home?' Cecilia corrects herself at the last moment. She cannot call her Claudine in front of this stranger – and she has not been Miss Hutton for many months. It is not an adjustment that comes easy.

The maid regards her blankly. 'May I take a card, miss?'

'Oh. No, I don't have one on me.' Cecilia stands there, with no coat, no hat, shivering in the wind that banks off the Heath. She has done this a hundred times – a thousand – the Hampstead house as much her home as the Gate House. 'Will you tell her it is Cecilia – Cecilia Moore. I am known.'

That is not true though, is it, not anymore. She is not Cecilia Moore but Cecilia Hart.

She is not known.

The maid looks sceptical, and Cecilia is flushed with humiliation. What does she think of her? That she is attempting some elaborate begging scheme? That she is a pathetic hanger-on come to beg a favour?

She laughs again, as she did with Leo.

After all, that is exactly what she is.

It is an embarrassing relief when the maid shows her in, and after a short while, Claudine joins her where she sits in the drawing room. She leans down to kiss Cecilia's cheeks in a gesture that seems directly copied from Lydia; it fits unnaturally with her stiff posture.

'Cecilia, what a surprise.'

Claudine does not sit. There is no offer of tea.

'I apologise. I should not have come without warning.'

'Don't be silly – you are always welcome here,' says Claudine, but there is no trace of warmth behind the words. 'How can we help?'

Cecilia does not know if she should stand, too, or if that would be too strange. Is it stranger to stay sitting with Claudine looking down at her like she is a child in a schoolroom?

Oh God – should she mention the governess position? No – no – she cannot bear it. She will not.

'I came to see if you had a forwarding address for Odette. I would like to write to her more fully.'

Claudine's expression sours. 'You needn't worry about her at a time like this. Think of your own situation. I am sure there must be much for you to consider.'

Cecilia ignores the bait. 'Only, I would like to ask her when she will come home?'

There is a flicker of irritation. 'Did George not speak to you?'

'No.'

Claudine sighs. 'I will have to tell you plainly, and I'm afraid this will upset you, but I can assure you this causes George and me far more distress than you. Odette will not be coming back. Not for some time.'

A flush of panic moves through Cecilia. 'I don't understand. Why not?'

'Odette is not *well*. That is abundantly clear. Her father and I came to the difficult decision that she would be better cared for somewhere that can fully meet her needs.'

'Do you mean a—'

'It is not the kind of place you are imagining. It is for the best. The girl is not stable, she could not control herself.'

The panic rises and rises, so huge and featureless and monolithic that Cecilia cannot see its edges. It is as though she is lost within it, swallowed up whole like an insect moving through a blank sky.

'I see,' she says, and she does not know where the words have come from.

Odette is gone. *Odette is gone.*

The world is split open. Her mother's death struck the blow that cracked the ice, and now Odette's departure has splintered it all into drifting fragments.

'Did she want to go?'

Claudine laughs stiffly. 'What a strange question.'

'Please. Tell me where Odette is,' urges Cecilia. 'I promise I will take her somewhere else, somewhere far away, you needn't send her to a – a—' The word is too terrifying to speak. 'I will make sure we never bother you again.'

'I would suggest you take a moment to gather yourself,' says Claudine, expression carefully schooled into neutrality.

'No – I don't think I will.' It is unlike her. But what would it be to be like herself now? Who is she? 'Tell me where Odette is.'

Claudine ignores her. 'Now, your brother has spoken to me of your situation, and I would be more than happy to write to a few of my acquaintances to find you a position.'

Odette was right. That is the only solution to this. Odette was right about Claudine and Lydia, so Claudine has exiled her. Cecilia laughs again. Of course she was right. She knew everything, and such knowledge drove her from her mind.

'You killed her, didn't you?' she says abruptly. 'Aunt Lydia. Odette worked it out.'

It is not bravery. It is only that nothing matters much anymore.

Claudine smiles. 'That poor, mad girl.' She leans forwards and wraps one hand around Cecilia's wrist as though in a gesture of comfort, but her nails dig into the delicate skin. 'No one believes her, you know. And no one will believe you.'

There is no point in hiding.

It is as Claudine said: no one will believe her. None of this is really happening. Claudine will magic it away.

So she says, 'You knew Leo and I were illegitimate, didn't you? That is how you blackmailed Mother to spy on Lydia and Odette. And now you use it to drive me and Leo out. We are the last ones you need to get rid of, and then you will have everything you wanted.'

It is the wrong play. Claudine bursts into anger, like a sail billowing in the wind. It is as sharp a sea change as a crack of thunder.

'A girl in your position shouldn't stamp on spring ice. Your mother was a useful idiot, but you are simply an idiot. Do not think I care for your fate, nor that of your brother. No one cared about my fate. Your mother called herself my friend once, but she proved the word hollow. Neither she nor Lydia knew what true friendship was, what loyalty meant. No wonder there was no one to mourn either of them, save their brattish daughters.'

Cecilia sucks in a breath in shock. There, the curtain drawn back.

There is no one now who stands between Cecilia and Claudine, not her mother, not Odette. She is unprotected. Claudine knows she has won.

She continues, all restraint gone. 'You are too like Odette – so self-righteous, though you know so little about that which you speak of. I suppose you have no idea that Lydia used your mother's secret to steal her from me, when your father died. She held it over her, promised her support if only she would help persuade George to cut me off and marry her. If she would take Lydia's side and spurn me in the scandal that followed. Your mother was my friend first, and she threw me away to save herself. Why should I not use my knowledge to my own advantage? You do not know the half of what was stolen from me – what everyone took from me.'

It unfurls before her: the anger, the hurt, the betrayal, the secrets. Claudine so trapped within her own pain that she is ruled by it, twisted into someone paranoid, jealous, vicious. The pain is a fist beneath her breastbone. Her mother, her poor, cruel, loving mother. She lost her life trying to protect Cecilia from this secret that will destroy her future all the same.

'You told my mother to follow Odette and her father that day, didn't you? You used her to spy on them as you used me. Could you not trust George to do your bidding unmonitored? Were you jealous of even that brief time he spent with his daughter? That is why my mother was on that train platform. You are the reason she is dead.'

Claudine's face is a scowl. 'No, that would be her own stupidity.'

'You and Aunt Lydia *both* used her,' says Cecilia, eyes prickling. 'She is not a pawn; she is my *mother*.'

Claudine shifts almost to lean over her, growing quiet in her menace. 'Tears again. All you girls know how to do is cry. Who cried for me? Did any of them cry for me? This is not my doing; it is *theirs*, for what they did to me when I was so young.'

Cecilia quails. There is a quality to Claudine's anger that brings up a visceral fear in her: that shimmering, latent tension like the shift of a crowd before a fight. They are no longer in a world of calling cards and tea and mourning wear. They are animals. Cecilia knows, so deeply and personally, that she is – and always will be – prey.

'George!' Claudine raises her voice suddenly. 'George!'

There are footsteps, then Uncle George opens the drawing room door. 'Yes? Oh, good morning, Cecilia.'

'Cecilia was just leaving,' says Claudine. 'Would you walk her home?'

'Of course.'

'We have agreed I will find her a place as a governess – isn't that right?'

'What a relief,' says Uncle George. 'I will be so pleased to see you well-situated.'

Cecilia is too cowed with fear to speak. George is not her ally. He is not the absent, kindly uncle she once saw him as. If he will cast off his own daughter, then she will mean nothing to him at all.

Everything so neat and polite. Tea. A chaperone home. A rest cure. No one here will wear their claws openly.

No wonder Odette has gone mad.

'I do not need to be delivered like a parcel,' she says plainly. 'I will go alone.'

'Well. If you prefer,' says Uncle George.

Cecilia walks, floats, from the door, across the rain-slick cobbles. At the Gate House, it is dark and the fires unlit. Perhaps they cannot afford coal. Leo has not said.

It is done, she thinks. No more. No more.

There is the terrible sense of a door having shut.

The chance to be happy, the chance to be loved, behind her, missed – and the rest of her life yawns open before her like a head-first tumble, over already.

She walks out again, walks onto the Heath and across its blustery grass.

Is she cold in her blouse and slippers? Does she cry?

What is a heart, that it can hurt so much?

There are burrowing creatures here for which she holds much envy. How warm and safe it must be under the earth, like all the corpses lined up in their coffins not so very far away. It is a kind thing, death, a good thing. A safe thing. Her mother is lucky. Aunt Lydia is lucky. Perhaps Odette will die, too, and they can be in the underworld together. It is the sad living who are abandoned to the relentless sky, the rain and wind of fate and chance. Far better to go under.

The ponds are unused on this blustery day. Reeds fill their banks; trees skim down to brush their leafless boughs against the murky water.

Here, she will lie flat in the shallows, like the painting, the one that hangs in Mr King's gallery, the last moment of Odette and Cecilia together, captured and unfinished.

She should have brought Malory with her – Lydia always preferred the Malory telling to the Tennyson.

The cold is just as much a shock as it was that day in the summer, but just as quickly, she finds she grows numb to it, and it is easy. There is a pressure all around her, the dense weight of her clothes pulling her down, and the sensation is close enough to an embrace that she laughs again.

If Odette were here, this would make the perfect play. Stones in their pockets and their hands bound tight together.

For a moment, she thinks: what if Odette walks out of the trees at this very moment? Imagines it so purely that it could be true. She will be seen. She will be stopped.

Someone must stop her. If there was someone who loved her, they would stop her.

Is there nothing she can do to be seen?

She has failed Odette. Her mother. Herself. Of course, there is no one here to stop her.

As the water closes up around her mouth and nose, she thinks:

Oh. She is not sure she meant to do this.

5

Odette

THE LETTER IS NOTHING in Odette's pocket. She can hardly feel it. And yet it weighs like a stone against her side, a stiff line in her skirts, and she is possessed with a fear that it will rustle or crackle each time she moves.

But she goes unnoticed.

The night train rolls out of Cologne, heading south and east through the smut and yellow light of the city into the dark countryside. They take dinner in the restaurant carriage, and Odette is thankful when Miss Rosebury takes out her book again and eats her soup without removing her eyes from the page. She treats Odette like something to be watched, monitored, not to be touched without terrible caution, like a pot boiling on a stove.

Odette pushes her sauerkraut around her plate, impatient for the evening to end. Her mother is not with her here, and it is a strange loss.

She thinks, again, about Cecilia. The curl of her hair that always came loose from its pins and fell across her eyes. The scatter of freckles along her breast bone. The hitch in her breath when she was surprised. What she would give to hold her again.

Eventually, they are evicted from their table for the second sitting, and Miss Rosebury retires to her own compartment and Odette to hers. While they were eating, the blind has been drawn across the window and the bed has been made up in the narrow space where the seats were, crisp white linen with the railway's logo embroidered on the corner. The steward brings a bowl of hot water for Odette to wash, but she knows at once what she must do with it. She shuts and locks the door and quickly takes the letter from her pocket before the water has time to cool. A thick head of steam rises, and gingerly she holds the letter over it, letting the glue soften until she can ease open the flap.

Light-headed, she sits on the edge of the bed to read.

When she is done, she folds it, puts it on the covers beside her, and digs her fingers into the hard mattress. She is shaking uncontrollably.

The letter is simple, direct, yet driven with an intensity of feeling that Odette recognises only too well. It is from Claudine to a Frau Sterne, the matron of a sanatorium – but Odette knows this means *asylum*. The letter speaks with carefully detailed compassion of a poor, troubled step-daughter, parted from her wits by a grief so strong it has made her mad and a danger to others. The incident with Cecilia and the pillow is written about at length, and Odette feels sick with the shame of it. She *has* gone mad, has she not? The letter calls her delusional, paranoid. There is with it a legal document half in Leo's hand, and signed by George, giving his permission for Odette to be detained. She does not yet have her majority; her freedom is not her own.

Not a health resort – a madhouse.

Not a rest cure – an incarceration.

So this is it. This is Claudine's final move.

Odette is terrified.

But there is something more to it than that. After so long in the dark, fumbling, here at last is something concrete. Claudine has shown her hand so openly, thinking that Odette will never return to confront her.

Odette *cannot* let that become true.

Somehow, she has forgotten how to breathe. Her chest hitches; her heart hammers. She is faint and trembling, desperately drawing at breath that does not come.

A weight settles on the bed beside her, then her mother's cold arm embraces her, and she lets herself be drawn down to lie with her head on her lap. She smells of rot now, carrion sweet and sharp, like the old city churchyards when the rain comes heavy and the ground splits to spill out fresh and decayed bodies alike. If she is truly mad, maybe that is no bad thing. In these moments, it is a muddled confusion between herself and her mother: did she die that day, too? Is she the ghost haunting the world?

Lydia runs her fingers through Odette's hair, and Odette thinks of the last time they were together like this, in the studio in Herne House, the nude propped against the wall, surely her mother's masterpiece.

'*Come and be with me, my girl.*'

'What do I do, Mother?' Her voice is a whisper.

'*Do not let them get away with this.*'

Odette presses her face into the shroud and sobs.

Words are all very well, but what can she do now? The trap has closed around her. They will arrive in Munich in the morning, and Odette has nowhere else to go: no money, no friends, nothing to do but keep going. It seems now a foolish errand to walk forwards into destruction. But has she not already done that? Is it not too late to turn away?

If she were a woman like Miss Rosebury, she would at least have the means to move about the world on her own.

Then, there, an idea – only the flash of it, but even in the moment she lets it rest in her mind, it grows, unfurls, each step falling into place.

There is one way out. One narrow, monstrous path along the cliff edge.

For a moment, she baulks at what she must do, then shakes herself. Is it any more monstrous than what she has done to Cecilia, what has been done to Odette and her mother? There is nothing left in life for her. There are no more consequences for her actions.

This is the only way.

6

Odette

MUNICH IS WET AND SLICK with the mulch of fallen leaves, piling in the gutters and turning the cobbles as slippery as ice. Even here, it has been a warm winter, and in places, browned and curled leaves still cling to the branches. They have arrived early in the morning, around eight, and the city is alive with people going to work or returning from the factory night shift. There are Christmas decorations in the shop windows, and a great tree set in the square. It makes no sense to Odette that her world and this one can occupy the same time and place. Things continue, normal lives are lived. How alien it all is.

She cannot look at Miss Rosebury. They are about of a size, though Miss Rosebury is slim at the bust where Odette is thick. Walking side by side from Bahnhofplatz, down Schützenstraße towards the Hotel Deutscher Hof, they match each other's pace, Odette's fitted coat flashier than Miss Rosebury's cape. Every time Miss Rosebury's bag knocks against Odette's hip, a shiver of anticipation snaps through her.

At the hotel, they are shown into a private sitting room that has been reserved for the meeting. Frau Sterne will take

Odette from here to the spa town, Miss Rosebury has explained.

Odette remains dumb. Nodding. Looking at anything but a face. Eyes. Her mother moves with her now, at her back, as though they are connected by string, Lydia a puppet animated by her own movements, or—

Frau Sterne is tall and broad and does not look unkind so much as disinterested. The sitting room is small but comfortably furnished, with a ceramic stove in the corner, as is the continental custom, throwing out heat enough to make Odette sweat. There is coffee set on the table and a plate of biscuits, and two men, smartly dressed, standing with their backs against the wall – to take her bags, Odette is assured, but from the thickness of their arms, she understands their real purpose, if she were to cause any trouble.

Odette sits in the chair indicated and watches as Miss Rosebury takes the letter from her bag and hands it to Frau Sterne. They make some small talk, but Odette can barely hear it. Frau Sterne opens the letter causally, skims the contents. There is only the slightest flicker of hesitation. She glances first at Odette, then at Miss Rosebury. Odette cannot breathe. This is it.

Frau Sterne folds the letter and slips it into her pocket, then turns to Miss Rosebury. 'You must have had such a terribly long journey,' she says, pouring the coffee. 'I hope our hospitality will be restorative.'

Miss Rosebury demurs. 'It is the nature of my work, and I am well accustomed to it.'

'I am sure you have taken exemplary care of your charge.' Here Frau Sterne flashes Odette a quick look, so brief it is almost unnoticeable.

Miss Rosebury seems reluctant to engage in the attention paid to her, rewarding it with only a tight smile.

'Will you take some refreshment?' Frau Sterne indicates the coffee.

'Thank you, no,' says Miss Rosebury. 'I trust all the necessary documents are in order?'

'Indeed, they are.'

Frau Sterne makes a little more conversation, all directed at Miss Rosebury, who, if she finds the situation at all disturbing, gives no indication. Odette is not acknowledged at all.

Frau Sterne replaces her coffee cup on the table with a finality. 'There is a carriage waiting outside, if we are ready to depart?'

There is a moment where nobody moves. Frau Sterne looks at Miss Rosebury expectantly, who in turn looks at Odette.

Palms clammy, Odette rises. 'Yes. It is time.'

The three women leave the private sitting room, repinning their hats, while the two men follow behind. The carriage is waiting around the back of the hotel, hidden from the busy streets. It is a plain thing, unmarked and sturdy. Here, the lie of the rest cure becomes untenable. Miss Rosebury appears unmoved. Odette admires her sang-froid. Hopefully it will serve her well in what is to come.

One of the men opens the carriage door.

Odette does not move.

'Come. We will travel together,' says Frau Sterne reassuringly. She looks meaningfully at Miss Rosebury, who, without hesitation, steps into the carriage.

The door is shut after her and fastened.

It is done.

7

Odette

In the depths of the night before, as the train rocked on its rails towards Munich and rain slicked along the windows, Odette wrote. It could be no desperate, quick or fumbling task. It required thought, precision, care – all in such terribly short supply to her. But this, of all the things she had done in her life, mattered. The train would arrive after breakfast, and by then it would be too late.

The plan that had come to her made her sick with guilt, but when she lingered before the fresh paper and ink, cold fingers twisted in her hair and her mother's voice was clammy against her ear. '*Do not hesitate, my girl. They all deserve it. They did this to us. Do not let them get away with it.*'

So Odette wrote.

She took great care over the shape of her letters, keeping her hand steady and even. It did not need to be a long letter, just as Claudine's was not, and she echoed its language. Driven mad by grief, a danger to others – delusions, paranoia. Then she wove in the new thread, a recent delusion: a girl who believed herself pushed out into the position of a lady's companion, and in turn, the real companion forced to travel as a lady of good breeding in order to bring about her charge's delivery into the care of the asylum.

When the first light of morning came, she held up both letters, overlaid against the window, and traced Claudine's signature.

It was only a moment's work to replace the letter in its envelope and reseal it. At breakfast in the restaurant carriage, she waited again until Miss Rosebury excused herself and slipped the letter back into place.

Now, she watches the carriage pull out of the alley and into the main street. There are no windows, so she cannot see innocent Miss Rosebury in all her confusion and fear. She did not deserve this. But neither did Odette.

The mistake will be worked out and Miss Rosebury freed, she tells herself, but the trick will give Odette enough time to return to London. In her pocket, she has Miss Rosebury's train tickets and a fold of money lifted from her bag when she replaced the letter.

Now Frau Sterne's demeanour changes. 'We will send a telegram to her family and assure them of her safe arrival. You are dismissed.'

Odette bobs an uncertain curtsy and does her best to walk calmly away and into the anonymous crowd. At every moment, she expects to feel firm hands close around her arms, to be jerked away into imprisonment.

She turns into Karlsplatz, where the crisp winter sunshine is glaring and bright. She has done it. She walks faster and faster, breaking into a run to dodge trams and omnibuses and carriages, then rushes across the square, up a street to the Hauptbahnhof. Her body shakes like a dog's, and it is all she can do to find herself a quiet café and tuck herself into a corner.

There is a train west departing soon, and though it will not get her all the way to Cologne, she cannot bear to stay here any longer. She drinks a cup of coffee and a glass of water and waits for her hands to stop shaking, then finds herself a space in a third-class compartment and does not breathe easy until they are pulling out of the station.

The journey is a blur. She joins the night train, and arrives in Cologne the following morning, after a ragged night's sleep. She falls into another café, hot from bodies and steaming coffee urns, the windows fogged like mist. There is a British family at the table next to her, newly arrived from England, as their conversation makes clear, and when they go, they leave a paper behind them. *The Illustrated Police News*, the most recent edition, published after Odette left.

The open page catches her eye.

She frowns.

She picks up the paper and glances over the image that has struck her: a girl surrounded by flowers, sinking into a pond.

Beneath it, the article is short:

Drowning victim rescued from Hampstead Heath Ponds – shortly after tragic death of the girl's mother in a terrible accident at —— station, as reported in this paper – admitted to Hampstead Hospital, thought to be in critical condition – attempted suicide or accident?

Odette's hands grip the paper so tightly it could tear. The sound of chatter and cutlery against plates and cups grows distant; there is only the ringing in her head, like she is a bell that has been struck, hollow and reverberating.

She has no doubt who this girl is. Her anger rips through her high and strong like storm winds against a sail.

Better anger, than horror, blame, grief.

No, she has had enough grief. She is sick to death of mourning.

Her mother coils around her, lank, rotting hair falling into her face.

She has her task yet: revenge.

Only Odette can put this right.

Everyone must pay.

8

Odette

THE BOAT TRAIN ARRIVES in London on time. The station is crowded with travellers, jockeying hansom cabs and newspaper and chestnut sellers, and the smell of the river rises rank and thick from streets away. There is a dense thicket of scaffolding around new houses, and in the distance, the spires of Parliament and Westminster thrust through the fog.

Home. What a strange word.

Odette has not slept since she read the paper this morning. Not washed, not changed her clothes. A rime of sweat sticks her underthings to her skin and her eyes feel coarse with grit. Her bags are lost somewhere. She has only the last of Miss Rosebury's money and the stub of the third-class return ticket.

Cecilia is drowned.

It is the only thing she can think of.

Her own dear, beloved, perfect Cecilia.

It is monstrous and unbearable, and the guilt makes her too sick to breathe.

She thinks she will kill Claudine with her bare hands.

She is owed that much.

There is a blessed crush of people who distract her with the smell of bad breath and hair oil and sweat rising from woollen overcoats, their elbows in her ribs, and someone steps on the hem of her dress as they are all disgorged at Victoria. She allows the flow of people to pull her down into the underground railway and onto a train on the Middle Circle route. People carry bundles of shopping – presents, she realises – and posters display advertisements for pantomimes at Covent Garden Drury Lane. Her mind is so full that she feels bloated, heavy, confused. There were moments like this in Cambridge, when she would find herself swallowed up, the world unreal, and she might lose two hours, more, walking in a circle around the market or rubbing her finger along the soft edge of a library book.

At Charing Cross, Odette comes back to herself with a jerk when a woman knocks into her hard enough that she cracks her arm against the side of the door, sending a wicked jolt of pain up to her shoulder. Shaking, she sits on the platform until it subsides. The next train takes the waiting passengers, and soon, she is alone.

Distantly, there is the rumble of wheels, and footsteps on the stairs to the ticket office. A mouse scurries over the tracks, quickly lost in the darkness of the tunnel. From the corner of her eye, something moves along the platform. Another mouse, she thinks – or a sheet of newspaper caught up in some subterranean wind.

She chances another look, sees pale skirts, white as a shroud.

Ah. Her mother is back. She lost her in the crowd for a moment, but now she comes to sit beside her and fold their hands together.

'*Why do you delay?*'

'I'm sorry, Mother. I'm so tired.'

A passing couple glance at the strange girl talking to herself. Odette ignores them.

'Hurry. She must see justice.'

'Yes. Yes, I will go now.'

She stumbles onto the next train and takes herself north, to Hampstead.

To Claudine.

To the end.

*

A cold wind races across the Heath and brings with it a clammy smattering of rain. Odette blinks it away like tears. Night falls early in December, and she is soon alone on the street. Her mother walks behind her like a shadow, matching her stride, their skirts and shroud blowing together and knuckles brushing.

The Gate House is closed up and dark.

So. They are gone.

Cecilia lies in hospital, all but dead.

Penelope is in the ground.

Where is Leo? Does she have it left in her to care?

If she thinks about Cecilia for more than a moment, the hysteria rises up around her like a fog, blinding her, turning the world to nothing.

It is impossible to cry for her. Odette does not deserve to.

The Hampstead house, in contrast, rises up like a fortress, busy with lights and the movement of servants. The jasmine and the wisteria have been cut back far enough that the brick is exposed like bare skin, the marks of the vines carved in like veins. She ignores the front door and slips around the side of the house, to the trellis that is still nailed into the wall, which Cecilia used to climb into Odette's room, in the days when they feared nothing. It is difficult work to lift the window from outside, and the rain begins to come down in earnest, making her hands slick and her hair straggle from its pins. She lost her hat somewhere – she is not sure when. Now she has only her fingernails. Her teeth.

With a screech, the sash jerks up, just enough for Odette to wriggle through and drop into her bedroom, dripping a puddle onto the floorboards.

Briefly, she catches sight of herself in the mirror. Gaunt, dark-eyed from lack of sleep, clothes dirty and tired, hair clinging to her cheeks. She is half revenant, more hate than human.

The room is cold and quiet, unlike the rest of the house. No fire lit, and already the walls have been skinned of the pictures she pinned up, the bed stripped, the cupboards emptied. There will be no memory of either Odette or Lydia when Claudine is done.

She feels her mother's hand on the back of her neck, pushing her forwards.

In the corridor, she slinks silently to the top of the stairs, listening for the tread of the servants, for the sound of glasses or voices. The gas is turned high against the dark, casting bright spots along the patterned green wallpaper, and she moves carefully, bundling up her skirts in her fist.

There they come. Voices. From the drawing room.

Claudine. George. Leo.

The only ones left.

On hands and knees, Odette slithers down a step or two, pressed close to the carpet, until she can hear. The entrance hall is empty, a few wet coats on the stand and umbrellas dripping into a pot. From the kitchens comes the noise of cooking, pots and knives and the whistle of a footman polishing silver or a pair of boots.

The drawing room lies through the door directly at the bottom of the stairs. She can picture the room: pale blue walls, long damask curtains, the sofas drawn close towards the fire, delicate colours that were out of fashion but pleased Lydia's artist's eye. Lydia had liked to read there, stretched out before the window. Cecilia had taught Odette card tricks sprawled in front of the fire during the cold winter evenings. All gone, all gone.

Now it hosts some conclave over Odette's fate.

They are talking about her.

It seems as though her deception in Munich has been discovered.

So be it.

'This is mad,' says Leo. 'Everyone has gone completely mad.'

His voice is hoarse, not that of the assured man she knows so well. He is taken apart, as well he should be. Claudine has destroyed his family as much as she has destroyed Odette's. Does he not see it? Perhaps not. Her childhood friend has felt like a stranger for too long.

They are all broken now. All in pieces on the floor, like smashed toys.

'Should we report her to the police?' Leo asks. 'Surely it is only a matter of time before she returns here?'

'No,' says Claudine at once. 'The police will hardly take this seriously.'

Leo is agitated, speaking too quickly. 'But she's dangerous – clearly, she is dangerous.'

Ah. He takes Claudine's line. Yes, Odette understands. It is easier for him. There is a singular evil amongst them, which can be sliced out like a cancer. Odette will be eliminated, then they can continue on, telling themselves they did all they could in the face of tragedy.

'As far as anyone knows, she is still abroad, and so the matter will be out of their hands,' says Claudine.

George has said little, but he speaks now. 'I must attend to some business at the Commons.'

'Of course you must.' Claudine's voice is ice.

'I am sure this is all sound and fury and will signify nothing in time,' he adds. Odette can imagine his bland smile, his pacifying hands spread wide.

There is no reply, or at least none that she can hear, and she has slid down another step to strain for softer voices when the door opens and George steps out.

Odette freezes, crouched on the stairs like some devil from Hell, clawed hands wrapped around the banisters.

Her father looks up at her, shock and distress plain across his face.

Odette cannot breathe. Any moment, he will speak, and she will be found.

Quietly, he pulls the drawing-room door shut.

The hall clock measures out the long seconds, the silence that lasts between them.

There is a blurring to her vision, dampness on her cheeks, and she is surprised to find herself crying.

Oh. Oh, there is some feeling spirit left in her still.

George hesitates a moment more, face twisted with pain. She thinks – hopes – for one wild second that he might come to her. Choose her. Listen to her. Together they might expel Claudine from the nest, bring her to justice. He might hold her as she cries for her mother.

But he does not.

Without a word, he puts on his hat and coat and lets himself out.

At the door, he gives Odette one last look, and she understands that this is goodbye.

This is all he can give her.

The door closes behind him.

Odette presses her hands into her face, hard, to hold back her weeping, to push against this weakness in her. She loves him – oh, of course she still loves him, her father, her useless, kind, deluded father. How awful it is to love someone who can only fail you.

When she can breathe again, see again, she turns her attention back to Claudine and Leo in the drawing room, now alone together.

They speak quickly, two strange bedfellows, in this to the end.

'So we do nothing,' says Leo.

Claudine, measured, careful. 'I did not say that.'

'But you said—'

'There is no point in the police. Yes. I stand by that.'

'But we must do *something*. I cannot bear the thought of her out there, roaming around as though she has not destroyed *everything*.'

Odette imagines Leo pacing, pulling at the lock of hair at his forehead that curls like his sister's, marching about the room as though he can demand the world stop and reorganise itself along the lines of his own wanting.

'I am so terribly sorry, dear boy.' Claudine's voice is soft. Does she place a gentle hand on his arm, an encouragement to sink further into his grief?

'What she did to my mother – my sister – the girl pulled my family to pieces, and for what? Her own mad delusions? It is – it is – I *cannot* let it lie.'

'And you are right not to,' says Claudine. 'She has done the same to me, though I am fortunate that things have not yet gone so far. George is blinded by his fatherly feeling, but you and I know better. The girl cannot be allowed to roam free.'

No, no, it is wrong, *wrong*. Everything laid at her door should rightly be laid at Claudine's. Odette cannot let it stand. She will no longer suffer the lie. They speak so boldly when they do not know she has the measure of them, that she spies on them even now.

Leo gives a bitter laugh. 'Well, you tried to lock her up, but fortune favours her even there. God, if any harm had come to that poor girl travelling with her I could never have forgiven myself.'

'I was a soft-hearted fool. I never imagined she would stoop to so evil a trick.'

'If she comes back here, I – I—' Leo stops himself, laughs again, choked and short. 'Well, I do not quite know what I would do, but perhaps it is better if she never returns to find out.'

A pause. Claudine eking out the tension. 'I cannot help but think – no, I should not say.'

Leo takes the bait. 'What?'

Odette creeps down another step. What? What is it Claudine plans now?

'No, I cannot bother you with my thoughts,' says Claudine. 'You carry too much of your own burden.'

'Please. I insist. There is no one else in this world now who understands me as you do.'

Odette frowns in distaste. How wholly Leo allows himself to be taken in. She expected more of him, though she is not sure why anymore. They are all fools, and they deserve what is coming to them.

Another pause. 'I feel the same,' says Claudine. 'Forgive me, but I find myself thinking too often that the wrong person has died.'

'You do not need to hide such thoughts from me.' Leo is soft now, confiding. 'I – well, I share them.'

Claudine sighs. 'We would all be better off without her. We know she is mad and dangerous. She will never stop. You saw how she hunted me.'

'Yes,' says Leo, 'yes.'

'And again, I find myself thinking . . . a mad girl like that could come to many nasty ends.'

Odette covers her mouth with her hands to hide her gasp.

'What are you saying?' asks Leo, hesitant.

'I am saying that it would be no surprise if she lost hold of herself and took her own life. Don't you think?'

'But . . . would she?'

Claudine is firmer now. 'We can make *sure* she does.'

'I don't – oh. Oh. I understand.' He is too quiet. Too calm.

Odette is dizzy, dizzy, slipping out of herself and half down the stairs, half into the street, with Claudine and Leo and their plan to murder her, with her mother waiting for her on the other side of the veil. What is she to do?

'In the drawer in my dressing table,' says Claudine, 'there is a revolver. It is only small – for a woman's protection, you must understand.'

'You mean—'

'I mean if – when – Odette returns here, there could be a tragic end. The key is to fire at close quarters, then place the gun into her hand at once.'

Odette holds onto the banister to anchor herself. It is only a plan. It has not happened yet. She can prevent it, she can fight. But how?

'I – am not sure I can do it.'

'Not for your sister?' urges Claudine. 'Your mother?'

'God. God, all right.' Leo is distraught. 'Yes – I can do it. I cannot let her harm anyone else. I will do it.'

Odette must get the gun first. That is the only path she can see. Get the gun and then – then – what does it matter after that? She can think on it when it matters. She must survive, second by second.

She crawls back up the stairs, carpet rough on her palms, then turns towards Claudine's room where the gun is stashed; but the sound of a maid coming down from the floor above sends her flying into the nearest room – Lydia's room – before she can think. There is the clank of the coal bucket as the maid reaches the landing – the fires are being tended. Surely they will have no need to come into this dead space, but Odette wriggles under the bed all the same.

More footsteps. Soft laughter. Two maids talking outside. She does not recognise the voices, which is as disconcerting as anything could be. It is as though she has fled home from the Continent and onto a different plane of reality, Alice's Wonderland or the backward world of fairy.

She breathes in the dust, the thick stuff of the mattress an inch from her nose. How long must she hide here? Will she be too late to seize the gun? How can she face them both? What is it she even means to do? There is something by her head, a sharp corner pressing against her temple; she pushes it aside, only to realise it is an envelope.

Strange.

An envelope beneath her mother's bed.

The voices grow quiet, as the clank of the bucket continues on.

She must go now.

She emerges, grime clinging to her damp skin, the envelope coming with her.

Odette.

There, written in her mother's writing: the only word on the plain paper.

What?

She turns it over in confusion. She recognises it and she does not. It is the same stationery used throughout the Hampstead house, the looping hand of her mother she would recognise anywhere.

And yet she does not know what this is.

Odette prises the letter open.

It is one short sheet of paper and a folded banknote.

My darling Odette,

This is the first of much more to come, or so I hope. Mr King is confident the exhibition will be a great success, and he has bought from me directly the Elaine piece, though it is unfinished, as a show of his firm belief. I enclose the money here, for you. It is all for you, darling. What else? What other meaning does my life hold?

When you were so small, I thought I could hold you in one hand. You would look at me in that fixed-gaze way that babies do, and I knew you saw right through me. I have never felt love like it. We are all unequal to the task of loving, I think, and I fear I have been poorer than most. But I do love you, my darling girl. If there is anything in this world I can give you, it is yours. I ask nothing of you.

You will live a happy life, won't you? Promise me?

There, that is enough for now.

We will have more time.

Your ever loving,

Mother

The note is for fifty pounds, many times folded and unfolded, but real. Solid.

She cannot breathe. She cannot breathe.

Oh, it is like seeing her mother's coffin go into the ground again.

For a moment, her mother was alive. She could hear her – not the coarse sound of the ghost but her real mother, her soft, mad, generous mother.

It is too much to bear.

She sobs again, skin raw from tears. They will hear her, they will find her, but she cannot control herself. She is cracked open, guts spilled around like confetti; she is a corpse already, she is a live nerve of agony.

The cold arms of the ghost settle around her.

'*Get up,*' the voice hisses. '*You are not done here.*'

No. No she is not.

Odette wipes her face on her sleeve, folds the letter and puts it in her pocket. Shakily, she stands, testing the weight on each of her too-human limbs. She will be equal to this task. She must be.

First, the gun. Then – the rest.

She eases the door open, and when she is sure it is safe, she darts from Lydia's room down the hall to Claudine's, opening the door just enough to slide through—

She is inside, but she is not alone.

Leo – with the gun – is staring at her, wide-eyed, his own hand on the door, about to leave.

A moment hangs between them, all the world in it, all possible worlds.

Then his face twists into a snarl, and he points the gun, at the same time as Odette grabs at his arm, his wrist, wrestling him back with all the weight of her.

There is one brief, frantic struggle, his hot breath on her cheek, the cold barrel of the gun grazing her temple, wavering back and forth between them.

The gun fires.

9

Odette

ODETTE IS PAINTED IN BLOOD.

It is hot and copper-smelling – tasting where it fills her mouth and spills over her lips – hot against her throat and wrists. Gunpowder is sharp in the air, and the shot has briefly deafened her.

Leo lies dead on the floor.

She does not know how it happened. The angle, the moment, whether it was her or him – she does not know.

The bullet has caught him under the jaw and burst out through his eye, like the bloom of a flower.

He slumps across the floor, wilted and limp, snuffed out so thoroughly. The carpet beneath him soaks through with red, and red stains his cheeks, his collar. He will not smirk again, not flick his cigarette ash in an empty teacup, or crack his neck or complain Lydia has made him too short in another painting.

Not Leo, no, not Leo. Do not let this be. She loved him once, and still, her brother-not-brother.

Where once there was light, there is now darkness.

Each star snuffed out one by one, till Odette is left all alone in the black.

How many dead bodies has she seen now?

How many her fault?

The ringing in her ears is so loud she cannot think.

What has happened?

Dead – dead again – all dead. Is she dead?

A cold hand grasps the back of her neck and shakes her.

Her mother brings her back.

She has seconds, maybe, before people arrive. The shot will have been heard throughout the house.

It cannot end now.

She is not finished. Not without Claudine.

On the landing she hears a commotion downstairs – people are coming, voices, a clamour. Only a split second to make her decision – so she runs, breathless, shaking, up to one landing, then the next, and the next, this endlessly tall house, these endless, useless rooms. Here a vase her mother purchased on her honeymoon, here a print of her father riding in the Herne Hunt. The sound of the gas burning follows her like a hissing crowd. She is the villain, she is wanted dead.

A scream comes from somewhere behind her.

They have found him.

What will they think?

A suicide?

It would not be so surprising, after all. Mother dead, sister drowned. A poor fool with no taste for life.

Claudine will know better.

In her mother's studio at the top of the house, Odette stops at last, breathing hard, throat on fire with the effort. The lights have not been lit here, so she slips through the dark, between the broken fragments of her mother's legacy. A torn canvas here, a broken brush there.

How long can she hide?

No – she cannot hide.

That will get her nowhere.

She has a better idea.

The subtlety of her hearing has slowly returned, and she listens more closely to the tumult of voices, all these new servants Claudine commands.

She is their mistress, but she stands alone.

They are not so mismatched now. Odette against Claudine. That is how it has been since her mother died.

Odette goes to the landing outside the studio and gives a knock on the banister.

It is not so loud.

She knocks again, slowly, steadily.

Does she have Claudine's attention? She does not know.

She goes to the centre of the room and taps on the floorboards.

Tap-tap-tap.

There – a creak on the stairs below. Someone is coming up. Someone scared.

Claudine knows it is a message just for her.

Tap-tap-tap.

Odette slinks back, towards the one window that is not yet fully boarded up. Rain lashes the glass, and the wind sends the tree branches outside clattering against the side of the house.

This time, she gives a quick and constant rapping, faster, louder, harder, until—

'I am here.'

Claudine stands in the doorway.

Odette forgot how much taller she is than Lydia.

She is dressed to receive guests, in arsenic-green silk with midnight-blue voided velvet in a brocade pattern like snakeskin.

Odette crouches by the window, back against the glass, a washed-out shadow.

'It is me you want,' says Claudine. 'Isn't it?'

Still, Odette says nothing.

She thinks, briefly, how foolish it was of her to drop the gun. It would be clean and quick. One bullet for Claudine. One bullet for herself. All of it over.

Claudine is shaken, she cannot let the silence stand. 'Messy, that you let so many others suffer and die for your impassioned cause.'

'You killed only one person, I suppose,' says Odette at last, a quiet voice in the night.

Claudine smiles coldly. 'We have sent for the police. I did not think you would be foolish enough to do something so incriminating, but you *are* Lydia's daughter. None too bright.'

What will she do, now she has Claudine? What does she want from her?

Her mother's cold hand at her throat.

Yes: a confession. The truth.

For Claudine to pay.

Leant against the wall beside her is a length of broken picture frame in heavy mahogany. A nail juts from one end.

'When the police come,' Odette says, 'will you tell them how you poisoned your sister? That is how you did it, is it not?'

'*Enough*. Why do you not know when you are beaten?'

Claudine's patience has snapped sooner than Odette expected, and she realises, abruptly, that Claudine is truly frightened. Odette wonders what she looks like, hunched and blood-smeared, wet hair plastered to her skull and nothing but desperation to drive her on.

Claudine is right to be afraid.

Odette smiles. 'Are you so sure of your victory?'

'There is no victory. Only fact,' says Claudine, though her voice wavers. 'George is my husband. This is my house. You are a child who has overstayed and refuses to grow up. Playing your silly little games with that lunatic Cecilia – you are a spoilt brat, and no one has had the courage to put you in your place.'

'So you lock me up as a madwoman.'

Claudine bares her teeth. 'I should have done it sooner. You have destroyed our lives – you have destroyed your father's life. You should be on your knees, begging us all for forgiveness.'

'And I should have realised sooner that you are a monster,' says Odette. 'Why am I such a threat to you?'

Her hand closes around the wood.

'*Yes,*' croons her mother. '*Yes.*'

'You are not a *threat*,' hisses Claudine. 'You are the cuckoo I must oust from the nest, but you are ever the victim, aren't you, stupid little Odette? You have had everything given to you while I have had to struggle and suffer and fight for any small scrap. I am *owed* this.'

'Why must you take it from *me*?'

Claudine stalks into the room, eyes dark with fury. Odette wonders for a moment if she will strike first.

'Take it from *you*? You were the one who took everything from *me*. You came along and took my fiancé from me, my home, my friends, my future, all because my whore of a sister could not let me have one thing of my own, could not let me be happy, be *separate*.'

For the first time, Odette falters. 'What are you talking about?'

'Don't you know yet? Have you not worked it out? I thought you considered yourself so clever.'

Odette shakes her head. What – took what?

Claudine is shaking with rage as she speaks. 'George was *my* fiancé. We were in love, we had been since we were very young. We were going to marry but – but Lydia never could stand to be excluded. If I had him, she had to have him, too, and then she was pregnant and that was that. I was thrown away, and she – *you* – took everything.'

Odette's mind races. 'That is why you left England.'

'Yes, I *left England*,' she echoes, mocking. 'If you can call it that. I say *driven out*. Exiled. My sister stole my life – because of *you* – and now I have come to claim it back.'

Odette feels so small.

So stupid.

The ghost stands beside her, teeth bared in a snarl. '*Murderer. Viper.*'

'By poisoning her.'

Claudine has stepped ever closer. The light from the window casts a long shadow of Odette across the floorboards, so that she has already blurred into one with Claudine.

'You are wrong. You do not know how wrong you are.'

'But you burnt the memorial. Why would you do that if not to hide evidence of your plot?' Odette sounds to herself like a child, naive and frightened.

'Because I was sick of your great performance of grief. As though no one had felt what you felt before. As if the world should stop and arrange itself around *your* pain.' Claudine laughs bitterly. 'Even after her death Lydia still found a way to ruin my life.'

Odette shakes her head. Tests her fingers around the wood. 'I don't believe you. I know you did something. She only became so gravely ill after you returned.'

Claudine throws her hands up. 'Of course she did! Lydia was herself until the end. She could never let anyone have *anything*. She was like that from the second she could speak. If I had a new toy, she wanted it, if I ate a cake, she must take it from my plate. She stole my jewellery, my ribbons, my books. One year, on my birthday, she contrived to fall down the stairs so the whole day was spent worrying if poor, delicate Lydia was quite all right, and I was entirely forgotten about. If I had a single thing for myself she wanted it and knew exactly how to get it. That is what she did with George. She *must* have done; he would never have left me by choice. She seduced him, to take him from me.'

'And you killed her to take him back.'

Claudine sneers. 'Stupid, again. That was never the plan. George told me if I came home with him we could easily live together as we wanted to, and simply push Lydia out to the country. I was a fool to believe it would be so easy.'

Odette frowns. George asked Claudine to return to England?

Claudine notices the understanding dawn across Odette's face with a satisfied look. 'Oh yes. Begged me back. Found me in Germany on one of his *business* trips, and told me he could not live without me any longer.'

'He wouldn't.'

Wouldn't he?

Odette does not know why she protests anymore.

'Came to visit me over and over, told me how miserable he was with his awful wife and maundering daughter. How he regretted it all. I could come back, we would find a way.' Claudine's expression falls. 'And then Lydia had to take even that from me. I should have known. She became sick, so sick the world revolved around her again. And then right as I thought I might finally be free of her, that she would die on her own – she began to get better.' Claudine snarls. 'She took twenty years of my life. I was not going to let her take the rest of it. I had to end it that night – she could not be allowed to drag on in a wretched half-life, destroying everything again. It was easy enough with a pillow. No one would know anything. Only a moment of struggle – then a lifetime of relief.'

Finally. Finally, the words Odette has known to be true. Finally, she hears them.

Just as Odette had play-acted with Cecilia. She was wrong about the poison, but the ghost had been telling the truth.

Oh, her heart is breaking. It is an agony, the death lived over again, as though the ghost of her mother has reached inside her chest and squeezed her heart.

The cold hand traces along her cheek.

Her mother's face is all but skull now. There are shadows at her cheeks, in the hollows of her eyes. The rot pulls back the lips from her teeth, wears away her nose.

She looks so sad.

Odette's soft mother is gone, and all that remains is grief and rage and anger.

'*She killed us*,' she whispers, her voice coming from inside Odette's own mind. '*She took it all. She cannot live.*'

'You didn't have to do it,' says Odette, one final plea. 'No one was asking you to give up your life to care for her.'

'She would have kept both George and me prisoner. Who else would be expected to do it but her spinster of a sister? She made my whole life a trap, then closed it around me.' Claudine shakes her head. 'She is better off dead. I don't regret it.'

Sorrow turns to anger like a match to oil.

So be it.

Odette swings up with the broken frame, aiming the jagged wood at Claudine's head.

Claudine shrieks, skitters back. Odette swings again.

A life for a life.

Odette's is already over. She will make the tally even.

'*Yes, darling. Only I ever loved you. Do not let me be forgotten.*'

They dance around the room, Odette throwing her whole weight behind the frame, Claudine stumbling back, in shock, then fury.

Odette lifts the makeshift cudgel, but Claudine lunges first, and Odette only sidesteps at the last moment.

Panting, chaotic, they dart and strike, unsuited to their sport but unable to retreat now. Odette's shoulders ache – she is clumsy and desperate. Her mother is at her back, arms braced against hers, lifting the wood and swinging it again.

Claudine comes to meet her, grappling with the weapon, her face wild and resembling her dead mother's far, far too closely. Now they back up against the window, neither one with room to manoeuvre. It looks down onto the long drop, the hard ground far below.

Odette thinks of Leo pressed up against her, the last few moments of his life, his beating heart, felt on her own skin.

Odette could do it.

Claudine would not see it coming.

Sideways, through the windowpane – a fall. The glass would break easily, she thinks, and it would only take tipping her own weight to bring Claudine down with her.

'*Do it, do it now.*' The voice is jagged and cracked, like something dragged from the deep. '*We can be together then. Please. I am so lonely; you are all I ever had.*'

Odette braces herself against Claudine's body, digs her heels in ready to fling her weight.

Then comes the thought: her mother would not ask her to die for this. Not her living mother.

It is cold water over her head.

The ghost wraps its strong and bony arms more tightly around her, crushing her chest until she cannot breathe.

Who is it who embraces her? Who is it who urges her on?

To stay loyal to the memory of her mother is to step into her own grave.

Oh, but some part of her wants to; she longs for it. It is the only thing left to her.

And she cannot do it.

If there is anything in this world I can give you, it is yours. I ask nothing of you.

Her mother would grieve to see her dead. Her real mother.

Not this creature.

This ghost is her own creation.

A twisted memory, guilt, anger, pain, all built up into the shape of a woman who would never wish this: who, for all the hurt she *had* caused, would never do *this*.

Odette lets go of the broken frame, and she and Claudine fall to the floor.

Claudine clearly cannot believe what Odette has done, and she clutches at the makeshift weapon greedily, eyes darting.

But Odette only edges away, one hand raised in supplication, shuffling back over the boards, through Lydia's scattered drawings, smudged charcoal sketches, rough studies for larger pieces.

Cecilia's face looks up at her.

There, by her foot, a lost page from a sketchbook. Cecilia's beautiful face.

Like the sun in winter. A desperate relief. A glimpse of hope.

Odette has been such a fool.

She has been caught up in a selfish madness, an obsession – but she did not need to look to her mother's ghost for love.

Cecilia has been there all along.

Cecilia, who has always come towards her, when others have turned away. Cecilia, who has held faith in her to the end. The only one who dreamt of a real future for them. The only one who ever truly saw her.

Cecilia, who lies in hospital not so far away.

Oh, if there is any chance at all that Cecilia still lives, then she must go to her – should have gone to her above all.

Claudine doesn't matter. George doesn't matter. All of this is nothing but the past, the echoes of the dead and dying, pain from lives that are not hers, pain that is not her duty to tend to.

Cecilia is hers. Odette has made such a monstrous mess of it all, maybe there is no way through.

But she must find Cecilia.

She must tell her that she is sorry.

Odette stands.

Claudine is on her knees, braced, clutching the wooden club, but Odette holds up her hands.

'You win.' She looks around at the chaos, the destruction. 'Have it all.'

'*No – no!*' her mother's ghost hisses, scrabbling at her.

Without another word, Odette leaves.

10

Odette

SHE WALKS, STEADY, UNBENDING, through the dank and lightless winter night.

The blood has dried on her hands and face, and on her dress, tacky and stiff.

If people look, she does not notice.

The pavements are slick with the runoff from the rain and rotting leaves pile in the gutters and against the walls. The rows of houses stand back from the street as though lifting their skirts from the mess Odette trails with her, shuttered and bolted against the chaos of the world.

Her mother walks behind her, plucking at her sleeve, pulling at her hair. '*You are not finished, my girl – go back, go back. How can you leave me? How can you forget about me?*'

Odette walks.

The streets change, the trees swaying bare-limbed overhead, narrow houses giving way to mansions and back again, a darkened school, a gasworks, the station still spitting out people and steam rising from the engines moving along the tracks. Gas lamps reflect in the puddles, cobbles smeared with horse dung and discarded papers. It is at once so familiar and like a world apart. Her feet are numb, her hands like marble. She does not belong here.

Still she walks on.

Walks and walks until she reaches the hospital where Cecilia has been taken.

There are so many people: doctors, nurses, visitors, patients – she cannot work out who is who, what is what. The lights are too bright, the smell of carbolic too strong. The corridors echo, all high ceilings and white tiles.

'Cecilia?' she calls, as though speaking her name will guide the way.

People turn to look at her. Someone screams.

A doctor comes up to her, in concern and fear. He says something, but she cannot hear it.

Odette walks through the crowd that parts before her.

There are voices – *Help! Call the police!*

She walks through the corridors, looking into wards of beds with stiff sheets and starched gowns.

'Cecilia? Cecilia!'

Too many faces, all wrong. Is she too late? Oh God, has she missed her?

Is Cecilia gone?

'Cecilia!'

She is running now, desperate. Please. She has to find her. Cecilia has to be alive. She cannot be too late.

Then – there.

A face she knows as well as her own heart.

Cecilia, laid out on sterile white sheets, arms above the covers, eyes closed and face ashen.

Odette flings herself onto the bed.

Living or corpse, she must be with her now.

'Cecilia. Please. Wake up, I'm here.'

She touches her face, the curve of her cheek, the swell of her lip.

She is cool to the touch – but not cold. There is the flutter of a pulse at her throat.

Odette sobs with relief. 'Cecilia, oh God, I am so sorry. I love you. I love you. I am so sorry I ever left you.'

She curls herself into Cecilia's side, fits their bodies together as they have done on so many nights.

Her mother stands beside the bed, staring at her. Perhaps it is the light, but she seems faded at the edges. Softer.

There is something of Lydia in her expression again.

Odette presses her face into Cecilia's hair. She must say it all now.

'I love you. I should have listened to you. I treated you so terribly. I do not ever deserve your forgiveness, but I am here to beg for it anyway. Please, Cecilia, wake up.'

Please still love me. Please do not leave me alone.

Beside them, Lydia's face has sweetened, the colour come back, her smile true and pained.

You will live a happy life, won't you? Promise me?

Lydia touches one hand to Odette's neck, familiar and tender.

Then she steps back. And back.

Begins to fade.

Odette presses her forehead to Cecilia's cheek. 'Please. Wake up.'

There is a clatter of noise in the corridor – shouts, footsteps.

Cecilia stirs.

Only gently, only the smallest movement, as she turns towards Odette.

Her eyes flutter open, her focus swimming until it fixes.

Odette's eyes are bright with tears.

Her mother steps back again – and is gone.

The door to the ward bursts open. There is a tumult of people: police in dark blue, doctors in tweed, nurses in their starched aprons.

What happens next, Odette does not know.

But Cecilia's hand moves, grasps Odette's.

She loves and is loved in turn.

Author's Note

My research process for my novels is always a little chaotic and ad hoc, half drawn from entrenched memory, half from books swallowed and forgotten as soon as a scene was written – so I wanted to stop and put together a record of what informed *Rottenheart*, for any reader who might be interested, and to beg forgiveness for all the places where research has failed me, or where I have taken liberties to suit narrative.

Rottenheart owes a huge debt to a number of works – most obviously, Hamlet – but also the film *Heavenly Creatures*, the poetry and essays of Coleridge, Keats, Tennyson and Malory, my grandmother's house filled with heavy furniture, Pre-Raphaelite prints, Tiffany lamps, thick Turkish rugs, books and books and books, the ghost stories of a host of Victorian writers, the sensation fiction novelists of the nineteenth century, the work of Bowlby and Winnicott, my therapist.

I will particularly highlight ghost stories of numerous authors that provided inspiration, including work by Charles Dickens, MR James, Mary Elizabeth Braddon, Henry James, Edith Nesbit, Sheridan Le Fanu and Elizabeth Gaskell.

Cecilia and Odette trade quotes and references from a literary world that women of their background would have been familiar with, though for them it becomes a shared language, a refuge. They quote from Keats' *Ode to a Nightingale* and *Ode on Melancholy,* Malory's *Le Morte d'Arthur*, Tennyson's *Idylls of the King*, Sophocles's *Antigone* and John Donne's *The Apparition* and *Holy Sonnet XIV*. At Waterloo Bridge, Odette thinks about the poem *The Bridge of Sighs* by Thomas Hood, which to the modern reader is almost embarrassingly sentimental and pious, but touched enough Victorian hearts that it inspired a number of well known artworks, notably, *Past and Present* by Augustus Egg, *The Bridge of Sighs* by Sir John Everett Millais and *Found Drowned* by George Frederic Watts.

Lydia was created with great love and respect for women artists of the period, with a particular nod to Henrietta Rae (who happened to paint *Ophelia*, now hanging at the Walker Art Gallery in Liverpool), and Evelyn De Morgan and Eleanor Fortescue-Brickdale, who painted ambitious biblical, mythological and literary works with clear nods to Pre-Raphaelite style. One of the most famous artists of her day, Rae's work has almost entirely gone into private collections and the location of several of her most important works is unknown. I would strongly recommend looking into the work of Rae, De Morgan, Fortescue-Brickdale and their contemporaries; I think you will be surprised to find more familiar pieces than you expect. I cannot list exhaustively all the women working in art in the nineteenth century, but if you were curious, I would recommend researching Emily Osborn, Sarah Setchel, Henrietta Ward, Florence Claxton, Joanna Boyce Wells, Rosa Bonheur, Elizabeth Southerden Thompson Butler, Annie Swynnerton, Laura Alma-Tadema, to name but a few. Women artists were talented, prolific and ambitious, but were excluded from establishment institutions like the Royal Academy of Arts, and prestigious watercolour societies, and translating their work into a career was fraught. Women had won entry into art schools but were still barred from life drawing classes on grounds of moral outrage. The nude Lydia uses Odette to model for is based on Henrietta Rae's *A Bacchante*, which was among a number of nudes exhibited at the Royal Academy and Grosvenor Galley that lead to a scandalised letter to *The Times* from 'a British Matron' scolding women artists for participating in 'the degradation of their sex'. The matron in question turned out to be a male academic supported by the Church Purity Society. Plus ça change.

The Deceased Wife's Sister's Marriage Act was a hot topic throughout the nineteenth century, being brought before the Lords and Commons no fewer than fourteen times. It was a fraught question for a long time. Consider the debate and repercussions of the marriages of Prince Arthur, King Henry VIII and Catherine of Aragon, for one obvious example. The reality was that despite one's siblings-in-law being within the prohibited degrees of kinship, as listed in the book of common prayer, which set out the laws of the church, it was a regular enough occurance to necessitate a lively and ongoing national debate. The law was eventually passed in 1907, and there were several further amendments to allow marriage with a deceased husband's brother, and with the brother or sister of a divorced spouse. George and Claudine marry before the bill was passed, so they use a loophole of marrying in Germany, where Claudine was a resident and such marriages were allowed. Foreign marriages were recognised in England, and so, they are able to skirt the law – though the risk of moral and social scandal was still present.

As ever I am in debt to a number of books for research, many of which I have mentioned in the historical note to *Hungerstone*, but I will repeat here. To create the material world of the period, I turned to a number of books, particularly Judith Flanders's very accessible *The Victorian House: Domestic Life from Childbirth to Deathbed*, and *The Victorian Girl and the Feminine Ideal* by Deborah Gorham. Food is taken from *Mrs. Beeton's Book of Household Management*, as well as much advice and detail from a number of contemporary etiquette guides too numerous to mention. I looked to fashion plates from the era for inspiration, as well as items from the collections at the V&A in London and the Met in New York City. Judith Flanders's *Rites of Passage* came along just when I needed it and made the process of research into Victorian customs around death and mourning eminently more pleasant and enjoyable.

I have taken a few liberties, either being vague to conceal unnecessary complexity, or siding with narrative satisfaction over strict accuracy in places, for example, men did not wear wedding bands as a rule at this point, but I couldn't resist the image of George having reused his ring from his marriage with Lydia for his marriage with Claudine. I beg forgiveness for any really grievous errors, they are all mine, and committed in service of actually getting the book finished, which at times I thought I might never manage.

Acknowledgements

IN '*THE NATURE OF LOVE*', PSYCHOLOGIST Harry Harlow presented to the sixty-sixth annual convention of the American Psychological Association the results of his experiments on rhesus monkeys studying their experience and formation of attachment to substitute mother figures. In his research, he gave baby monkeys two mother options: a wire model of a mother with a bottle of milk, and a cloth model of a mother with nothing, and recorded the monkeys' preference. He found that the infant monkeys spent significantly more time with their cloth mother, though it offered no sustenance.

Harlow's research is a disturbing read. He went on to perform ethically and morally repulsive research on the early development of rhesus monkeys, which I do not suggest you look into. The devices used, and the experiences these monkeys were subjected to reads, in cold scientific language, like unspeakable torture. I find myself very angry at Harlow quite often.

And yet, he has given us the most bleak, uncompromising and powerful way to articulate that strange bond we are forced into from birth: the experience of having a mother.

My point is this: we will love our mothers even when they starve us.

It's really bloody hard to have a mother. I find myself reading work on attachment theory, on early childhood development, on human love, to try to unpick what it is to be a person, what it means to be born human, deeply, radically vulnerable, dependent, into the arms of those we did not choose, who may or may not be up to the job. It can be a comfort, a place of great solace – and one of absolute madness and suffering. And we do not know any other version than the one we get. My blue is not the same as your blue. When I say mother, I mean something unique, as do you.

Rottenheart is a book, first and foremost, about having a mother. Perhaps, a little, about being a mother, as these two things cannot but go hand in glove. Each mother we experience was also mothered in turn – even when there may have been a void where mothering was supposed to be, our motherless mothers have their own unique relationship to it. I suppose, then, *Rottenheart* must also be a book about love. Love is like water. We cannot live without it, and we will swallow it down even when it is poisoned.

Hamlet can be considered a play about fathers – but it was not so difficult to turn things over and look at these questions from another angle. What is it to be a child of a parent? What do we owe the dead? Can we ever truly be our own person? (Indeed, Hamlet and Old King Hamlet cannot even separate their names). Who rules us? What do we do with suffering? Where can it be tolerated? Who must carry it? Who is allowed to suffer, and who is despised for it? Is there space for us, as well as our parents? Must we always clasp the knife to our breast? Can we escape our mothers?

I first saw *Hamlet* as a teenager, at the Old Vic in London, with Ben Whishaw in the title role. It was one of those seismic experiences you have growing up where the world changes shape, your own mind expands to allow something new in. The kaleidoscope is twisted, and the patterns of life reorganise themselves. I have been in pursuit of Hamlet ever since. I have no pretensions to have done anything profound in *Rottenheart*, or even to claim to be 'in conversation' with Shakespeare. It was, at heart, a deeply personal problem I worried at, and shaped it out on paper so I wasn't alone with it in my head. In my acknowledgements, I often talk about what personal experience led me to write the book in your hands, but today I find myself unwilling to do so – though, if you have read *Rottenheart*, I don't imagine it is too difficult to piece things together.

So here it is, as a book. I hope it made some sense to someone.

I want to thank my agent, Hellie Ogden, for her tireless support from the start, and always having faith in me when sometimes I have so little, as well as my US agent, Caitlin Mahoney, who is a great source of enthusiasm, passion and astute guidance. Thank you to the wider teams at WME, Ma'suma, Frankie, and everyone behind the scenes.

Thanks to the wonderful editors who have worked on the book in the US and UK: Sophie Orme, Zoe Yang, Masie Cochran, Katie Burdett, Erin Wicks, Katie Lumsden. Thank you to the teams at Bonnier: Helen Reith, Beth Whitelaw, Flora Willis, Tamara Douthwaite, Kelly Samler, and Zando: Zoey Cole, Julia McGarry, Christopher King, Jennifer Freilach, for the huge amount of talent and dedication you put behind all your work; I feel very grateful to get to work with such a fantastic team.

Particular thanks are due to some very dear friends who dug me out of several holes along the way: Harry Catlin,

Lizzie Huxley-Jones, Lucy Rose, Madeleine Beresford, all of whom read drafts at various points and set me back on track.

Thank you to all the authors, booksellers, bloggers (are we still calling you that?), who I have been lucky enough to meet, be supported by or, gasp, call my friend. I'm not going to write a big list of publishing people because I am too frightened of leaving someone off, but there, you are very thanked and appreciated.

Thanks also to the WEJLU Discord, who know who they are but will not be named, for joy, encouragement, patience, niche research and bad jokes.

Thanks to my friends and family who have nothing to do with publishing, and make me very happy.

Thanks to my silly little cat, Effie, who knows nothing about anything and should not have to. I love it (hate it) when you scream at me at four a.m. Never change (please change).

If you enjoyed *Rottenheart* don't miss the captivating debut novel from Kat Dunn, a compulsive, fierce and powerful reimagining of sapphic vampire novel *Carmilla:*

Hungerstone

For what do you hunger?

Lenore is the wife of steel magnate Henry, but ten years into their marriage the relationship has soured, and no child has arrived to fill the distance growing between them. Henry's ambitions take them from London to the Peak District, to the remote, imposing Nethershaw estate, where he plans to host a hunting party. Lenore must work to restore the crumbling house and ready it for Henry's guests - their future depends on it.

But as the couple travel through the bleak countryside, a shocking carriage accident brings the mysterious Carmilla into Lenore's life. Carmilla, who is weak and pale during the day but vibrant at night, Carmilla who stirs up something deep within Lenore. And before long, girls from the local villages fall sick, consumed by a terrible hunger . . . As the day of the hunt draws closer, Lenore begins to unravel, questioning the role she has been playing all these years. Torn between regaining her husband's affection and the cravings Carmilla has awakened, soon Lenore will uncover a darkness in her household that will place her at terrible risk . . .

Available now in paperback

Read on for an opening extract from *Hungerstone*...

1

It starts with blood.

In the middle of the night, I wake, like a hound scenting the fox, and place a hand between my thighs. It comes away sticky and dark.

I used to feel grief about it, once. Now, I am numb. A task my body gives me to dispense with: a rag, the awkward fumble with the safety pins and the belt that will lie against my skin for five days, bringing up rashes around my unused belly and hips.

There is an echo of a dream in my mouth, a copper taste on my tongue and the prickle of the skin of my throat. I cannot recall more.

Henry is sleeping in his room; I can hear his soft snoring through the dressing room that forms the connection between our two private spaces. I still think softly of him, too, though I have come to doubt the strength of his regard for me after so many years.

I squat over the chamber pot and arrange my business. The nightdress is not stained; nor are the sheets – such is my intuition at thirty, when as a girl of sixteen I ruined so many bedclothes that my Aunt Daphne made me sleep with the belt on for a week either side of my courses as a precaution. I am mistress of my own house now, and I have sympathy for her pennypinching. If I had a daughter, perhaps I, too, would begrudge her any accidents, wish her to hasten into adult responsibility.

I have no daughter. I have no child at all.

Leaving a bloody splatter against the porcelain, I place the lid on the chamber pot and push it beneath the bed. This is no quiet loss; I have not lain with Henry in many months. There was no hope to lose.

As my head crests the bed, I see something.

So fleeting. Just a flicker of movement, and the soft creak of weight on the floorboards.

I go still.

What was it? Where?

There – the corner of the room, where the darkness seems deeper.

I hold myself as quiet as I can, waiting for it to come again. My heart is clenched tight.

On the mantel, the clock ticks out the dead seconds.

Nothing.

There is no movement, no sound of the boards.

Fear seeps away, and I feel foolish. This house makes noises; every house I have ever lived in has eased and groaned with the wind and the damp.

I will not sleep again; the pain woke with me, so instead I furl myself in the quilt like an oyster in its shell with no pearl to show for the grit that works through it. Pain and blood, grief and hunger.

To be a woman is a horror I can little comprehend.

Blood has marked much of my still young life. Bleeding at twelve – younger than my mother had expected, an advent into a new age of motherhood she had not anticipated so soon. The absence of blood on my wedding night – Henry searching for it on the sheets in the morning, and finding none, pricking my finger on a penknife to smear a bright stain for the servants to find and know he had done his husbandly duty.

The blood that came each month after. At first, a disappointment, then a fear, then a grief, then an inevitability.

I was good for nothing but blood.

*

It is high summer, and the London house will have no more glory. We will close her up for the summer and retreat to the edge of Derbyshire and the new estate Henry has acquired, away from the smog of Sheffield proper. With ten years of migration, I am well used to the ebb and flow of the nomadic season, but there is still much to do. There are clothes to be mended and brushed, silverware and china to be counted and packed, clocks to be wound, dust-sheets to be hung across Chesterfield and sideboard. My desk is cleared, menus stacked and correspondence filed. There are no more invitations to be sent, no more seating plans to be decided. This anxious work of mine that has driven me for ten years, the precise and unassailable positioning of Henry and I both in the upper ranks of society, gives the meaning to my life, makes walls and floors and borders in a borderless, insecure land. But it exhausts me. Once we settle in the country, a new round of social obligations will commence, but until then I am granted a reprieve: for a few weeks, it is enough for me to be only what I am.

I rise, aching and sluggish, and add a wrapper over my nightdress. The weather teases summer in bouts of bold sunshine and heat that sours the milk before it arrives from the dairy, then retreats in a flurry of grey skies and a heavy humidity that lies across the city like a fog. Between my curtains, there is a slice of white stucco and green bough. Our house is a fine building in the square near Holland Park, which Henry purchased from a drawing shown to him in Sheffield. We are surrounded by artists, about whom Henry is occasionally ungenerous.

Molly puts a slug of laudanum in my tea without my asking, and I am glad of it. My body is my enemy, and I will use every weapon in my arsenal against it. I breakfast lightly on kedgeree and strong tea, and remain in my bedroom, tending to correspondence.

Molly returns sooner than expected, something in her hand. 'Miss Lamb has given her calling card.'

Cora. I should have known.

'I am out to all visitors today, Molly.'

I return to my letter writing, but Molly lingers at the door.

'Yes?'

'She's talking to Mr Crowther in the hallway – he was coming in when she arrived.'

Of course she is. Cora knows how to make herself at home anywhere. Though she is more than half a decade younger than I am, it is one of many talents she wears lightly, which come at so high a cost to me. Pretty, accomplished and reassuringly conventional, the world seems to rotate around her every whim and delight. Sometimes, I feel too aware of her friendship granting reflected glory.

I do not look up. 'Let him deal with her. I am occupied.'

Molly bobs and slips away.

I am riled at the intrusion, too much in pain to be generous to those who lay endless demands at my door. On my writing desk is a tin of pastilles, and I put three into my mouth at once, letting the overwhelming rush of sugar blunt my mind.

To business: Henry's secretary has arranged a first-class compartment on the Midland Railway and our departure from St Pancras is set for the morrow. I do not know what to think about Nethershaw, the moorland estate for which that I am now responsible. I have seen but one smudged photograph of its exterior: a long, low stone edifice of medieval and Tudor foundation that, unlike its distant neighbours, Chatsworth and Lyme, has not been wrapped in a Palladian façade. Its arched windows and crenelations give rise to images of monks and knights, an England we have long fled. Its position on the rising bank of hillside, leading to what is called in those parts an 'edge' – here, Hungerstone Edge, flanked by Stanage and Burbage Edge – seems a bleak, alien landscape to me.

Until now, we have summered in rented houses in fashionable areas, but Henry is not satisfied. He wants his name on deed and register: on the marriage banns that joined my ancient family to his, and on the contract leasing four thousand acres of Derbyshire.

If I can become a woman in no other way, then I shall make it this: I am an unerring general in the campaign for our social standing. No rule of etiquette is obscure to me, no occasion too difficult to host.

I ignore the scatter of calling cards that arrive throughout the morning and think instead of the shirts and petticoats that came back from the laundry with scorch marks, the new gown that the dressmaker has yet to deliver and my summer hat that on second look seems a little out of style. Is there time to order a new one before we go? Or should I give instruction to a milliner in Sheffield? No, it must be London. The steel wives of Sheffield will all have hats from the same establishments in York and Harrogate. I must come with the London fashions of this year, 1888, and not a single thing that speaks of a moment earlier. That is what Henry bought in me: taste, refinement, high birth and good blood.

I take a moment to write a letter to my hatmaker with my request: whatever is considered the appropriate fashion for a married woman of thirty to be made up in my size and sent north.

A little before the luncheon bell, I dress. I have kept a tea-gown apart from the rest of my wardrobe, which has already been packed into trunks. This one is striped pink Liberty silk over a light corset, with a train trimmed in black velvet and a boned collar that sits tight around my throat. I am a beauty. It is well known. My eyes are cornflower blue and my skin like spilt cream. When we were courting, Henry would take down my hair from its pins and wind its heavy locks around his fingers like honey around a knife.

I was pretty then; I am beautiful now. My waist has thickened and my figure filled in the decade since our wedding, but it has only flushed my looks further into delight. There are perhaps some graces to being un-mothered. My body is as unused as a dress not yet worn, and so remains as crisp and fresh as the day it was bought.

When I descend, it is to the hushed tones of a voice seeking privacy. Henry is in his study, and I linger outside, straightening a vase of dried flowers.

'. . . grand gift . . . no . . . surprised.'

I can picture him, mouth cupped close to the telephone receiver, teeth yellow-stained by coffee and port, glistening with spittle when he runs his tongue across them, as he does when he is addressing a matter of urgency or importance. The telephone itself was installed only a few weeks ago – the first on the street – and Henry was as delighted as a school boy with a new toy, delaying the workmen at every turn so their cart could be observed outside our house the whole day.

It is our ten-year wedding anniversary in three weeks. The tin wedding. Perhaps Henry is telephoning Cutlers' Hall to insist the year be renamed steel.

We have spoken of no plans, but the words *gift* and *surprise* linger with me as I pass from the sheet-covered house into the tranquillity of the garden. The dining room was amongst the first to be prepared for our absence, so we must take our final meals at the iron table on the terrace or else like breakfast, on a tray in our respective rooms. Or at least *I* must – Henry will dine at his club or at a chop-house no doubt.

I wait for Henry with my eyes closed, willing away the pain in my stomach, frustrated by my weakness. The table on the terrace has been laid with the worst china for luncheon, the gold leaf flaking from the rims, along with a set of Sheffield steel cutlery from Henry's Ajax Works, and a selection of dishes repurposed from dinner last night: a little pressed beef, a coil of tongue, a small pot of shrimp beneath the oily plug of butter that seals them in, a dish of mashed potatoes, a shining glass of jelly, stewed fruit, cheeses and biscuits. It is proper; I am pleased. I think of Aunt Daphne and her swollen knuckles rapping the etiquette book. *An elegant disorder is perfectly distinct from a vulgar confusion.*

My plate is too empty, and there is so much I want, but I must not start without approval. There is a note of my half-remembered dream in the metallic taste in my mouth – perhaps a storm is coming, the low pressure bringing the blood to my tongue.